ADVENTURERS BORN

BOOK 1: TAKING THE HIGH ROAD

BY MALCOLM HARRIS

Dedicated to
Mary McKissack

My first dungeon master, mother of my
best friend, artist, and genuine good person.

Gone too soon, but never forgotten.

Adventures Born book one: Taking the High Road by Malcolm Harris
Published by Relentless Fiction
510 E. Woodin Dallas Texas t5216

Join us on Facebook at : https://www.facebook.com/theworldofAerix/
Contact Malcolm at : Macielmallusdie@gmail.com
Cover by Malcolm Harris
Illustrations: Malcolm Harris

ISBN: 9781980745457

Book 1: Taking the High Road

Book 2: Across the Emerald Sea (Coming Soon)

Book 3: The Great Northern Campaign. (Coming Soon)

Aerix: Adventures in the Free kingdoms tabletop RPG (Coming Soon)

NOVEL SPOTIFY PLAYLIST
(Adventurers Song)
https://open.spotify.com/user/21uc7aw74ibfgrdq4juauazoy/
playlist/2lOIIX3RMgdgMd5rYUiK48?si=CK6OkOLWQg-TiX9H84K5yw

TABLE OF CONTENTS

Chapter	Page

WELCOLME TO AERIX

A FANTASY MELTING POT

Hello,

I'm writing from the past in hopes that in the future someone is reading this book. Maybe you downloaded off a futuristic database or library or your holding a real copy of it in your hand as you float about weightless?

Your future I'm sure is better than my present, and my today is better than my past and the past of my parents or their parents. But fantasy tends to take place in a past of sorts, and while that history usually involves a Eurocentric medieval world, it doesn't always have to.

You see, I wrote this book to rebel against that concept. I wanted to make a fantasy world that's not your typical fantasy world. I wanted to do something that embraced the past, while still being hopeful and full of adventure magic and monsters. I wanted a world that was diverse, and that tapped into the legends and mythology of Africa, Meso America, Native Americans, India, China and more. I wanted a fantasy melting pot, and since no one was doing it the way I wanted, I decide to do it myself.

What if North America was the fantasy world, and not just any North America but one that avoided many of its original sins. That would be the foundation that I would build my world. And so Aerix

was born but not as a novel , not at first. I'm a game designer, not
video games, but tabletop Role-playing games. You've probably head
of the most famous of its kind involving various dungeon and dragons. I've written a fair amount of tabletop RPG content, some did
great, others not so much but for a time I avoided writing a non-
modern fantasy setting for my rules. However, eventually I did just
that, and so I wrote DDF (Drama Dice Fantasy) and Aerix (the setting was born) about ten years ago.

  The project wasn't my best, and I never pushed it as I pushed other
projects because I never saw its real potential. Then the world
changed. That change was the real world political climate and the rise
of open racism, gender bias, anti LGBTQ and more. It was like everything we thought we had conquered was now returning, and an angry
and evil voice that was once silenced had returned

  Things were going dark and terrible for a lot of people and as a
writer, I decided those who were marginalized and those seeking
something new and different needed a world to escape the real one.
So I looked at Aerix, and I expanded on it. I started creating stories
and characters and a timeline for those characters, and after some
contemplation I thought to make my characters young and embrace
the "Young Adult" concept. And thus after many updates and
changes, I can now say, welcome to Aerix.

  Aerix or the "Newlands" was discovered in the 1400's by multiple
human kingdoms. It was the home of ingenious human kingdoms,

confederations and tribes, the mighty Mytec a cross between the Mayan and Aztec Civilizations) empire and the haven for those of the old blood. The magical peoples who had left the "Old Lands" fleeing human expansion.

To the east coast came the Gilden (Europeans) and the Nyumbani (the Africans) To the west coast came the Wu (Chinese) and the Raahtr (Indian). The migration of these great kingdoms and noble houses changed a continent as the "Newlands of Aerix" was settled equally not only by them , but unlike our world after some early struggles the native humans maintained many of their native lands and cultures.

Conflict, of course, was inevitable, but instead of using gunpowder it would be fought with magic and steel. Magic was the great equalizer, it changed the world millennia ago, before recorded history and that one change, sparked more changes. Gunpowder was never invented, after all, it was an alchemical attempt to make an elixir of immortality which was precisely what it did (The one the that has kept the emperor of Wu and his court alive for hundreds of years). Healers stopped many diseases that would have wiped out nations including the black death and heroes outfitted with magical items and mystic arts helped changed history.

When the story starts it's 1874, four hundred years have passed. Most of Aerix is now united as the Free kingdoms, a loose confederation of kingdoms divided by the wilds between them. The Free kingdoms is not a single governing body; they are separate kingdoms who try to keep the peace between each other, promote trade and protect each other from the wild lands, the still mighty Mytec empire to the south and the Giants and Estahutten raiders (think Vikings) of the north.

Helping keeps that peace , explores and protect are the Adventures Guild. Think of them as heroes for hire, well-trained people with unique skills and powers that do the deeds kingdoms can not openly do, protect those crossing the wilds and hunt creatures that an ordinary local militia could never defeat. The guild reports what they find to all members of the free kingdoms equally and does it best not to take sides in conflicts between kingdoms.

In this world, The guild members are celebrities second only to royal and noble families. For that reason, hundreds of young people seek to join and test themselves against its tasks and trials. And like all such organizations, it attracts the outsiders, those on the fringe and those trying to escape their lives be that life too hard or too soft.

In the guild all members at there respective levels are equal. A lord may find themselves taking orders from a freeman or peasant. A rogue who see Gods as not being worth the trouble stands equal with the most devoted follower of Alomeg (The Aerix equivalent of the Judeo-Christian-Islamic God). Mystics work side by side with device building tinkersmith, mighty uneducated warriors get the same cut from the booty of a delve into the unknown as a haughty educated witch.

And so our story starts with a group of young people on their first guild mission. To say more would mean spoilers and we all hate spoilers.

CHAPTER 1:
VALLUS PROPER

Seamus and Callum had been friends all their lives; They had grown up in the southern lands of the Mwamba Wa Mwaloni. Callum was the third son (Fourth of six children) of the local lord which meant that he had very little to look forward to as far as ruling the land, and when asked about the subject he would often say, " I wouldn't want the job anyway,"

Tall, barrel-chested with a bald head, dark brown skin and eyes he stood just under seven feet despite only recently celebrating his eighteenth birthday a few months past. His heritage was mostly human with a little Titan and some (much less than this Titan Heritage.) Djinn (A rare form of Oldblood that despite legends could not grant wishes.). Most people had a little magic folk in the blood in the south, it was a land full of old standing stones, hidden valleys, and magical wilds settled by those with an adventuring spirit (most like Callum were descendent from the Nyumbani people). Small lordships and kingdoms filled the area, and while it wasn't as populous as the Northen lands or magical as the vast central wilds, it was a near perfect mixing of the two.

"I don't think we're going to get picked," Seamus looked at the large wooden boards were dozens of names were written on small black slate cards in white chalk and slid in and out of oak grooves.

Seamus was the opposite of his friend of almost ten years; he was born to a peasant family, his father worked on a road gang, smoothing dirt paths and setting cobblestones and slabs twelve hours a day, his mother took care of the small family farm where Seamus and his younger brother and sister helped. Standing at a little over average height with long blond hair fair skin, a thin face and blue eyes, his slightly pointed ears marked him as having some fae heritage as did his aptitude with magic.

The eighteen-year-old had learned some basic magic from his mother and had self-taught himself enough to catch the eye of a local mystical supplies shop owner who taught him more complex spells. His specialty was elemental magic, although he was well adept in divination and some fundamental necromancy and defense.

"We're a good duo, Magic, and Muscle," Callum smiled wide as he spoke. The usually high-spirited young man nursed a cold cup of Zazoo, a cold drink that mixed copious amounts of cream with strong coffee and honey.

"You can heal too," Seamus, "That has to count for something," the young magician adjusted the staff in his lap made of pecan wood and brass.

"I heal as good as you swing a sword," the larger one laughed, " Both our secondary talents are measures of last resort, at best,"

The blond smiled, "That's true" he said picking up a small cup of fruit juice and taking a sip.

Looking around the Adventures hall he saw dozens of people just like him and his friend. Some were armored, some held staves and wands, a few bows and exotic weapons or holy symbols. All of them, him and the young man he thought of as a brother had come to seek fame and fortune as adventurers, an occupation both revered and frowned upon by those in power.

Adventuring was an age-old service. Those with the skill and might would be hired by those in need to do a job, be it dealing with bandits, slaying or capturing terrorizing beasts or helping out on a military campaign or journey of exploration. It was a dangerous job, and most of those taking on the "questing life" lasted ten years at best and retired due to a healthy dose of common senses, death or in rare cases acquisition of great wealth. Those that endured long enough ,were powerful enough and good enough at their job became famous and found themselves hired out by kings, queens, and nobles court, becoming magicians and, priests and generals. Some even manage to found noble houses of their own.

The Vallus adventuring guild house was the closest to the Mwamba wa Mwaloni, it was three days by land and another two upriver by barge in the city of Vallus, a river port city, and one of the three largest in the southern nations. Here three great rivers met, canals cut through the busy city streets and for two boys from a backwater land it was a place of wonder, and their first look at a real royal castle, more people than they could imagine and the world they only dreamt of.

" Thunder-rear," A woman in the green and white attire of the Guild staff, called out to the crowd of young and low rank -adventurers. In her hand was a slate tablet with the number two on it. Nervous laughter followed as eyes darted about looking for the person or persons who had chosen such a ludicrous name for the guild group registry.

"Thundereers," called out both friends standing and raising their hand with looks of nervous surprise on their faces's. The woman waved the two young men forward, One was wearing clean, but worn black tabard and breaches over a hand-stitched red and blue robe that was a hodge-podge of cotton and silk. With gold inlays, he had a staff in one hand, and a large leather bag slung over his shoulder. The other was tall and wore a red tabard with a black bull rearing on it over a chainmail shirt. He had on black breaches and metal-shod leather boots that matched his fingerless gauntlets.

When the two made it to her, she leaned in close and growled. , "I could give the Fallen's own hells what your name is, get to room two," The woman pointed to the front of the large room where a hall lead to small meeting rooms marked one thru ten.

After traveling down the high ceiling hall, the two would be questers found room two but instead of entering both young men stood outside the door as their dreams now reality turned eagerness into nervousness.

"You open it," Callum looked at his friend.

"No, you do it, You 're dad's a Lord" Seamus motioned at the door.

"Lord of one of smallest land in the south, to the nobles and royals here, were just peasants with indoor plumbing and delusions of grandeur," The larger of the two said looking at the wooden door as if it was made of flame instead of wood.

"Sword, Parchment, Storm?," Said the young magician was holding out his palm in a preparation of his friends choosing to decide the issue with the childhood game. The two looked at each other and started, not noticing a young woman their age dressed in a green and black dress, and corset with a wide brim pointed hat walking past them into the room they were so nervous about entering. Both young men looked at the now open door and with a deep breath followed the well-dressed girl inside.

The room was small, with a ceiling just a few inches above Callum's head, lit by light crystals. In the middle of the room taking up most of the space was a table with six seats, at each place on the table was a simple drinking cup and in the middle a pitcher of liquid.

"Hello," Callum spoke to the girl who was now sitting. His mind floated back to growing up in his families home; an old building part frontier Keep, part old manse. Their his father's mother, a former Vallus court healer, and a lady in waiting taught the six children of House Wimbowaradi how to be young lords and ladies as best she could. One of those things was being able recognizing those of an equal or higher station including knowledge of other nobles heraldry. Theirs were the raging black bull rearing on a background of red trimmed in gold. The young woman wore a clasp of an owl on a stylized wheel that attached her cape on the left side. He knew it was a southern noble house but because of nervousness couldn't for the life of him remember it's name or any other pertinent information about it.

"Lord Wimbowaradi," the young woman spoke with soft confidence.

"M'lady," he said in return trying his best to remember the heraldry and feeling embarrassed by the fact she recognized his, and he hadn't the foggiest of what her's was.

Seamus looked at his friend, recognizing the frustration on his face, smirked as he sat across from the young woman in green. The larger man, following his friend's example, sitting down in a chair made for a much smaller person,

The trio remained silent, Seamus at first wondered if the young woman was the client that would be interviewing them, then he noticed the thin silver and ivory wand holder attached to her belt and the mystic energies swimming around her. "Two magicians," he thought, wondering what kind of assignment required two spellcasters. Curious about her power level and specialty the blond magician released a sliver of his power to observe hers. His minor spell met a well woven protective ward designed to not only stop such prying but other things as well.

"Stop," said the young woman, in a manner that said, "That's the only warning I'm going to give you,"

"Sorry," Seamus.

Callum looked at his friend and the girl, he wasn't exactly non-mystical and knew something had happened.

"What just happened?," he asked.

"Your friend was prying," the girl.

"I said I was sorry," Seamus.

"You're lucky I didn't turn you into a toad," the young woman glared at both the men at the table with piercing blue eyes, her pale round freckled face framed by the ginger hair in perfect long ringlets.

"You're a witch?," Seamus, spoke up feeling her magic become more focused as she spoke as well as the magic coming out of her body, which was one of the things made witches different from other spellcasters, that along with their gender (all witches were female). The "kind ladies" as they were often called often in a sarcastic tone were said to not only have the magical talent like most wizards, but a spiritual bond to magic like a priest/priestess did to their deity. The combination made witches their own thing in the mystical world and allowed them to do things other spellcasters could not dream of they were adequately trained.

For a magician, like Seamus, magic was learning rote and mastering one's energy and the magic in the world and weaving that energy into specific shapes focused on gesture and words. For a witch it was more emotional and primal, confidence, belief, and understanding of the true nature of reality allowed her to do her spells.

That's not to say she was more powerful than the blond wizard across from her. Training, in fact, had always been the equalizer between magicians in wizards as most witches were self-taught while mostly most wizards were trained from an early age in their art with exceptions existing on both sides.

"Yes," the young woman said as she placed a gloved hand slowly on her wand case. 'Do either of you have an issue with that?" The witch knew even among other magic-using folk her kind was feared. Witches were often vilified, and while yes, many a witch had made a name for themselves by vexing entire lands and even taking over kingdoms, most lived quiet, solitary lives fearing their potential and the adage, that a witches power corrupted far more than that other magicians.

"Not at all, you're just our first Witch, at least my first witch," Callum.

"Mine too, I've read about you... witches but never seen one in person".

The girl relaxed and managed to smile, "Well stop staring, Or I'll make maggots out of the both of you,"

"I apologize, lady"..," Seamus.

"Xarona, of House Belasona," the red-haired girl replied before taking a sip of the watered down wine, And you are,"

"Seamus Pathson," the young magician.

"Callum Wimbowaradi, Son of Lord Vilheim Wimbowaradi and Lady Greta Wimbowaradi," The armored young man smiled shyly after speaking to the young woman.

"Wimbowaradi? timber, and crystal, right? , the young woman spoke up.

"Timber and... yes, that's what we do, Cut trees, Mine crystal, and harvest, walnuts, and pecans". Callum felt prideful as he spoke. His families lands were thick with hardwood trees as well as a few crystal deposits on the cliffs overlooking a deep bend in the central river. Despite being a lord's son he and his father and brothers would spend time helping their people mining and cutting as the season warranted. The timber they would ship upriver , the crystals they would sell to private parties or ship to sell in larger markets for their magical qualities. Most of their stones glass was Clear, which meant it was suitable for storing and focusing mystical energy and little more, Occasionally they would find a red flame crystal or a silvery lift crystal, but rarely anything more exotic than that.

"Belasona, You're family are rookers and timber," Callum spoke quickly as he finally remembered the crest,"

The young woman nodded, "Training birds, oak trees, and our wheel-wright works," her voice wasn't as prideful as the other lord at the table, in fact, it was it had just a hint of shame in it both young men noticed.

Before the three young would-be adventurers could speak the door opened again, "Am I late?," A willowy young man with the suntanned skin of a farmer, dark hair, and a slim face entered . He wore a vest made of hides over a handstitched buckskin shirt and pants . on his back was a cape made of leather patches of various greens and browns, a longbow was slung over his shoulder, and a belt festooned with small pouches was worn around his waist.

"Not unless you're the client," Seamus.

"No, I'm Jase, " said the earnest-looking young man shaking the hand of the blond, and the hulking young man in armor earnestly. However, when he turned to do the same to the young woman he was met by a steely gaze that told him, she wasn't the handshaking type.

"Well will you look at us, all first timers I wager," the thin young man turned his chair around and sat on it backward.

"I think so," Seamus.

"This is going to be great," Jase smiled wide.

"One can only hope," Xarona, "I for one am starting to wonder if we were sent here to meet a client or to sip on this horrid wine till we gave up and left."

"I bet they just needed to put together a proper party," Jase reached into one of his bags and pulled out a hand full of dried berries and nuts.

"Snacks anyone," he said. holding out his travelers meal for all to see.

Seamus nodded and took a small scoop as did Callum and to no one surprise, the young woman kept her hands to herself, a look of disgust on her face.

"Sorry, I'm late," an older voice from the opening door.

The man entering was six feet tall, medium build with the deep tanned skinned of someone of Myberian heritage, with dark hair graying on the sides. He wore a purple surcoat with gray and lavender shirt and pants.

"Had to wait on a carriage from the Inn," he said, as he sat down on the other side of the table and took a leather messenger bag off his shoulder.

"I'm Vinceno Salazar; You might have heard of my business Salazar Silks," he said. To his surprised the young people before him were silent.

"Never mind, You'll know of me soon enough," he said with a smile. Opening his bag, he took out a printed folded paper map of the central wilderness with a red line drawn in wax tracing the high road from Vallas-Proper to Arden Proper to Kascee-Proper.

The line then cut cross the wild lands of western Kascee territory into Colos and then to the Grey keep, it's capital.

Each kingdom center was marked by its hearldy. For Vallus it was A single gold star on a traditional Nyumbani shield colored red on one side and blue on the other. Behind the shield where two long-bladed spears. Like, Vallus Arden, had the Same spear crossed hold only it colors were red and white and instead of a star there was a stylized gold griffin. Kasee's heraldry showed its native heritage with a round disk representing a drum head with three dangling feathers. On the drumhead was a stylized winged horse.

For Colos was the Broad Gilden style Shield flat at the top with curves leading to a point at the bottom. On it was a green background with a Stylized white mountain and great Roc Claw.

I'm looking for a small escort group to accompany me and family plus three wagons and their drivers from here to Colos Manse. That's thre hundred and sixity miles along the Highroad and another five hundred across "wilder" lands. Vinceno looked up after speaking seeing all eyes were on him and the map. He then continued, " I'm paying a standard one gold sovereign a day, plus standard bonuses for dangerous duties. Also, as a bonus, I'm throwing in two bolts each of silk, of any color if we arrive on time".

"What grade silk ?," the young woman spoke up.

"Noble grade," the man spoke up, "You can have a nice dress or two made from it,"

"Or sell it, right? That swag has to be worth almost as much as our regular pay," Jase.

"I'm no expert, but I would think so" Seamus.

"Mr. Salazar, can we talk about the nature of the trip?," Callum looked at the client.

"Good question my large friend, My son youngest Bernardo is getting married, to The Colos' youngest daughter. You'll be escorting not only my family but gifts for our new and incredibly wealthy. In-Laws. "

"Well, congrats sir," the dark-haired young man with the bow shook the client's hand, "It'll be my honor to help you reach your destination,"

The client smiled and looked at the other three, "And the rest of you?," he asked.

"Seems like a good way to get our feet wet," Seamus looking at Callum,

"I'm game if you are the friend," the big man nodded at his old friend then looked the red-haired young woman.

"One gold a day, and three bolts," she said., "These idiots may not know it but we'll be crossing some less and hospitable areas even on the High Road and far worse once we're off it,"

The young man looked at the woman, "Nothing we can't handle right?," Jase.

"Maybe," Callum spoke both amazed at the young woman's moxie and ashamed at the fact he didn't think about negotiating.

Vinceno looked at the young woman and smiled, "True, But you're all rank ones, untested".

"Which means you wanted us because we were cheap or expendable," said Xarona standing as if to leave, "I was trained at the Coventry of Evershade, I'm ranked high adept in four schools of magic. I have no idea who these three are, but if you picked me, then they are not as incompetent as they seem. regardless, two gold, three bolts or I decline,"

The merchant looked the group over; If he paid for a higher rank he would have to pay more, he had thumbed through the available adventures picking the best he could for their level.

"One gold, four silver," Vinceno.

"One gold, eight silver and Three bolts," the young witch was now at the door,

"Gentleman, before I leave, here's some advice, always negotiate,"

As she opened the door, Vinceno spoke, " One gold, Six silver, and three bolts," The young woman stopped, " seven silver" she commanded.

"Seven," the merchant agreed.

The three young man looked at their red-haired teammate with reverence.

After the negotiation was done, the adventures and their client walked to the to the contract room where a guild employee wrote out the terms of the contract and all involved signed their signature. Vinceno then handed each of the young people five silver for supplies and sundries for the road. They would have only two days to prepare for the journey.

Once done with signing Vinceno left leaving instruction with the young witch on when they will be starting and from where. It was evident at least to him that she was the one in charge.

"What you packing big man ?," Jase looked at Callum, "You doing sword and board?" The guildhall policy against carrying melee weapons into the adventures hall or meeting meant that all such weapons were stored at the front of the building in lockers sealed by magical locks over-seen by guild register and guard.

Callum smiled as he stood at the registers desk, I don't do shields, "If you need a shield your armor's shite," he said.

The register took the metal numbered tags from each of the young men as the woman they were with watched unimpressed.

First, he came back with Seamus' simple short sword and scabbard. The young magician drew the blade to show it to his new friends,   It was, well made of it had a clear crystal embedded at the bottom of its hilt.

"That's a mighty fine blade," Jase

"Callum made it; he's a pretty good smith". The young magician spoke with such pride his large friend had to turn his head away out of humility

"I'm not that good, That's just northern steel, I folded a few dozen times before shinning it up nice, nothing fancy,"

"I have no idea or care what any of that means," the red-haired girl scoffed, "Anyway, he's a magician If he has to swing a sword we're in trouble anyway,"

"That's true," Seamus.

The registered returned with Jase's quiver full of Arrows, Two curved swords, and six daggers. "There's my babies," he said carefully looking them over before sliding quiver on his back placing the swords in two sheaths built into the quiver and the daggers into sheaths on his belt, boots, and lower back.

"You have enough weapons there ?," Seamus.

"I have a few more I left in the stable I rented," Janse.

"That explains your smell," The young witch.

"If you're going to hunt, you can't smell like a princess, princess," The young man in leather.

"I'm a lady, not a Princess, Peasant," Xarona placed a hand on her wand handle and started to focus her power.

"M'lord, some help," The register stood at a large locker. Callum walked over taking from it a large crossbow and a quiver that attached to his belt. He then reached in for something even bigger, From inside he pulled out a great hammer with a milky white Pure crystal head a foot and half wide and a brass coated steel shaft some three feet long.

"What the hells," the Hunter turned from the young witch to look at the massive weapon. "Is that Pure crystal ?" he asked

"Yeah, from my family mines, only Pure we've ever found there, I carved the head and forged the handle myself, My brother, a Minster of Alomeg blessed it and "cured" it in holy water,"

"You an ordered Crusader," the dark-haired hunter asked?

"No, I'm not part of the official the order, but I know the rites and the works of the path,"

"So you're not just a warrior?," the witch.

"No, I'm a Free Crusader," Callum lifted the hammer as if it weighed far less than it did and slid it into a chain attached to his belt.

"What's your healing skill," the woman asked.

"I can keep you from bleeding to death if the wound isn't too too bad and I can handle normal cuts and wounds, purify things, basic lay on hands. Healing isn't my specialty". The big man spoke humbly knowing unlike his older brother or grandmother he could only perform basic body mending and cures.

"Well, that's better than nothing," Jase.

"Indeed," Xarona, " I've read something of the Crusaders orders, The Hand is the healers, Voice sings their magic, and I'm guessing your more fist?"

Callum acknowledged her words with a knowing nod of the head.

Hunter, Crusader, Witch, and Wizard, not bad ," said Jase, Before heading out the door. "Now if you don't mind let's get out of here and finish this talk over some food and good ale,"

*****

"They are so frustrating" spoke Xarona, pacing in her in-room her irritation barely contained.

Who's frustrating?," A tiny voice from the bed

"Boys," she called out, "I'm not going to call them men because a man would use their heads for more than a bloody hat rack! Not that any of them wore hats, but it's obvious they're not very smart," The red-haired young woman stopped her pacing and sat on the bed. Allowing a creature that resembled a winged cat with three tails and oversized eyes to crawl into her lap.

"They can't be all bad," The creature.

"I thought the wizard would be the smart one, but he's little more than a self-taught hedge magician, I bet he can 't even perform a basic astral evaluation. The Lord is from some little backwater land I've only heard of because my tutors forced me to. He's almost as big as a troll and probably wants to burn me at stake. And the other one is a smelly, loutish peasant hunter" The young woman stroked the creature as she vented.

"I'm sure they have good qualities," the cat-creature.

"They didn't do that boy flirting thing," The girl's eyes grew wide as she spoke to her friend. "Am I ugly Sani? "

The creature looked at the young woman, round freckled face, piercing blue eyes, long red hair in ringlets, a soft build with slim curved shoulders and wide hips. "I have no idea what humans find attractive, ," said Sani,

"But you are intelligent, powerful and confident. most of the time, Those boys should count their lucky stars that you're traveling with them".

"True, I did graduate at the top of my circle at the coventry," the red-headed girl voice sounded more upbeat as she spoke. Her cat purred and turned on it's back to her belly could be scratched.

"And if they prove truly thick-headed, you can always make mice of them for me," Sani closed her eyes as she enjoyed the undivided attention of her mistress.

"Mice ?," laughed the witch, "Maybe the wizard, But the big one is a toad waiting to happen, and the other one... a dung beetle,"

Xarona smiled, "But I doubt if it'll come to that,"

"You never know, and I do like the tastes of mice and the occasional toad and bug," the cat creature purred.

*****

"What do you think of her?," Callum looked at Seamus who was busy reading from a large book as he sat on a rickety old bed, one of two in the small inn room.

"Her ladyship?," Seamus looked up and saw his friend was sitting on his bed using a tool to work on the rings in his chain mail. , "She's exactly what I expected from a noble,"

"I'm a noble," Callum

"You know what I mean, Your family didn't put on airs, you worked alongside the rest of us and just because I was low born no one in it treated me any different from anyone else. " The wizard spoke calmly, remembering the times he spent over at his friends Manse. It's tall red walls, single courtyard, and attached buildings, it wasn't in the best of shape, but it was always welcoming.

"My family had to work for our lands and title; My grandmother was gifted the old keep by her friend, the queen of Vallus When she arrived with my father as "maiden mother " with a bastard son it was just a run down wild land fort with and a few farms. Over time the two of them tamed the land, attracted good people like your family to it and started our trade.

Seamus nodded, he remembered coming to the "Mwamba wa Mwaloni," His father had been told that the lord there was offering jobs and land to farm to anyone that came with "good intent," They traveled in a rickety cart into the hills and the forest for almost two weeks. Eventually, they came to the Wimbowaradi family keep. There they camped outside with a few dozen new families as had been the tradition for the thirty plus years of the land. Seamus and his two younger siblings were playing with wooden swords, and he mistook Callum and his two younger siblings for peasants like him as they wore simple clothing just slightly better than his own. When he asked to join them, they said yes, and soon they were playing a small scale war with ten other children.

Callum's Grandmother, Mother, and Father then appeared with the three older children and a small retinue to hand out directions to parcels of lands for those present, gifts of a cow, some chickens, a house, feed and two bags of milled wheat. The Grandmother also made sure every child and the sick was given a basic healing touch by her.

Seamus said goodbye to his new friends still not knowing their place in his "new world," and traveled for half a day to a small farm where a simple house, barn, and fences were built. It was simple two room home, but it was his families for as long as they paid their taxes, worked the land, and his father helped out on the crew making sure the roads were well kept, and that path to the grand high road was built. And maintained.

"So you don't like her?," Callum, "I think she's somewhat pretty, but then again I always liked girls with hips. The large young man smiled.

"You know she's not my type," Seamus, "And before you ask, Jase isn't either, I don't like people that smell like horses,"

"But Jase seems okay as a person; we could have done worse," The large, dark-skinned young Lord carefully added new rings to his mail as he replied. Seamus' eyes widened as he finally realized the magnitude of his friend's first question,

"Wait do you like-like her?" he asked

"No," Callum growled.

"Can you do that, isn't there are rules of celibacy? ," Seamus decided to goad his friend some.

"No, I'm a Free-Crusader, I follow the path but not the order," his friend replied quickly, "Not that I'm thinking of that.. or her that way or..,"

"Sure," The Magician. , "I guess Free-Crusaders don't always have to tell the truth either,"

*****

"Will there be danger?," the blond haired girl looked at Jase as they both sat in the stables on a small bench.

"Possibly, But It's nothing I can't handle," The dark-haired young man moved ever so close to the girl as he spoke, "But don't worry, I'll return to you safely.

" Good," the girl leaned in and kissed the hunter softly on the lips.

"Are you sure your father is asleep?," Jase asked looking and listening about and hearing only the girls heartbeat and the animals resting.

"Yes, he is," The girl kissed him again after speaking, Jase returned the kiss and pulled her forward, rubbing her back and stroking her hair.

*****

The cloudy sky spat rain down as the rooster crowed in the merchant part of town. The great southern city like most was laid out in various quarters based on the wealth and standing of those living in it. The Salazars were merchants of a high price commodity and could afford if they like the very best of things. The "Welcome Rest," was the best inn in town with large rooms, indoor plumbing, good food, and amenities second only to a manor of a powerful noble house.

"I don't love her," Bernardo, tall aristocrats in lavender and purple doublet, dark gray pants, black boots and purple cape.

"Love will come," His mother Isabella was of medium height and thin , with tan skin, dark hair and wore a purple and lavender dress, black gloves and a hooded purple cloak.

Next to their mother stood two identical 13-year-old girls in Purple dresses, head scarves, gloves, and cloaks. One was reading from a small book while the other was enjoying her brother's predicament with a smile on her face.

Vinceno looked at his son from where he stood next to a wagon where he watched his driver check the ropes and wheels.

"I brokered this marriage, and you'll learn to live with, your wife's family is rich and the gateway to selling our silks in the central lands,"

"I'll run away father I swear it," the young man spoke dramatically as he stared at his father.

"No you won't, You're the too spoiled son, you couldn't last a day on your own," said the merchant., " And by Alomeg, I'll hobble you myself, before I let my son break off an engagement and embarrass our good name,"

"You'll do no such thing, my love," the wife spoke up, "Bernardo is just nervous, once he sees the girl he'll fall in love with her,"

Before anything else could be said the Salazar's family noticed two people approaching one was a long haired blond boy in red robes leading a saddled gray horse packed with bedrolls and , full saddle bags. Next to him was a tall bald dark skinned youth leading a large odd looking thick leg black bull saddled for riding, drawing a small two wheel cart loaded with supplies.

"Mr. Salazar" Seamus nodded as his employer as he greeted him.

"Young master Seamus and Lord Wimbowaradi, It's good to see you,"

The man's wife looked at the boys, who looked no older than her own son. , Vince, they're children".

"Well paid and skilled children," he replied to her.

"What's this? You two are actually on time?," a familiar aristocratic female voice. Xarona rode sidesaddle on a white horse with odd cat shaped eyes.

"And we can read and do arithmetic too," quipped Callum causing everyone but the redhead to giggle.

"Isabella, Bernardo, Kisa, and Lisa, this is Lady Belisona. All the women curtsied. And Bernardo did a quick bow.

"I'm in your employ, not the other way around. , You may call me Xarona, ," the girl graceful slid off the horse to her feet.

"Good Morning Xarona," Callum.

"You three dolts can still use my title.. and speaking of three where's the archer?"

"Technically I don't have to use your title," Callum, left the back of the bull and walked to the Salazar women and bowed, then shook Bernard's hand after speaking to the witch a polite yet condescending manner.

You're a big one," said Isabella to the young man in front of her.

"Thank you, Ma'am," returned the young lord.

"Are you a Giant," asked Kisa looking up from, her book., "

"No," said Callum, "But my great, great, great grandfather was a Titan or so my grandmother's story goes,"

"We have Wildkin blood," Kisa, "Not a lot, though, just enough to do this. the girl's eyes turned cat-like for a second.

"Not in front of strangers," said her mother sharply.

"It's ok Ma'am," Seamus left his horse and walked it closer to the group, "Most people have the blood of some of the old races in them. I have a few fae bloodlines in me".

"Actually, it's about 75% of people". , Xarona, This land was full of the old races when most of our ancestors arrived from across the great sea centuries ago. "

"That's what I said," Seamus.

"And I elaborated," added the redhead.

"What about you Red, what do you have in you aside from ice," , Jase who to everyone's surprise was sitting on a bench outside the inn.

"You will address me properly," Xarona.

"I'm sorry, your royal highness," the dark-haired young man stood and bowed as he spoke with a mocking tone.

"Lady, Lord and Gentleman, shouldn't we be readying ourselves for the road, it's looking as if the weather may be against us," Isabella spoke like a mother talking to her children, whom the four young people reminded her of.

"So can we eat it?," Jase looked at Callum's Bull as the group headed towards the cities northern wall and the High road.

"He's a Bomax, their bread for heavy labor and war" Callum.

"I bet he tastes good," Jase, "

"I've never seen one before," Bernardo road up to the adventure to observe the creature closely. " Is it tamed?"

"Like a Puppy that can pull three trees and gore a southern bear with its horns," , Seamus

"I think it's silly, riding a lumbering animal like that," Said Sani to the surprise of everyone.

"Did your weird horse just talk ?," Callum.

"She's not a horse she' a Chimera and my familiar," Xarona

"Incredible, what kind, A Manticore? Griffin," Seamus looked at the witch and spoke with reverence and wonder.

"A felix ," the young woman looked at the young man, "And do you have a familiar wizard?"

Seamus met the girls gaze, "Not yet, but then again I haven't needed one,"

"If you like I can show you the binding rites, maybe we could use your horse or the lice in the Hunters' hair," joked the lady of Belasona

Seamus looked at the girl and smiled.

I believe a familiar finds it's master, not the other way around.

Sani noted and giggled knowing that's exactly what happened between her and Xarona. The witch was in the middle of her with the year when she founded the scared and wounded creature that had run afoul of the many groups of owls that perched on and around her families home.

Xarona spent days reading books on chimera and mundane medicine to keep the creature alive and was surprised by that Sani had, in turn, learned the girl's language. To the young Wizards surprise the witch just nodded at him in a manner with a civility he did not expect.

" We best get moving," said Jase looking at everyone, I smell rain building up in the north," he said . Vinceno nodded and looked at his drivers who immediately headed to collect the wagons and prepare for the trip north.

*****

"Documents!," called out an armored wall guard standing at one of the five gates exiting the city.

Two of the gates were for entry, two for exit and third for official travel. As was the law in most kingdoms, those entering or exiting a kingdom seat needed to show their travel documentation, for some of it was a piece of paper or vellum with their name, place of birth and their lord's seal, for other it was a grand patent of nobility.

To help expedite things the Adventurers guild gave their members folded leather bound books identifying them as guild members along with any pertinent information. The information stamped with the guild seal and magically enchanted to make altering it nearly impossible.

The line to exit moved far quicker than the entrance as large wagons full of various items being shipped from other lands needed to be inspected and their tax information verified. Contraband was a big problem as was everything from untaxed cheeses, to illegally summoned imp workers. A combination of guardsmen and magicians specializing in mind reading and divination inspected horses, carts, and large supply wagons. On the ground, while a smaller group did the same at the cities towering airship tower port where magically powered and expensive galleys and barrages locked, loaded and unloaded.

The party passed through the gate quickly; adventures were often rushed out of cities due to the issue of having powerful and well-skilled people in towns with nothing to do was usually seemed as potentially dangerous. Once out of the city gate the group crossed a bridge over one of the multiple rivers leading into the city and headed to the official start of the southern –central branch of the high road.

CHAPTER 2:
CROSSING THE CRIMSOM

The High-Road was first constructed five decades ago when kingdoms realized that while rivers were convenient for shipping, roads were cheaper. Several members of the Free-kingdoms decided to put aside differences and build a road between them with stops at their most magnificent cities. The first version of the road was just a well-kept wide packed dirt road. Eventually, however, the road was improved upon with stone.

The High-Road proved to be worth its expense but not without its problems. Such a well-maintained road was perfect for armies to travel on and maintenance was high. The first issue was solved by the roads not being allowed to go directly into cities but curving around them three to five miles away. Cities and towns build their roads to connect to the high road, but those roads were usually well guarded or designed in such a way to give the city an advantage in case of attack.

Past travelers on the road started to add their own "amenities," camp-sites were built near the roads, with some lords providing stone or wood "Travel houses" they maintained. Enterprising merchants rented lands from nobles to build inns and taverns and as was expected, small towns sprung up along the road. Yet, as the law-abiding and the lordly found the road a boon to their travel and finances so did the criminal element. Bandits preyed on travelers, smugglers drops and caves were placed near the road is hidden by crafty artistry or magic.

Members of the old races such as trolls, ogres, and the smaller more brutal giants found the road an easy place to gather "food," Still, despite all of the potential dangers the High Road was the easiest and cheapest to travel for most folk.

*****

Jase rode out in the front of the odd little caravan as the drizzle fell. His old gray horse was more used to traveling through the dirt paths of the woods near his families home and while many saw the southern lands as being just as civilized and populated as the north, it wasn't. In fact, while it wasn't as wild as the central lands, it was still in a lot of ways pristine grasslands, forest, mountains, and rivers. Jase grew up in a small isolated forest that while officially control by Lord and Lady Ausnorbi it was so remote and so far up in the tree-covered hills that the people there never paid taxes, and had lived in relative isolation for almost a hundred years. Most made a living farming, trapping, hunting, and in less than lawful pursuits.

Jase's father made his living as a hill raider. " The old man" as Jase called him and his crew would travel far from their home, rob from the "Bottom Folk," what they called those that didn't live among them and bring back their ill-gotten gain. They did this with more stealth than bloodshed, but they were not afraid to fight, especially when it came to Adventurers and guards sent after them. Jase learned everything he knew about moving quietly, noticing what's around him and how to use a bow from his father. The "old man" could be stubborn, drank too much and had more than once struck him out of anger, but he knew what he was doing and unlike most raiders had never been caught.

He also saw his son's potential. Jase was "touched" as they called it in the hills. He could see, hear and smell farther and with more details than most people. He knew when the weather was about to change and he could shoot a bow better than just about anyone in his village.

The "old man," knew his son would be a great Hill-Raider, maybe the best, but he also knew how dangerous the life was. Those that were captured were hung or died working under a lord's lash as part of a farm or road gang. Those that lived risked death by accident or by the hands of a friend or rival wanting to take what they had. When his son turned fifteen, he told him son to leave the hills, to see the world and if he didn't like what he saw he could come back and be a raider. Jase left with only his bow, horse and knives and traveled into the bottomlands living off nature's bounty and honing his abilities as a hunter and tracker.

"Don't you think we should move slower', Xarona called out from her place riding near the enclosed purple and lavender wood and metal wagon that held the Salazar women and acted as the entire families home on wheels. The wagon was pulled by two large draft horses controlled by a grey-haired man who whistled to himself.

"No, The roads good and the rains not too serious yet," Jase called back, his eyes still on the road and not on the fussy red-head who was holding a well-made parasol in one hand and her reigns in another.

"We'll be fine young miss," said the old teamster.

" That's Lady to you," said the witch.

"Yes M'lady," said the old man quickly, acknowledging her position while still enjoying her obvious discomfort at being on horseback in the rain.

Seamus rode next to the two large wagons full of supplies and gifts. Both were made of wood with large iron and wood wheels. Stacked high they goods were protected from the elements by canvas tied down with ropes. His cloak's hood up for the first time since coming to the city with his best friend he allowed himself to embrace the fact he was now an Adventurer and doing what he used to read about in the books read as a child. His emotions now ran the gambit between excitement, and nervousness as he watched the mist-shrouded lands around him, would there be bandits, would there be monsters? Or would it be as they had told him in the guild, just a long, uneventful, boring trip like most were?

"Callum, you okay," the young Magician called back to his friend who was at the end of the caravan. Callum, wearing a red leather hooded surcoat over his armor, rode quietly missing his home more than he had thought. The Old red keep was never quiet, either his mother was talking to their few servants about their various duties or general gossip, his father was bellowing at their small militia or talking to various foreman and visitors. His siblings also kept up a fair amount of noise especially his younger brother and sister who were now well into their teens but still enjoyed tormenting their older siblings especially the eldest son an Acolyte Of Alomeg in training at the keeps temple, a steepled building connected by a covered breezeway to the rest of the buildings. Yemen was the future Lord of the keep and a talented singer and musician, tall (but not as tall as Callum), handsome and very even-tempered. While their parents tried not to show favorites, in moments of weakness when they did it was Yemen they favored as he was the future of the House.

Older them him, but because of family tradition not in line to rule the house was the eldest child Yvette. She was the second tallest child, but where Callum had the with of a titan, she had the thinness of her all but forgotten Djinn ancestors as well as some of their angular features, and like them, she could talk to plants and winds, but that was the limit of her abilities. Still, her talents came in hand and made her an expert gardener and allowed her family to avoid diseased trees when cutting timber as well as coaching trees to grow after being cut.

Third in line was Mareen If the family was said to have a black-sheep, it was the athletic child with a love of gambling, petty crimes, and a good fight. Many would also remark he was most like their father in his youth, Maureen didn't avoid trouble, in fact, he made a fair amount and might have come to an early end if his parents had not intervened and forced him into the militia. The military tempered him some but more than anything taught him to be a better fighter. In fact, he would make a living traveling the south as a bare-fisted fighter picking up new moves and new troubles along the way, and when things became too troublesome, he knew he could always find sanctuary in his family's home.

After Callum (by one year) came to Erv. Who was an odd child growing up, having imaginary friends and spent most of his time alone? His grandmother thought for a time he had the sight and could see spirits, but that's was not the case, Erv was just an odd duck. An artist and perfectionist he spent his free time painting murals inside the keep, organizing things and helping out as needed. Then puberty struck, and the awkward boy learned another talent, he was fast and witty and good with the ladies. This mother's disappointment Mareen taught the youngster how to fight, not with his fist but with swords and Erv took the blade as swiftly as he did to painting. Luckily he wasn't as short-tempered as his older brother and still saw himself as more of a lover than a fighter.

Being the youngest daughter by five years left Vimi or Vee for short was isolated from her siblings. The hardy youngest daughter grew up mostly alone as her siblings were in classes or helping their parents most of the time while she was stuck in the keep learning to be a lady and though she didn't know it would most likely be the daughter married off for family advancement. Vimi eventually figured out her lot in life and rebelled by becoming as unladylike as she could. Against her mother's wishes the girl learned what she considered the worse possible lessons from her siblings, From Erv, she learned to speak her mind, From Callum a love of reading books about things a courtly lady shouldn't such as adventure, sciences, and philosophies. Mareen taught her to fight, Yemen, to seek her path and Yvette not to be afraid to explore the wilderness.

Callum giggled to himself as he thought about how at such a young age his sister was spending more in time at lumber camps and could wield an Axe as good as any man.

As his thoughts gathered back into the present the big man saw the clouds above darken as thunder rolled in the distance,

"Looks like we're in on a roll, Enkidu," he said to his bull who unlike the horses seemed unbothered by the growling sky.

"Should we stop?," Vinceno called out to Jase from his horse. "The Weather is about to get nasty.

"It won't last long, just a little shower. ," the dark-haired hunter smiled as the rain started to increase, "Just watch the road and follow me,"

The caravan moved along the road past trees that among farmlands as the rain poured , increasing every minute and reaching a point where only Jase could see more than a few feet ahead.

We need to stop," called out the witch, "I'm getting soaked!".

"This here is nothing, I've seen harder rains in the Hills," the caravan's guide called back just loud enough to be heard over the near torrential rains.

"We'll catch our deaths of cold," Bernardo.

"We got a healer," laughed Jase picking up his pace a bit. , "And It's about to break," Just as he said the words, the rain started to slow down.

In a matter of minutes, the rain was back to a drizzle.

"Told You," the young man called out, Should be like this 'til nightfall, He added. Xarona glared at the hunter and resist the urge to curse him on the spot. Instead, she pulled her wand and focused her magic on herself and remembered what it was like to be dry and clean. Green energy swirled from her wand around her fading as it rose, leaving her, her clothing, horse, and belongings both dry, clean and refreshed.

"That's a useful spell," Seamus from behind her.

"Refresh," It's little more than a cantrip, the witch spoke with her usual highborn manner.

"I know, I can do something like that... but, It's a waste of energy, It hasn't stopped raining, and once we stop we'll have a fire and dry out on our own and as it has". The blond did his best not to sound condescending; there was something about the redheaded witch that still intimidated him despite the fact her fussy nature made her an easy target for various barbs.

"I refuse to go about like a drowned rat," the girl insisted despite the fact she knew he was right, once spent even a witch's magic took time to recharge. If there was an emergency, a vain glamour like the one she just cast could be far more costly than remaining wet.

"How far are we traveling young Master Jase," Vinceno.

"Well Mr. Salazar, I was going to go till you said "stop," the hunter replied, "Cause if it were up to me we'd go till we cross the Crimson-River, after that can camp and I can do a little hunting,"

The silk merchant nodded, despite the discomfort of the rain, he wanted to make it to their destination on time and felt more assured of the peasant boys abilities after he predicted to the second the weather's mood.

"Sounds good," said the merchant with a nod to the young hunter.

As the rain lessened the group's pace increased as they made their way past more farms and a work-gang huddled by fire to the side of the road. They then past a sign letting them know that they've traveled almost eight miles and that the Rojo river (Often called the Crimson or Blood river by locals) was less than two miles away. The livestock was starting to slow as the group had yet to stop to rest or for food hoping to push past the river before doing so.

"There is such a thing as Lunch," Xarona.

"This is barbaric," Sani growled in in her horse form.

"We need to cross the river before there's more rain and we have to deal with..,". Janse words stopped as he came over the rise and looked down a slight hill to see the Crimson river, so named because the red dirt it flowed over in parts made it red when it was moving fast, was partially covering a stone bridge.

"Hell Fire!," he exclaimed raising a hand to signal the caravan to stop.

Leaping off his horse the hunter walked towards the bridge, The river had over flooded its banks covering the stone bridge in a foot of water.

"Looks like all the rush was for nothing Bernardo," looking at his father.

"Maybe we can go around it," the older man reached for his saddle back, opened and pulled out a rolled up damp vellum map.

Spotting the river with his eyes, the man backtracked with his finger they way they came and to a small road, they would take them to another less well-kept bridge crossing to the west and a low creek crossing (most likely flooded also) to the east.

"Damn the Devils, Almost a day's ride back and across either way across bridges and creeks that are mostly like as bad or worse than this,"

"Master Salazar," one of the drivers spoke up., We're loaded good, and our carriages are pretty high, we might make it".

Salazar shook his head, " It's not worth the risk, we might be able to wait it out," said the merchant in a dour tone.

" Can't the Lady and the magician magic us away across," The voice of Isabella who had exited her wagon along with her daughters only to see most of her group gathering to look at a river cresting over a bridge.

" I'm no wizard, but I think that'll take a load of magic," Jase,"

"Maybe we can set up a guideline with ropes. ," another driver.

"Lady Xarona, do you think you and Seamus can do something here," Isabella looked at the redhead with who's ringlets were now a frizzled mess on partially held down by her pointed hat.

"I'm not much of an Elementalist, but I might be able to move a few things across or shrink some of the supplies to make them easier to move, maybe even a wagon, but that would exhaust me for days,"

"I know my elements and movement; I might be able to slow the river down, but not for long," Seamus.

"How about, I unhitch Enkidu, walk him across, you throw a line, and we help guide the wagons?," Callum.

"That could work if Seamus can do what he says he can," The witch looked at the magician who glared back at her.

"Of course, I can, I think," he said sounding far less sure that he would have liked.

"We'll do it one at a time," Jase spoke up then looked at Xarona. "Fussy britches can you help get Ms. Isabella and the girls across?,"

"What did you call me," growled the young Lady.

"Just wanted to see if your listening," quipped the hunter.

"Yes, I can do it that," the young woman took out her wand," That's simple levitation.

"Then we have a plan," Salazar looked at the group. " and Let's hope to Alomeg, the Lady of the crossroads and any anyone else listening that it works,"

Callum crossed the bridge river slowly, leading Enkidu across. And carrying with him two large rolls of rope. After a couple of near slips, he made across. Tied a rope to a part of the bridge above water and the other end to a large rock and threw it back across. He then did the same thing on a similar raised portion of the bridge. This created two guidelines showing the width of the bridge and something to grab on to if someone slipped. He then tied a piece of rope to his bull and tossed the other end tied to rock across.

"Tie it to the first wagon!," he said.

Jase and one of the teamsters tied the rope to the Neck of the first wagon.

"How strong is your friend," Vinceno looked at Seamus with a worried look on his face.

"Very:," said the young man as he started to focus on the river, reaching out with his power he began to feel the flow of the river as moved along the bridge and river itself. The water like all elements did what they did; Fire burned, Air wanted to fill up everything, earth wanted to be stable, and water wished to move. Convincing it not to do so was not an easy thing as it was telling it not to do what it saw as its primary duty. In fact turning water to ice or steam would have been easier than to tell it not to be what water was at its center.

" Holding his staff, the young magician walked to the water and dipped it in a few inches, touching it saved energy, which was basic magic knowledge.

"Something's happening," Bernardo watched from his horse as the water slowed.

"Hurry," Seamus spoke calmly maintaining his focus but knowing slowing so much water would in time start to back up the water on one end and the more that happened the harder his task would become.

"Ready!" shouted Jase as he took a smaller rope tied it around the head of one of the wagon's horses and started to lead it across slowly.

"Come on a girl; you can do it," he said to the creature. His keen senses could hear the horse's heartbeat quicken as hit's hooves touched the water.

Slowly the young man led the wagon across with the help of the driver, the tall lord, and the bull.

"Steady," he said as they reached the middle of the river.

"This is exciting," said Kisa

"But scary," added Lisa. As the watched the wagon make it a third of a way there before it started to slide to the side pushing. With the slowed but still mighty river.

"Seamus!," Jase looked back at the magician who was standing at the river's edge, which knuckled hands on his staff, a grimace on his face.

"Trying," grunted the blond magician.

Feeling the rivers growing weight and strength, the wizard knew he had to try something different least the river break free of his grasp. Focusing harder he pictured the river in his mind's eye, he could feel its flow, and it's wanting to be free. He could also feel the wheels and horses in the river as water moved around him. Releasing the water that no longer affected the wagon or the travelers he was able to slow down and divert water around where and near where the people and carts were.

"You're quite good," The witch spoke to the wizard with surprise and admiration. The wizard ignored the compliment, focusing on his duty and feeling the wagon and horses leave the water on the other side. Relaxing he heard the bridge creak under the water; he could feel the weight of the water being held back now starting to shift the bridge.

"Unmoor the horses and use them to help pull the other wagon across," Vinceno to the men across the river., "I'm coming across next,"

Bernardo looked at his father took a deep breath and as the stone tied to the rope came flying across he grabbed it and tied it to the Wagon with the help of the next driver. As his father readied his horse, the merchant's son climbed on his and started to lead the wagon, "I'll take this one, father," he said

"Bernardo mi nino," called out the woman in the language of her ancestors. Bernardo slowly walked his horse between the guidelines slowly, his eyes darting between the men and animals on the other shore. Seamus and behind him to his worried family.

"Be careful Master Bernardo," said the teamster handling the wagons reign as he felt the force slip slightly along the currents.

"I can do this," said the tan skinned young man, feeling the pull of his horse against the current.

"You're close Mr. Bernardo!," Callum.

"Good job son," Vinceno spoke with pride. His son had always been a shy boy and had never shown any interest in anything athletic or dangerous beyond horse riding. He had tried to get the boy interested in swordsmanship and even hired him a tutor but to no avail. The fact the young even wore a sword was more for show than anything else.

Ten feet to the shore Bernardo, pride fully raise a hand in triumph and smiled, he didn't seem or notice that under the murky water a stone had loosened and risen enough to trip his horse causing it to stagger and rear. Unable to control his stead the young man was thrown into the water causing screams on both side of the river.

"Seamus watched as the handsome young man slid into the water and tried to stand only to be dragged across to near the guide rope. flailing about he tried to grab the rope but couldn't reach it and slid over the bridge itself into the river. Xarona raised her wand, her eyes darting about for the young man if she could see him she knew she could grab him, but he was underwater already.

The young magician focused his thoughts, feeling through the water and finding the young man. Dividing his focus between the wagon and Bernardo, he strained to find the young man so he could will the water to raise him up and swing him near the far shore of the river.

Jase looked about for any signs of the boy in purple and lavender, seeing a ripple and a purple sleeve he moved quickly diving into the water almost on top of Bernardo. Swimming in the river and with the help of Seamus's magic he slid the young man near the shore and along him was tossed out of the river by a large eddie.

Upon seeing his successful save, Seamus felt his knees buckle, and he saw his vision blur as the ground moves towards him quickly.

"Got you," Vinceno grabbed the young magician by his clothing pulling him away from the river.

On the other side, Callum ran to Jase and Bernardo and with one hand lifted the coughing hunter to his feet. He he then looked at the other soaked young man was laying on the ground. Quickly he knelt and checked for a pulse.

"My son?," called out Isabella, pleading to all that could hear her for his safety.

Callum turned the boy over and looked for cuts, broken bones, and bruises and upon seeing none, he turned the young man on his side and tapped on his back, the boy started to cough up water. Looking at the frantic woman the young lord raised a hand and nodded at those on the other side. Sign things were fine.

"Did you give him the healing touch," asked Jase now standing straight.

"No," Callum looked at the soaked hill-man. , "Healings more than calling the divine to mend bones and seal wounds it knows the body and how to help it without prayer and powers,"

"Thank you," Bernardo spoke between coughing.

"Jase and Seamus did most of the work," Callum.

Jase nodded at the scion of the Mwamba wa Mwaloni and patted him on the back, "I owe you," he said, the dark-skinned young man looked at him and waved away his pledge, " We're a team, we have to watch each other;'s back right?'. He said. The young hunter nodded, he could see being in the guild was different from being a raider, raiders cared little for each other and always had an angle, but it seems for now, or at least with the Crusader, that wasn't the case.

Xarona stood looking at the predicament on her side of the river; Things weren't working out as she had planned. She had thought her first mission would not only get her away from her troubles at home but be easy.   However, less than a full day in and she was stuck on the far side of a raging river with her client, his daughters, wife; a fainted magician, a scared teamster, and a posh travelers wagon.

"Mr. Salzar, please help me tie the remaining horses to the last wagon," she said. Moving towards the connected lines.

"We can't risk the bridge again. ," The merchant looked at the girl who was already heading to unity the first rope.

"We won't touch the bridge," the witch.

"What are you planning mistress," Sani looked at the redhead who was struggling with the knots on the rope.

"I can't let a country mage outdo me," she said in her typical haughty tone" as she grew flustered with the rope. Pulling her wand she tapped the bundle of knots causing them to unravel and float to the large wagon's neck and tie themselves.

The merchant looking for something to focus on other than almost losing his son and the so far folly of his trip easily untied his ropes, he, after all, was a sailor long before he became a merchant, he then tied his lines next to the girls.

"I would love to know your plan Young Lady," the silk merchant looked and sounded worried.

"I could, and would most likely end looking like Seamus there If I levitate the wagon across. , but as I might be needed for other magic later, I've decided just to levitate the wagon off the ground and have the others

pull us across, " Xarona tried not to sound as nervous as she felt. The
Merchant's eyes widened. "Is that safe?" he asks.

"Of course not, We'll be weightless, and the merriest strong wind could
tip us or worse. But I will do my best to keep us steady," Xarona walked
over to Sani and whispered in her ear, in less than a second the house
flowed back into the multi-tailed winged cat and started her flight over
the river.

"Don't shoot," said the creature as it made its way over buffeted by the
growing winds.

"That girl turned that horse into a talking cat with wings," said the
driver after observing what he saw.

"No, You dolt, I can change my shape," Said Sani landing near Callum,
Bernardo, and Jase.

"That's different," The hunter looked at the other young men.

"Incredible!," Bernardo.

Yes, Yes, I know you're in awe, but my mistress is about to do something... unpractical, and she needs your help".

All eyes fell on the cat creature as she took a breath and started relaying
instructions.

Xarona made sure The Salazars and Seamus were secure in the Lavender and Purple wagon and instructed the Teamster to tie The merchants
and the young Wizards horses secure to the wagon at the rear by ten feet
of rope, no more and no less. Walking around the Wagon and looking at

the four horses attached to it and the driver Xarona started calculating the exact amount of energy she would need to do what she had promised. The Coventry taught witches not only how to use magic but how to apply mathematics to its use. Climbing into the front of the Wagon and sitting next to the driver who smelt of cheap ale and tobacco their head closed her eyes briefly, she focused on the wagon and horses in the same way Seamus did the river.

She started to feel them in her mind's eye, feel everyone in the wagon as well as every piece of wood and every metal bolt. She could feel the horses and the ropes and even the driver next to her.

"Well. let's get started shall we," the girl pulled her wand from its casing, It was ivory and onyx with a dark green crystal at the end tapering to a point.

"I'm not sure about This M'lady," said the driver.

"Nor Am, now hold tight to the reins, keep the horses calm, or I'll turn you into grub worm," The young with voice was cold, she didn't want to threaten the man, but knew it would help him focus on doing his best.

With a flick of the witches wand, green energy started to flow from the air around the wagon and horses. As well as through them. Xarona then raised her wand causing the wagon and horses to rise and bob like a ball in the water. She could feel the wind moving them about and used her magic to compensate. At first, the wagon only hovered a few feet off the ground then with an upward flick of the wand it floated higher. "Sani it's time," she thought to her familiar as she floated and straightened the horses and wagon," The creature heard her telepathic command and related to those on the other bank.

Slowly they started to pull everything across making sure the lines didn't tangle. Xarona knew her mind had to remain a focus; there were so many variables that nothing could be left unnoticed.

"Steady," she said to herself as she moved her wand rhythmically in her gloved hand. The wagon despite its weight was behaving as was to a lesser degree the horses being controlled by the driver. The rear horses, however, were not, they moved and kicked and whined as they floated above. The witch could feel their fear and knew it had to be dealt with, taking a breath she sent calm through the spell to everything it was connected to, it would cost her more energy, but the horses and even the humans panic would lessen.

The Wagon and horses came to the shore yells, and bellows of victory arose from the drivers and three young men on the ropes. Xarona released her spell as soon as it was safe and did her best to draw in whatever lose magic she could as she was taught. Spells occasional left small amounts of residual energy about and even more rarely attracted like energy into itself.

"Good job," she looked at the pale man sitting next to her.

The man nodded, You too M'lady," he said relieved.

Not long after the wagon landed and was driven down the road to join the others, Isabella opened the door of hers, leaped to the ground looked about and ran towards her son.

"Bernardo," she called out as she threw her arms around him, "You silly boy, don't ever do that again,"

The young man smiled," Yes mother," he said hugging her back.

Vinceno upon exiting looked at his son with pride bringing an even more significant smile on the young man's face. He then looked at the wagons and started inspecting them and to his surprise found almost no damage.

Seamus exited the wagon using his staff to stand, he felt drained and was still unsure what had happened. Looking around he saw Bernardo hugging his mother and then Callum and Jase walking towards him and suddenly felt relief.

"You okay," Callum to Seamus.

"Just tried," the blond returned.

"Well holding back a river will do that," The Crusader patted the Wizard on the shoulder and hugged him, "Didn't know you had that in you," he said before releasing his friend.

"I didn't either," Seamus.

"Neither did I," Xarona climbed down from the wagon awkwardly almost falling, "You have the basics down, and you know your craft, with some advance energy working you could be a collegium quality wizard,"

Seamus nodded at the left-handed compliment figuring it was just the ladies way of doing things.

"You did pretty well yourself Fussy Britches," Jase.

Xarona smiled, "Thank You, but call me that again and you'll not live to regret it," her voice showed both annoyance and amusement.

"No kidding, that was incredible," Callum.

"As I said on the other bank, I couldn't let your friend show me up," the girl smile over rid her arrogant tone in the eyes of the bald young man.

Sani floated over to her mistress and into her arms,

"Can we go home now? " the creature asked.

"No," the witch responded.

"Seamus laughed and for the first time took stock of everyone and everything and realized something was missing.

"Callum, where are our things?" he asked his oldest friend.

Callum slapped his head, "Alomeg 's tears, Their still on the other side in our cart. Vinceno looked at the young men, "Do not worry; I'll replace whatever you lost in the next town, It's the least I can do," He said his wife was nodding in agreement.

Xarona rolled her eyes and walked back towards the river, seeing the cart on the other side she pointed her wand. She just made a travelers cart, its occupants, and four houses weightless; Her confidence was up, and for a witch, her conviction was just as much a tool as her wand, in fact in a way it was fuel. The cart stat to float upward and across as green energy moved about it. Landing softly on the other back she then willed it to roll up next to her.

"One cart full of what I'm sure is useless minutia, safe and sound".

"Thank you M'lady," Callum.

"Was nothing," Xarona found herself smile again and realized she had not smiled this much since leaving home.

After reordering the caravan the group headed north up the tree-lined road for another two hours. Needing to rest the found a stone campers circle to the side of the road with a bare fire pit, stones for seats and a makeshift wooden table; a dugout latrine sat about 20feet away with a two crude stone and wood seats with holes in the bottom at one end.

Jase made sure the immediate area was safe before signally the group it was okay to set up with a whistle before heading deeper into the woods. The wagons were moved off the roads, and their wheels hammered down into the soft ground with foot long "U" shaped spikes designed to keep the wagons from rolling off and making them harder to steal.

The travelers wagon was set up close to the camper's circle allowing for easy access. The drivers then started to gather firewood despite the fact a small pile was already present. It was common courtesy to leave some wood out at stopping areas along the High Road. Vinceno and Isabella sat on a two of the stones and quietly, their daughters made their way to the latrine while Bernardo stood guard up wind, his eyes were fixed not on his surrounding but on Seamus who was taking chalk and etching sigils on the road near the wagons and near the stone sitting area. He knew the young magician had saved his life and was not only thankful but found his eyes were drawn to him for reasons he didn't quite understand.

Once the firewood has gathered the drivers set up their simple tent while Callum did the same for him and Seamus as his friend finished his sigils and recovered from his ordeal at the river, the medium size tent was "modern" model designed to be set up quickly. It was sewn together with a canvas floor, walls, and sloped roof. Held together by a simple wooden frame and rope. Inside the tent, the young lord unloaded the supplies off the cart and then lifted and moved the cart closer to the tent. Before spiking its wheels.

"You need help setting up your tent Xarona?" The Crusader asked the witch. "And that I 've asked that... where are your things".

The Witch smiled and took a small velvet pouch off her belt and placed it on the ground. With a point of her wand, the bag expanded till it was now as tall as it's owners waist and just as wide at the base.

"No thank you, though I appreciate it, I think I can handle things on my own. ," the witch reached into the bag and pulled out a roll of green canvas and tossed it at an empty spot nearby, in mid-air, it unfolded into a tent setting itself up and even spiking itself to the ground in a matter of seconds.

Callum smiled and nodded before leaving the witches side and walking over to Seamus.

"She throws magic about like a generous king throws around gold coins," The crusader said as he sat next to the magician.

"No. it just looks like that, I can see the enchantments on her things, the spells were pre-cast and set to do their magic on command. Each command takes hours to set and powers itself off the magical natural energy found everywhere. Its good work and-and shows she has no problem putting time into her workings. "

"Why didn't you do that with our stuff?," Callum.

Seamus shrugged, "Didn't think of it till now, once I get back to full power I can start on it a little bit at a time,"

After the camp was set and everyone had gathered around the fire to dry the drizzle slowed some, and the sun could occasionally be seen peeking through the clouds. Jase returned, heralding his arrival with a whistle before appearing from the forest carrying a wild piglet about the size of a medium-sized dog and two plump pheasants. Arrows had clipped the bird's wings, and their necks rang while the pig showed signs of being shot in the throat.

"Forest clear, just some deer, a small pack of wolves and small game. ," he said placing his catch on the damp wooden table in the stone circle.

"Give me a second to clean up my arrows, and I'll get started on skinning my catch,"

"Isabella looked at the dirty young hunter and his game with disgust, " I appreciate the effort young man, but we brought ham, flour and a few other things for our dinner,"

"Well, it's going to go bad if we don't cook it or cure it," Jase.

"I'll take care of it," Callum.

Jase nodded and took three bloody arrows wrapped in cloth from his quiver and started to clean.

"You got it," he replied wondering what his teammate had planned.

The drivers sat up the fire pit, then set up a pole and hung the pot over it, filled the bowl with water and placed in cubes of ham, potatoes, beets, and onion with a large helping of salt and started a stew for themselves and the rest of the party.

Not far the drivers fire, Callum waited for Jase to pluck the pheasants and drained the pig's blood into a small bowl before taking the blood it back into the woods. The Crusader then took the meat and laid it out on a piece of vellum he had laid on the table using coals from the fire he burnt off most of the sparse hair on the piglet before taking out a small sharp knife and water to shaving the rest. He then opened the creature up, and innards on the side were making sure the pig's intestines were intact.

"That's disgusting," Xarona.

"It won't be in an hour," Seamus

The crusader then Walked into his tent and came back with a large fry pan a hinged metal grate and clay bottles full of oils and spices. He then reentered the tent and collected a small metal tin full of butter, some apples, potatoes, onions, carrots and long finger-shaped red peppers.

With a knife, he removed the pigs head, butterflied the pig, cracked its bones with a mallet so it would stay flat a, oiled it, coated it with spices, placed it on the metal grate and lay the unfolded grate over the large fire.

He then took the pheasants quickly, opened them stuffed them with sliced apples, onions, and carrots, stitched them closed with twin, placed them in a pan with melting butter and dried rosemary, thyme, and garlic cloves. He then put the potatoes on clean stones in the fire.

"That's some fancy cooking," Jase., "I didn't think lords do that kind of thing," Callum smiled, he had moved a large stone to sit near the fire where he was mixing corn meal, wheat flour water, soft butter salt and sugar into a mix.

"Not all lords are rich enough to have lots of servants," We had a few for stable work and cleaning, but my mother and grandmother does most of the cooking, I had a big appetite as a kid, and I used to watch them, I picked up a few things, and eventually they started teaching me".

"Spicy-corn cakes!," Seamus walked near the fire exited.

Callum placed the batter on his lap and started cutting the Pepper into tiny rings into the mixture.

"While I'm sure that stew tastes good, I'm sure there's enough food here for everyone," the large young man said as the smell of his meal filled the area and flowed into the forest.

CHAPTER 3:
LESTER BOUND

The following morning a fuller and dryer group awakened. The stew was left eaten only by the Drivers who found Lord Wimbowaradi's too fancy. The group ate a quick meal of Sausage links made of pigs and birds livers and kidneys, ham and spices smoked overnight smoke over a covered fire pit that night and honey-cornmeal mush. The camp was then struck, and the wagons placed back on the road and hitched for travel.

Still traveling north the caravan saw their first kingdom marker, a large log set in a stone stand. On the stand was carved Vallus South, Arden North. On the trunk was engraved the names and miles of various towns, the first being Lester and the last being Arden Proper. Placed around the stone and tacked to the logs were multiple papers from recent travelers letting anyone who cared to read it know they had passed that way.

"The Vu family by wagon. from Vallus to Wykota, 1872)," Kisa read one of the letters. "I hope they made it," said the young girl before moving to the next sign. The group had stopped as many did to look at the marker and place their names on a piece of fancy white paper and tack it to the log. Seeing a chance, Callum kneeled for a quick prayer and was surprised to see Isabella and two of the drivers join him. After the prayer and a few more readings by Kisa the group once again started up the road again, following its path north than ever so slightly west.

When the Sun marked noon, the group stopped at a small creek to water the livestock and have a quick lunch of Ham stew heated in the bowls with a wave of Seamus's hand.   When the overly salty meal was done, the group continued on the road, occasionally passing wagons heading south and travelers along the route. As the marker for "Lester 40 miles" came into view Jase noticed three horses at nearby a tree line.

"On the right," he said pointing the men out and placing his hand on one of his swords.

"You think it's trouble," One of the drivers,"

"Not for us, three men in broad daylight? They're looking for easy picking". Jase spoke without taking his eyes of the men for as long as he could. , "Still if they're stupid, they may still give us a try. "

After the horseman, there was very little for the group to do but ride until sunset, camp and rise the next morning to more grey skies and dust blown off the road. And so it went for the next three days until the flat terrain revealed a wide river that matched the High-Road after a turn in the bend.   The travelers watched boats flow up and down the wide river before it snaked away towards the town of Lester.

Tired of the road the Salazars decided to head towards the small town that sat on the Matope River in hopes of a bath and resupplying. Vinceno had seen towns like Lester before in his youth it was surrounded by farmlands and rice paddies that fed off the river. It held multiple small docks where supplies and travelers using the river did their business, and the rest of the town was mostly wooden houses and buildings a few were covered with red clay that once dried gave the buildings a ruddy color.

An ill-kept dirt road connected it to the High Road marred by the dried groves of multiple wagons, potholes and other forms of disrepair. Thankfully, however, the really bad parts were covered somewhat haphazardly by halved logs that were starting to show wood rot. So ill-kept was the road that the caravans riders and drivers were more than once forced to leave the road and travel the trampled grass nearby which was only marginally better.

At the entrance to the town, the group found a gate that also acted as a checkpoint guarded by dirt covered guards in black tabards with a silver coiled snake painted or stitched on the front that matched the town raised banners.

"Welcome to Lester," a tall man in his fifties with only a few yellow teeth remaining in his mouth spoke standing next to a three younger guards.

"Greetings," Vinceno, who had maneuvered to the front of his group spoke from horseback, "I'm Vinceno Salazar, my Family, servants and contracted adventurers are traveling to Colos lands for a wedding," He said.

The sergeant at arms grinned, "A Wedding is always good news," he said, "Now are you carrying anything for shipping or anything you shouldn't " The man looked about during his best to read the riders as he spoke.

"Nothing to ship and no contraband," Vinceno.

"No Imps, unmarked spirits, poppy or black crystal?" the man asked ignoring the merchant.

"Nothing of the sorts," Vinceno spoke with contempt to the guard.

"Ok you lazy dogs, look it over," he signaled to the three guards near him, and immediately they started to inspect the caravan.

"Is this necessary," asked the graying man in purple and lavender.

"Yep, thems my orders and I always follow my orders," the Sergeant at arms watched his men look the caravan over, look under the-the Canvas and even inspect the inside of the Traveler's wagon much to the annoyance of Isabella.

"They got a few locked chests and lots of silks on one wagon, and that ginger girl in the funny hat's horse looks kinda weird, said the eldest of the three guards, a ginger himself who seemed to be in his late twenties.

"Well, Silks and the likes that could be smuggling, you have papers on that" The sergeant at arms.

"How much is this going to cost me?," Vinceno .

"Now, that's a might rude, We're not burglars and brigands," said the man. , "But In all fairness, and as it seems you look like you're in a hurry. Copper a horse and silver, a wagon including that little cart". The Guard nodded at his men slyly.

"Fine," Vinceno reached into his coin pouch and felt around for four silver and copper coin for every horse,".

The lead guard looked over the money then waved the caravan through as its leader mumbled angrily under his breath.

Once in twon, the group made its way to the stable where the horses and bull were unhitched, and the wagons moved near a barn to be guarded by the drivers.

"If it's anything like the guard, this place is full of ill intent, girls, you stay close to me or one of our escorts. Bernardo don't wander, and everyone watches each other's back ," Vinceno.

The former sailor had not only sailed the sea but had his fair share of travels along the river. He knew some small towns like Lester made their living robbing and stealing from travelers by both illegal and semi-legal means.

"I need a Bath," Bernardo.

"Me too," said Seamus.

"Never liked them myself," Jase, "My Paw said a man only need to take one once a full moon and on his wedding day,"

"That explains so much," Xarona.

Callum giggled, looking at the girl he quickly turned away and sniffed under his arm revealing he too was "ripe" with the smell of travel.

"Yeah, I think a bath is a good idea," Callum.

"I'm sure we can find an inn or a private bathhouse," Isabella.

"I'm not so sure about that," Kisa words were full of doubt as she looked at the walls, outside fixtures and people of the riverside town.

The travlers moved through the muddy streets and wood-planked side-walks of the town, discovering that despite its condition it was full of people going about their daily business ignoring the fact they were walking in mud and muck.

"I used to live in a place like this," Seamus spoke to no one in particular., Before coming to the Mwamba wa Mwaloni, I don't remember its name, I was very young, but I do remember streets like this and the smell".

"It's not too bad, reminds me of some of the hill villages only bigger," Janse.

"Good people," a man in a long faded gray coat and mud-covered shirt and pants walked towards the group holding necklaces of shimmering crystals," ,. "Can I interest you in a clear-crystal necklace, guaranteed to extend your life and bring good health," He said.

"Jase hand slipped to a dagger and Vinceno, and his son's hands moved to his their ornate and unused swords. ".

"No thank you," Bernardo.

"Can I see, Lisa," rushed forward to look at the necklace, the man handed one to her and smiled with brown teeth.

"It's from the mines of Geaholm across the sea," the man added.

"What do you think mother?" the girl turned towards Isabella holding the necklace composed of silver wire and tiny four-sided pointed transparent crystals.

" See M'lords and Ladies, the child has the fine taste," The salesman bowed and briefly and returned to his spill, " Normally a necklace like that would cost 50 nay, sixty gold coins, but I'm a generous man willing to part with it for twenty".

"How about copper," Xarona spoke up, That's, not crystal, It's glass," she said.

"You are mistaken M'lady," the man glared at the redhead who met his gaze with one far more intimidating. "That's clear crystal, mined by the stout folk themselves,"

"Poppycock," Xarona took the necklace from Lisa and handed it back to the man,

" I know a magic crystal when I see it; I know how the light hits it and how the facets align. Now away with you ," the young woman looked down her nose at the man who reached a hand into his jacket.

"Move your hand slowly mister," said Jase calmly "Or the next thing you see will be the pit itself,"

As the false-crystal salesman didn't see the youth draw the thin tapered dagger, but he did see the big armored boy in the rear move towards him. Both actions caused him to back up and lose his footing and landing on him on his rear in the mud.

Xarona looked at Jase and Callum, "While I did not need your protection it's appreciated," she said to their surprise.

Over the past few days on the road, the witch had started to become less abrasive, and while she still threatened to turn her teammates into toads and bugs when they annoyed her, she had become slightly more polite.

After the man ignored a hand up from the free crusader, The group walked past, not noticing the man sitting in the mud look of embarrassment suddenly turn into a smile.

"Fish on a stick, Roasted fish on a stick!," A barker cried out as the group entered the town market. Wagons sat alongside small makeshift booths and wears were placed on old boxes and rugs. Locals and visitors moved between merchants, the smell of fresh cooked meats and bread filled the air and even managed to block out the smell of mud mixed with animal manure.

Callum moved to the front of the group forcing everyone in front of him and his group to either get out of the way or move ahead. The polite young lord with every bump, apologize and smile at anyone who made eye contact. He knew he could be intimidating and knew around strangers he had to make a conscious effort not to be seen as such.

"Giant!," a man called out from the crowd.

"I think he's talking to you," Jase tapped Callum on the shoulder and pointed at a man covered in mud and tattoos, he was tall, well muscled and had dark hair, beards and the blue war tattoos of the people who lived north of the Free kingdoms.

"Me ?," Callum pointed to himself.

Aye, You Shadowskin," said the man walking from a ring of people that surrounded him and a man lying in the mud.

"I don't like that word," Callum.

"What word? ," The Northman walked up to the young lord whom height he matched.

Jase could tell by the healed cuts, tattoos and the way he moved that he was a fighter.

"Mr. Salazar, we might be in a little trouble". The young hunter stopped and placed his hand on the hilt of his sword. Seamus moved to the rear and set his staff in the muck, Vinceno, and Bernardo nodded at the hunter and stood on each side of the females of the group. Xarona moved forward closer to Jase, her fingers touching her wand case.

"Shadowskin, It's an old word that was meant to hurt," the Free Crusader spoke calmly.

"Do you hear that boy, I hurt the Giants feelings," laughed the tattooed man to the group behind him who themselves started to giggle.

Callum smiled and raised his hands in placating gestures as he spoke, "Look, Friend...,"

"I ain't your friend," The burly Northman moved closer standing just a few inches from Callum, "What I am is a fighter, and I bet you six silver I can tbeat you in under 100 stones,"

"I don't fight for fun," Callum.

The man placed a finger on the young lord's chest mudding his dusty stained red and black tabard.

" What's wrong big man, afraid of looking bad in front of that plump little ginger bird," This time, the man looked past Callum and at Xarona, "I bet she'll even let me snog her right good once I take you down,"

Xarona eyes widened, her cheeks grew flush, and her anger started to build. She knew from her brief time traveling with the large man he wasn't the violent type and that he would do his best to keep the situation from escalating. She on the other hand always had a temper but knew a situation like this called for restraint and for that reason, what came out of the young lord's mouth next surprised not only her but the rest of his party.

"Touch her, and I swear to Alomeg and his Archangels I'll tear off your head and shove up your arse," Callum lowered his hands and balled his fist as he spoke in a low, threatening tone.

Lisa and Kisa stood between their father and brother; they could see something was happening up front. As they craned to necks to look, they didn't hear or notice the men moving in from the side. The first one grabbed Bernardo by his doublet pulling him close as another pushed him away into a merchant's stall. Another one placed a dirty cloth bag over Lisa's head, struck her in the face and started to drag her off.

Jase shifted his weight and drew both his swords and turned towards the girls just in time to see another man push Vinceno towards him while two more grabbed Kisa, place a bag over her head and start to run away.

Seamus sat frozen, till Isabella called out breaking his shock.

"Vinceno, the girls!," she said. , The young magician raised his staff, heat gathered around the tip, looking about for a target he found one, a middle age man pulling a struggling Kisa away.

The ball of heat shot from the staff ignited and hit the man in shoulder setting fire to his dirty shirt and burning his arm.

"The blond pup's a caster," he called out before pushing Kisa closer to his comrade and quickly pulling off his shirt off.

Callum turned his head upon hearing the sound of the fireball, seeing his chance the tattooed fighter pushed into the big man, sweeping his legs and sending him to the ground on top of Xarona.

"Mistress!," Sani flew up to get a better look, To her most humans looked alike, from her point she now saw the Big one smiled a lot at her Mistress was now on top of her mistress while the skinny little ones were being pulled away from the group by other humans.

"Got you!," a burly woman slammed a staff into the cat creature knocking it unconscious and to the ground, she then scooped it up in a bag and started to run, "Wonder what you taste," like she said smiling as she disappeared into the growing crowd.

Seamus could smell the burning flesh and cloth from his first fireball even though the man had vanished into the crowd. Looking for another target, he saw a man standing over Bernardo about to kick him. Pointing his staff again, the young magician released another self-igniting ball of heat at the hood. But before the spell could be released a sharp pain in his back between his ribs broke his concentration.

" Squeal Blondie," said a man behind the magician as he prepared to stab him again. Rearing his bloody dagger back as he smiled the man wearing the blue face paint of a northern folk didn't see the young dark-haired hunter drop his swords, draw his bow, cock an arrow or fire.

He did however, see the shaft in his chest.

Jase saw Seamus fall forward a bleeding wound in his back had matted his robes. Preparing another Arrow he turned to fire, but the only targets he could see was the crowd around him, the Big Northman was gone as were the others and the girls. Callum turned over to start stand and saw Xarona doing the same. Frustrated and embarrassed he couldn't look the young witch in the face as he rose from the muck.

"They took the girls," Isabella screamed, tears rolling down her face.

Vinceno was back on his feet and looking about his sword now drawn.

"Where are my daughters, speak up," he said brandishing his weapons and being mostly ignored.

"Bernardo looked to his side at the corpse of the man on the ground, his body still smoking and blackened from the waist up.

"Lisa, Kisa !". he called out as he tried not to gag on the smell of burning flesh.

Jase supported Seamus, to keep his torso from falling to the mud that was now mixing with the magician's blood.

Xarona upon Callum moving off suddenly rose to her feet without the use of her hands. "Sani," she called out, before spotting Seamus. Her eyes then turned to the Free Crusader who though standing was looking lost.

"Lord Wimbowaradi, your friend needs you," she said,

"I'm so sorry," Callum.

You can be sorry later," the girl grabbed the man by his by the hem of his glove and started to lead him towards the bleeding magician.

"It was an ambush; no one saw it coming," Vinceno spoke hoping to calm his wife.

"I did," Jase, "But I didn't expect, it'll be for the kids," the dark-haired youth thought back to things he could have done differently.

"You should be trying to find our daughters not trying to help your incompetent friend," Isabella growled .'

"Mother, he saved me twice, and they will need him to save Lisa and Kisa," Bernardo walked over to Seamus knelt and took the young magician's pale hand into his.

Callum mind snapped back from his melancholy upon looking at Xarona who was despite being covered in mud was focused on her wounded ally. And the young lord's best friend.

"Hold him, he might kick a little," the young Crusader said kneeling down and placing his hand on the wound.

"Alomeg, To whom I beg, creator of all, Just and right with you I shall not fall. In the name of the Seven angels who guard the world, bring healing through me, let your light unfurl," Maciel's voice grew deep louder with each word till it could be felt in the very chests of those around him. As they watched a feeling of peace and calm flowed from him. White light erupted into Seamus, causing him to shake and kick briefly, his jagged breathing started to calm, and his eyes began to open. He could feel his wound heal, not entirely but enough to stop the bleeding and close the slit in his lung.

The young wizard looked around; He could see Jase steadying him and Bernardo at his side.

"Thank you. ," said the tan-skinned man in lavender.

"Did it stop him?," Seamus.

"Fried him like fish," Jase, helped his friend stand.

"What?," Upon Standing, Seamus caught a whiff of the smell, his eyes turned to see the corpse of the man on the ground, burned from the waist up.

"What's going on here," said the leader of three men and two women in the guard attire marked by black tabards with silver snakes.

"Some Brigands took my daughters and stabbed this young man!". Vinceno sheath his sword and gestured to Seamus.

"Two girls you say?," the said leader of the group of guardsman could barely hide his apathy.

"And my cat," Xarona spoke up.

One of the guard guards snickered but stopped quickly as the red-haired witch drew her wand.

"Please, help us find them," Isabella.

" We'll do our best but, two girls of obviously well to do types like you folk are most likely just going to be sold back to you," The leader of the guard looked eyes darted to Xarona's he spoke, "And it's best you just wait to be contacted and not cause any more trouble,"

The witch lowered her wand, "I think you're right, maybe we should just return to our wagons and wait," she said to the surprise of her guildmates and the Salazars.

"Exactly," the spokesman for the guard nodded and waved a hand signaling his men to fan out, "Like I said we'll look, but your best bet is just to wait," With those words, the man bowed and left the way he came.

Isabella started to cry, as did Vinceno. Bernardo, who was standing next to Seamus nervously pulled his hand free of the magician's after realizing he was still holding it and turned to meet the witch's gaze. "Why did you say that," he demanded with an accusing looking at the adventurers.

"Because it's pretty obvious they had no intention of helping," said the young lady.

"I think her Ladyship is right," Jase spoke up. , "In places like this guards are usually as shifty as any thief and more than likely taking a cut of every crime,"

"So what do we do ?," Vinceno .

"We find the cowards and get the girls back," Callum replied, pulling his hammer free of its chain holder.

Kisa felt there was something wrong with her face, it was hurting especially around the jaw. An awful tasting rag was in her mouth, and she could not scream. Look around she could see very little, but she knew Lisa was near, she and her twin could always feel each other no matter how far away they were from each other.

Looking about in the dim light she saw a shadow of someone in a chair across from her.. Adjusting her eyes using her paltry magical talent she could see better and see that the person in the other chair was Lisa. In front of them on the floor was a bag, something squirmed inside. Looking about she could see she was in a room with a low ceiling and a wooden door, a light came from under the bottom. Jars sat on shelves on the wall to her right in left, she couldn't tell what was in them other than liquid by the way the dim light moved across one. Looking at her sister she could see they were tied to the chest and legs with rope.

"How much should we ask?," a man's voice.

"Hurd said they had silk and chests, so a lot, twenty gold each at least," a deep voice.

"Hurd's going to want his cut as will Lucas and his people," a woman's voice.. 'So maybe thirty gold each.

"What about the cat," the first voice.

"I'm eating that critter," the woman, "I heard if you do, you gain its powers,"

"That's a fairy story," Another voice.

"Still going to eat it," The woman.

"So what do we do If they don't pay?," the deep voice.

"They'll pay, and we'll do what we're gonna do if they pay," Sell them to The Cap'n of the River-Runner," Another voice.

Kisa heard everyone start to laugh and the clanging of metal on metal.

Jase moved following the footprints and the signs of struggles. He could tell what prints were fresh and what ones were the dragging heels of a girl. The kidnappers first dragged them to an alley near a tavern, where they met up with two more people who helped him carry one of the girls to another alley where they met up with two people and the other kidnapped girl who lost a shoe. He figured it was Lisa's shoe as she was the most active of the girls and the heel of the shoe was more worn from use.

He then followed the footprints to the dock to a small worn down building painted brown and green, men sat on the porch rolling dice, drinking and smoking pipes and cigars. The young hill-man could see candlelight from inside through the shutters.

"There," he said to Callum, Seamus, and Xarona as they walked up behind, he had told them to follow but not too close just in case he was spotted.

"I can feel Sani; she's afraid," Xarona,

"So am I ," Seamus.

" If you don't think you can handle yourself wait here, we don't need to be watching out for you and the girl," The hunters readied an arrow.

"I'll be okay, it's just that man I .," Seamus spoke softly.

"Alomeg will forgive you," Callum patted his friends on the shoulder," And may he bless us with keen eyes, fast legs, strong hearts and righteous fury," His words took on the deep tone they could all feel in their bones. A tone that made them feel more focused and less nervous despite the situation.

"When I shoot, you follow, don't stop moving and don't go soft, those bastards tried to kill Seamus, and they'll kill all of us and the girls if given a chance," Jase.

The three other adventurers nodded after hearing their friends words. Other nodded.

"I can make a diversion," Seamus spoke up softly.

"Then do it," Jase.

Seamus looked at the river and the porch, raised his staff focused, The river started to ripple as a fog built on the surface.

The fog started to move quickly onto the docks and towards the building where it slowed began to creep up on the porch. The magician then raised his staff cutting a corridor through the fog from where they stood on the porch.

"That's some good cover," Jase released his first arrow, a man rolling dice felt a prick in his back and then on a shoulder.

Drel, you've been shot," said another dice player seeing arrows stick out of his friend who was now falling to the ground. Drawing a dagger and moving towards his friend the gang member felt something he couldn't see grab him and lift him as he glanced behind a nearby building and saw four people running through the fog towards him.

His first instinct was to warn his friends, but to his surprise, he couldn't feel a tongue in his mouth, and his mouth was ceiling shut as teeth and skin that made his lips merged into a seamless, smooth surface. Xarona waved her wand from the man she had levitated to the one on the ground sealing his mouth. The third man on the porch didn't have time to scream as Callum's Callum hammer hit him in the stomach and sent him flying into the air emptying the contents of his guts and rolling him into the street.

Jase Then signaled for the group to wait on the porch. Quickly he shimmied up a drain pipe to a shuttered window on the second floor. Taking an arrow he slid it between the shutters, opening the hinge and tas quietly as he could entered the room. Inside a man slept on the floor. Heaps of clothing was piled against the wall, and empty bottles of ale were everywhere. Looking at the man, the young hill-man readied an arrow. Jase considered shooting the sleeping man but instead crept to the door, unlocked it and snuck out.

A passed out the man holding a half consumed bottle of clear liquid sat on the floor against the wall, Jase could hear multiple voices from the ground floor, smell liquor and tobacco smoke in the air and hear an accordion playing. He also saw two more rooms on the second floor and could see stairs leading down.   Quickly he moved to the two-rooms inside one he could hear snoring, inside the other nothing. Slowly he opened the door. Inside was a windowless room with barrel, and boxes on the floor.

As he went to exit the room he heard someone coming up the stairs. Peaking he saw the big Northman that had confronted Callum tossing a single-bladed ax and catching it as he went up the stairs and towards where Jase was.

Ignoring his nerves the young hunter and readied an arrow, he was pretty sure unless it was a perfect eye or headshot one arrow wouldn't do. As Jase watched, the big man walked past the door, found a corner and urinated there before turning around and heading downstairs. Seeing his chance, Jase followed closely as quietly as he could and hoping his luck and skill would allow him to get the drop on the ax-wielding man.

FROM GOODWIN'S TRAVELS OF THE FREE KINGDOM.

Lester

I'm not sure what kingdom claims Lester. While it well within the land claimed by Arden and less than ten miles from land controlled by the Jesnumi noble family, there are no documents claiming the small river town.

Upon was entering Lester you see why no one claims it as it seems populated by what one could at best called "unsavory" and at a worse criminal. Traveling light, my wife and I had little more than our horses, saddlebags, and clothing but were accused of smuggling Poppy oil until I paid a bribe.

Inside we found a town that seemed to cater to river sailors and the criminal element. Twice someone tried to sell man angel's feather that was little more than owl's feather painted silver.

It was not long after that we found a place to stay, a small red clay covered in called the bleeding-eye ran by a man whose eye had been cursed blood red. The Inn was a bad as you would guess and doubled like most taverns and such in the town as a gambling den.

CHAPTER 4:
FIGHT AND FLIGHT

"You think you're good don't you pup!," The Northman turned on Jase halfway down the stairs. Turning the tattooed man threw his ax at the young man who dodged and fired hitting the big man in the shoulder. He then quickly moved past him. To the bottom floor, The man selling the crystals, two of the men who he recognized as kidnappers took the girl sstood about looking at him. As he went to readied and fired another arrow the men and women around him started to move, some drew swords, other grabbed clubs, one even picked a meat cleaver from a large half-eaten roast. Surrounded the hunter chose his target and fired.

Jase watched his arrow fly across the room just as the massive ax-wielding Northman tackled him.

"Boy, first I'm going to skin you, then I'm going to get creative," said the warrior . Jase dropped his bow and went for a dagger, but it was too late the man was on top him, and in a matter of seconds his arms were pinned down by one of his opponents arms and knee. Jase could smell fish on the man's breath and see the murderous rage in his eyes.

As the Ax-wielding Northman prepared to end the young hunter, the door leading into the criminal den exploded open, and Callum walked in, drawing everyone's attention including the warrior pinning Jase.

"Well looks like the real fight's here pup," he said coming to his feet and raising his Ax leaving the surprised hill-man.

The Ax wilding northerner swung at the Free-Crusader, who moved back out the blades range before stepping forward to ram his hammer into the stomach of the attacking man, lifting the man up, Callum then grabbed the raised man and be slammed into the floorboards.

"You got the touch, Shadowskin!," The man called out; he could feel the faith flowing through the young lord making increasing his already prodigious strength.

"And so do I," The blue man eyes bulged, veins appeared on his body as he used his magic to increase his rage and drive him into a frenzy," Raising a leg, the berserker warrior kicked Callum off him and scrambled to his feet.

" He's a Rager !," Callum

Xarona who had entered the room wand at the ready could see Jase now on his feet shooting Arrows into the mob and Callum facing off against a hulking berserker.

"Time to do what witches do best," she said to herself. The redhead thought back to her time at the Coventry, and how it was often said a witch need not worry about being outnumbered. Their reputation alone could turn the tide of a battle or reduce the most arrogant lord to a syco-phant servant. Xarona had no reputation, but standing in that room ar-mored members of a gang of kidnappers already here she decided to make one.

"You worthless mortals, You have managed to annoy me, and that's a mistake you'll only make once," she hissed, pointing at the man with the meat cleaver and turning him into a small brown toad on the spot.

"Did you see that!," a man called out dropping his club and running for the door.

"I don't want to be a critter!," said someone else before running and leaping out of a open window. Another window opened, and someone jumped out, another man ran upstairs. "I'm glad you're on our side," Seamus walkinged in behind the Xarona his staff glowing. He was searching the room with his power for the girls using his memory of them as a guide. Across the room, a door glowed golden.

"There," he said the young wizard pointing his staff at the glowing door.

"Get them out!". said Jase to Seamus.

Seamus nodded, he was glad he wouldn't have to participate in the bloodier aspect of the rescue as the-the burnt man's corpse appearance and the smell was still fresh in his mind.

Holding his staff close Seamus sheath himself in silvery energy and started to move towards the door, an attacker moving towards him bounced off the protective shield.

"A wizard too," cried out the would-be attacker, "This ain't worth it," said a man before he scrambling for the door that to his sorrow had Xarona near it. The witch smiled wickedly at him causing him to retreat into a corner drop his weapon and calmly sit.

Callum struggled with the Berserker; He could tell they were evenly matched and knew if he fell the Northman would decimate his friends with his rage-fueled magical strength and speed.

"Forgive me Alomeg, For today I must be like Mizeriel your angel and sword," he said.

"Praying already?," The Berserker grunted, with a smile.

Callum pushed the man off and took a fighting stance, The Berserker stagger backed a few steps before attacking. The young lord remembering what his older brother taught him and waited for the Berserker swing his ax which heads whirring wildly. The crusader blocked the attack with his hammer but allowed the momentum to continue.

The maneuver allowed the free-crusader to spin the Berserker against the wall and by adding his strength pushed him and his foe through it first onto the porch then into the street.

Callum rolled to his feet but not before a fist caught him in the nose breaking it. The young man with the hammer swung wide hoping it would just get his foe to step back.. instead; it made contact hitting the other man on the side

"I'm going to kill you hard," said the berserker after spitting out blood.

"Please stop," Callum

"Gone from praying to begging?," The Northman grabbed his ax and rushed in as he replied. He could feel his ribs were broken, but the rage allowed him to ignore the pain. In fact, he felt very little other than the need to destroy his opponent.

Callum for the first time grabbed his hammer with both hands and lowered it and as the Ax came down biting into his shoulder through the chain mail. Ignoring the pain, the young lord brought his weapon up into the man's chin snapping his neck and crushing his jaw. The raging warrior flew back landing in the mud blood bubbling in his mouth and streaming down his nose. His body twitched twice be for stopping and releasing a wet death-rattle. Tears in his eyes the Crusader knelt at the man side and placed his hand on his chest.

"Forgive me and forgive him," he said, "Alomeg be praised," Rising the young lord gripped his Hammer and headed back to the building were his friends were.

Jase could see the room was the thinning out; magic didn't frighten him, he knew given the right conditions he could take down a caster without them even knowing it. The people here had no such confidence, and upon seeing Seamus and Xarona in action and with the big Northman out of the room, their spirits were starting to lose any desire to fire.

"You can't come into my house like this!," Screamed a woman standing a club in hand.

"And you can't steal girls," Jase," The woman looked at the three young adventurers as Seamus touched the lock on the door he identified causing heat it up till the wood around it charred and burnt away.

The magician then released his finding divination and opened the door, inside the small room was a bag with what he assumed was a struggling chimera and two tied up and gagged, frightened girls.

Seamus walked over to the girls and with a touch of his staff, willed the rope to loosen with a touch; he then removed the gags.

The girls started at crying.

"It'll be okay," Seamus said helping Kisa stand just as Xarona arrived.

Kisa, Lisa, did any of these bastards hurt you? ," Xarona looked the girls in the eyes in a way that made them shudder. The young witch knew the perils of kidnapping she had read stories and had even been instructed on how to deal with being kidnapped as part of her training as a Lady of her noble house. In most cases, death was preferable than being taken and used by brigands as a way to make money or worse.

"We're fine," Lisa.

Xarona looked at their girls, their dresses were muddy but mostly intact, and though one of them sported a face bruise, she seemed to be walking fine.

Seamus looked at the red-head, "We need to get them out," The Witch allowed the wizard and the girls to exit. She then knelt down and opened the bag on the floor. Sani scrambled out.

"Mistress you saved me!," it purred out.

"My poor dear, I'm so sorry," The witch picked up her familiar and hugged it and exited the room.

"See The girls are fine," said the woman with the club

Janse looked at the rough looking woman and raised his bow at her, "Still doesn't mean I shouldn't take an eye for our troubles," he said.

"But, kind Sir... I'm truly sorry, nay repentant ," the woman.

Xarona looked at the woman as did Sani; She wanted to eat me, said the winged cat.

"Really," said the witch, Maybe you should eat her instead," Xarona placed the familiar down and drew her wand.

"What shall be a mouse or a fish?," she asked the cat as the woman looked on in horror.

"Please M'lady, I'm sorry," begged the woman.

Sani looked up at her, mistress " A Mouse, a plump mouse," she said.

Jase was about to chime in on the frightened woman behalf when he saw the glint of steel near the stairwell, the man he had left asleep had stumbled downstairs with a knife and was preparing to throw it.

"Knife," he called out, aiming and firing and to his surprise missing, his arrow hitting where the man and avoiding the cowering mice on the floor.

Xarona chuckled. "Well I did have the spell ready," she said.

"Can we go now?," Callum walked through the hole he made with a bloody nose and a wound in his shoulder. Seamus moved quickly to his friend and offered him a shoulder to lean on as did Lisa.

"Thank you all so much," said the dark-haired girl,"

Jase looked at the room, "I'm going to head upstairs to make sure there are no surprises and meet you outside," he said heading towards the stair-well.

"And you'll sit here quietly for the next few hour, and If I ever see you again, I'll turn your blood into maggots," threatened the witch to her pet's kidnapper. Before turning to escort her charges outside

Jase was climbing out the window just as his guild-party made it past the porch. Reaching inside he pulled out two small iron shod wooden chests,

"For our troubles," he said.

Seamus rolled his eyes as the young man dropped the chests to the ground into the mud. And then gracefully leaped down after them.

"How are we going to carry those, Callum is in no condition to lift anything, and we need all eyes and hands-on duty till we get back to the stable,"

I can take care of them," The witch spoke taking off her pouch and returning it to it's true to size. She then levitated the chests into them closed it and returned it to belt size.

Once the pouch was attached the group begun their slow walk through the alleys of Lester back to the stables and hopefully safety.

Vinceno sat on top of Travelers wagon a worried look on his face. He had allowed his greed to once again lead him astray. Bernardo's marriage was to be a celebration, it was to make his family even richer and makes his son and grandchildren nobles. His new in-laws also had connections; they could help him ship his Silks across the western deserts and to the eastern coast. But now his unwillingness to book his family on an expensive airship or boat, his willingness to pay four children instead of adults and his foolishness to stop at Lester had cost him dearly.

"Father!" Bernardo called out from the stables gate where he stood guard with a driver and a stable hand they had paid to help. Vinceno stood to look down over the nearby run down one story housing into the street.

Seamus and Lisa helped a slouching Callum move up the street, behind them were Kisa and Lady Xarona and at the rear Janes was walking, ready to fire. Vinceno wanted to cheer, but instead, he clambered down off the roof of the wagon and to the ground, knocked on the wagon door. His wife with a mournful look opened the door, she could tell by the look on his face it was good news. Taking her hand the merchant helped the woman out off the wagon, and the two of them ran to the gate, a driver carrying a club at their side.

By the time they reached the gate The daughters were there hugging their brother.

"My hearts!," called out Isabella running up to the girls. The girl's left their brother to embrace and ran towards their mother almost knocking her down as they hugged her.

With no one to hug, Bernardo turns Seamus and the others, "Let me help," he said taking his sister's place under Callum's right shoulder touching blond the magician on the left hand quickly as he passed.

"I can walk on my own," Callum

"No my friend, let us help you," the merchant's son and his friend led the large man to a bench on the side of the stable and sat him down.

Xarona still holding Sani walked over to the large young man.

"That's what you get for being all so foolishly noble," in a concerned tone.

"You turned someone into a toad, That's both scary and amazing," Callum returned struggling to talk despite his pain.

"Of course, I did, Witches unlike most, don't have to lie," the young woman spoke in her typical haughty tone. , "Now don't die, I've yet to turn you into a toad, and It's something I'm looking forward to,". said the witch with a mischievous smile.

Callum nodded and closed his eyes; he could feel the blood flowing from his wound on his shoulder and could feel his consciousness slipping.

"Alomeg, I've taken a life, I dare not ask for my own," he said to himself," raggedly, "But If they will is to heal me, then I shall see amends," Xarona watched as the young man fainted.

"Callum!" she called reaching towards him and noticed his nose no longer looked broken, and though the gash was there it was no longer bleeding.

Jase knew that there was a chance the kidnappers might retaliate that night and that staying in the town was a bad idea. Still, Callum needed to rest as did the girls. With the help of the drivers, He and moved his friend into a stable Xarona had set up for him. The witch said she would guard him as he slept and used a spell to clean his clothing and wounds as he slept. Seamus once again took chalk and drew sigils on the wagon and ground, when Jase asked what did they do Seamus just smiled and said,

"Nothing, their just gibberish really, but most people don't know that and think they are magic and avoid them,"

That night the stable owner and his wife provided the meal, Vinicio paid them well to make sure they accepted no more trade for that day and night and ordered their two hands to help with security. Jase spent his time roaming the stable yard looking for any sign of trouble.   There was none, in fact, it was pretty quiet save for the animals. Seamus and Bernardo talking while the magician guarded the front gate.

Sani, in the form of a large wild cat, prowled the ground, it was then Jase discovered the creature could only change shape at her mistresses command, which is why she was little help at the kidnapper's nest.

*****

"Sit down," Xarona called out just a few minutes after sunrise.

"I need to... relieve myself," Callum looked at the young woman, "And I feel better,"

The free-crusader tried to rotate his wounded left shoulder and found it stiff, painful but with full motion.

"Fine but If you don't come right back I'll put a curse on you so you'll relieve yourself through your nose,"

The redhead allowed the big man to pass and move towards the rear of the barn before he exited he looked back at the girl.

" You are beautiful when you're all flustered," he said smiling at her.

The Young woman's eyes widen, and her pale cheeks turned ruddy. "I'm so going to turn you into a toad now," she said playfully, "or maybe a capibara, decision, decisions".

Seamus yawned as he awakens by a snoring Bernardo. The two had fallen asleep leaning on each other sitting at the front gate. Across from them stood a driver half asleep holding a pitchfork.

Looking about he gently pushed the young man off him and looked about. He wasn't sure why he liked the young and handsome dark haired boy so much. There was something about him that was just kind and gentle. Looking at the sleeping young man, Seamus tried to push back his feelings, he knew that his predilections while not unknown weren't always welcome.

"How are were feeling Hoss?," Jase saw his friend walking towards the stables tying his trousers front.

"I'm not dead, but I am hungry,". Callum

Jase nodded and walked towards the Crusader, "I have a question, but you don't have to answer it, though," said the young hunter.

"Ask," the Big man looked at the young man in buckskin as he spoke.

"Was that your first kill?," he asked.

The young lord took a breath and looked at his feet before facing his friend and talking, "I've killed animals, but never a person," he said slowly.

"I figured," he said, "The thing is it might not be your last on this mission, There are a lot of bad people out there, desperate people willing to do anything to take everything from you," The hill-man looked at his friend.

"I know, but I have to give them a chance.., it's my way," The crusader replied, "It's how I was raised,"

"Some won't give you a chance," Jase.

"That doesn't mean I shouldn't try," Callum response held the conviction, and while Jase knew it could well cost his friends life, he acknowledges with a nod it was something he respected.

After a breakfast of boiled eggs and porridge the town guard visited the group and to their surprise seemed happy the girls were found and more thrilled that the Salazars and the adventures were leaving Lester as soon as they were packed. Xarona recognized two of the guards as men who had run from the kidnapper's building not only by their appearance but by the fearful way they would look at her or at least tried to avoid catching her gaze.

Just to be sure there were no hard feelings, Salazar slipped the Sergeant a silver coin for their "service," during their final handshake and received a knowing smile in return.

Once the meeting and breakfast were done, the group started to pack their wears. Seamus helped Bernardo prepares the horses along with the drivers. Callum at the urging of a stable owner and out of gratitude for his help "blessed," a pregnant horse. Xarona cast her refresh spell on Isabella and the girls, it wasn't as relaxing as a hot bath, but it did clean them from head to toe. Isabella also as the group passed her in the stables thanked each adventurer for saving her daughters and promised them she'll personally write the guild about their heroism.

As the sun reached the zenith and chimes of noon were rung in the town the group left Lester, heading down a road that followed the River east for a bit then north and west. Crossing a bridge they once again found the High Road. From there they traveled till nightfall , putting as much distance between them and the dirty little town as possible before finding a camping area of the road with a rickety wooden pavilion and a stone fire circle. Tithe group moved the wagons off the road, and Callum cooked his version of the drivers Ham stew, combing his spices with the Salazar's supplies. The adventures instead of camping huddled around the fire (augmented by Seamus magic) for the night, telling stories and sleeping in shifts.

Despite their best efforts the group was so exhausted that even Jase fell asleep, awakening the next morning and finding nothing out of sorts. The sun was long up, and the fire was almost out. Quickly he reignited the kindling with a few logs. Once done with the campfire, he left the camp, relieved himself and then walked to the high road. Ahead he could see the foothills of the kingdom of Arden and above them the mak-ing of a storm followed by drizzle. Looking about he could both see and smell old pine trees and that reminded him of home.

He remembered being young and his Father coming home after raids with gifts. His first bow was one of those gifts. Not long after getting it and almost killing a pig practicing on his own, his father took him out into the woods and taught him how to use it, how to breath when pulling it back and firing, how to feel the wind and know how to compensate for a breeze. His father wasn't surprised his son became a great archer, but he was surprised by how great. Jase was taking down full-grown deer at a hundred paces in one shot before he was nine and killed his first bear at ten. One shot through the creature's open maw into his brain. Jase often juggled the good with the bad of his father in his mind, but the thoughts he was having now were all good, and he knew it was because it was that skill that the girls were saved and his new friends were safe.

As the hunter mind turned from his past to his present, something blocked out the sun. It had the body of a great lion, easily, twice the size of Callum's bull. , Large bird-like wings, a head that like a great hawk and feet that were a mix of talons and claws and a long tail. The creature paid him no mind to the hunter and just flew over the trees and then veered out of sight as the hunter watched.

He had heard tales of the great beasts but had never seen one, Man it seemed had killed and scared them off most of them off, occasionally, however, someone would say they saw something, but such talk was often ignored and attributed too much drink. For the young man seeing the beast was as close as he ever had a religious experience. It was nature, magic and the drive all rolled up into one in his eyes, and though he didn't know till he had stared off into the distance for some time, it had brought a tear to his eye.

*****

"A Griffin?," Seamus looked at Jase as the road next to him at the head of the caravan., "..are you sure?".

"I'm not sure what to call it, but it was a Bigger than a grizzly and part wildcat and hawk. I didn't think things like that still existed," he said the young hunter.

"They do, but only in the untamed wild, which I guess the forest here qualifies as," The young magician looked up at the sky, hoping he too would see such a magnificent beast. His tutor in magic had lots of old books on the great beasts, everything from dragons to chimera to wooly mammoths and leviathans. Hundreds of creatures magical creatures that roamed the new lands and old.

Hearing the conversation Bernardo, rode up to the two adventures and spoke up, "I once saw an Ogre in a traveling show along with a mermaid in a large glass tank" he said wanting to join the conversation.

"Ogres are more old-folk than beast and Mermaids, I hear they are still plenty of them in the Sea of Topaz," The blond young man looked sad as he spoke, "The great beats and the old-folk shouldn't be locked up or hunted, they should be free like we are,"

"I would still like to hunt a critter like that," The hill-man looked at a glaring Seamus, " Now, I didn't mean kill it, just hunt it, get close enough to it so I know I could kill it if I wanted," Seamus looked relieved, he hated the idea of hunting for sport and was both gladdened and surprised by Jase's words.

Callum rode in the rear of his group making sure to rotate his shoulder every few minutes to help with the stiffness. He knew that such a wound could cause lifelong problems if he didn't work on it. Ahead of him and to the side of the wagon road Xarona who was dressed in a dark blue dress with puffy sleeves and high collar rode her familiar (back in horse form) . She carried her parasol in one arm and held a book in other. While to many outsiders it looked like she was controlling Sani, in actual reality the familiar did most of the work.

As he watched, Callum found himself fascinated by how the sun played off the young witches copper colored hair.

"M'lady," he called out, to her.

The young woman sat silently for a second, "I'm not sure I'm talking to you M'lord," she returned coldly.

"Why not M'lady," he answered playfully.

The girl flounced her hair, "I watched you as you slept after being wounded and I cleaned your wounds, yet you did not thank me," she said.

"True, But I was waiting till I could find the proper words or a gift to do so," he responded.

"Thank you, would have been a good start," The girl's voice held less announce than before.

"Thank You, would not have sufficed M'lady," The young Lord spoke nervously. Despite his position, he wasn't used to talking to girls other than those related to him. Work and training ate up a lot of his time at home and while occasionally the visiting noble families would bring daughters it his brothers, not him they talked to.

Xarona smiled, she wasn't exactly sure why, but the provincial lord words had made her do so. Serious minded and studious, the witch was amused by only a few things. Sani, her sisters, and the vexing her parents by being far more outspoken than they would have liked.

Belasona house sat on a hill overlooking the walled town around it and the timberland and farms beyond that. A river cut through the walled city and was used to power the vast wheel works of Belstone where Trees were cut, rubber was melted, and bands of iron were formed into the various hubs and axels of wagons and carriages. And steam was used to soften and bend temper into circles for It was hard work, but work her father oversaw and worked he wanted a male heir for.

When Xarona was born, the first child of the lord and lady a grand celebration was thrown. Lords of the land came or sent gifts, and even the king and of Queen sent gifts from the castle in Vallus. But in the middle of the celebration after the lord and lady presented their daughter who even at birth had a mane of red hair three change women entered the hall and declared the child was a witch, putting a damper on the festivities.

Witches, unlike other casters, started their training early, not because of their magical talent but the danger that came with it. A witch if left uncheck might curse someone by accident or conjure a creature or fire during a tantrum. Magic was as much a part of them as it was a dragon or a pixie, without magic they could not live, with it, they were forces of nature in need of being tamed. This gave her very little time for frivolity during their training, and in fact, as she grew up she found levity to be a distraction she thought she could live without despite her younger sisters antics and Sani. Still, she was on the High-Road smiling and thinking very frivolous thoughts.

CHAPTER 5:
SMUGGLER'S SHORE

Kisa and Lisa splashed in the lake fully dressed as their mother watched. Isabella knew that the girls' childhood had been coming to an end for some time and while they seem over their kidnapping eight days ago, and were splashing each other like children now, she could see the signs of adulthood slipping in.

Vinceno sat next to his wife on the grass looking over the map. They would go to Arden, rest for a few days and then travel to Topic the second largest city in Kascee (after Kascee-proper.) where they would rent a boat and travel westward for the second half of their trip . Despite what happened in Lester, they were still on schedule and could, in fact, take an extra day in either two large towns head and still be on time.

"You look worried my love," said Isabella to her husband.

"No, Not worried just a tad road weary," The merchant rolled up the vellum map and placed it in his map case and picked up a cup of wine off a tray laying the grass.

"Well since the girls are occupied, and the drivers and our escorts are busy maybe we should go in the wagon and ... rest". The woman spoke softly and leaned over to kiss her husband. The man smiled and kissed his wife back before coming to his feet and offering his wife his hand to help her stand.

Bernardo stood in front of Jase his long sword drawn, The hunter held only a dagger and moved slowly in front of the tanned skinned young man looking for an opening. Seeing it he moved, Bernardo swung, Jase rolled past his swing and placed the dagger to his throat.

"You're getting Better," said the hill-man.

"You could have killed me," Bernard stepped back.

"You almost hit me, at least this time you kept an eye on me," Jase smiled Both men stood on a flat area near the lake under some trees. Jase was shirtless while Bernardo was in a white short sleeve shirt, his dark purple pants, and boots. Callum and Seamus watched nearby. Seamus practicing with his sword against a log his friend had driven into the ground while the tall, dark-skinned lord enjoyed his time off the road finishing up the repairs on his armor.

Xarona sat nearby on cushions reading while Sani swatted at tiny fish in the lake. "Lady Xarona, Do you want to give it a try," Jase held one of his sleek slightly curved swords at the witch.

"Did my ears deceive me or did you not call my Fussy Bridges?" the girl looked up from her book. on leyline theory and celestial alignment.

"Just trying your proper name on, to see how it works," the Hunter smiled at the girl who lowered her head and returns to her book. " No thank you, I don't need a sword I have a wand," , she said.

"And if you lose the wand, M'lady?," Bernardo.

The girl looked up again and smile, "Sani, Protect me," she said to the cat who turned around from her play and grew into a white three tailed mountain lion.

Jase and Bernard looked at the creature that was starting to circle them,

"Finally, I get to eat them," said the chimera.

"No, While Mr. Salazar might be tasty, I'm sure eating Jase will just make you sick".

Seamus looked at the situation and laughed. He then lowered his sword and picked up his staff and pointed it at the cat, a stream of sparkles rain from it forming a ball that danced in front of the familiar catching its attention and leading it away.

"And If your cat is occupied... Fussy Britches? ," Jase spoke after giving Seamus a wave of appreciation.

Xarona closed her book looked at Callum who smiled at her and shrugs.

"Fine, you had this coming anyway," The young woman came to her feet straightening the simple light green dress she wore under a brown vest. Taking her wand off her leather belt and dropping it to the ground she looked at the boys.

"The first one to get to me will revive a kiss," she said.

"This sounds like a trap," Bernardo sheath his sword, "and I'll pass.

Seamus looked at the merchant's son and smiled, "I'll pass too," he said.

Callum stood and stretched, his shoulder was almost fully recovered, and though he was larger, he was closer to the young witch.

"I'll take the risk," he said placing down his armor and tools.

Xarona wiggled her fingers as if stretching them.

"Very well, On your marks, ready... set.. go!," she said with a wicked smile on her face.

Jase sprinted at full speed knowing that while Callum was fast and if need be could be faster, that the free-crusader would not use his faith abilities just to earn a kiss.   As the Hunter reached out to touch the witch on her shoulder, he was surprised to see her levitate upward and over to where he started.

"What!," he said surprised, " I thought you needed your wand!"

Upon landing gracefully, the girl placed her hands on her hips,

"A wand helps a witch focus magic energy and its materials can enhance different types of spell, but a witch doesn't need it to do magic,"

While the witch talked Callum almost cleared the distance between him and the young lady, who upon seeing him pointed in his direction. Suddenly the man stopped unable to move. She then flicked her wrist tossing him into the shallow edge of the nearby lake

"I'd stay there if I were you Lord Wimbowaradi," she said playfully as the third Son of the Mwamba wa Mwaloni sat in the water for a second before rising to his feet just in time see Jase almost upon Xarona. To his surprise, the thought friend kissing the Lady Belasona made his heart sank.

Jase smiled as he reached out his hand only for the girl to playfully gesture at him. He felt his body convulse and painfully start to collapse in on itself as the world around him expanded hundreds of times its normal size in less than a second. From his point of view, Xarona strode towards him, her body so tall he couldn't see all of her till she leaned over to look down at him. Fearfully he backed away and realized for the first time he wasn't standing but rather on his belly with his limbs sprawled to his side and something attached to his rear. The grass about him was almost as tall as trees and the only sound he could make was a dull hiss.

Xarona looked at the bright pink and blue lizard. In front of her.

"And that's why I don't need to know how to swing a silly sword," she said.

"Got you, M'lady," Callum had quickly moved behind the witch wrapping his arm around her waist and spun her up into his grasp.

Sani upon seeing what happened started to laugh as did Bernardo and Seamus.

"You Brute," Xarona said in mock protest.

"I win," Callum put the girl down as he spoke grinning wide,"

"Perhaps, but is your victory worth this," The witch gestured at the man causing him to spin and shrink till all that was left was a small brightly colored frog. "Isn't that a tad cliche M'lady?" Bernardo said walking towards the witch.

"Yes, but It'll teach him a lesson," she returned picking up the frog then walking to pick up the lizard. , "And him too I wager,"

" You are way more powerful than me," , Seamus walked towards his friends.

Xarona walked back to her cushion to sit placing the frog and the-the lizard on the tray where her teacup, kettle, and pour over sugar and cream sat.

"No, I'm not, well at least not that much more..," the redhead looked at Seamus as she blew on her cooled cup of tea heating it back up.

"I can't throw fireballs or hold back rivers," you are very talented at what you do. Witches have an advantage, access to more energy and an innate understanding of magic, but we have to study. I also have formal magic training and while I'm sure your mentor did their best. I trained at the Coventry with dozens of teachers for years.

Seamus nodded, "But transmutation, I heard that's the most difficult of magics," he spoke with a reverent tone at the tea drinking Lady.

"Yes, It's difficult but not the most difficult, there are types of magic, bending distance and time, Conjuring living beats and more that are far more difficult," The young lady looked at the frog and lizard as she continued. "People are beasts, higher beasts but still beasts. Making a person into a lesser beast like a toad or caterpillar is just convincing that someone to take a lesser form. Right now their bodies and clothing are convinced they are in the right form and shall stay convinced until I allow it to know it's true form again. Of course granting something a new form takes a great understanding of that form, knowing how it's built, how it acts and thinks. " The witch turned to face the young magician, "It takes years to learn,"

"Can you teach me?," Seamus.

The witch took a sip of her tea and thought for a second before replying, "Transmutation, as I said, takes time, I can't teach you anything worth using in less than a year of intense study, I can, however, teach you some energy work that will help you conserve power and use your rather considerable talents with greater ease.

"Thank you, M'lady," Seamus.

"Wagons on the road!," called out a driver to the group," in a panicked tone.

"Oh Pooh," the witch placed down her tea and looked at the lizard. Gesturing she returned it to normal. Jase scurried across the grass on all fours before standing.

"I take it that's why some people still burn witches," he said stretching and getting a feel for his body.

"And why some witches eat the people that transform," Xarona hissed at the hunter before turning to the frog, picking it up she kissed it softly releasing her spell.

Callum found himself on his knees kissing the red-haired young lady far longer than was needed before they both pulled away shyly.

"We've worked to do," said the young witch blushing.

"Yes of course," said the young lord standing.

Seamus took his friend by the arm and lead him back towards his armor and hammer.

"You like him," Bernardo to the Xarona who was coming to her feet and placing her wand back in its holder,

"That's silly; we have nothing in common:," The young witch, "And I have other obligations," she added.

"I understand obligations, but I 'm starting to see that love comes re-gardless of them," The merchant's son bowed to the young lady before heading up towards his family and their wagons.

Six Wagons moved off the Highroad to the small dirt one leading to the lakeside rest spot. The large wagons were packed with wooden kegs. Each wagon had four people two up front at the reigns and two on the rear sitting on the kegs.

The lead driver of the wagon raised an open hand to Vinceno and Jase as they made their way to the rest stop signaling in the traditional manner of travelers, he had peaceful intentions.

"Well met," he said looking at the aristocratic man in purple and the wiry young man with dark hair wearing no shirt but carrying two swords.

"Same to you, I'm Vinceno Salazar, a merchant traveling north," said the man to Jase's side. "This is Jase one of our hired adventures,"

The man driving the large wagon stood, "I'm Aldis Manohierro, chief teamster of the Arden wine and vinegar, I'm heading south to Vallus," He said, lowering his hand as the wagons came to a stop.

The broad but short man jumped from the wagon dressed in the dark gray jacket, brown shirt, pants and black boots. He had a round face, dark eyes, long dark hair and long sideburns that almost formed a full beard but didn't quite meet on the chin. Once on the ground Aldis signaled to the other drivers to line up next to him before striding off towards Vin-ceno and the adventurer.

"We've been driving for four days straight and would like to make camp here," the man said.

"Of course, as long as long as you come with no hostile intent," the merchant spoke calmly as he tried to read the man. He could tell by his hands he was indeed a teamster and by his clothing, he was a freeman of moderate income. His accent marked him as someone from the north, and his height and complexion said he had stout blood in him, not that many generations removed as well as Mytecian.

"I intend to feed our horses, eat and get some sleep," Aldis said with a smile.

"Pop, are we stopping here?," A girl walked from the second wagon, just a hair taller than her father with the same completion short dark hair wearing a brown bibbed dress over a white blouse and black coat. Broad shoulder and-and , she had the build of someone used to working for a living.

"Mr. Vinceno, this is my daughter Clare," said the Aldis.

Jase looked at the girl, she was apparently his age or maybe a little older. Her round face and large dark eyes had both a prettiness and toughness about them.

"Hello Clare, I have two daughters myself as well as a son," Vinceno walked up to the girl to kiss her hand, but instead, the girl took him and shook it with a firm grip. She then walked over to Jase who placed his swords down.

"So you're his boy?," ask the girl

"No Miss, I work for him," said the hunter.

"Make senses; you look nothing like him," she said with a shy smile.

The girl shook the young man's hand squeezing hard enough to turn
them red.

Looking past the dark-haired young man Clare spied four other people
walking up. A tall and broad dark-skinned man clad in Chainmail shirt,
dark pants and reddish boots carrying the biggest hammer she had ever
seen. A thin blond man dressed in a yellow shirt, brown pants and carrying a very ornate staff, a tanned skinned boy in purple with a sheath
sword and a prissy pale skinned red haired girl who was full of hip and
round of face dressed in green.

"Is everything fine, Mr. Vinceno," Callum spoke with authority.

"Everything is fine, my friend," the older man returned. "These people
seemed to just good folk traveling south,"

The free-crusader nodded, looked at Jase who also nodded. Lowering
his Hammer and placing it in its chain holder the young man walked up to
Aldis.

"What's your name youngster?', he asked looking up at the smiling teen.

"Lord Callum Wimbowaradi, but I'm fine with just being called
Callum," He said. Looking about he pointed at the others that had joined
him, "The one with the staff is Seamus, The noblewoman in green is
Lady Xarona Belasona, and the one with the sword is Bernardo, son of
our employer,"

Aldis nodded to the group, "A lord and A lady working for someone, That's different," he said.

It's the Adventures life," Callum turned to Clare who was already at his side looking over his Hammer.

"That's the biggest whammer I've ever seen and is that Pure Crystal... It has to be worth a small fortune. ," The Nyumbani looked down at the tough looking girl as she spoke, "Alomeg script, high-grade iron shaft, brass fittings, and coating, that's good work,"

"Thank you, I did it myself," Callum.

"I tinker and do some enchanting myself," said Clare.

"Enchanting?" Callum looked at the young lady, "Well It's just a little dedication and power aligning, nothing big,"

"It's a good start," the girl patted the hammer and could feel its energy, the growing power of the divine in it.

Aldis looked at his daughter, "My daughter has the makers touch, like me. ," he said out loud.

Xarona looked at the girl her eyes narrowing. The way she spoke to Callum made her almost instantly dislike her despite the fact she had done nothing to earn her anger.

Clare turned to look at her father, "Well let's get the horse hitched and set up, Pop," said the girl.

"Let's do that," Aldis nodded at the other campers again before turning to walk with his daughter back t their wagons. Clare started to bark orders at her father watched occasionally commenting.

The group moved their wagons horizontally to the slope leading to the lake, spiked the wheels and united their teams tying them to a tree on rope long enough to allow them to graze.

"Should we trust them?," Seamus looked at his friends as they gathered near the Salazar's traveling wagon.

"They seem fine," Jase looked at Seamus, "But try to stay close just in case,"

"I suddenly regret using up all that energy up just for a little amusement," Xarona sounded surprisingly humble as she spoke.

"Is that the only thing you regret about that?," Callum looking first to Jase then to the witch.

"Yes," Xarona replied with a slight smile.

"Maybe we should keep them close where we can watch them," Bernardo.

Everyone looked at the young man, who despite not being an adventurer had shown both loyalty and some usefulness.

"Not a bad idea, Jase,"

"I'll talk to my father, See If we can lend some of our supplies to a group feast of sorts," Bernardo., "That should keep them close and let them know our intentions are good,"

"Jase can you get me something big, a deer or maybe a pig?," Callum looked at the hunter.

"Odd thing, looking about there no sign of any big game around," The Hillman looked at the-the Crusader, " Might be able to get some more peasants, though,"

"I'll watch the girls and Isabella," Xarona.

"And I'll keep an eye on Bernardo.. and his father," Seamus.

"Sounds good, I'll try to get back as soon as I can," Jase.

With a knowing look from all present the group quickly split up without another word. Jase placed on his shirt and his quiver, grabbed his bow and headed into the forest that boarded the lake. Callum started preparing his menu. Knowing he could resupply in Arden and have picked up some wild herbs, mushrooms, and garlic along the way the young lord looked through his supplies. Two bags of potatoes, Some bacon, Apples, some lemons, butter, peppers, lard, flour, cornmeal, oats, some maple syrup, some dried fruit and two bottles wine and over two dozen spices secured in a tiny chest of draws. Walking to one of the three fire pits in the area he started to set up his kitchen in hopes his friend would find some meat.

"A feast"?," Vinceno looked at his son, "I'm not sure that's a good idea.

"Father, It'll allow us to keep track of the others, and it's not so much a feast as a communal meal," Bernardo spoke to his father as the two sat outside of their home on wheels.

"What do you think Seamus," the older man looked at the magician.

Seamus looked at the man than his son, "I think it's a good idea," said the blond young man.

"Very well, I'll let Aldis know," the merchant to his son, "And Bernardo, your idea is very shrewd, if it weren't for the fact you are about to become nobility I would say you would make a great businessman,"

Vinceno rose to leave, not noticing the crestfallen face of his son.

Seamus stood looking at friend stare with sad eyes at nothing for a few minutes before speaking up.

" What's wrong?," he asked.

"Nothing," Bernardo.

Seamus walked over to the small wooden and seat Vinceno was sitting on and sat.

"I haven't known you long, but I can tell," Seamus.

Bernardo sat quietly gathering his thought before speaking, "It's the marriage, I don't even know the girl I don't even want to do it," he blurted out.

Seamus looked into the young man's dark eyes and replied, " I'm sure your father is doing what he thinks is best, and who knows she might be beautiful.

Bernardo stood quickly, "But What about my feelings, my plans, I'm a man, I should be able to love who I want to love and do as I please," he said. Seamus just nodded and listened knowing right now the young man only needed to vent.

"And I do not care if she's beautiful or not, I know she's not for me," his voice calming Bernardo sat.

"I'm sorry," Seamus.

Bernardo looked at the blond and slowly reached out to touch his hand, "I know, and I wish things could be different," he said. Seamus placed his other hand on his friends while keeping eye contact.

"So do I," The young magician's tone was sad yet, for some reason he felt a part of him, a lonely part fade away.

Looking at each other and holding hands the two young men leaned in towards each other and closed their eyes, they knew what was about to happen was wrong and could, in the end, cause all manner of trouble, but as they kissed for the first time in both their lives they felt complete.

*****

"So do you live in a castle?," Kisa looked at Xarona who was sitting across from her in the witches tent.

"She's a lady; all ladies live in a castlem,'" Lisa.

"Girls, do not bother her ladyship," Isabella stood behind the noble-woman brushing the witch's copper colored hair. She had seen that despite the magic that kept it clean it was becoming more and more tangled and brushed it in hopes it would make amends for her angry words after her daughter's kidnapping. For her part, Xarona loved having her hair done, the lady had considered on more than one occasion just cutting most of it off or dying it a less vibrant color, but her mother who was a redhead like her loved her daughter's hair. Overtime, Xarona had come to appreciate it despite the insults it garnered when she was a child and the way it made her stand out.

"Teach AilleachtIt... our home is more of a large Manor house, It sits on a field surrounded by an orchard and open fields," said the young lady.

"Do you have servants? We have six house servants and two to take care of our fields," said Kisa.

"We had a dozen in-house and ten more outside," plus guards and the like," Xarona, " And we needed it, our home was always busy with people visiting my father, guests from other noble houses and kingdoms,"

"If I had all that, plus magic like you, I would never leave," Lisa.

Xarona looked at the girl, she knew her life as the first daughter of Belasona may sound like a fairy story to other but the obligations involved was something that she didn't like nor like to think about.

"Stop it you two," Isabella look at her daughters, "If I was the Lady and you were asking me questions like that I would turn both of you into chirping little birds,"

Xarona thoughts of her family and her obligations were left behind as the woman's remarks made her smile.

"Can you turn people into birds?," Lisa

"Yes, Turning people into animals is relatively easy. " Xarona.

Kisa liked where the conversation was headed, she often wondered about magic, especially spells, she had read books on magic and even tried it, but she didn't have the talent to be a magician let alone a witch.

"I read some witches can turn people into furniture, or bowls of fruit. is that true? ," she asked.

The witch was glad the subject was changing and could see Kisa was curious, something she appreciated.

"Yes, To turn the living into unliving and unliving to living takes a lot of energy and understanding. I'm not quite there yet. , but I know witches who are". Xarona .

"Like Duchess Indra and Queen Maeve of Phelix," Kisa spoke energetically, "I read Maeve once turned her army into gold coins and sent them to her enemy, the soldiers then turned back and killed the enemy and took their lands.

"Two things Kisa, never speak a witches name, especially a powerful one you don't know, she might have enchanted it so she'll know everyone saying her name. ," said the Lady of Beleasona, "And second that's a bit of an exaggeration, it was only twenty men, one would hardly call that an army,"

*****

Jase knew how to hunt, he knew the signs to look for, and he knew that the forest near a lake that size should be teaming with animals. However, after two hours of hunting, he had found nothing more significant than the six pheasants he had slung on his shoulder on a rope tied to their necks lived there. No raccoons, no possums, no deer, boar, badgers or elk or bears. There was, however, lots of squirrels and birds and small mice and toads. In fact, it was a paradise for, little creatures, as there was nothing big around to eat them.

"It's not right," he thought to himself as he followed old game trails that told him once, not to long ago there was something substantial in the area.

Coming to a clearing The young hunter heard something moving, Stopping he stood still feeling movement through the ground, smelling the air and above all listening. Out of the corner of his eye, he saw another pheasant moving along the ground. Reading his bow and arrow, he aimed and fired at the bird. The Arrow flew true striking the creature and sending it into a bush. Jase moved towards his quarry when suddenly there was rustling in the forest, and the hunter saw something, or rather the outline of something move from the underbrush and up the back of a large oak. , the Pheasant was nowhere to be found once the Hillman arrived at what he thought was it's resting place.

Looking for the creature, Jase hunter found grooves on the ground twice the size of his leg and circular spots on the back of the oak than where the bark had been removed or pressed inward.

Once again the Hunter knocked an arrow, he could feel something was nearby and watching him, something even his keen eyes couldn't see.

CHAPTER 6:
OF MONSTERS AND MAGIC

"Callum I think I did something stupid," said Seamus walking up to his friend who was slicing up onions with a small sharp knife.

"That's never a good way to start a conversation," The young lord looked at his oldest friend from where he sat at his makeshift prep table.

"But I knew it was stupid, and I did it anyway," The magician looked at the ground across from his friend and concentrated briefly and tapped his staff on the grass-covered earth, causing a rock to rise from it so that he could sit.

Sitting in silence, the young man looked at his hands. He had never talked to his friend about his romantic life and truthfully was pretty sure his friend wasn't interested. Callum was one of the few people aside from his mother that knew of his "attractions," and while neither his friend of his mother would ever judged him on it, he didn't feel comfortable discussing his desires out loud.

"I kissed Bernardo," he said quietly before looking about to see if anyone was nearby.

The young lord kept chopping, in silence for a few seconds before looking up, "I figured he was sly," Callum.

"You knew he was.. like me?," Seamus.

"I think the only person that doesn't is his father and that just maybe denial," Added the Free Crusader with a smile, "Regardless of that, what you did was pretty stupid," Callum.

"I never met anyone, like me, you know who liked me," Seamus.

"Let no sinner, mock the sinful" Callum.

"What does that mean," Seamus' voice held anger, "are you calling me a sinner because I'm Sly?"

Callum stopped cutting, "No I'm calling us both sinners for acting like two boys from backwoods lands getting all heartstruck the first time we leave home," The young lord also spoke quietly.

Seamus looked at his friend with a curious countenance as he spoke., "Wait...Bernardo's sisters are a bit young, I mean their not overly young, I heard of lords three times your age marrying girls that young but...,"

Callum rolled his eyes, "Xarona," he said.

Seamus, "Are you mad... she's...'

Callum, "Let no..,"

"Oh I get it now," The young magician smiled, " Does she know, Have you two.. you know? Wait, no you're still alive, ,"

 "No, no and what?' Callum.

"Witches devour the souls of their paramours," Seamus.

"Dragon dung," Callum

"Maybe not, but she seems a little cold for you," Seamus,

'And Bernard seems a little too... engaged for you," Callum

The two friends looked at each other and suddenly started to laugh at their follies. It was the kind of laughter only old friends could share and the kind that melted away all nervousness or fear of judgment.

"What are you two going on about?," Jase spoke as he walked up carrying his catch of six pheasants and catching both young men by surprise.

"Nothing," a smiling Seamus.

"Uh-huh," Jase.

Callum looked at the birds; they were each about half the size of a chicken. " Is this it, oh mighty hunter," he said hoping to change the subject.

"Fraid so, not much to hunt out here, which has me a tad nervous," The hill-man's voice turned serious, "Normally a place like this would be full all manner of critter . But it's not. Which means something is scaring them away or hunting them".

"I'm no hunter, but couldn't it just be locals overhunting," Seamus.

Jase shook his head in disagreement, " This place is pretty isolated. No sign of people outside this area and even the fish here are small a lake that size should have catfish as long as his lordship's arm.

"I would kill for one of those," Callum, "But I can make due to Jase,"

The hunter nodded, "Just do me a favor and keep a look out for anything strange, I think whatever is hunting here isn't exactly a mundane sort of animal,"

Both young men nodded as their friend left.

"Start plucking," Callum.

"Wait, I'm not here to pluck, I'm here to pour my heart out," Seamus.

"Well do it while plucking" Callum.

Clare sat leaning against a wagon wheel tinkering with a set of goggles with smoked red lines and tiny gears and springs built into the band. She had always loved creating and building; it was something that drove her and kept her quick mind from becoming bored.

Her father used to tell her. It was a gift, the ability to see connections in machines and how to connect it to magic as a source of power.

Placing on the goggles, the young lady adjusted a dial on the lenses turning her red-tinted dark till only things that are living shown as bright white blobs. She then turned the dials again allowing her to see the lines of magic itself briefly before the goggles gears started to whirl and sizzle.

Taking off the glasses and rubbing her eyes the first thing Clare saw was Jase looking at the ground with a worried look on his face.

Coming to her feet and gathering her tools and goggles and placing it in shoulder bag the young woman walked towards the hunter.

" Names John, right?" she said to the young man.

"Jase," corrected the hill-man.

"Sorry, I'm bad with names," said the girl.

" It's fine, John beats plenty of things I've been called before," said the young hunter smiling.

"Well, some people are sensitive about names, titles and the like," Clare

Jase nodded and looked at the dark-haired girl, "Where I come from most people have a couple of names, one they're given at birth, one they earn and one they keep secret to help hold off hexes.

So which one is Jase?," Clare.

"One my parents gave me," The Hunter started to walk, in hope, the girl would follow, which she did.

"And since I know you're not going to tell me the last name on the list, do you have an earned one," Clare walked with the wiry young adventurer to a tree where most of his supplies laid.

Jase sat down on a rolled up bedroll leaning against the same tree and relaxed.

"What's in it for me?," He asked with a smirk.

Clare looked up at him hands on hips, the bangs on each side of her head partially obscuring her face but not hiding her smile.

"I would say a kiss, but that didn't work out for me earlier today," the hunter picked up a long blade of grass and held it in his teeth.

"Well how about if you do I'll sneak you some of the stuff my dad's hiding," she said.

Jase eyes widened, "Your paw's hiding something?," he said.

"Name first,". the girl.

" Twack," said the young man.

"Twack?: the girl looked puzzled.

"My name...Twack, because of how I'm pretty good with a bow, and that's the sound a bow makes when you shoot it," he said.

"Twack Huh?," Clare spoke only slightly less puzzled, "Is that a word? Must be a local thing,"

Jase pretended not to care what the girl was saying and leaned his head back against the tree and closed his eyes. He heard the girl stand there for a few seconds then walk off quickly. He listened the teamsters talking and the start of a card game among them and their group's drivers he even heard a bird fly over. He had learned how to focus his senses, listen for things between and around background noise, he had to, his senses were both a blessing and a curse when he was young, the local conjure-man said he had the blood of the wolf-kin in him on both sides of his family.

"You fell asleep," Clare sitting across from Jase trying throwing acorns at his mouth playfully hoping to awaken him or at least land one inside.

"I guess I did," the young man felt an acorn hit his forehead before he awoke and pretended to sleep while the girl had her fun.

"Want to see it?," she asked.

"See What?," the young man said yawning.

'What my paw was hiding," the girl reached behind her back, and retrieved paper wrapped dark bottle, it's corked top sealed it wax and its a crude paper label on the front showed a winged goat.

Jase looked at the bottle and smelt the top; there was the slight hint of rum.

"Rum?," he said.

"Not just Rum, my family's rum, We make it ourselves and drive it south in a few barrels under the high and mighty Lord of Arden's vinegar and wine," Clare spoke with pride, taking away the bottle and open removing the wax.

"You're smugglers?," Jase.

"Just a little, if we paid the road tax and city taxes, we wouldn't be able to turn a profit, and It's not like we sell a lot, just a few dozen bottles," said, Clare

"So why you telling me," the Hunter leaned forward, "As far as you know I'm a spy for the lords and the like," he said looking into the girl's dark colored eyes.

The young woman relaxed appearance turned serious,

'You tell anyone, and I'll cut your throat". she replied as intimidating as she could manage.

Instead of being Intimidated Jase started to laugh at the girl's surprise.

"You know I'm the last person to turn on your Paw," he said.,

"Hells, if you knew some of the things my Paw did..,"

The girl suddenly relaxed and reached into her pocket for a tiny device placed it over the bottle top, a whirl and a click later the cork popped free. Between her and the young man.

"Now that's new," said the adventure.

"Just something I made," said the Tinkerer.

Jase took the bottle from the young woman and moved in closer to her, "You're just full of surprises," he said.

"You have no idea," she said pulling him close but just out of kissing range.

"Just as the two traveler's lips touched a woman's scream chilled the warmth in them.

"Ms. Isabella," Jase knew the sound and sprung to his feet.

Having time to focus and looking about he figured he had dozed off for just over an hour, during that time who knows what had happened. His mind raced, was the girl sent to keep him busy, was the rum poisoned. He didn't know and didn't have time to think about it. Grabbing his bow, quiver, and sword, he headed towards the noise, Clare behind him.

Isabella stood not far from a makeshift latrine, Kisa stood next to her and the hanging cloth they used for privacy.

The older woman looked pale, tears rolled down her face. Callum, Seamus, and Jase were bounding towards the woman in her daughter, while in the bushes came a scream and purple light followed by the cracking of wood.

"What's wrong!?," Seamus.

"Something touched me," Isabella.

Kisa looked at her mother, "Mother is ok, Lady Xarona is after it," she said.

"Xarona?". Callum looked at Seamus; the large young man speed increased, while the others stopped he plowed past into the bushes and past the Latrine only stopping to see a frustrated looking red-haired witch and Lisa heading his way. Callum stopped and took a breath, looking about he smelt ozone in the air and saw multiple tiny purple fires flickering out the ground and trees.

"What was it," Lisa looked at the witch.

"I'm not sure" Xarona "In fact, I'm not sure I saw anything other than ... where it was or what was moving around it. Seamus looked about and raised his staff. Concentrating he connected with the air around him, increasing the radius till he could feel everything moving in it and taking the breath within hundred feet. The breath of everyone, their livestock, birds, small animals, but nothing large enough to cause any real damage.

"Jase, Callum, are we safe here?," Vinceno looked at the adventurers.

Jase thought about what happened in the forest, a feeling of regret built inside of him as he didn't think to consider that whatever he saw would be a threat. Looking at everyone he pondered his options. before speaking.

"We're leaving in the morning anyway, So as long as we stick together and take precautions, we should be okay," looking about at everyone and the latrine, "That means if you have to go, do it before dark and make sure you're not alone,"

Callum nodded, and the merchant nodded just as Seamus' eyes opened.

"Nothing nearby other than small animals.

"I'm going to look at a few of my books," Xarona, "It might give us a clue on what that thing was,"

"I can help with that," Kisa.

Lisa looked at her sister then looked at her mother who was reaching behind herself rubbing her bare back where her shoulders and neck met.

'Mother what's that?". said the girl moving closer and sending a circular bruise about the size of her fist.

Isabella could feel the raised bit of skin and an itchy sensation but nothing more. Upon seeing Lisa looking at her mother's back, Callum noticed the bruise too and quickly walked to the woman,

"May I look Ma'am?," he asked.

The woman nodded, and the free-crusader lowered the back of her dress an inch and saw the size of the reddish fish bruise. It was if she had been struck by something perfectly circular.

"What is it lord Wimbowaradi," Vinceno asked while holding his wife's

"Looks like a bruise of sorts, My guess would be, the creature made it," replied the young lord. "I'm going to need more light to be sure, so let's get her back to the camp,"

The merchant his son and one of the daughters escorted the large man and the injured matron back to the camp while Seamus,

Clare and Jase discussed what had happened and future precautions including setting fires around the field.

Clare took an immediate liking to Seamus, for some reason. There was something about a wizard who came from nothing that appealed to her working class sensibilities.

However, She wasn't sure how she felt about the rest of the groups. While Callum seemed to be a good-hearted, he wore the symbol of the Crusaders and the symbol of their god Alomeg. The Crusaders while claiming to be a force for good had a reputation of forcing their rules on others and treating those not of their faith as inferiors. Stories abounded of Crusaders slaughtering the old blood and "heretics" in the name of their god. And her grandmother's words and the words of almost anyone in her community was "Never trust a witch," Magicians despite their powers were seen as people, they lived and died a person's lifetime depending on bloodlines and the like. Witches lived hundreds; some said thousands of years and that detached them from short-lived folk. Witches also according to what Clare was told as a child tended to be very mercurial creatures and would, "Cure you with one hand and curse you with the other. "

"We're going to need a way to detect this thing because apparently, It's hard to see," Jase looked at Seamus who was deep in thought.

"If I knew what it was, I could do that, but as I don't the best I could do is a basic alert spell over a small area," the blond magician looked at the hunter rubbing his chin and, for the first time realizing it was starting to grow from the lack of shaving.

"I think I might have a few trinkets that can help If you can cast a spell on them," Clare.

Seamus looked at the girl and nodded, despite the fact he had no idea what her trinkets what he knew he would need all the help he could get.

Showing off her work was something Clare rarely had a chance to do. leading Seamus and Jase to a wagon she opened up a large hidden panel under its front driver's seat. Inside there was a wood and brass chest. The stout young girl pulled the chest out and placed it on the ground. Moved a few dials on the brass locks and it popped on the revealing dozen of small clockwork devices.

"That's a lot of doohickies," Jase.

Seamus looked at this rustic friend and rolled his eyes; the young magician has always been interested in tinkersmithing. The craft combined artificer with engineering and clockwork gears and sciences. Most magicians saw it as a poor substitute for outright magic, but those who understood it knew it had its uses.

"How long have you been a Tinkersmith?," Seamus

"For as long as I could remember," she answered reaching down into a box and pulling out a brass cylinder, " My father's pretty good at it too, he taught me, and I learned a few things on my own,"

Twisting the device in her hand on both ends it started to buzz and hum, a small door opened in the machine and a red balloon unfolded and inflated. The girl released it, and it stood at her eye level hovering as small brass and paper wings buzzed on its side.

"Amazing," Seamus

"Like a big airship, only smaller," I figure we outfit this with a clear crystal, you cast into it, and we have it buzzing about over us looking for whatever it is that's out there," the young woman smiled wide as she spoke.

"I guess," Jase, "This kind of thing is above my learning,"

"I think we can do that," Seamus looked at the young tinker smith then to his friend, "It's a really good idea, I'm not sure how long it'll last, though,"

Clare smiled and reached into the box and pulled out a silver box about as wide as her hands, opening up she revealed it contain six crystals in slots two were clear, one was red, one brown, one an amber color, another silvery. Each one was round about half an inch wide mounted in an octagonal silver bracket.

"Ground these myself," she said, "Curved cut, silver mounted, should hold a spell-like yours for a day at least,"

The young woman took out one of the clear crystals and held it up, the light hitting it caused it to twinkle.

Seamus' eyes widened, the only crystal he owned was on his staff it was a gift from the Wimbowaradi family on his sixteenth birthday. It was of the highest quality and worth more than his family's land. He was honored to get it and knew the Wimbowaradi mines rarely produced anything beyond a grade one crystal which was suitable only for alchemical mixtures and basic trinkets that one could purchase in a market. His and Clare's where grade threes at least possible fours and were not only rare but could channel magic far more efficiently than lower grades and even enhance it, depending on the crystal type.

Clear crystal was the most common type of "mana crystal" and could store magic as well as enhance a person's health and fortitude if worn as jewelry. Magicians drunk pure crystal based mixtures to restore lost energy due to casting and the rich wore it to increase health and even slow aging. Spells cast into pure crystals stayed there and could be set to cast under a specific set of circumstances by the casters will or by an enchanter or tinkersmith.

Seamus focused on the crystal weaving his will into it, What he wanted to do, how to do it and how it felt, how the spell when cast feeling was important as it gave the energy a kind of life. As he focused, Clare reached out with her energy to help him align his own and allowing her to feel the energy's pattern so she could best etch the runes with a metal pen on the silver base holding it.

*****

Xarona laid out every book on Cryptozoology she had in her possession on a blanket. Liddle's guide, The complete dragonic, Tainted by darkness and thirty-three other books laid out before her organized as best she could by likely hood of having information ion the creature she had faced but not seen.

" How many magical creatures are there," Kisa.

The redhead looked at the young girl in glasses and smiled,

"Thousands, possibly more than non-magical, sadly most are so afraid of humanity we'll never see them," the witch said thumbing through "Kyren's Aquatic Aberrations,"

"I wish I could see them all," Kisa., "But once Bernardo is married Lisa or I will be next.

Xarona looked up from her book, "Duty isn't the only option," she said.

The girl looked at the redhead and nodded, "But, my family, our business it means so much to all of us especially father,"

Xarona nodded, she knew what duty was and she knew the cost of running from it. Kisa was an intelligent girl, not a noble but a free-woman from a family that despite their place in society had gained wealth beyond some noble houses and could buy what name did not grant them. Xarona wished that their culture wasn't one where a child's life was linked to a families legacy or desires.

"Fathers tend to mean well despite the things they do," the witch spoke softly. Together the two read through the books over the next two hours quickly, following leads and moving on through almost a dozen books before the dinner chime ringing.

****

"If you ever give up the adventuring business, I'll spot you the coin to open up a fancy restaurant," Aldis.

"Not if I do it first," Vinceno chimed in relaxing on a blanket and cushions, his wife, noticeably more relaxed at his side.

"It's spices, You can make tree bark taste good if you have the right spices," the young lord replied with a smile.

"This is the fanciest meal I've ever had," said one of the vnegar teamsters. and cooked by a lord to boot, ain't no one going to believe this,".

"You better stop it, before you destroy any humility he has left," Seamus took a sip of rum, the Teamsters had brought to the meal.

"I can humble him," Xarona spoke up regretting her words immediately as all eyes fell on her.

Kisa eyes widened with delight and recognition as she saw the witch blush.

"Of that, I have no doubt," Callum spoke up, adding to the redness of the pale young lady.

"So those two?," Clare who sat next to Jase leaned towards the young man whispered.

"I didn't see it coming at first, but It's pretty obvious to everyone, except' maybe them," The hunter smiled as he spoke. When the adventure started he didn't consider the two nobles as friends, but now they were, and their awkward joy delighted him.

"So how about a song?," Bernardo, "That what people do after a good meal with friends and family right?'.

"I usually go to sleep," Seamus looked at the dark-haired young man.

"With critters about, maybe a little noise will help keep them away," One of the merchant's teamsters spoke up.

"Sounds like a good idea," Isabella.

"Let me get my squeezebox," The eager to please teamster came to his feet and headed away from the large fire towards the wagon he drove.

Once there he opened up a small chest near the front he took out a well-used concertina given to him by his uncle who had brought it over from the old lands.

Leaving the wagon, the teamster turned back towards the fire down the hill and near the lake. The moon shone down as did the stairs and it was to his surprise that after just a few steps he tripped. Landing he turned expecting to see a small branch or root but instead saw nothing starting to rise he felt something move to his back and what felt like large smooth ropes snake about him, grabbing his chest and pushing all the air out of him before he could make a sound. Out of the corner of his eye, he saw something move then vanish it was the size of a pony, mostly head with large inhuman eyes on the side and eight thick tentacles supporting its body; its skin was red and blue swirls that quickly blended into the scenery and vanished.

Struggling the teamster tried to pull the invisible tentacle from around his chest only to find another one grabbing his arm and dragging it to the side and back behind him with ease. He then felt another tentacle snake around his neck and squeeze. The world around him started to tint red then darken as he lost consciousness dropping his "squeezebox,"

With a snap, the Teamster's neck broke just as his prized musical instrument hit the ground letting out a high pitch whine.

Startled, the attacking creature backed up into the wagon striking it and causing it to shift.

Jase came to his feet suddenly, he heard something large move and the whine of something from the way the driver went, "Quiet down," he said to the group, who upon seeing the serious look on his face did precisely as he ask.

Reaching near to where he sat he grabbed his bow, quiver and one of his swords. Callum came to his feet and grabbed his hammer.

Clare came to her feet and whistled, her clockwork machine flew from where it was searching nearby for her, another whistle sent it towards where Jase was looking.

Bernardo and Vinceno stood drawing their swords, Aldis reached into the fire and pulled out a piece of wood to use as a torch with one hand as he picked up an iron-shod club with another.

"Protect the lady folk boys," he said to his men.

"Poppycock," Xarona came to her feet and drew her wand, "I'm not some useless damsel," she said releasing a spell that shined a purple cone-shaped light that gave specific colors hit by it a strange glow.

"Stay behind my barrier," Seamus held up his staff, summoning up a silvery glow that grew out to surround those around the fire.

The argent glow then started to stabilize into a glowing ring as the wizard willed several protective spells into it.

"Can I get past it?," Jase

"It'll let us pass and keep hostiles out, I hope," The magician spoke nervously as Jase, Callum, and Xarona exited the circle. Looking at Bernardo who nodded at him, Seamus followed at did Clare to the surprise of her father.

"Come back here you fool girl," he said softly but angrily, only to be ignored.

The five young people headed up the hill. Xarona's light shone brightly from her wand. As it reached the wagons it spied the missing teamster standing his back to him; his head turned oddly.

"Is everything okay," Jase called out.

Silently the man raised a hand to at them, his back still to them.

"This looks wrong," Callum.

"Very wrong," Clare whistle a new note, causing her whirling flying machine to move closer hoping the spell in it would tell them something. As it approached the driver it started to glow and chime.

"It's here," Seamus.

"I don't see anything," Jase spoke calmly as he nocked an arrow.

The flying device moved closer to the man before suddenly being knocked to the ground.

"There !," Xarona called out, under her light, they could see a large tentacle hit the whirling machine.

The teamster turned away from them suddenly moved and floated up, turning to face them they could see the look of dead horror on his face as he bobbed like a puppet on strings.

"What the hell is that!," Seamus screamed in horror.

"Alomeg, Protect us and let us do they will!," Callum spoke his prayer out loud, forcing his faith past the fear he felt and into himself and those around him.

Jase could feel the fear inside him ebb, He knew it was Callum's prayer, and why he wasn't keen on his friend's religion, he has had no doubt there was something to it. Looking about he saw under the witch's light the grass under the man was flattened, something was there. Aiming at the flattened area, he fired. At first, he thought the arrow was in the wagon, but then the arrow moved showing it had hit something else.

Suddenly the creature came into view, Five feet tall head, an odd side facing eyes, eight tentacles, he was using three to hold the Teamsters, the other five he was using to support itself and move.

"What the hell is that!" Clare took a step back reaching into her pocket and drawing out metal tub that telescoped into a staff with a small blade on end.

"Of course, it's a cephaterram!," Xarona shouted out.

"What's that?" Seamus

"There sometimes called "Hide-behinds, They are related to squids, octopi, and Kraken, they live in freshwater and are amphibious, odd they are usually described as pack hunters,"

As the witch spoke, she felt something move across her feet, briefly becoming visible in her wand's light. Suddenly she could feel something wrap around her ankle through her boots and pull, sending her to the ground.

Upon seeing the witch fall Callum started to move towards her but was blocked by something he couldn't see, as he started to move around it something grabbed his arm and wrapped around his waist.

"Their's more than one," he called out struggling.

Jase looked about and could see multiple signs of things moving in the grass; they were being surrounded.

"They're everywhere," he said pulling his sword and swinging wide and hitting nothing.

"I know," the blond magician stood drawing a circle around himself on the ground with his staff, green energy marked his spell on the ground. He then stuck his staff in the ground and closed his eyes, he did his best to ignore his friend's words as he reached out trying to connect with the creatures, to find their energy. He could feel the earth and the worms in it, the roots and trees, he could feel his friends footsteps and their energy, but the creature's energy though there was hard to connect to, it was like trying to grab the smoke.

As he worked his spell an invisible tentacle lashed at him, but upon entering the circle, it became visible as it hit a barrier of green energy and pulled away as if stung.

Seamus felt the attack and his spell on the creature. Changing his focus, he focused on the part of his spell on the monster and willed it to spread. Suddenly the beast though invisible was developed in translucent green energy.

"Get it!," the magician called out to Jase who without hesitation started to cut at its large head only to be blocked by its flailing arms.

Clare moving quickly joined in the melee with her bladed staff.

"Let's see if you can bleed," she said stabbing at the creature and drawing blood from a blocking tentacle.

Callum struggle as the creature tightened around him, He could feel the arms reaching under his arms and around his chest, If he were a smaller man, he would be fully constructed by now, but his Girth and strength made it a struggle for the creature.

"Get off me!," he said straining himself, and knowing that despite his strength it was his two arms against eight and without his armor he knew wouldn't last long once they wrapped themselves around his chest or neck.

"Burn," Seamus called out as he fired a fireball at his friend. The bolt struck near the Free Crusaders feet, igniting the grass but causing the creature to pull back in fear and revealing itself fully.

Callum staggered through the knee-high fire in front of him and lifted his hammer, turning he struck at the creature, hitting its head and sending it staggering to the side.

"They're afraid of fire," he called out," maneuvering around the fading flames to the staggered monster kicking it with his large feet and penning a tentacle under his boot. He then raised his hammer and brought it down on the creatures head between its large eyes, he didn't feel any bone but could feel the thick muscles and then the earth as his hammer reached the ground with a sickening thud.

Upon hearing about the fire, Xarona held her wand up and started to rise, the weight of the tentacles slowing her flight,

"Let my mistress go," Sani leaped from the darkness in her wild cat from scratching at the creature's eyes after using is shapes changing powers to adjust her eyes.

"Sani, get away," the witch called out just as the creature struck the cat sending it flying against the tree and back into its winged cat form.

Xarona could feel her familiar's injuries and pain and strained to maintain her spell. Taking a deep breath she channeled her anger and flew up higher, the creature grabbed her legs with three tentacles then four, looking at her with it's now one good eye as the strain of its actions made it fade in and out of view.

The witch knew creatures with so much control over their forms like the one trying to murder her were hard if not impossible to transform and it's exotic mind would be tough to control, leaving her with less refined options to get rid of it.

Pointing her wand at the creatures good eye, she fired a bolt of purple lightning, the bolt of nearly pure magical energy mixed with anger and electricity cut through the creature's head. Xarona then moved her wand, cutting the creatures across the head and through the tentacles till it released sending her up into the air where she continued to rain down the death till she landed next to Sani.

Jase had hit the monster holding the driver with his sword multiple times as he moved to dodge it's attacked by feeling the air move just before it struck. Not blessed with such senses Clare was grabbed by the arm and struggling to pull herself free even as she could the creature causing welts and bruises going her captured limb.

"The bastard has me!," she called out kicking and pulling

Jase moved towards the young artificer. Grabbing his sword in both hands he swung, severing the thick meaty tentacle in two.

"Theses things are tough," he said sheathing his sword and once again drawing his bow and firing first at where he thought the base of the creature was then up the feed.

Clare kicked away the visible floating tentacle and came to her feet. Looking about she ran next to Jase and pulled two arrows from his quiver. Quickly she reached into her pocket and pulled out a rough looking red crystal.

Focusing her power, she etched the symbol of fire into the arrows flat heads transferring the crystal 's powers and causing it to crumble.

"It's a quick and dirty enchantment," she said handing the arrow to Jase who was so focused on the monster into of him he didn't notice her into she spoke.

Jase holding both arrows in his hand knocked one and fired, In the air it burst into flames, hitting the creature where the tentacles and body met.

Screaming, the cephlatherum rum released the dead driver and pushed past Jase and Clare knocking them to the ground. Rolling across the ground and to his feet, Jase fired his other enchanted arrow, this time at the creature's head, which was now partially visible. On contact, the arrow hissed and sputtered flame then exploded.

"If that's quick and dirty, I hate to see what you can do if you had time," he quipped at Clare.

"There!," Seamus announced firing a bolt of flame down the hill, The small fire revealed another creature briefly as it turned to avoid the flame in a mad dash for the lake.

"Put it down!," Jase called out, preparing another arrow.

Seamus could feel he was running low on energy and couldn't manage another fireball. Concentrating he released his protective spell down the hill and drew in as much energy as remained. Ppointing his staff he fired a jet of cold at the creature slowing its pace and causing it to reveal itself as it suddenly felt the need to hibernate.

"So it doesn't like Ice either," Clare.

The frost covered creature moved about slowly and was unable to dodge the barrage of clubs and sword strikes from Alvis, Vinceno, and two teamsters. Seamus soon joined in drawing his mostly unused sword to cut at the creature to a combination of wounds and hibernation instinct left it motionless. Vinceno and Jase's swords finished it off with stabs into the eye. Allow Alvis and the drivers to move to the other downed creatures, pounding them and making sure they were dead.

"You got yours big man?" Jase looked over at Callum who was still pounding on his, "I think so," said the burly young man, "It seems to be a bit less vulnerable to hammers than fire and cutting,"

The free-crusader on seeing the creature had stopped moving save for twitching in a few tentacles knelt and gave quick thanks to his God and touched the animal and said a quick prayer for its soul in case it had one".

It had shown far more intelligence than a beast of burden or a wild animal, and it was only right it was given a chance for redemption in the next world.

Clare walked towards Xarona who was holding the body of a Shani in her laps, the cat wings looked broken and blood leaked from its mouth.

"Great gear!," she exclaimed running up to the witch.

"Are you hurt," she asked looking at the redhead.

"No, but she's dying," Xarona could feel her familiars soul slipping as much as she could feel her pain. Tears welled up in her eyes.

"Help !," called the dark haired girl as she knelt in front of the witch with a feeling a sympathy she didn't think she could have a creature she had been taught not to trust.

Seamus, Jase, and Callum soon joined her, the young lord pushing past the others and Kneeling reaching a hand out at the tiny chimera.

"Save her, please," please the witch.

"I'll try," the Free Crusader looked at the freckled face young woman who for the first time since they've met looked vulnerable.

"Alomeg is good," he said loudly as his hand started to glow.

He could feel the wounds now, crushed ribs, a punctured lung, broken wings, cracked skull, and spine.

"Alomeg is kind," he said out loud focusing his faith and the energy it drew into the creature, starting with the most severe wounds first then moving to the next till his energy waned.

"That's all I can do," he said, looking at the cat who was sleeping peacefully. , "I can try so more after I rested up," he said.

"Thank you," Xarona said looking at Callum and placing her hand on his.

22

CHAPTER 7:
AT LAST ARDEN

Jase watched the sun over the trees from where he sat perched in a small pine tree, his bow at the ready. After the encounter with the Ceph-latherum, it was decided that the camp was to be patrolled and watched over till dawn. Vinceno and Bernardo took the first shift, followed by Seamus, Callum and a Driver with Clare, Jase, and two more drivers taking the last turn. Before that, the creatures bodies were taken away from the camp, stacked and burned adding more light and a pungent smell to the area. To everyone's relief, the night was quiet giving those not on watch time to rest.

Isabella and Kisa tended the fire and prepared coffee and hot chocolate from the family's private supplies for all along with a cornbread and Arroz con leche filled with nuts and berries. Isabella had grown tired of feeling useless. When her daughters were taken all she could do was cry and place blame and when the creatures attack she panicked like a scared child.

To her, her actions were disgraceful as her family had its fair share of warriors, both male and female and as a girl she had been taught how to protect herself with a rapier , sadly easy living had taken its toll.

"I'm sorry," she said to her daughter.

"Sorry for what?" Kisa looked at her mother bewildered.

The older woman looked at the fire and cooking quietly for a few seconds before responding, "For not protecting you, for not helping,"

Kisa leaned over and hugged her mother, "Mother, It's not your fault,"

The older woman smiled touching her daughter's arm as it wrapped around her from behind.

"Yes, It is, In my youth, I would have been at the forefront, but now look at me, I'm soft," said the dark-haired woman.

" Forefront?," Kisa

"Yes, I used to be very good a with a sword, better than your brother and father combined," Isabella.

Kisa looked her mother over, she had never seen her do anything overly active or athletic and couldn't picture here as a swordswoman.

"Why did you stop?," she asked.

Isabella looked turned to face her daughter, "My family told me, that female fighter intimidated men, That if I were a fighter, I would never marry,"

The girl rolled her eyes, she had read of many great female warriors, and while a few remained single, most found love and had children and fought until they were old and gray.

"Mother, I'm sorry," Said the girl in glasses. To her surprise, her mother smiled and looked her in the eyes,

"Don't let that happen to you, be who you are meant and show the world how brilliant you are," She said, embracing her daughter again.

"Is that Coffee," Xarona dressed in a green robe and long white dress walked up cuddling Sani who was sleeping peacefully in her arms.

"How are you M'lady," Isabella looked at the witch who eyes showed she had not slept well. , "and how is your friend?"

Xarona sat on a stone, "She's better, Lord Wimbowaradi laid hands on her again late last night, and she sleeping peacefully.

"That's good news right, She's going to be okay?". Kisa

Xarona smiled, "I think so, but it could be weeks before she can change shape, which means I'm out of a horse,"

Isabella looked at the young woman, "Don't worry, we'll figure something out," said the older woman the older woman as took the witch's hand and smiled.

*****

"But father!," Clare looked at her father with malice.

"No buts, Vinceno, and his people are to escort you back to Arden, in exchange you'll drive his wagon there.

"I'll make sure she gets home safe and sound Aldis," The Merchant looked at the shorter man and shook his hand, " I'll keep an eye on her as if she was one of my own,"

"Father I want to come with you," the young woman pleaded with her voice and eyes.

Aldis took both his daughter's hands " I thought you would be safe, but, It's far more dangerous out here than I thought. " he said, I can't risk losing you like I lost your mother,"

Clare lowered her head, "Yes father," was all she could say before walking away to gather her things.

Not far away, Seamus looked at the remains of the burning creatures. They were little more than ash now. He knew the remains of magical creatures maintained some of their magic even after death. Taking a small jar, he gathered together some of the ash and collected a few dozen small sharp teeth he had no idea the creatures had. He could feel tiny bits of magic in them and knew that given time he could figure out what kind of potions or charms the remains would be good for.

Turning to walk away the magician saw something move across the ground towards the ashes. It was tiny, purple with orange spots and no bigger than his fist.   Hurrying to get a better look he saw a tiny Cephlaterrum with large eyes and eight stubby limbs moving up to the smoldering ash, stopping and staring.

"Hey little guy," he said to the creature who upon seeing him turned and back away.

The creature looked up at the human with what could only be interpreted as sadness. Seamus' eyes moved from the tiny beast to the corpses and back, in his mind he instantly made the connection or at least a logical leap, The small helpless thing was most likely the child of one or more of the creatures they killed.

"I'm sorry," he said out loud reaching down and picked up the little creature who immediately attached itself with tiny suckers to his hand and started to gum it.

"I'm not food ," said the magician, "But I can get you some".

Callum stood next to his tiny two-wheel cart tying down his supplies. He hated using his powers to hurt people or things but knew that as an adventurer it would be a part of the job and had accepted that. He also knew that he needed to make a conscious effort not to let stop affecting him. He was taught, part of his faith and power was based on empathy and understanding, guilt was a buy product, and that guilt should be accepted as should understanding that sometimes the greater good meant doing things that caused guilt. The creatures had killed a man and would have killed them or others and had to be dealt with,

Alomeg would understand, in fact, Mizeriel. The Archangel of heroes was often invoked to for help in ridding the world of dangerous and dark creatures. But to invoke Mizeriel meant a commitment to his ideas and dedication to being a righteous warrior that the young lord wasn't sure she was ready for. Still all crusaders in time choose their Archangel and made their cause, the crusader's cause, Callum wondered was Mizeriel calling him.

"Hey Callum, do you have any leftover raw meat?," Seamus looked at his old friend who seemed lost in thought. The young lord looked at the magician, "No, I'm out, I do have some bacon, though, are you still hungry after Ms. Isabella's corn cake?" he asked.

"No not for me, for him.. her it," said the magician revealing his pet.

"Is that a..?," Callum.

"It's baby. ," Seamus.

"It's parents... or whatever tried to eat us". The free-crusader said walked closer and looked at the thing, he could feel upon touching its large soft head it wasn't malevolent, in fact, it was quite innocent.

"Come on, It's cute," Seamus.

"Very, but maybe it has other relatives," The Lord of Wimbowaradi rubbed the creature's head with its large fingers causing it to make a cooing noise.

"I doubt it, it was hanging around the pyre, and I think it knows on an instinctive level what happened". The magician pulled the creature back from his friend and pulled it from his hand and placed it on his shoulder, Crawling clumsily the eight-legged started to move, seeking bare flesh. Seamus picked it up again and allowed it to rest on his hand again.

"We're just ripe with good decisions. ," Callum said sarcastically, looking through his cart, finding a small bag, opening it and removing wax paper wrapped bacon. Taking a small knife he cut off a piece and handed it to Seamus.

The Magician pinched off a soft piece of fat and held it near the creature. The tiny cephalopod detached from the young man's hand and reached out with stubby limbs for the meat revealing the tiny mouth under its head/body. Seamus placed the meat in the mouth but found that despite chewing it could not swallow its breakfast.

"This isn't going to work," Seamus.

"Yeah, the little guy has fewer teeth than my Grandmother". Callum thought for a second, "Which means... it most likely either drinks some kind of milk or needs someone to chew on it".

Seamus looked at his friend who was now smiling.

"I'm not going to chew its food," Seamus.

"If you don't he'll probably starve," Callum.

The magician looked at the bacon, placed it in his mouth and started to chew. After making sure the meat was little more than mush he placed it in his pet's mouth. The tiny creature slurped the meat up and made a playful cooing noise.

*****

Jase rode his horse along the Caravan, Making sure everyone was ready. Clare sat at the head of the middle wagon with a look of betrayal on her face. He knew from a brief conversation with her what had transpired. A part of him understood her anger, He had left home years ago seeking his way, he knew that the young artificer wanted a chance to see the world, but a part of him wanted to protect her.

"I think we're ready," the hunter rode to the front of the Caravan where Vinceno waited.

"How far to Arden?" asked the merchant.

"We'll make it in an before sundown day after tomorrow , ," the hill-man replied. looking down the Caravan.

"Good, I think a few days off the road will do us good," Vinceno started to move his horse forward, Jase followed as did Seamus on his horse, the wagons, and Callum and his cart in the rear.

The group left the lakeside traveler's campsite, traveling up to the high road and turning north, behind them Aldis and his company turned north. Bright blue skies hung above as the northern heading group watched the forest to their side grow thicker. For the rest of the day, the trees seem to get taller and taller feeling the air around them with the scent of pine.

"Look at that one," Lisa called out as she looked out of the wood covered Wagon. A great pine stood above all the others off in the distance. It was so tall it made trees as tall as their caravan long looked like saplings.

Kisa leaned over their sister spying the tree off in the distance, "It's a Mother tree, The kind the fae used to live in back in the old lands," she said.

"You think there are fae in the area?," asked the twin.

Xarona looked up from where she sat next to Isabella, Sani asleep in her lap, "No, The fae like most of the Oldblood is either out west or up north, Even this wild land is too close civilization for them," she said.

Kisa nodded, she had read over a dozen books about the Oldblood, and how they were pushed across the sea by the humans only to be pushed further into the wild again once the humans crossed the sea leaving great abandoned cities catacombs and more. The thought of such great ancient peoples being driven away because they were different or didn't conform to human "civilization". made her sad as she watched the great tree in the distance.

As the group moves along the road the once great forest started to thin, an hour after the Mother tree a road veering left into the woods was marked by a sign that said Arden Timber camp and barrel works in the common tongue and a few others. Not long after that more small road

going across and to the left and right started to appear as did more sighs
including one saying Arden Proper in 35 miles as well as one that
said:"No unauthorized poaching, violators will be hung". Next to it was a
pole from which hung the remains of a man, his skin dry and pecked at,
his clothing tattered.

The two mornings later the Salazars and their party were exaausted
from almost nonstop riding woke early to grey skies and mist in stone-
floored travelers stop surrounded by trees just off the High Road. The
stop was exceptionally well kept with walled latrines; Several metals lined
fire pits and covered stalls. Knowing he would resupply in Arden, Callum
emptied his pantry into breakfast cooking flat cakes, ham, sausage, eggs
and a potato and vegetable hash that even manage to bring a smile to
Clare's dour face.

After breakfast, the group broke camp, watered the animals and returned to a much busier high road. The road which after Lester was
barely wide enough for a wagon and a half was starting widen not unlike
it was outside Vallus. The packed dirt started to give way to stone and dirt
then stone. Logs carved with the Griffin of Arden and mounted light
crystals started to appear every few hundred feet.

Of in the distance large and small farms dotted the lands as did roads
leading to them.

"Bullocks," mumbled Clare under her breath as the all to familiar land-
scape of her homeland started to appear.

Looking at Jase and the others on horseback she could see, that for them this part Arden was something new and different, but for her it was the same small world she grew up in.

"It's starting to smell like a city," Jase.

"Yeah, the same city I'll be stuck in all my days," Clare.

Jase looked at the girl and smiled, "I'm no fortune teller but pretty sure still got plenty of days on you," said the Hunter slowing his horse, so he was next to the dark-haired young woman".

"I guess ," she said. looking ahead as they came over the hill and looking at the walls of her home city off in the distance.

As the caravan moved closer, they could make out in great detail the great city of Arden-proper. Even though it was much smaller than Vallus, it had the look of a great city in miniature with a large surrounding stone wall covered in plaster with red stone inlays at the top. The buildings were also white with red slate roofs that matched the tall multi spire castle near the city center.

"That's no Lester," Jase.

"No, it's not, Arden is the largest kingdom between Vallus and Kascee, it's small but from what I hear very rich in timber and other resources," said Vinceno.

Jase nodded, heading down a shallow hill he could see the twisting me-andering road leading to the wall meant at least two more hours of travel past two small hamlets.

The caravan moved closer to the walled city passing other travelers going to and from their destination, mostly local farmers and work gangs heading to the to cut timber. A half mile to their destination banners mounted on wooden poles with a white griffin holding a small symbol of Alomeg on a red backdrop started to appear on the side of the road taking the place of the lighted poles. , some were new others worn by weather but obviously repaired. Approaching the wall the great gates, open for entry could be seen as well as soldiers in red tabards with white griffins on them at the gates themselves and along the top of the twenty feet walls.

"They look antsy," Seamus said riding next to Xarona who had moved to sit next to Clare after a brief stop before arriving at the gates for inspection. "We've had had a few raiding parties seen in the area, mostly to our north, but nothing like this, maybe something happened after we left," Clare looked at her home city worried.

"Well that's not good either," The redhead pointed at an arch over the gate, Clare looked and saw nothing, Seamus saw the vague wavering image.

"It's something... I think, I can't make it out," said the magician, but I can feel it from here, it's some kind of notice.

Xarona nodded, "It's whyk, the language of witches, well not language, more writing, she said, "It's there to tell visiting witches, visitation is mandatory".

Seamus looked at his friend, he knew that as wizards had their customs so did witches, chief among them was a visiting witch having to go to a town's senior witch and let her know what she was doing in that witch's are

"I don't see anything," Clare.

"That's the point, It's made for witches only, even the most skilled magicians will just some gobblygook. ," Xarona did her best not to sound insulting, She had spent very little time with Clare but despite the dark haired girl mostly silence on their travel to Arden, the witch was starting to take a liking to her. Not just for her skill as an artifice,r but because Clare was brave and tended to speak her mind without fear something the Lady of Belasona respected.

"You know that's why people don't trust witches, too many secrets," said the dark-haired girl, "That and the whole powerful, Immortal, poof you're a two-headed cricket thing".

Clare smiled, and so did Seamus and to the surprise of everyone so did Xarona.

"We're not Immortal, We just live as long as we wish and age as we choose after we reach adulthood. And Yes, we are powerful, but it comes at a cost, We tend to, how do I put it, become capricious over time, our magic our abilities separate us from our humanity, that's why so many of us eventually leave civilization and isolate ourselves from... everything. " Xarona sounded melancholy as she spoke before perking up and saying, "As for the last part, guilty as charged" she laughed.

"So do you ever fear that?, "Seamus looked at the redhead, "I sometimes fear my power, not so much losing control but becoming one of the wizards where magic ceases to become something they do but rather something they keep secret and just learn about as an for academic pursuit,".

Xarona agreed, "I fear becoming someone I don't like, letting my anger, my frustrations drive me,"

Clare rolled her eyes, "Look at you two, A fireball tossing wizard and an honest to goodness witch being all sad-eyed about their powers, I swear to the great gear in the sky If I had half your powers I wouldn't have another sad day in my life.:

The magician and witch looked at each other and started to laugh and was soon joined by the straight-talking artificer.

"Now that's something," Callum spoke to himself as he came to the gate. like most city gates there was a marked side of exit and entry. Those entering who the guard recognized or who wagon bore the seal of Arden could go freely, those who didn't were ordered to the side by guards. and a well-dressed man in red and white robes holding a huge ledger. The low-level bureaucrats inspected the cargo, asked questions and took down the name, occupation, titles and estimated time of stay of visitors quickly and efficiently. Callum watches the man in the robes and guards move towards him as other groups of guards and bureaucrats took care of another group ahead of his.

"Name, Occupation, Title, no need to answer how long you are staying, your employees said three days".

"Lord Callum Wimbowaradi, I'm an Adventurer," The Free crusader spoke casually,

"Ahh, Wimbowaradi, Small House, but respected, your travel papers please," "," the thin dark skinned middle age man held out a hand, Callum handed him his paper, a guard walked up and placed a stamp on the back folds showing the Griffin of Arden.

"You're good M'lord," said the functionary after a quick cursory look at the small cart being pulled by the riding bull. Callum nodded and followed his Caravan through the gates and past a row of six sentries in light armor, wielding long spears, Beyond them, were three heavy armored warriors, one female, two males standing next to their steeds talking. They wore Arden tabard, but the marks on their armor shoulders marked them as Crusaders dedicated to Araiel, the voice of Alomeg.

"Will you look at that," said one of the men, tall with brown hair and a purple long-healed scar ran down the left side of his face over an eye that had healed shut marking the wound as being caused by powerful magic and one that could not be healed fully

,"A whelp in arms".

"Belay that talk Franden," The woman, dark hair, dark skin, dark eyes and a square chin spoke up and walked towards Callum.

"Welcome to Aerden, brother?," she said, "From where do you hail?," she asked.

Callum had never seen another Crusader before, he had gotten the call, but like most free–crusaders that and what he read about the order was all he knew at the start of their careers.

"I'm from the Mwamba wa Mwaloni," said the young lord, "House Wimbowaradi... I mean I'm Callum of House Wimbowaradi".

The woman looked the tall young man over, He wore a simple red and black knee length leather vest over a simple chain shirt, over a dark grey shirt. He looked unsure in the saddle of his great best and she concluded had never experienced mounted combat, he had the hands of someone who had worked hard but not overly hard and raised chin of someone not used to looking down, so a freeman at least or low noble.

"Wimbowaradi, That's that's Vilheim the Cyclone's land ," she said.

"That's my father," Callum. It had been a while since he heard his father calls the Cyclone, in his mind, his father was gruff but fair graying man who while in good shape for his age was far from the warrior he had once been. But he heard stories of how his father, wielding two great maces in battle would fight with such speed and abandon he was like a cyclone on the battlefield.

"You're Father owned the battlefield against the trog's at Ranger's Rock," the woman spoke then looked back at her men who nodded, What we would give for him now,"

"He never talked about Ranger's rock," Callum.

The young lord thought back to his family meals and talks, while his father was honest when answering questions, he never spoke about his past beyond saying it was a tough life and occasionally did some terrible things to get to where he was now.

His mothers were more open about her life as was his grandmother. His father's past, however, came almost strictly from friends of the family, old soldiers, and adventurers who would come to their home while traveling or looking for work denied to them by bad choices and old age.

His mother called them "Sword bums," military men and warriors who careers were squandered and long over. His father would call them by their nicknames from days long past, The Grave Digger, Red Randy, Peace-mill and so on, dozens of men and occasional women talking old times knowing their best days were behind them.

" It was one the last time the Trogs tried to fight back in mass. Vallus, Arden, and Myzonna sent twenty thousand men that day; only four-thousand," The one-eyed Crusader spoke up. Callum nodded, he knew his history, The Trogs were one of the many old-blood races that controlled the south before humans, and the other people arrived from their land. Brutish in the body, they were mighty and cunning warriors who used their strength and strange magic to fight back against the push of civilization.

"I never expected to see Trogs in my lifetime, but a few days ago a raiding party of them and few fae got one of our villages," the marked crusader continued to talk to the woman next to Callum raised a hand signaling him to stop.

"It was nothing just a raiding party that wandered too far east," she said, "We're on alert now, But I'm sure we've seen the last of them".

"We're traveling north then west," The young lord looked at the woman with a worried expression.

"As I said, I'm sure it's nothing," The crusader replied then looked at the hammer tied to the young man's bull. , "Anyway with that whammer of yours, I almost feel sorry for the soul's of the buggers if they cross your path".

Callum nodded, he then looked at their weapons, the woman had a sword, golden handled with pure crystal on the pommel. One of the men had poleax with red crystal mounted on the shaft. and the one-eyed man a single bladed curved ax with red and clear crystal mounted on the handle. Proper crusaders weapons powered by their faith and their augment by their crystals.

"I doubt the High-Voice himself has a Pure that big," the other male crusader finally spoke looking at that hammer. , "If you ever want to put it to good use, M'lord, I'll be more than willing to take the son of the Cyclone as an acolyte,".

The young Lord looked up and saw his group had moved on without him, he could see one of the wagons nothing down a crowded street some hundred or so yards away.

"Thank you, brother, But I have my obligations, and I must be going," Callum held up a hand and placed it over his heart, the other crusaders

174

did the same.

"Glory be to Alomeg, may he shine on you and yours," said the three Crusaders.

"Alomeg is Good," Callum said in return before riding off.

*****

The busy streets of Arden made catching up with the party easy for the Free Crusader, in fact, his caravan had stopped and was waiting for riders to lead a large herd of sheep at a crossroads. Once past the crossroads, the group headed north from the low section of town through an open gate with a sign that said "closes at sundown," Into the freeman district, houses and businesses became larger the smell of dung, and burning wood decreased, and the dirt roads became stone. Two canals cut through the area.

Vinceno lead the group to stable, The woman running it took stock of the wagon, horses, and single riding bull talked to the silk merchant offered a price and a quick handshake later she was signaling her workers to take the reigns and-and lead the livestock into stables and the wagons to large secured stalls.

Vinceno then gathered his family and employees, His drivers (except Clare) he told not to get too drunk and to be back an hour after sunrise in three days. He handed each man two silver, and gleefully they thanked him and ran off towards the low district. He then leads his family and adventures to a nearby well-kept inn. The Red framed building with white walls and the red slate roof was three stories tall with a courtyard with both public and private hot spring baths.

"Now this is fancy," Said Jase entering the inn and seeing a middle-aged man behind with light tan skin, dark hair and dark almond-shaped eyes behind a counter between the front doors and large glass and wood doors leading into the inn itself.

"Welcome to the Nesutohōmu, how may I help you," said the man with a smile.

Vinceno started to move towards the desk but was beaten to it by Isabella who placed her hand-stitched velvet and silk money pouch on the counter first.

"We need rooms for three days, One for my husband and I, one for my daughters, one for my son, One for Lady Xarona and one for the three young men in the rear," she said surprising her group and delighting the inn manager.

"We can manage that, I can put you and your Husband up in our two silver room, Your daughters, son and the young lady in one silver room each and we have large bunk room with four beds, just for a two Silver for the young men, Since you're staying for three days and renting so many rooms I'll let you have that one for a silver too. All of them include one bath, cleaning once a day and breakfast and dinner," The manager took out a ledger as he spoke, "That's a total of eighteen silver,"

Isabella smiled, and took two gold from her purse and handed it to the man, "Here you go no change," she said.

"Thank you Ms. Isabella," Seamus spoke up.

"It's nothing, you saved my daughters, you saved all our lives," she replied before turning from the blond magician to Clare, "And I have not forgotten you, she reached into her purse and took out a gold coin".

"I can't take that, you've been nothing but kind to me," said the girl.

"You take this, use it to do something fun," said the woman thrusting the gold into the girl's palm and closing it. , "Something that makes you happy".

Vinceno looked at his wife and for the first time in a long time, saw the spark that first attracted him to her.

"I agree, I told your Father I would make sure you got home safely, give us time to unpack and I'll walk you there personally". Vinceno

"You don't have to worry about that Mr. Salazar, I'll make sure she gets home," Jase smiled and looked at his employer as he spoke.

"Very well, thank you Jase," he said as he took his wife's hand while holding his and her travel bags in other.

Isabella looked at the adventures, "You four are not my children, you are adults, but I feel I must say, please be careful while we're here," she said before entering the Inn's second set of doors.

*****

Xarona took out the two tiny chests from her pouch, each no bigger than pebbles and placed them on the clean wooden bunk floor. Her three teammates and Clare stood and sat nearby as she placed them on a floor and released the magic that kept them so small.

"So you four of you took on kidnappers, rescued those girls and walked away with some loot," Clare looked at the four Adventures," That's just crazy, amazing but crazy".

"I almost forgot about this," Callum.

"While I'm not one for ill-gotten gain, I am a bit curious," Xarona.

"You want me to melt the locks?," Seamus pointed his staff at one of the chests.

Jase looked at the Tinkersmith claim "I figure If it's okay with the rest of you Clare can do her doohicky thing on the locks".

"That's a pretty good idea," Seamus.

"Why not, I mean if Seamus melts it and it's full of pouches of alchemist fire..," Callum.

"I'm still stunned at the fact, the hunter had a good idea," The witch smiled and looked at Clare.

"Me too," said the tinkersmith walking over to the first box and checking the locks and doing the same to the second one.

Reaching into a pouch, the young girl removed some wire and a few small tools. Carefully she fiddled with the lock on the first chest popping it with ease, the other chest had not only a padlock but one built into the container. The padlock was easy, but the eternal one took a few minutes and revealed a hidden spring-loaded blade that could have severed a finger if the lock was picked incorrectly or forced.

"Normally I wouldn't charge, but I think I want this chest, just it, not what's in it, as my payment," quipped the dark-haired girl. , "It's some top notch craftsmanship. "

"It's yours," The witch.

Clare Opened up the second chest, inside was a series of wax tubes as wide as coins, some six inches tall each. On the end of the Tubes was a seal of a serpent eating a hawk.

"Coin wax," Jase took one of the tubes and cracked its ion, revealing it to be a stack of silver six-sided coins bound together in wax.

"That's a Mytec seal," Xarona spoke recognizing the symbol of the empire to the far south. The ancient civilization empire was one of the oldest human ones in the new lands and while known for their warlike ways and blood magic rarely crossed the aptly named "Big River" that divided their lands from the southern kingdom.

"I heard their coins was cursed," Clare.

"I don't feel any magic in them," Seamus.

"There has to be thirty silver in each stack," Jase exclaimed as he picked out the seven other tubes. That's two each,".

Seamus smiled, his family could use the coin, he would have to figure out how to get it to them safely.

Under the tubes was a stack of six lead boxes sealed closed and bound with cold iron. Each had the seal of a Dragon on a spire.

"I know what those are," Callum.

The broad young man picked up one of the boxes, "That's the seal of The kingdom of Manheim," he said peeling back the lead with his hands, Inside was three jewelry quality pure crystals.

"Now that's something," Jase.

"We use boxes like this for crystal shipment," said Lord Wimbowaradi., "The crystal worth twenty gold each".

"Open the rest". Jase.

Callum nodded and started opening the rest. The second one contained three amber colored crystal, The others a single crystal each, Red, blue, dark green, light green.

Seamus was about to speak when something ran from under his robe sleeve crawled across the floor to get a closer look at the blue crystal.

"Where did that thing come from," Xarona pulled her wand and was about to blast the tiny orange cephalopod to add when.

Seamus reached down quickly to pick it up.

"He found it," Callum looked at Xarona as he spoke, "I think It thinks he's it's mother now".

The Witch lowered her wand and smiled, "Well sometimes you don't get the familiar you want," At the Witches word Sani looked up from where she rested on one of the beds.

"Shhh, sleeping," the chimera said.

" So what do we do with these?," Jase.

"Three jewelry quality clear, three lightings, a fire, water, serpentine, and flora ?," spoke excitedly to the group, "You either sell them or mount them or better yet make a nice alchemical mixture using them, oh the things I could do.

Callum nodded in agreement as he replied., "Mounting and dedicating them, would be our best bet,"

"Well, who gets what?," Jase.

"I'll do the work, for one of the lighting and one of the pure," Clare.

" I was hoping you would say that I would be too afraid of messing them up," Callum sighed with relief,

"Don't short yourself Lord Wimbowaradi, That Hammer is class work. ," Clare looked at the free Crusader as she spoke.

"If no one has any objections I would like the Fire and Water," Seamus.

"I have no one idea what would be good for me," Jase.

"I'm thinking A clear and since you're a hunter, the flora". Xarona,

" I would personally like a clear and the serpentine., added the witch

"Two lightings?', Callum smiled, "I'm good with that".

Clare smiled and looked at the young lord, "Oh I can merge those into thunder," Clare looked at Callum, "Put that on your hammer and boom!".

The group laughed then looked at the other unopened chest.

"By all rights, as good as that chest one, this one should explode and kill us all when we open it," said a Seamus in a worried tone.

Clare walked over and opened the Box, inside was two bundles folded scaly hide, the set of ivory combs and brushes, a small pouch with three gold coins, two small bottles of pure liquid, a large pouch full of copper coins from various kingdoms. A folding fan made of bamboo and silk, and a black metal dagger in a blackened bone scabbard.

"Jase gets the knife," Seamus., "Man loves sharp things".

"Jase smiled and picked up the knife, unsheathing it he looked at the wicked and curved blade, "Shadow metal," he said softly.

"Most people call it night metal, " Said the free crusader, "Metal mined from a place of dark magic, wounds are given by it don't heal normally and scar horribly even with magic or faith healing".

Jase carefully placed the blade back in its scabbard. "I heard the stories, never thought I would own one," he said.

"Those vles are magic," Seamus.

Xarona nodded and levitated them to her and sniffed the closed tops,

"Aspron by the smell," she said.

"Used for instantaneous travel spells and for portal maintenance," Seamus.

"Can any of you use it," Callum.

Both the witch and Wizard shook their heads negatively.

"If I may, I need to present the local city witch with a gift, That might do". Xarona.

"I'm good with that; we can sell the rest and split the coin," Jase.

"I need to tithe something at the church, That's a lot of copper to be carrying about," Callum.

"I'm all for paying off any god that might help us survive this trip," Laughed Jase.

"It's not a Payoff," Callum.

"Take the copper," Seamus, "And I'm calling it a payoff too".

Callum ignored his two friends and looked at Xarona who stood and stretched, "My goddesses don't take tithes, do as they will " she said in a manner more humorous than condescending.

Clare looked at her friends, "I'll need your things," she said, 'to do the work".

"I'll help you carry them," Jase.

Clare nodded and smiled at hunter as they gathered the witches wand, the hunters bow magic staff and the free-crusader's hammer. The chest who contents they were selling and headed downstairs.

CHAPTER 8: TALES AND TIMES

Xarona moved along the streets of Arden a upbeat stride. She hadn't felt truly clean in what seemed like months. Magic, while useful was never as good as the real thing, her refresh spell kept her decent but it didn't provide the relaxation and the satisfaction of an hour soaking in hot springs warmed bath while Sani was playing with the flower petals floating in the water.

After the bath, the oldest daughter of the Belasona's returned to her room and placed a simple peasant blouse, dress, vest and-and leather buckled shoes and sought out the services of a lady groomer. The Inn-keeper was more than happy to give her instructions on finding such a place and told her of a small shop not far away that had two chairs and smelled of strawberries. For three copper the tall elegant Nyumbani lady running the establishment coiled her hair back into ringlets with hot curling irons, buffed and reshaped her fingernails and arched her eyebrows. As a lady of standing in her home city, this was a daily occurrence and while it was appreciated she knew that in her new occupation it would be a rare luxury.

Once done with the groomer, the red-haired witch made her way to a seamstress. The store, catering to well-off free-people offered pre-made dresses and accessories for ladies of means, and while not exactly, the quality of a noble could manage with a private dressmaker it was close enough to what she needed.

Old world styles and new world styles mixed as did styles from various cultures. The Seamstresses on seeing the curvy, freckle-faced redhead could tell by her walk and her odd-looking pet, that despite her simple attire she was a woman of means and jumped to help her showing her the latest styles and taking quick measurements.

"What are your colors Madame," said a thickly oldland accented slender man in heavy makeup dressed in a black gentleman's coat, white shirt, and white pants and shoes.

"Hunter green and Olive," said the young lady watching her cat chimera drink from a silver bowl of milk given as a courtesy by the staff.

The man nodded and started to show the witch designs in her size and sizes they could easily alter. Xarona picked out a high collar dress, green with puffy shoulders, tight sleeves, a tulip-like skirt over frilly petticoats, a wide brim hat, white gloves, and boots. The man then placed the dress on a table and started to wave his hands over it. He wasn't much of a magician, like most people blessed with magic he lacked the potential of a true wizard . So instead he trained on his own as best he could and focused on using his magic to augment a useful mundane trade. In the store owners case, it was dressmaking, cobbler, and haberdashery.

"Now for a little magic," he said sensing the woman he was dealing with was herself a magical practitioner and one of far more power and skill than he could dream of having.

The clothing colors flowed from white to greens as did the hat. Moving his hands over his work the man weaved brocade into to outfit and added designs to simple silver buttons.

He then expanded and shaped the dress to fit the client.

"I'm impressed," Xarona looked at the result, "Could you show me the fitting room?".

The man smiled and nodded as the woman entered the crystal lit room and returned a few minutes later dressed in her new outfit.

"You look like a jewel M'lady," said the slender sorcerer.

"I had no idea this kind of service existed outside of the larger kingdom seats and the oldland empires,"

The man smiled, "The number of free persons of wealth is increasing, the world is changing," said the man. "Add in ladies of smaller houses springing up as the wild is tamed and even here in the back end of the south me and those like me can not only make a fine living but fine-tune our arts,"

Xarona nodded looking in a mirror, feeling not only clean but pretty. Giggling to herself she wondered for a second what a certain free-crusader would think, but quickly locked the thought away along with all the complexities it would bring.

After paying the seamstress five silver for the dress and another two for his services, the witch, cat in hand walked outside the seamstress and closed her eyes, reaching out with her power she sought the willful power of nearby witches. Different types of magic left different markers in them, witches knew their kind, it was power, will and finely tuned chaos woven together. Arden would have at least a handful of witches each one casting spells daily leaving its signature. More common magicians magic once used faded quickly unless the spell was granted some permanence through ritual and practice. A few such spells were found first lingering on the streets and further up in the noble areas and the Castle of Arden itself. Minor magics were like tiny sparks of eldritch fire fueled by focus and Xarona felt them too, mostly from the seamstress nearby but a few others. Digging deeper she found old magic dancing about, from long ago and the innate magic all around her, from there she searches till she found a witches signature, then another and among them one of power, one the other energies respected and fear and an energy who had "noticed" her search.

"This way," A male peacock perched on a hitching post spoke to her. In a flash it transformed into a brightly colored bird of paradise that took to the sky, Xarona followed on foot through the Freeman quarter to an area populated by taverns.

Xarona slowed down, wishing she had her wand, she knew she could do magic without it, but the energy expenditure would be higher. Moving along wooden sidewalks and stone streets the redhead watched as free-men of all types male and female entered the taverns and gambling houses of the area she was lead into. The smell of liquor, cooking food and to-bacco filled the air. It was the kind of place her parents would warn her against and be outraged if they saw her there.

The bird of paradise flew to a two-story building with glass windows, red curtains a beautifully carved door and red crystal powered lights illuminating the front. Young men of every size and skin color her age, and a few years older stood out front or reclined on chairs. They were dressed in matching red pants, red vests, and no shirts.

"You lost M'lady," said a blond young man with short hair,"

"No," Xarona spoke to the handsome young man, "I'm, just surprised," she said.

The bird of Paradise landed at the front door and transformed into a young woman in a blue dress that matched blue hair, pale eyes.

The Young man stepped back, "Ms. Azure," he said surprised.

"Get back to work, She's a guest of the Mistress," said the familiar.

"She can turn into a person, Why can't I turn into a person? ," Sani looked up at Xarona. The witch knew that as a witch power grew so did that of her familiar. Taking the form of a person was hard for the creatures and meant their caretaker had power to spare. Some witches familiar could become great beasts like leviathans, juggernauts, and dragons or so she was told at the Coventry.

Xarona was lead through the beautifully furnished front room and up the stairs.

"The Mistress says you have potential," Azure.

"Thank you," Xarona.

"You're familiar not so much," added the blue haired female.

"What? I'm quite full of potential," Sani.

Azure chortled and walked down the hall to another set of stairs going up. Xarona swore the building only had two stories but followed anyway to a small hallway on a mysterious third floor. The strange woman who looked mostly human, but who on close examination had pointed ears, large eyes and long fingers changed shape again, this time, becoming a peacock again. Before entering the door at the end of the hallway followed by Xarona and Sani.

Inside the door was a large apartment with hanging gossamer dividers, marble floors and pale yellow walls. Paintings showing various parts of Arden moving every slow slightly. The witch knew the magic being used and that each painting was allowing the viewer to look into a specific place.

"You are lovely," a woman's voice from behind one of the gossamer curtains.

Azure turned into a bird of paradise again and flew forward, the curtain parted revealing a sitting room. A tan skinned woman with dark hair, dark brown eyes, a red jewel on her forehead reclined on a divan. She was dressed in a red and yellow sari and smoking a thin cigar in a long gold holder.

Xarona could feel her power, she looked to be in her thirties but was much older two centuries at least. The young witch could feel the elder sorceresses apartment was as much a part of her as her skin, created by her and augment by her magic, it was her place of power.

"Madame, I come to you in accordance with the tradition of visitation," said the redhead girl.

"Sit" a chair was behind Xarona now, and a tray full of finger foods and one with tea appeared between her and the other witch .

"Eat and drink with me my child," said the woman.

The young witch sat, Sani, Leapt to the floor and curled up at her feet wishing her wings were working correctly.

"Thank you," Xarona sat and willed a cup of tea to pour and prepare itself for her.   Despite doing her best to look comfortable, she was afraid,

At the Coventry, she was taught by powerful witches, but they were teachers and despite being taskmistresses when it came to their lessons most were refined ladies and free women. They would not harm her, this witch, however, was not only more powerful but had Xarona in her place of power where she could if she wished to wipe her from existence with a thought. For the first time in her life, the young with knew what mundanes felt like around her.

"So why are you here?," The witch looked at the young lady, "Arden is mine," she said as if she was talking about a trinket she owned instead of a city.

"I'm passing through, I'm with the Adventures guide," Xarona

The woman smiled took a drag off her cigar and smiled, "You young girls, testing yourself like common wizards and conjurers," she said with disgust.

"Yes, Ma'am," was all the young witch dared say.

The witch in red and yellow sat up, "How many days," she asked in a bored tone.

"Three," Xarona.

The woman smiled, "Good, Three days, it is, You will use magic only to protect yourself, and for trivial things, the people here are mine, not yours to play with," she said.

"Of course Madame," Xarona saw a look of mischief cross the woman's face as she answered her.

"Madame Arati," corrected the woman.

"Yes, Madame Arati," Xarona.

The redhead reached into a small pouch and pulled out two purple potions and placed them on the silver tray the tea kettle floated on.

"A gift, for your hospitality," she said.

Arati gestured causing one of the potions to float to her, taking a sniff she smiled, "Very nice," she said.

Xarona nodded.

"You are a courteous child, a lot of young witches don't follow the old ways, they come here to my city with no visit or no gift," The witch gestured, causing a tiny statue of a woman screaming in pain float from an unseen shelf in another part of the apartment to a table that may or may not have been next to her divan a second ago.

"This one was very rude," she added.

Xarona could feel the statue was once a witch, her body petrified and shrunken and in constant pain for months, perhaps years,

"I'm sorry she was rude to you," Xarona said, "but don't you think she's suffered enough,"

As the young witch spoke, the blie birds wings fluttered, and its mistress scowled.

"Would you take her place," The older witch asked.

Xarona heart sink, she could feel the suffering, the pain, but couldn't see find the bravery or the want to take the others place.

"No," she said.

"Good," the older witch gestured shattering the statue to dust, The petrified witch didn't die, as Xarona had hoped, her suffering was not over, but instead her thoughts shattered and very being was now spread over hundreds of pieces.

"You're smart, you are practical, you will go far," said Madame Arati.

Xarona disgusted with herself and what she saw came to her feet and prepared to leave. Sani leaped into her arms.

"May I leave," the redhead spoke softly.

The older woman nodded, "Yes but before you do, may I ask a favor," She said.

Xarona stopped cold, a chill going up her spine.

"But of course," said the redhead.

Arati smile wickedly at her guest, She could tell the witch, though skilled had yet to embrace her true nature fully.

"There is a man downstairs in the gambling parlor, His name is Iven," said the woman. "He's winning far too much, Be a dear and do away with him for me please,".

Xarona felt a chill up her spine, nodded and left the room quickly with Sani in tow, She wasn't sure exactly how she would do what ask. Saying no wasn't an option, she and Sani were in Arati's place of power. Also knowing the witch had a way to view different parts of the city she couldn't take the man outside and send him off with a warning.

"What are you going to do," Asked Sani who spoke into her mistresses mind for the first time since her injuries.

"Shh, she could be listening," Xarona cut the connection quickly and looked at her familiar with a sorrowful glance. Sani looked back worried as the two left the hidden apartment and head downstairs, but instead of landing on the second floor they found themselves coming down the stairs to the first floor, a sign the young witch thought that she was being watched.

Xarona walked into the business' sitting area and asked one of the young male employees the way to the gambling parlor, the young man motioned to his right and the young witch without any acknowledgment head that way. Finding a curtain, she walked down a small hallway that ended with a door where she could hear voices . Slowly opening the door she peeked inside, the room was much larger on the inside than the dimensions of the building would allow on one side. Entering a young man walked up to her.

"How may I help you, M'lady," he asked.

"Your mistress sent me here for Iven," said the redhead coldly.

The young man nodded and pointed out a fat older man with long graying hair balding on top dressed in a leather doublet over the gray shirt and brown pants. He was drinking from a dark bottle and smoking a large cigar.

Xarona went over her options and came up with an idea, it was a dangerous gambit, but if she were fast enough with her magic it would work. Sadly she didn't have a wand, so her success wasn't guaranteed despite her skill.

"Iven," she called out walking to the table.

The burly man and the two other men and one woman playing cards ignored or didn't hear the young lady.

"Iven!," Xarona spoke louder, over the din of multiple card games and games of chance.

The man looked up at the girl calling his name, "Well thisis new, I thought the flavor her was strictly young men," he said with a lewd look.

Xarona raised her hand and purple lighting shot from it striking the man and from those around him appearing to vaporize him. The Witch then commanded with a look her pet to check the smoldering spot for any remains before turning and walking away with an unconcerned look on her face. Once outside she looked at Sani, got her bearings and headed towards the inn.

****

Jase discomfort at cities showed in Arden, He was so used to his senses guiding him to a destination, smelling the water and hearing its movement lead him to rivers, a footprint or a broken branch told him what food was available and the humidity and the way the clouds moved told him what the weather would be. But here in the city most of that was lost to him, and Clare became the guide for the helpless hill-man

The broad shouldered young woman lead him through the freeman area to where it met the peasant wall to the east. There sat a great series of factories powered by one of the canals. The air was full of the smell of vinegar, freshly sawed wood, and general muck.

"Do you smell that? ," he said.

Clare stopped sniffed the air and smelling nothing but fresh air

"No," she said walking towards a small group of Cylinder shaped houses near one of the factories, the white adobe covered homes sat on bare earth with small wood framed flower beds, with stairs leading down to below ground level doors

Clare walked up to the house carefully stepping stones that made a click-ing noised.

"Follow me, " she as she moved to the steps and grabbing the handrail and twisted a brass knob and causing the ground to vibrate briefly.

Jase did as she asks half as he carried a massive Warhammer that actually managed to seem to weigh more than it looked over his shoulder.

As he moved down the stairs, the house lights came on and the door opened on its own.

Entering The hunter and tinkersmith were greeted by a house with dark hardwood floor, and paneled walls, all manner of devices lay in cluttered piles, and the crystal drove lighting glowed brightly. A sizeable mechanical spider, the size of a small dog, walked up to Clare.

"Hey, Scooch," she said to the creature who upon hearing her voice made a melodious hum.

"What is that," Jase laid down the hammer and the other things he carried. and looked at the metallic spider formed from gears and springs.

"That's Scooch, He's my... pet and assistant". Clare.

"Did you make i?t," Jase looked at Clare who had plopped down on a large comfortable looking chair.

"Pop and I did," The girl whistled, and the mechanical spider ran to her, crawled up her leg and turned upside down showing its belly. Clare flipped back a few connectors and slid open a panel revealing two jewel quality crystals one a shimmering gray and the other a translucent green with shimmering clear veins, "A soul crystal and a life crystal, rarer than a righteous witch. ," she said.

Jase smiled, "Oh fussy britches isn't that bad," he said.

Clare nodded, "yeah, she's okay, But like I said rare, witches around her are nothing but trouble,"

Jase smiled, "So what now, is your Ma home?" he said looking around and noticing despite the clutter everything looked clean.

Clare's head lowered, here upbeat look darkened, Never knew my mother, She died right after I was born. ". said the young woman.

"I'm sorry," Jase.

"Nothing to be sorry about, My Pop and the other stoutkin around here was all I needed," she said.

"Stoutkin? The old blood miners, a lot of that blood 'round here?".

Clare stood, causing the spider to leap to the ground. Walking to the wall, she pointed at a painting of a broad-chested man with a thick beard with a large blood covered metal weapon over his shoulder, one head of it was an ax, the other a large wrench.

" Uriz Manohierro, pureblood Mytec Empire stout. ," she said. "Married Marcella Martinez an Iberian Enchantress. Their son, Magu came to the Freelands and Married a Half Stout Blood Mytec warrior woman, My Grandmother Dara, mother of my father and my seven uncles and six aunts. All of them came north, and most settle near and around Arden, building for the nobles, working and improving the wine, vinegar, timber and waterworks. I have almost thirty cousins in the city, not to mention other distant relatives my family called upon when they found work here.

"That's incredible, My folks are mostly human stock from Ire mostly, some of the old tribes and a little Wolf kin." said the young hunter sitting down on a well cushioned wooden stool.

"Well you're cute for a mutt," said the young woman.

Jase upon hearing the young woman's words blushed, Clare upon seeing his face turn noise and walked over to him, leaning over she kissed him on the lips. Jase joined in the kissing, not noticing the girl; was pulling him over to her larger comfortable chair in preparation for what she saw as an extended romantic interlude.

*****

Callum walked through the streets, dressed in what his grandmother would call his "temple clothes," a long black vest over a white shirt, black pants, sandals and a black leather skull cap. Around his neck was a circular sun hoop of Alomeg made of gold. The temple to his surprise wasn't in the Freeman or Peasant area its walled circular section where all three social classes could gather. The gate entrance was open and unguarded, beyond it was a small orchard. People in the clothing that marked them as the poor moved about gathered fruit under the watchful eye of vicars who sent them on their way once a hand full was gathered.

The temple itself stood in the middle of the Church's land. Made of white stone, with gold framing it had a triangular spire and multiple stain glass panels and windows.

For the provincial lord, it was a thing of beauty, far from his family's keep temple and the larger one outside their wall that served the masses. White marble formed the stairs, statues of the seven archangels stood in along the stairs, each made of bronze with their weapons, wings, and eyes gilded in gold.

Araiel Mizeriel Vivael. Fariel, Geaiel Boriel and Zolaiel.

Walking up the stairs, Callum said one of the many the prayers he was taught as a child.

Araiel bring us Unity

Mizeriel bring us Bravery

Vivael bring us Life

Fariel Bring us good news

Gaeal Bring us Bounty

Boriel Bring us light

and Zolaiel take us home.

At the top of the stairs on columned porch circling the church, pilgrims and practitioners gathered, most looked as poor as the ones in the orchard, a few showed signs of injury and sickness, Alcolates moved about handing them water and saying a quick blessing.

"Gretting brother," a dark-haired acolyte, her hair and neck covered by a white and gold silk hijab.

"Greeting Sister," Callum smiled at the pretty young woman, with a round reddish brown face, big brown eyes, and high cheekbones.

"In what way may I serve you?" ," She said reaching out a welcoming hand and feeling the faith-filled power of the young man.

"I bring tithes, and seek to pray," the young lord said.

With a smile the young woman did a quick bow, "Come, follow me," she said.

Callum followed her through the front doors into the large chamber or worship, where practitioners would come and stand during an end of week service to hear the head vicar or an assistant speak from the Book of Alomeg and the Song of the Angels.   Callum though a follower, had no love for services, he remembered standing for hours listening to his grandmother proselytize, then his older brother. On a rare day, he was asked to speak, he would keep his readings to less than an hour, and since during so brought no plagues or curses he decided that was all one needed to have one's faith properly recharge.

"Why are you smiling Brother?," The acolyte looked at the young lord.

"My family we have a temple in our keep, I was thinking about it," he said.

"Keep? While it matters not, are you a noble," asked the young woman.

"Barley," quipped Callum, " And in Alomegs eyes and glory we are all the same,"

"Amen," the young woman lead the free-crusader past the choir stands where those inclined to do so would sing the hymns and blessings during service, to a side door. Sliding the wooden door open the two entered another room, this one smaller. Round like the building, in the middle sat a fountain, above it a hovering gold sun orbited by seven smaller silver stars.   The floating sculpture was powered by faith-based power and filled the room with a silver-gold light. Placed in the room where solemn stone statues of great prophets and minor angels.

"The Prayer sanctum is yours," said the young woman., You may leave your tithes in the fountain".

"Thank you," said Callum looking bout and feeling the power present.

Callum walked to the fountain and poured in the copper coins and half of his share of the silver. Tradition stated all monies must be washed with holy water before the church could use it to cleanse of the influences of greed.

From the fountain the young man walked around the sanctum, stopping at each prophet and angel to kneel seven times. Out of the corner of his eyes, the girl watched her head down, singing a single beautiful note. Callum then looked for a prophet or angel to stand before and confess, He had dozens of options, or if he chose he could go to the fountain and confess before Alomeg and his Archangels which he did. Removing his shoes, he stepped into the water on the coins never looking down as he was taught.

"Alomeg and your host I do confess my sins," He started, "I confess to killing a man who took two girls by force and who tried to take my life. I confess to taking the lives of one of your beasts in the protection of others," his words echoed in the chamber. It was the tradition for there to be a witness to confessions so that the confessor would be humbled and shamed.

The killings were easy to confess, as much as he detested it, Callum accepted they had to happen for the greater good and to save lives, his other sins, however, were different and took more out of him as he spoke them.

"I confess arrogance for my strength and skill, and avarice for the payment and prizes won in my travels," He started building up to what he saw as the biggest sin, "And. I confess my amorous thoughts for Lady Xarona, a child of the daughter of the crossroads. I confess my sins and seek forgiveness, I confess my sins in the hope of your mercy and grace".

Once done Callum exited the fountain and placed his sandals on without looking down, Listening he could hear the accolades tone, unending and perfectly pitched follow him towards the door where he exited.

Once outside the young woman walked to his side,
" Love is love," she said with a smile.
Callum looked at her, "I'm not sure I know what love is? Look at me, and It's not like women would be chasing me". Said the Free Crusader.
"Nonsense," The young woman spoke quickly," You are handsome, broad of shoulder, tall and noble, You confess your heart, and I can feel your grace, growing stronger".

"What is this..," A voice from across the large temple room, a Man short, dark-skinned, his salt and pepper hair cut short under a gold skull cap, he was dressed in white robes with gold trim and wore a golden amulet of Alomeg festooned with five pure gems.,

" Young Sister Labibah talking to a visitor and not just singing. said the man.

"I'm sorry Patriarch," said the girl.

"Nothing to be sorry about," the Man spoke as he walked up to the young people. His dark eyes looked at Callum with warmth.

"You're the one the crusaders spoke of, the one on the bull," he said.

"Yes Patriarch," Callum lowered his head briefly in acknowledgment of the High-Vicars position.

"Wimbowaradi, Son of Vilheim, Grandson of Soru the soulful, War Healer and keeper of the faith," the man words brought a look of surprise to the young lord. , "Is she well?".

Callum had never heard his grandmother be called a War Healer or that term used at all. As far as he knew she was an Acolyte-healer of the Church, turned royal healer and lady in waiting.

"Last I saw her; she was in good health for a woman of almost a hundred years," the young lord said.

The Patriarch laughed, "She'll bury us all, I was but an Acolyte when I met her, She taught me prayer-craft and did not spare the rod if I got one syllable wrong. She would have made Vicar or High Vicar if she did not leave for Vallus to serve as midwife to the old queen and in times of battle heal he fallen and protect the just. Against the heathens, " as he the man spoke Callum could tell he respected his grandmother but revered here. .

" I didn't know that, but then again, it seems recently I'm learning more about my family history than I ever imagined," The second youngest Lord of Wimbowaradi looked at the Patriarch as he spoke.

The older man nodded, " Alomeg reveals the past; he prepares you for the future for, your next step in faith and his glory," said the head of the church reaching out and touching the young lord's chest and closing his eyes, "Alomeg, Bless your child, watch over him, care for him comfort him, show him his path and guide him to your brilliance" .

Callum did not expect a blessing from the High Vivar or any vicar and did what was expected of him by closing his eyes as the man's faith flowed about him, Once done the Vicar removed his hand and spoke one phrase, "Your time comes soon,"

Both surprised and wary of the words Callum said a quick goodbye to the Patriarch and the acolyte. Heading back towards the inn he found his mind wanting to push what the words meant away. Was it a prophecy, or just words of advice, some of the Faith powered could see glimpses of the future or speak prophecy without even knowing it. Was it a death that would come soon or something else, was a crossroad in his life or a crisis in faith. By the time he had gone over the what he was sure was every possible meaning he was back at the Inn,

Entering the manager greeted him "Lord Wimbowaradi, your back just in time," he said.

"In time for what?," said the tall young man.

The dark haired older man walked to the door leading into the inn's large common room Standing there was Xarona in front of a boy, no older than 12 dressed in Red and White with a floppy red plumed hat holding a scroll.

Upon seeing the free-crusader the boy stood at attention, Xarona turned to see Callum and both looked at each other with a questioning expression.

"By order of king Galen Nyekundu the second and Queen Osa, Lord Callum Wimbowaradi, and Lady Xarona Belasona presence are requested for dinner tomorrow night at sundown at Arden castle, one guest or retinue member may also be received. The boy read from a small leather-bound book. Upon finishing, the young page bowed deeply and left.

CHAPTER 9:
COURTLY IN ALL THINGS

"I'm so jealous of you two," Bernardo walked next to Seamus talking animatedly.

"It's not big of Deal," The blond, magician carried two rolled up pieces of leather made from a scaled creature through the market a few hours after sunrise. vendors sat at stalls showing the seal of Arden, which according to what the two travelers overhead meant the inspectors have agreed they have quality items and that the stall owners are paying taxes.

"What?," Bernardo stepped in front of Seamus facing him to speak., " You and Kisa are going to see the king and Queen tonight,"

Seamus smiled, "What were their choices? Callum is like my brother, I spent almost as much time in his family's keep as I did on my farm, His mother and grandmother taught us both courtly etiquette at the same time and if we got so much as a bow wrong, whack, a willow reed across the knuckles,"

Bernardo stepped back to his friend's side briefly passing his hand close enough to touch the other young men.

"I'm jealous of that too; You have a best friend and someone who does-n't judge you for being you,".

Seamus blew a strand of hair from in front of his face, "He judges, just not for me be sly," said the young magician, " He thinks my swordplay is shite and my choice of pets and whatever we're doing are multiple cases of bad life decisions,"

Bernardo looked into his friend's eyes, "And what exactly is that?"

Seamus grimaced and spoke walking past, "I don't know, what can it be ?" , You're getting married, and I'm working for your parents".

Bernardo quickly strode to catch up, he could see that Seamus was vexed by the situation.

"I'm sorry I said anything," said the merchant's son.

"I'm sorry I'm not sure," Seamus.

The two young man then continued in silence, looking at the busy market. Walking past people sell all manner of crafts from dyed wool to food, to handcrafted mirrors and homemade liquor.   Half an hour later and of quiet sightseeing the Merchant's son and the magician found what they were looking for, a tanner selling rolls of leather and handcrafted leather bracers, doublets, corsets and more. The blond woman of medium height looked at the young men with gray eyes as they started going over her wares.

"I can dye them any color you like, even that purple you're wearing m'lord," she said looking at Bernardo.

"Do you buy hides?," Bernardo asked.

"Only good ones," the woman replied.

Seamus took the hides off his shoulders and laid them out over some vellum rolls in front of the woman.

The woman looked at the hide; it was thick but flexible with green scales and purple blemishes and veins.

"Looks a little worn," said the tanner.

"I don't know leather, but I know silk, and that's in no way worn, and is far more subtle than most leather," said Bernardo.

The woman cocked an eyebrow, "Well, I can take it off your hand for one gold each, she added, 'Basilisk leather is hard to come by,"

Seamus jaw dropped, Basilisks were rare magical creatures, known for their robust hides that were corrosive and transfiguration magic resistant.

"We're heading to Kasscee; I'm sure we can find a better price in a bigger city," Bernardo spoke and started to gather up the leather only to be stopped by the blond woman

"three," she said.

"three," Seamus blurted out taking, "But only for one," he said.

Bernardo looked puzzled.

The woman reached into her pouch and counted thre gold pieces and ten silver coins for one of the hides which by the look of it was all she had.

Before Bernardo could say goodbye, Seamus had grabbed him by the arm, picked up the other piece of leather and the gold and walked away half dragging the young man in purple.

"What's the matter?",Bernardo.

"Basilisk leather, You know what I can do with that?," Seamus.

"Make really lovely boots? said the other young man.

"I can make potions with it, cures for poisons and transfigurations"
The magician smiled and kissed the other young man's hand quickly,

"And it's all thanks to you and your salesmanship,"

"Well I guess," said a grinning Bernardo.

"So two gold and ten silver, I can get a new outfit for the night, and take at least twenty silver back to the others to split up, I'm sure," the blond spoke and started walking towards a row of shops they passed on the way to the market.

"I saw a place selling flavored snowballs, do you think they'll mind if we take a little of the money and splurge,"

"Only if we don't bring Callum one," said Seamus.

****

Jase hated sleeping inside, even in his home in the hills he would climb on the old roof if it wasn't too wet or cold and sleep. Clare's cylinder-shaped home had access to its flat roof where Clare kept various plants, and her father came up to smoke his pipe.

The hunter awoke to a gray sky and sound of the nearby factory and a vibrating floor. Coming to his feet, the hill-man placed on his shirt and headed downstairs. On the first floor, he found a berry muffin and a warm cup of tea and note, "Working in the work-room,"

Never one to turn down food Jase ate his breakfast and started looking for the Artificer he had kissed and caressed for hours while trying not to see her as anything more than playful infatuation.

While Jase didn't find the Clare on his current floor, he did discover a door near the kitchen with steps leading down; the fact Hunter of his skill had no idea the house had a basement made him despise what the city did to his senses even more. The vibration increased as he came down the stone stairs to another door, this one with a small barred porthole. Light flashed from the circular window, and the sound of buzzing and grinding could be heard from the other side.

Jase pulled the lever opening the door and the smell of melted metal, ozone and sulfur bombarded him as he entered to see Clare at a workbench, and a strange device sparking electricity in her hand. Before here was Callum's hammer in its component pieces.

Upon seeing Jase, the short, board shouldered girl raised up her dark glass and leather goggles and smiled. Placing the sparking device down, which Jase could now see was connected to a cloth covered cable that ran to a loud whirling device that glowed in the front and back. Pulled a lever on the large device turning it off and then walked to Jase,

"Big man's hammer, is a piece of work, and I mean that in a good way," she said.

"Good morning to you too," Jase.

"Sorry, I just woke up early to start working," Walking up to the Hunter, the dark-haired girl hugged him and kissed his cheek,

"Got a lot done too," Turning she walked towards a workbench and picked up a bow Jase barely recognize, what was once one made of simple wood now was made of multiple types of wood with metal screws and bracing.

214

Jase picked up the bow, thinking it would way more but found the weight had decreased and the balance improved, and he could feel something else. A connection to it he couldn't quite explain. .

"You work fast," he said.

Clare walked to the bow, opened up a slot near the hand grip showing the flora crystal mounted inside in a silver frame along with a clear crystal and an empty crystal frame.

"Crystals are odd things, They know the bow is yours, and they tend to have their idea what they want to do. I read once that bonding is a matter of making connections between the spirit in things, That's how I work, I think of you when I worked on the thing. I think of it's connection to you through those thoughts," said the tinkersmith as she smiled as she closed the slot and found her and Jase holding the bow together.

"So what does it do?," asked the hunter.

"I think it's the wood, it makes it live again. It might affect your arrows, make them fly straighter, keep your strings from ever breaking. Regardless, it'll take time for it to fully bond with you and reveal itself," Clare.

"Speaking of bonding," Jase spoke kissing the girl on her lips.

"Really, you're leading with that?" replied a playful Clare pulling away.

Jase stood holding his bow looking at the girl, "I took the shot,"

Clare stood in the well-lit room hand on hips, "Do all the girls fall for lines like that," she asked.

"Most," Jase.

"Lucky for you, you're handsome, traveling with a sly magician and a half celibate crusader pining over a ginger witch," she replied sarcastically.

"Sly... Seamus is Sly," Jase looked on surprised.

Clare walked over to the hunter, "Eyes like a hawk, yet you're blind as a mole rat," she said.

" Are you sure?," Jase.

"Yes, you don't have a problem with that?," the young woman asked.

Jase had never known a Sly man before, It was something he never thought about, and something after hearing about it didn't bother him too much.

"Not really," Jase, "As long as a man has your back, who cares,"

Clare nodded, "And what about a woman," she said.

Jase looked at the dark haired girl puzzled.

"Having your back?" Clare spoke to herself and lowered her goggles as she spoke., "You know, my father sent me home, he never said I had to stay,   All you would have to do is add me to your contract ..,"

Jase took a step towards the young lady as he realized what she meant and the ramifications of their relationship.

"You want to join us?," Jase, "On the road, through the wild,"

"Clare nodded again, grabbed her electrical tool, started her engine and went back to work with a smirk on her face, enjoying the look on Jase's face as he contemplated what she said.

"Ms. Isabella, I don't think this is necessary," Xarona stood on the stool in noticeable discomfort as the older woman tightened her corset.

"Yes It is M'lady," the woman tied the redhead's corset and tucked the strings. , "You're taking my daughter to her first royal dinner,"

"A dinner I rather not attend," the witch found breathing challenging but manageable.

"What, how many young ladies would kill to attend a dinner given by a king and Queen with a strapping young lord on their arms none the less. ". Isabella smiled and started adjusting the green blouse making sure every fold was perfect.

"Lord Wimbowaradi is not on my arm," Xarona.

"More around your pinky finger," said Isabella jested, "I've seen how he looks at you, It's obvious,"

Xarona blushed, "Well if he's fascinated with me, that's his problem," she said as the woman powdered her face.

"And I see how you look at him," Isabella.

Xarona stood silent, she had a lot on her mind, as her past obligations, current ones and future ones collide. Looking across the room, she saw Kisa dressed in greens like her, the young girl's hair was done up by her sister, who was currently adding makeup to her face.

The lady of Belasona at first thought the other twin would be jealous and at first, she was upset until she realized how frightened her sister was about the situation. Kisa was never quite as outgoing, and Lisa knew this might be the only chance she would get to dine among royalty (unless she father married her off too).

"I feel silly," Kisa.

"You look pretty," Lisa said, "Now shut up while I do your lips,"

Xarona giggled at the twins banter, while she wasn't exactly happy about the event, it didn't frighten her. She had gone to multiple balls, noble feasts, and royal dinners, she knew how to behave. She knew how to tell a Queen's mood by the flowers she wore or her style of dress, she knew what was a polite conversation and how to properly use the multiple cutlery and glasses found at the high table, her mother and had made sure of it.

After dressing her employee, Isabella fretted over the hair of her daughter, and then Xarona's making sure not a single strand was out of place.

"So what is Seamus doing for clothing?", Isabella making small talk.

"I sent him to this sorcerer-clothier I discovered , I know he specialized in dresses, but by the owner's garb I'm pretty sure he can come up with something passable," The witch spoke as the older woman checked her make up.

"Callum?," Isabella chuckled, "What did he say?"

"He argued, he had proper clothing, Showed me what passed for high-garb in his lands. It was wrinkled and threadbare in some parts". She said smiling.

"I told him, he'll not embarrass me and that If he didn't go, I'd give him a pig's nose and a Jackasses ears for the rest of his days," the witch voice slowed as she talked. "Then he said something like, " Fine woman, but this isn't over,"

"Around your finger," Isabella.

Before Xarona could protest, there was a knock at the door.

Lisa walked to it and opened, Jase stood there holding something a foot long object wrapped in leather.

"Afternoon ladies," he said with a smile.

"Go away Jase," Xarona, "We're getting ready for,"

"The Shindig at the castle, I know," He said peeking inside the room., "Clare sent me back with your hexing stick,"

Xarona eyes perked as did Sani who was sitting on the large bed. The witch stood and walked towards the door, the dark-haired young man upon seeing her fully gave her a sly glance, "You look like really nice, M'lady Fussy britches,"

Ignoring his words, the witch took the leather wrapped and unfolded it, it looked the same except the grip was now silver lace with a three crystal mount, one with her green gem the other two empty.

Holding it, she could feel not only the focus it provided but a new magic coursing through it and into here.

"Tell her to thank you Jase," said Xarona. , "It's beautiful work,"

Jase nodded, "Wait don't I get a kiss for delivering this," He asked.

"Of course," Xarona pointed at the wood floor with the wand turning it into a liquid version of wood that allowed the hunter to fall through into the kitchen and frightening two cooks.

The floor resolidified a second later, just as Bernardo and Vinceno walked up.

"Their ready and the coach from the castle is coming down the road," Bernardo looked at Xarona, "You're going to be surprised," he said.

The witch raised an eyebrow and slid her wand into her handbag. Making sure not to hit its other passenger. Sani closed her eyes and focused, training she started to change shape, her body twisting folding in on itself until she became tiny white owl with pink highlights on the end of her feathers, flying up she perched on her mistresses right shoulder and sat quietly.

"Are birds on shoulders still in among ladies at courts," Vinceno spoke up, " trends come and go so fast,"

Isabella walked her daughter to her husband, "yes it is, now look at your beautiful girl,".

Kisa stood in a green dress with gold and green corset, her hair up with green silk woven into it.

"You are stunning my child," said the man.

"Thanks, Father," the girl spoke shyly.

"Vinceno we should hurry," Isabella moved past everyone to clear a path, heading downstairs she saw Callum and Seamus talking to Jase and the Inn's Manager.

Callum stood fiddling with his outfits high collar. He was dressed in a red double-breasted frock coat, black high collar shirt, black pants with gold trim, on the left breast of the jacket was a Nyumbani shield with a black bull stitched in gold thread on it.

Seamus was also in similar pants with a starch white shirt, ascot and red vest with a matching bull.

"I feel like I'm going to a funeral," Callum.

"It's just one night," Seamus.

"Look at you two, looking like fine upstanding young dudes," Jase.

"This going to make us famous!', exclaimed the Innkeeper., "We've never had people from here be invited to meet the king and Queen.

Isabella looked the young men over checking for lose threads, hairs out of place and any sign of body odor. , "It'll do," she said.

Everyone watched as Vinceno escorted his daughter down the stairs like the proud father he was, He had every confidence Kisa would bring only honor to his family at the dinner. Behind them came Bernardo escorting Xarona.

"Araiel is praised," exclaimed Callum, softly in awe of the redhead. Upon reaching the bottom of the stairs, Kisa linked arms with a shy looking Seamus who smirked playfully at Bernardo at the change off.

"You look gorgeous," Callum to Xarona.

" As oppose to what I normally look like," she asked.

"No, I mean you look extra Beautiful," Callum kissed the young woman's gloved hand.

"Good answer M'lord, Shall we leave," Xarona smiled, hiding back the nervousness she felt under her bravado. The thought of a friend or associate of her family seeing her at the royal event and telling them was a though she wished she could lock away deep in her mind.

The couples left the Inn, outside a red and white covered carriage awaited with a driver and two footmen.

"Please don't trip," Kisa said to herself boarding the carriage, Seamus followed. Callum and Xarona entered after that and as everyone watched the carriage headed down the road. From there it turned up the main thoroughfare towards the wall leading to the noble's section of the city.

The gate at the wall was engraved at the very top with the griffin of Arden, while along the wall it's six minor noble families seals sat three on each side of the room for more to be added as the kingdom expanded.

Xarona had thought she knew noble family in the south and most of the ones in the New Lands ever; she recognized none of the minor ones listed. According to her education, Arden was itself an insignificant kingdom between Vallus and Kasscee, she never expected it to be so well organized beautiful and thriving,

The carriage entered the gates onto a well-lit road surrounded by green trees, and flat gardens and small fields with well kept little creeks, with the homes of nobles and the embassies of other kingdoms sitting in serene comfort. Then passed a small area with beautiful shops, an amphitheater, and fountain sitting area before turning towards the last wall and the castle.

"This beautiful," Kisa looked about at awe of surroundings.

"Vallus' noble quarter is a lot like this, only larger," Xarona spoke up, " Only I didn't have the time or inclination to visit when I was there last. "

Seamus sat with a sullen look, "If they spent more gold helping their people and less on things like this, things would be much better," he said.

"Life isn't fair Seamus, very few people can change their place in the world or want to help others do the same," Xarona didn't mean to sound so cold, but her nervousness was making her far less charitable this evening.

"I don't know," Callum spoke up, "My family helped hundreds of people, and while we don't live nearly this good we do live pretty well,"

Seamus nodded in agreement, "That's what I'm talking about, The Wimbowaradi's is looked down upon as, peasant-nobles and copper-lords yet they work with their people, help them and are loved for it. The magician spoke as he started to feel magic about him, the castle wall of Arden, like most he had heard was protected from magic aimed at those inside and had spells to help deflect or stop spells that would harm the walls or allow people to teleport into the castle or magically enter unnoticed.

"My family isn't perfect," Callum words broke his friend's fascination and with the magic about them.

"No noble family is," Xarona added looking outside as they entered the walls surrounding the castle and up a slope past, well kept white-walled and red slate roofed guard towers, trees, lush garden and grassy areas, small ponds and beautiful topiaries.

The carriage came to a halt in front of the castles large wooden doors, swung open, low functionaries milled about as guards , all pressed in polished Arden tabards, shiny plate armor, and clean curved pikes stood at attention. With the footman's help, the group exited the carriage, Two pages one boy and one girl, dressed in red and gold Arden griffin Tunics red pants and white shirts ran to the part, bowing.

"M'lords and Ladies, welcome," said the pages almost at the same time.

"I'm not a lady," Kisa.

The boy, red hair and freckled face looked at the dark-haired girl who was just about his age, "You are an honored guest of the king and Queen " he said bowing and blushing before the girl.

"Come you'll be announced," the female page moved towards the door, past two statues of on the inside stone walls.

Callum hooked his arm into Xarona's followed.

"I hope I don't do anything to embarrass you," he whispered to her.

"You'll do fine Callum," she returned patting his hand before holding it gently. .

The group walked past more stone walls full of banners depicting Griffins, the Archangel Araiel slaying a hydra with her great broad Katar and defending a wounded Nyumbani knight with her chakram. The last banner was dedicated to The battles that formed Arden, one of a mighty army vs., Trogs and another of a great king on Griffin fighting off fae Airship and fae riding winged horses.

"The male page opened asmall sliding door no taller than him in, stood on his gold slipper-clad toes and whispered to someone beyond it. The sound of violins welled up inside followed by flute and horns as the door open revealing the castles beautiful wood and white stone hall. Lit by dozens of illumination crystals. At the far in sat the high table, the king, a man tall athletic middle aged with skin as dark as Callum' s and long braided dark brown hair stood next to his golden tan, dark hair, and dark-eyed queen.

"At the court of Arden, before His Majesty Galen Nyekundu the second and Queen Osa Nyekundu, we hereby announce the presence of your honored guests, Lady Xarona Belasona, and Lord Callum Wimbo-waradi," called out a herald dressed in attire similar but more elaborate than the pages called out to the hall as the door open. Callum and Xarona took a deep breath and entered to melodious display by a group of small musicians positioned in an ornate viewing platform in the corner of the fall.

Ladies, Lords, their children, Free people, military, and clergy all bowed as the husky young lord and the red-haired lady entered arm in arm.

"A t the court of Arden, " The herald started again, " , before His Majesty Galen Nyekundu the second and Queen Osa Nyekundu, we at this moment announce the presence of your honored guests, Magi Seamus Pathson of the Mwamba wa Mwaloni and Miss Kisa Salazar of Vallus," the herald spoke again, While there were no bows, there were nods of acknowledgment of the two non-nobles.

"I feel like royalty," Whispered Kisa, her words brought a smile to Seamus' face and the will to do everything he could to make sure Bernardo's sister would enjoy this night.

The male page walks alongside Callum and Xarona leading them to chairs next to the right hand of the king. Standing before the royal couple the young lord and lady knelt.

"Rise My friends and guests," said the king of Arden.

The adventurers stood, suddenly and surprising king Galen embraced Callum, "Good to see you cousin," he said.

"Cousin?," Callum took the embrace as he spoke surprised.

The king took a step back, "Yes, We both share a great-grandfather, your grandmother's younger sister married into the Nyekundu family.

"I did not know that," The surprised Free Crusader looked at the smiling king and beyond to his beautiful queen.

"It surprised my husband too, but our scholars made the connection once we knew you were in town. ," said Queen Osa who was now walking over to Xarona, "And you my dear are just as welcomed, your family's wheels move our kingdom," she said taking both the witches hand.

After everyone returned to their seating, the king held up his glass and gold goblet high, "To our guests, my cousin, Lord Callum Wimbowaradi and the beautiful Lady Xarona Belisona," he said, "May Alomeg bless them in all they do," Everyone held up the drink, including Seamus and Kisa who sat at a nearby table next to The Grand-Magas of Arden, his wife and children and a local lord and his family.

Once the toast was given servers appeared bearing trays of fresh cheeses, bread, wild smoked boar, yams, vegetables and-and more.

The king and the high table that consisted of the royal family, guests, The High Vicar of the Church of Arden, the general of the Arden Army. At the end of the table sat a woman in a beautiful red and yellow sari that no one made eye contact with that. Xarona instantly recognized her of as the witch Arati, who had a small blue bird perched on her shoulder matching the odd style of many of the other women present.

"So what brings you to Arden, Cousin," Galen spoke after taking a few hearty bites of food.

"I'm hired out as an adventure, escorting a family across the wilds from Vallus to the high seat of Colos your grace," Said Callum.

"No need for formalities between us," Said Galen, "It's rare I see distance relatives, and rarer I see ones living life instead of living off their names and titles,"

Callum nodded, "Be careful what you say, once I tell my family, we are related to the king of Arden, you should expect visitors," jested the young lord.

"And they will be more than welcome," The king said, "I have nothing but respect for the Wimbowaradi family, my family titles come from old ones in Mother Keygiro, in oldlands, forged from the old tribes that became kingdoms thousands of years ago. But you, your Grandmother took a gift of granted by the Queen of Vallus to her and with your father forged it into a legacy,"

Callum beamed with pride that a man of royal blood would have so much respect for his family and their story.

"Thank you for Your G.. I mean Cousin Galen".

As Callum was about to continue the Queen leaned over towards him and her husband, " So, are you and Lady Xarona, betrothed or just traveling together," she said.

"Just traveling," said both young nobles at the same time.

The queen nodded and smiled, "Well if that's the case, we do have a daughter, our third, Liani, She'll be seventeen soon..,"

The king looked at his wife and raised a hand signally her to stop talking before speaking himself, "My love, he's an adventurer, let him have his time of daring do on the road before he settles down,"

"Of course dear, I'm just trying to see if there is interest," Osa watched Xarona's face when her daughter was mentioned she could see the redhead's eyes narrow, years in the royal court had taught how to read the subtle signs people give. , "And mow I see there is.. interest in him already".

Seamus ate slowly at his table making small talk, laughing at jokes and nodding during the conversations. He was terrified. Especially by the fact, the Grand-Magus of Arden, a gray and brown-haired man with a mani-cured curled mustache was sitting just two seats down from him dressed in ornate red and white robes worth more than his family's farm.

"So young Magician, Where did you train," said the older magician.

Seamus looked up, meat still in his mouth, slowly he swallowed, and took a drink, "I had no formal college training, But my teacher was Cass-bell Pann, but I'm sure you've never heard of her Grand-Magus," Seamus.

"The magical world is a small one," The Grand Magus said, "I've heard of her, She was bounced out of the Collegic if I remember correctly for disciplinary reasons some twenty or so years ago,"

Seamus' eyes widen, Cassbell, was a tad eccentric but didn't seem to be the type to be removed from anyplace for disciplinary reason's, in fact, she was a pacifist and would be sad beyond measure if she knew what her apprentice had done with what she taught, thought the magician.

"Still, I heard she was talented, and I can in no way tell you're a back-wood sorcerer by reading your aura," said the Grand Magus in a way both condescending and complementary.

"Thank you, said, Seamus,"

"He stopped a river to save my brother's life," said Kisa, "And help saved my sister and me from vicious men,"

Seamus looked at the girl and eyes all eyes fell on her.

"Now that sounds like a rip-roaring tale," Said the heavy set lord across from her.

Kisa nodded took a sip of her drink and started telling a story, embellishing some but keeping the most pertinent facts. The Grand Magus, The Lord, their families and even Seamus listened intently as they sat, mesmerized by the tale as the girl told a tale of tentacle creatures, kidnappings, raging rivers and high adventure with the skill of a master storyteller.

After The appetizers and main dishes were consumed cakes were brought to the high table, The largest one was Red and White with a Griffin made of sculpted transparent sugar on top. The smaller cakes were of the Wimbowaradi, and Bellasona colors with sugar spun bull on one, and an owl peached on a wheel on the other   The castles pastry chef entered the room, tall thin and androgynous was the first full-blooded fae Callum, Seamus, Kisa and Xarona had ever seen in person. With a Silver knife, the green haired chef cut the cakes.

"That's a fae," Xarona to Callum.

The lord to her side nodded, "I thought they were in the Wildlands,"

The king on hearing the whispered discussion leaned towards his guest, "Vasir has been a cook for my family for generations," said the Galen as the Fay gestured at the cake slices to send them spinning out to multiple tables landing on small saucers.

"That magic is so graceful," Xarona.

"You know Seamus is part fae, from way back in his family," Callum.

"Your Magician friend?," Galen, "Then I shall arrange for them to meet,"

The king waited till the cakes were served then gestured for the chef to come to him, leaning over he whispered into the Chef's ear and pointed to Seamus. The fae nodded and walked towards the table.

"Come to my love, finish eating so the dancing can start," Queen Oso.

"Dancing?" Callum looked at the Queen.

"Of course, and as our guests, you and Lady Xarona will be the center of attention when it starts," she said.

Sani, who had been utterly still on her mistress' shoulders giggled, she knew Xarona was talented at a lot of things, she was a witch and noble-woman with numerous skills and aptitudes, dancing was not one of them. In fact, her dancing instructor had described her as ponderous on the dance floor as a drunken mammoth, up until the redheaded witch turned him into a goat for his constant insults.

"I have a confession" Callum to Xarona

"I can't dance," said the couple to each other, before giggling at simultaneous confession.

"Well this is going to be embarrassing," Callum said taking a bite of the best cake he ever had, a chocolate cake with pureed strawberries between the layers coated with white chocolate frosting.

Though the news of dancing gave her a nervous stomach, courtesy demanded she takes a bite, and she did before responding, "I agree, we have to find a way out of it, and my goddess this cake is good,"

The two smiled at each other, despite their nerves and they found the fact they were eating the best cake of their lives next to each other something to be cherished, something special they would never forget.

Callum's hand moved over Xarona's.

"You know, If you turned me into a frog, We wouldn't have to dance, and I 'll get a kiss out of it at the end of the night,"

The witch smiled playfully, "You may get a kiss at the end of the night anyway. She said. For the first time in a long time, the Lady of Belisona felt her obligations and worries slip away, all that she cared about was th moment she was in.

*****

After The dessert was finished, and the plates gathered by dozens of porters who also moved the tables in preparations for the dance, Seamus stood next to Kisa who was now talking about astronomy with the Grand Magus, who seemed fascinated by her knowledge on the subject as did his wife.

"The king said I should talk to you," a light melodious voice behind him caused Seamus to turn and see the chef in his double-breasted red jacket, a red skirt that reached the top of his gold slippers.

"Hello," the magician, eyes locked with the pale but vibrant blue eyes of the person he faced. Suddenly he smelt pine around him, felt the moon

232

high above him and a haunting music all about him.

"Hello, I enjoyed your cake," the magician felt as if he was drunk, tired or a bit of both and had said the first thing that came to mind.

The chef sensed something in the young man, something that reminded him of his people, of the life he once lived in a mother tree of the old lands. Taking Seamus by the arm, he pulled him away from the crowd to hallways and up stairs to a secluded balcony overlooking the large garden in the blink of an eye, moving as he could for short periods of time.

"What was that?" Seamus looked about and realized he was no longer in the great hall, "How did I get here.

"I brought you here, using the silver stride," the chef, "It's an old talent of our people, we can only use sparingly.

"Wait, our people?" Seamus.

The Chef nodded and spoke, "You have fae blood in you, It's mixed with different bloodlines, but enough to matter,"

Seamus knew he had fae blood on his mother's side, but his father claimed no such heritage and would say he was "all human,"

"I doubt it, I have about as much fae blood as a pigeon's fart," he said,

The chef smiled at the joke, "I'm Vasir, Of the great Pine of Ereisle," he said. "And you are more fae than human,"

"Bullshit," Seamus, "And my best friend rides a bull, so I know what a bull's shit looks like,"

"No it's true, I've met others of mixed blood, they are more like your pigeon's fart, but you, you had at least one full fae parent and the other, is quarter fae blood at least,"

Seamus took a step back, His mother said her Grandfather was a fae, she even had an allergy to iron and could talk to animals. But his father, short, sticky, long red hair, and beard had no such allergy and worked on the farm and road crew with metal weapons and wore an iron symbol of The green mother around his neck.

"I don't look overly fae," Seamus.

"You have lived among humans so long you are locked in a seeming that's not your true form, And I senses your human blood has taken some of your other abilities, part of your heritage is in you, locked away," Vasir touched the young man's shoulder.

"If you like, I can start the process of awakening it," the Chef spoke to the young magician softly.

"If It helps prove, I'm not what you think, sure," Seamus suddenly felt the need not to be special, to not be something more than he was, he also felt a memory he had forgotten start to rise in him, something that was sealed away long ago. .

Seamus knew magic was about connections and knew that the fae had a natural connection to nature, he, however, didn't think it extended to others and when Vasir touched his hand the smells and feelings he had when he first saw him returned and engulfed him.

"I'm married," said a female voice in his head, "You're no longer the father,"

Seamus realized his eyes were closed and when he opened them, he was standing in behind a rain barrel at his farm . The barrel was as tall as him, and the voice he heard was his mother standing outside talking to a man who Seamus could not make out beyond the fact he was tall and thin.

"He needs to know," the man spoke, his being becoming less a shadow and more real, Tall pale with, yellow-white hair worn long, large almond shaped eyes, long pointed ears. Seamus thought of him as he despite the fact his features merged male and female perfectly. He was dressed in a Green long coat, Brown vest, a brown skirt that touched the ground.

"Go," said the woman now in tears.

Seamus could feel himself crying as the fae lowered his head and walked away.

"Seamus still small turned to see the "Man," behind him looking at him.

"You will find your way back to what you lost," he said before blurring away again.

Seamus now stood crying on the balcony, a feeling of betrayal in his heart and the sound of an orchestra warming up in his ears.

"My father," he said sobbing.

"I saw, By his look, he was one of the MotherAsh fae," said the chef.

"No, My Father wasn't my father, My mother lied," the young magician said retreating the way he came quickly but far from as fast as he arrived.

Is this mind the magician fought against the memory he had just re-lieved, He knew it was the truth, he knew it's what had happened, but he didn't want it to be true, he wanted his father to be the human man he once knew, not the fae he had seen.

"No," he said his sobbing easing. as his hand slammed into a wall,

"Are you alright Magus," the female page that had escorted him and Kisa to their table entered walked towards him.

"Yes," he said.

"Good, the dancing is about to start," she said.

CHAPTER 10:
A DANCE OF GRIFFINS

Seamus stepped into the great hall and stood quietly at the door.   All the magician could think about was what he now knew and what he now felt. A knot in his stomach formed by a sense of betrayal and loss grew in him as the music started and though he wanted to hate him, he knew Visit meant well, that he only wanted to enlighten him, not hurt him.

Across the room Callum and Xarona stood in the middle of the hall, moving as best they could as Sani whispered the timing of their steps to them.

"One, two, three, to the left, one two, to the right," said the tiny bird knowing neither of the couples werw great dancers or evening passably average ones. Still, both knew, if they could manage not to step on each other's toes and not run into anyone they might be able to survive the night with their dignity intact.

As they swayed to the music the southern lady and lord looked into each other's eyes

"Isn't there a spell that can help us?," Callum.

"Isn't there a prayer," returned Xarona in a playfully sarcastic tone, " I mean according to some beliefs, one of your bloody archangels invented music,"

"Heathen," The young lord smiled after speaking.

"I was raised to respect your church. My parents, gave tithes and would visit the temple on holidays even though they thought gods, in general, were far more trouble than they were worth," Xarona replied

Callum thought of her words, His father wasn't traditionally devout either . He believed in Alomeg, but instead of seeing him as a loving father
and creator, the high jord of the Mwamba wa Mwaloni and Urefu Nyekundu, thought Alomeg just wanted you to do your best and do good
and beyond that didn't care. He hated the ideas of prophecy and destiny
and taught his children, you have to make your own way in the world.

"What about your goddesses, or goddess, I forget how that works,"
Callum shot back playfully.

Xarona chuckled, "Look who's the Heathen now, She's complex, or
they are complex, and she doesn't expect us to be devout, just be what we
are and in that we do her will. "The couple continued to talk enjoying
each other company, not noticing the first song ending or the second.
However, upon the, ending of the third song, they decided not to push
their luck and retreat from the dance floor. Xarona to the "Powder
room," with a smiling Kisa by her side while Callum sought out Seamus
wondering if his friend was having a good time. Not wishing to brag, but
state his surprise he also wanted to tell him about the king being a distant
relative, and other local gossip gleaned at the high table.

"It was like, The story just came to me, I never talked that much in my
life," Kisa spoke as the women entered the Powder Room past a female
guard at the door. Inside was a white tiled wall lit by illumination crystals,
small porcelain sinks with continually flowing water sat in raised counters
under mirrors, a female servant sat in the corner next to a cabinet, seeing
the ladies enter she jumped to attention.

"How may I be of service," she said.

"Get me out of this so I can use the loo," Xaronae said," I forgot how much how much drink and corsets don't mix," she asked politely.

Kisa smiled as did the servant girl. Together they went to work.

The witch was removed from the corset and petty coats and placed them back once she was done.

"Thank you," Xarona said looking at the girls

"Thank you, M'lady," said Kisa, "This is the best day of my life,"

The redhead smiled and hugged the girl, not noticing a lady in a sari entering the room.

"Lady Belasona just who I wanted to talk to," said Arita walking into the room.

"Not here," Xarona.

The witch looked around the room, 'Oh yes, the help". She said before gesturing at the Kisa and the servant girl, causing them both to vanish. "Better?" she said.

Xarona, drew her wand, "I've had enough of you and your games," said the young witch.

Arita raised her hands in a placating manner, "I'm not here to fight," I'm here to talk and the sooner we do that, the sooner I undo my spell," said the amused witch.

"Talk," growled Xarona lowering her wand.

Arita walked to the counter and said, "What do you know about the Wimbowaradi family," she asked.

The redhead's hand looked at Arita coldly, "Do anything to him and I'll kill you and bind your soul to a latrine," her voice didn't hold anger but instead spoke as if her words were just a fact being stated out loud.

"Oh no, never," said the witch, "I'm just asking a question,"

Xarona rolled her eyes, "They rule the lands of the Mwamba wa Mwaloni, and Urefu Nyekundu, they are sworn to Vallus, just like my family.

"Yes, they are, but did you know there are six children? Six children, they're a large noble family in the making... ," the witch smiled knowing, "Like many families, it's the first son who inherits most of the land, not that your Callum is ambitious, he isn't, but you see there's the rub,"

"What are you talking about? ," the redhead looked at the woman in front of her annoyed and spoke in a manner that showed her indignation.

"I'm getting to that," she said. "You see High Lord Vilheim Wimbo-waradi, Is in good health, So It's not an issue now, but one day, It will be and on that day which one will become High Lord?," the older witch asked.

"The eldest son," Xarona.

Arita looked at the young lady and gestured, The servant girl and Kissa appeared in two of the four mirrors behind her, their eyes closed, their images mere dull reflections of their flesh and blood form.

"Wrong answer," she said snapping a finger and shattering an empty mirror.

"The Eldest son is dedicated to Alomeg, rumor has it he plans on be-coming a missionary and taking his wife and soon to be born child into the western wilds, The eldest daughter , again this is rumor is being married off to a noble family in Lasana daughter, a situation you can sympathize with yourself and the son after that is a known, a ruffian, No way his family would let him rule. So who happens to be the dependable, oh so earnest and next and line? Said Arita snapped a finger, shattering the other empty mirror, " silly me,"

The lady of Belisona knew how the magic at work, she had bound the two girls to the mirror, their bodies and souls stuck as reflections, it was powerful magic that made her realize that she could no more defeat the witch in front of her than a single termite could beat a mammoth.

"Callum, He would be a great ruler," Xarona

Arita stood and walked towards the redhead circling her slowly as she spoke, "Yes, humble and good-natured and just, his lands would prosper, maybe even matching your Father's in time, but that's keeping in mind there's no scandal to mar his good name. A scandal of say involvement with the eldest daughter of a larger noble house, running from her own betrothment to become a dust worn adventure ".

Xarona eyes grew wide, "Please don't," she said softly.

"I won't, and I won't bring up the fact that their daughter's future husband is the nephew of a member of our illustrious sorority who will not take to kindly to her beloved relative being left at the altar for a copperlord," Arita stopped and faced Xarona, she could tell by the look of defeat on her face she had succeeded in her task.

"Why are you doing this?" the younger witch asked.

The woman in sari pretended to yawn before answering " One, I'm oh so bored, too, Your betrothed's Aunt and I went to the Coventry together and three, I truly dislike, young witches who thank they can trick me with fast casting and diversion".

Xarona looked at the woman in front of her, "I'm sorry, I couldn't," She said in a pleading tone.

The older witch looked back, "Yes you can, so much potential, so much training, so much anger and you hold on to a moral structure not meant for our kind," she said, "And for that someone has to pay, It can't well be you, The mother would frown upon that, but one of these trapped children, she would care less".

The redhead looked at the mirrors knowing despite the knot in the stomach she felt or the anger, loss, and frustration she was being buried under she had only one choice.

"Spare my handmaiden," she said.

Done," said the older witch snapping a finger and shattering the mirror with the Powder room servant girl in it. She then gestured, causing the image of Kisa to pull free of the mirror and return standing next Xarona, dazed, but alive.

Arita then walked up to Xarona, "Don't fret child, this lesson though lost on you now will serve you well in the future. " With those words, the witch's form swirled and vanished in a blur of colors, leaving Xarona standing there, fighting back tears as Sani sat leaning against her trying to ease her pain.

"What happened?," Kisa looked about at the four shattered mirrors. , one of which was tinted red.

"We need to go," Xarona spoke up grabbed the girl's hand and dragged her out of the room and down the hall, through the great hall and towards the door they were announced at.

"What about Callum and Seamus?," Kisa.

"They'll find their own way," Xarona.

Kisa stopped moving, causing Xarona's hand to let go of hers. Looking for her friend's eyes all she could see was sadness and pain. Reaching out a hand she took the witch's left hand.

"M'lady what happened?," she said again slowly.

Xarona wanted to speak, she wanted to confess, but she knew Kisa, looked up to her and the burden of what she had done and was about to do was for her alone. Taking her wand by handle she pulled it from her corset and pointed it at the girl Before Kissa could react she found herself once again groggy. Xarona carefully filed through the girl's thoughts removing the memories of the powder room and replacing them with Kisa, find Xarona feeling unwell and wanting to take her back to the inn.

"Mistress, this isn't right," Sani.

"I know, but it's for her own good, her curiosity might undo us both," said the witch finishing the spell and sheathing her wand quickly. Kisa blinked twice, then a look of urgency crossed her face.

"I"m sure the boys can find a way back to the Inn," Kisa said suddenly.

"I'm feeling better," Xarona.

"No, I'm taking you home," said the girl. Kisa leads the young lady through the crowd of the great hall and towards the way they entered. The female page assigned to them spied her charges and ran towards them.

"There you are," she said, "I could have sworn I saw you head towards the powder room,"

"Lady Belisona is ill; we need a carriage to take her back to the inn," Kissa.

"I'm sure one of the castle healers or apothecaries could help:, said the girl.

"Kissa shook her head, "No, Please just find us a carriage," she said.

The page girl, knowing she had no choice, helped Kissa lead the Xarona down the entry hall and then ran outside to gather a driver and a footman to take the Xarona and Kissa back to the inn.

Callum found Seamus sitting in a chair in the rear of the great hall half listening to a young lord and lady talk about their lands being attacked by Trogs. Their land according to them was now cursed, every tree flower and a plant were now growing faster and larger than normally possible, vines covered homes and roads, livestock once tame was now wild.

"Seamus, have you seen the girls," Callum asked for the third time finally getting his friends attention,"

Seamus looked up at his friend, "No I haven't," he said

Just as Callum was about to say something, the crystal lights of the room brightened. The crowd started to part and moved closer to the walls of the great halls.

"Thank you all for attending this dinner," said Queen Oso. "May the Blessing of Alomeg go with you.

From the rear of the great hall near the where the high table once sat came a great screech, curtains sat against the wall there opened. Another screech and a great Griffin leaped into the hall ridden by Galen. The Creature was twice the size of a draft horse with the body of a great lion, the head of an eagle and great wings that buffeted the air in the room.

"A Griffin," Seamus stood. He could feel the creature as it entered, feel it's majesty, strength, and sadness.

"That's a... real Griffin, A real great beast," Callum started to move through the crowd, followed by Seamus.

"It's sad, It hates being confined, it hates being ridden against its own kind," Seamus muttered as the emotions from the creature flooded into him.

The young lord looked at his friend, "What are you talking about," he asked concerned and annoyed by the fact his first viewing of a great beast was being ruined by a friend he thought would love nothing more than to behold such a creature.

"I'm sorry, I just don't feel well," he said.

"It's almost over, His Grace loves to strut out Razorwing at his parties to end them on a high note," said the page boy who had remained quietly at Callum's side.

"Can you gather the ladies than," asked Callum, "So we may leave,"

The boy page looked at the men puzzled then realized they didn't have the information his sister had relayed to him almost half an hour ago

"Lady Belisona and Kisa have already gone, It seems her ;adyship wasn't feeling well," said the young page.

Seamus and Callum looked at each other, both suddenly feeling as if they had done something to make their escorts evening less than perfect.

"We should go," Seamus.

"Yes, we should," Callum agreed , Making a mental note to write his cousin and his wife a thank you letter, the Innkeeper would most likely want to deliver it personally in hopes it will help promote his business thought the young lord as he walked towards the entry hall, hoping against all hope Xarona was actually ill and not crossed with him for some reason.

*****

The witch walked into an alley behind the Inn in the morning just before sunrise. , Reaching into her pouch, she removed the tiny brown bug and placed it on the ground. Pointing at it, she watched it return back to its true form. A large man with long hair who smelt of tobacco and liquor.

" I was a bug," said the man standing up, chilled by the cold morning and fear.

"And you'll be one again, or worse," Xarona said angrily, "Unless you leave Arden and never return" .

Without a word the former bug started to run, The witch stood watching, unable to feel empathy towards the man, because if she allowed herself to feel anything right at that moment, she might start to scream and never stop.

*****

Jake and Clare found Seamus and Callum sitting in their room. The young lord was writing and the magician reading from a book. The Hunter opened the door using his key.

"So how was it?," the Hunter asked.

The two men remained quiet.

"Must have gone bad," Clare.

"You could have knocked, what if we weren't decent," Seamus spoke up from where he sat before summoning a gust of wind to close the door behind the hunter and tinkersmith.

Clare, wielding Callum's Hammer far easier than Jase Placed its head down at its owner's feet, "Here he goes Your Loudness," she said with a smile. Callum looked at the Hammer then returned to his writing, "Thank you," he muttered.

Jase handed The magicians staff he carried back to Seamus, who looked at it as if a part of him had just been grafted back on, yet there was something else there, something that made the staff more focused and complete.

"I tweaked its focus latus some and added the crystals you wanted," said

Clare, "No offense ".

Callum remained silent while Seamus just nodded.

"Wait, What happened last night?," asked Jase, " The Salazars are downstairs grilling Kisa, Seems Fussybritches got sick, but aside from that she seemed to have had a merry old time,"

"So she was sick," Callum.

"That's what the kid said," Jase, "and she didn't sound like she was lying,"

"That's a relief," Seamus,

The hunter started to laugh, "You really have it bad for fussy britches," he said to the young lord, " Sitting up here writing bad poetry worrying about her not enjoying your company,"

"Jase," Clare looked at the Hillman, " Leave him alone, It's sweet,"

Jase looked at the stocky young woman and did as requested before walking to the middle of the room, "So now that we've got that done, I have news," he added

"You took a bath?," quipped Seamus.

"Yes, I did at Clare's house.. they have this room that makes water rain from a spout," he said. 'But That's not it".

Clare reached into her pocket and pulled out her Adventurer's Guild papers, "I'm an official adventurer,"

Seamus and Callum looked at the young woman surprised.

"Congratulations," said the Free Crusader,

" She wants to join us, strictly for a slice of any future booty," said. Jase quickly

"And you thought to get us to say yes before taking this up with Xarona?"

"Xarona's not our party leader," Jase said after looking over his shoulder just in case, "But as per the rules, If the three of us agree, she's in,"

Callum smiled, "I'm fine with it, but the Salazars need to agree with it too".

"We already ask, The mister didn't like it at first. , but Ms. Salazar... Isabella and Bernardo made him see it our way," Clare spoke up.

"Then welcome on board," said Seamus, "And by the way, You two are going to have to tell her ladyship. "

The Magician placed his staff upon the wood; he could feel the wood, more asleep than dead under his front, the wooden framing of the inn, the stone, the hot springs, he could feel the energies of everyone in the inn, even Xarona who was laying in her bed, awake.

"She's in her room," he added.

"How do you know that?," Callum looked at Seamus, one eyebrow raised questioning.

"Things are just so much clearer now," said Seamus. The magician stood up, he had suddenly realized he never felt better or more connected to magical energies,

"You know Blondie, I never noticed your ears," Clair

"What About them," said Seamus checking his ears and noticing they where not only longer by pointier. .

*****

Xarona laid in her bed, quietly as Sani sat on a nearby end table.

"Please get up Mistress," The chimera in its true winged cat form sounded worried. She had never seen the young woman like this before; she always had confidence, always had a plan and liked it or not an opinion.

Now, however, she just laid there, eyes open, quietly.

"I'm a monster," said Xarona softly to her familiar, "I'm not a human, I'm not old blood, I'm the daughter of a mysterious lineage, cursed to never know love and sow only chaos," she added.

Sani lowered her head, "No you are not," said the chimera.

Xarona turned away from her friend and faced the wall.

"If that's my lot in life, and that's not a lot I'm sure I can live with," Xarona wanted to cry some more, but she was out of tears.

" It's not," Sani

"Yes it is," The young witch covered up her head with a pillow in a manner she knew was childish.

"Fussy Britches," Jase said playfully knocked on the door.

"That's not her my mistresses name," Sani called back, And she's she's Asleep,"

"No she's not, she snores in her sleep," Jase returned.

Xarona sat up in her bed and shouted, "I do not Snore, you lout!"

Sani realizing the insult had succeeded she smiled, started to grin despite the fact her mistress still looked as melancholy as ever.

"Lady Belasona, can we talk," Clare.

"Go away please," the redhead said.

"We just wanted to see if Clare can join the Party," Jase spoke up.

there was a moment of silence as the two young people outside the door waited for a response.

"I do not care; In fact, I'm not sure I'll be traveling with the group any further," Xarona blurted out to everyone's surprise even herself.

Again there was silence, then the door lock click.

"You stay," said Clare

Clare opened the once locked door she had easily picked and peeked in to see the redhead noblewoman sitting up in bed in layers of white under-garments.

"And if you peak, I hope she turns you into a trout," the tinkersmith added.

Clare walked in and closed the door behind her.

"Get out this instant," commanded the witch.

Clare pulled a chair from the corner towards, dragged it closer to the bed and sat facing the witch.

"What happened," The dark-haired young woman spoke calmly.

"I'm keeping my own counsel thank you very much," Said the witch, and anyway, I don't know you,"

Clare looked at the young noblewoman, she could tell she's been crying

"No you don't, which means you can talk to me and I won't judge you" the young woman softly.

Xarona looked at her Clare, and though she didn't know her well she needed to talk, Sani would have been her first choice, but the chimera didn't understand the complexities of obligation or human emotions.

Clare looked at Xarona relived, "It's a boy right, It's always a boy," she said.

The witch sat in thought, until recent romance or the complexity of them had never entered her mind. Like many a young lady, she read the famous romance books of the ages, although her reaction was usually contempt or bewilderment as the heroine after heroine made bad decisions or allowed a boy or man to manipulate them or make them do something utterly stupid.

"It's complicated, but yes boys are involved," Xarona.

Clare suddenly felt a pain of regret, "Is it Jase and Callum, because, Jase didn't tell me anything, not that we're doing anything other than flirting" said the dark-haired girl quickly.

Xarona looked at Clare as if insulted, "No, But Callum is involved as is, another," she replied, "Someone I knew before I left home, well not knew but was meant to know,"

"So you're cheating on this guy with a Crusader who's all moon-eyed over you?" , Clare

Xarona took, a deep breath and wondered, was Arita watching, should she cast a ward to prevent spying, would that help.

"Ever heard of the Phelix's? , Xarona.

"Yes, there some big deal royal family up north, If I remember, they are, all are gingers like you," she said

Xarona nodded, "Where most noble houses are patriarchies or ran equally by lord and lady, they are matriarchs, and with good reason, The queen of their lands is a witch,"

Clare had heard that not only did the Phelix's have money but they were the most magical kingdom in the lands.

"Are they relatives?" the young woman asked the witch.

"No, Not yet, The Queens third daughter, has a son and it seems they like marking their progeny both past and future with ginger hair," she answered. "They made my parents an offer while I was at the Coventry... my training. My parents accepted, and now I'm promised to Daschle Phelix.

Clare held up her hands at the witch, "Wait, You're engaged?" she said surprised.

Xarona scowled at her guest, "You don't have to say it like that.

Clare smiled, "No, I mean I'm surprised that you're an adventure, being that you're engaged and all that,"

Xarona lowered her head in shame, "I don't even know Daschle, I've only written him twice, he seems very.... simple, he likes dueling, and hunting, riding his horses and wants to be a knight. "

"While Callum is all, honorable, kind of smart and a just a big old kind-hearted hoss," Clare.

"Yes, I was content to run from the engagement, but recent events could drag Callum and his family's name into my situation, and I can't hurt him.. them," Xarona.

"Because you more than just like him?". Clare looked into the witches eyes, though Xarona remained silent she knew the witch loved the crusader. "What do you think Callum would do?" she continued.

Xarona thought for a second before speaking, "He's still a boy, He'll want to fight for me or do something stupid and noble instead of just washing his hands off me,"

Clare chuckled, "That sounds about right. Still, that's something on his part,"

"True. Still, I can't let him do that, so It's best I leave," she said.

"Or," Clare spoke up.

"Or?," Xarona.

"Or you can stop worrying, live your life and not leave me alone with three boys and a family of rich no-nothing free folk. " Clare smiled as she spoke.

Xarona thought over her options, She didn't want to hurt Callum, but she knew the Phelix would not take her being with him lying down. So that meant she had to keep their relationship professional. She also knew after returning to Vallus she would have to return home and marry Daschle. It's wasn't what she wanted out of life, but it was the only way were everyone but she would get what they want and not be hurt too much.

"Fine, I'll finish this," said the witch, "And then I'll see to my obligations,"

Clare looked at the redhead, she felt selfish, yet she also felt that sometimes despite what one thought some problems needed time to work out and even though Xarona may not know it, she was far from figuring out hers.

*****

Jase stood next to Vinceno as the new driver stood ramrod straight.

"What's your credentials Mr. Bhang," said Vinicio.

"It's Bhang" corrected the dark-haired lightly tanned skin man in his late twenties man with brown eyes. He was dressed in a Red tabard, white pants, and red shoes and wore a necklace made of wooden beads. ,

"I finished up my four years in the Arden army; I was a war wagon driver sir," he added.

The merchant smiled at Jase, he knew that war wagons were expensive pieces of equipment, pulled by muscular bulls not unlike Callum's.

The armored wagons carried, massive ballista, and alchemy fire launchers into the field.

"What was your rank," Vinceno.

"Sergeant," said the man.

Jase looked the man over, he could tell by his eyes, he had seen battle and that he responded he was used to following orders.

"Ever been in the Wild?" Asked the hunter.

The Man nodded, "My family and I crossed from the Western Dragon coasts across the western steps and Sapphire mountains to here when I was a child," Bhang stated. The former Sergent though proud of the journey had lost both friends and family on the way.

"Do you drink spirits ?," asked Isabella from where she sat.

Bhang looked at the older woman and smiled, "No Ma'am, Nor do I smoke tobacco or gobleaf. said the man with pride, "My father was an acolyte of the lotus garden,"

Isabela nodded and looked at her husband, "I like him, He's hired," said the woman. Vinceno looked as if he was about to protest but instead calmed down. She after was not only the woman he married by a great judge of character far better than him in some cases.

"Thank you, Ma'am," said the Bhang looking relieved.

*****

Callum walked through the market, smelling the air, he had come early knowing that in a few hours he would be leaving Arden and his chance to gather spices and other cooking supplies would most likely have to wait till Kascee, yes there might be villages and towns with markets but they would be expensive and the selection less than great.

Bernardo walked next to the Free Crusader admiring at how the big man would at a glance look at vegetables, mushrooms, and dried or smoked meat and know their quality. His mother had asked him to go with Callum to pay for any supplies the adventure deemed was needed.

Callum had agreed to it in hope to get a chance to talk to the young man in private.

The Crusader pushed a small cart ahead of him he had borrowed from the inn, Already it held bags of wheat flour, corn mill, salt and sugar, two hams, four slabs of bacon, olive oil, butter, bread starter. And two dozen cans of various foods Over his shoulder was two large bags full of dried fruit and potatoes and onions.

"So Bernardo, may I ask you a personal question?," Asked the young lord.

Bernardo smiled, though they haven't talked at length, he considered Lord Wimbowaradi, a friend.

"Of course, M'lord," said the young man with a smile.

"Seamus is my oldest friend; and like my brother, you know that right?".

Bernardo nodded even as he felt a knot grow in his stomach. , "Yes," he replied.

Callum stopped walking and lowered the cart he then looked at the young man in lavender and purple. "You and he are grown men, You can do what you like, but when it comes out and will, you have to promise Seamus won't take the fall alone," said a concerned Callum.

"I have no idea what you're talking about," Bernardo.

Callum smiled, "Sure," replied the adventurer. "That's all I had to say,"

Callum adjusted the bags on his shoulder, picked up the cart and started to walk, behind him, Bernardo stood for a few seconds in stunned silence.

By the time tanned skin merchant's son caught up with his friend, Callum was standing smiling and giggling like a child in front of a market stall selling spices and peppers. The stall was manned by a family consisting of mother, father, grandfather, grandmother and three children.

"I've gone and joined the light," said the young lord smelling the air filled with the scent of saffron, curry mixes, turmeric, basil, star anise and more. Along with spices was. Dried ground garlic, peppers, and smoked and flavored salts.

"I see you like spices," said the gray-haired man behind the counter.

"Where do you get all of the theses?," asked the young lord.

"Some we grow, we have a small farm that grows the peppers garlic and some of the less exotic herbs, and we make our own flavored salt, The more exotic spices we buy off caravans heading east or the occasional airship," The old man took a small spoon off a necklace dipped it in a purplish salt and handed it to Callum who took the salt poured it in his hand and licked it, "Coriander, black pepper and.. something else" he said.

"Lavender," replied the old man.

"I want some of that," Callum, "I want some of everything,"

The old man grinned and was about to speak when a tall, dark-haired woman in the armor of a Crusader walked up.

"Brother Wimbowaradi," she said

"Sister of the faith," he returned," looking at the leader of the crusaders who had greeted him when he first arrived in the city.

"I 'm glad I saw you, I wanted to talk to you at the king's Dinner, but my company and I were called to the west on an urgent matter," said the woman.

"I'm sorry I missed you, I'm just shopping for supplies before we head north to Kascee," Callum replied still slightly in awe of the woman and her position.

"Kascee?," Said the woman walking up to the large young man then slowly pulling him away from the stall away from the Bernardo and the family of spice sellers., "Trogs have come east across the western steps and out of the sapphire mountains. You and your people have best be careful," she said.

Callum thankful and surprised by her words responded, " We shall be Sister, thank you," He said shaking her hand. "Alomeg bless you"

"And may he watch over you brother," replied the woman.

After the elder Crusader left Callum returned to the spice merchant and Bernardo, feeling the urgency of the message he knew he could no longer savor the spices. He instead purchased his usual cache of Crimson cry, Green burners, and tiny orange screamer, peppers, three kinds of smoked salt, turmeric, nutmeg, ground cloves, cinnamon, saffron, basil, oregano peppercorns, ginger, and paprika. The family children placed each handful of spices in tiny double layered cloth bags, tied leather strings around the openings to seal them and handed them to their customer.

CHAPTER 11:
A WARRIOR'S WHEEL

Clare watched Arden grow further behind her in the distance. She had always traveled with her father and had in her own way depended on him for the small things her fast-paced mind would sometimes forget. As the three wagons and the seven riders (including one on a bull pulling a cart) reached the top of the first northern hill outside of Arden the young woman could not help but wonder, what she forgot.

She had loaded onto the great mountain goat she road three boxes full of devices she might need, equipment to repair it's about anything, supplies, clothing and more. She also left a letter for her father explaining she wanted to try the adventurers path and see more of the world beyond the road between Arden and Vallus. He, of course, would be angry at first she thought, but she hoped over time that would change, and he would come to respect her decision.

Callum had told Vinceno, Jase and the others what the Crusader of Araiel had told him. Everyone agreed that they had no other viable paths and left Arden quickly. Thankfully he had time to write his "cousin," but not to talk to Xarona in anything other than passing. She was uncharacteristically polite to everyone, not a single snide glance, job or treat of transfiguration. Taking up his position the young lord's mind kept floating back to what the Arch-Vicar said and what it meant as well as his brief talk with Bernardo, did he do the right thing? Did he have the right to say anything?

From the rear where his bull pulled its cart, Callum could see the land ahead growing hillier and greener . From what he saw of the map in a day or so they would be in the actual wild lands between Arden and Kascee, unclaimed and with only the high-road showing any sign of human civilization. The lake where they fought the eight-legged creatures while isolated was still claimed land, but what was to come would be their first taste of a land without rules or law. The kind of country his father helped conquer decades ago.

The party pushed themselves hard the first day, making it out of the hills and to an overgrown travel stop. Jase used his swords to clean it up as best he could while Seamus used his magic to help with small controlled jets of flame and magical lifting of upturned stones that boarded the area. Callum then prepared a quick meal of bacon and potato stew designed to counter the growing cold as skies darkened and the north wind started to blow.

"Is it, It's too early for snow ?," asked Isabella to whoever was listened as she huddled near the fire in a heavy cloak.

"I'm not feeling the snow, but it's going to cool off even more, and we have lots of rain coming," said Jase.

"I'm not cold," said Seamus, "I mean it' cool, but I'm not cold,"

Xarona looked at Seamus from where she sat Sani in her lap and a hot cup of tea in her hands. There was something about the magician that was different, something more connected, something older. His hair was a tad lighter and his to have longer points and his eyes more angular.

"Lord Wimbowaradi, this is delicious," Bhang.

"It's Callum, My father is lord Wimbowaradi," said the young Free-Crusader.

Bhang smiled, in his life, he had met nobles of all kind but had never met one as openly humble as Callum, Nor had he met a witch as somber as Xarona or anyone like Seamus who from his point of view was as close to a fae as he had ever seen up close. The group seemed to be less a group of travelers and more like friends and family and while the other drivers were more than welcome into the group, they chose to keep to themselves and sip cheap liquor and smoke near the wagons.

The next morning as predicted it was raining steadily and cold. The group packed and headed up into the hills. The normally well paved and traveled Highroad was full of uneven places, its stones uprooted in some places parts of it overgrown in brush or covered in mud or water. A wagon headed south drove past quickly, pulled by one mule it contained what looks like an entire house of furniture, a family of five and a large hunting hound. They didn't look at the large group headed north but focused on the south and what they saw as safety.

For three days the group traveled into the hills their days blurring together, rain, meals and travel, wolves howling at night and a bone-chilling damp cold. The Salazars when they could huddle in the covered wooden wagon, everyone else near fires. No one talked beyond exchanged pleasantries as the weather and the rough terrain had started to take its toll. Clare would occasionally huddle with Jase but that time was cut short when Jase went into the woods hunting. Callum would talk to Seamus between making sure the cook fire stayed lit, everyone was fed and the night's watch schedule and Xarona become even quieter and more distant, to the point that Sani spoke more than her and also at times spoke for her.

As the group started down the hills to what would turn into the Western Steps, they could see the land leveling off, in the distance green lands and a river could be seen as well as the surrounding forest thinning out. By the end of the second week out of Arden, the clouds started to part occasionally, and rain ceased, though cool, the wind brought less of a chill, and the hills lay far behind. The group approached a river feeding into a lake. Around it, a group of a few dozen Bison gathered along with some great elk and to everyone surprise, mammoths.

The mighty beast moved like a herd of eight, six adults and two calves, towering over the Bison they sauntered along the lakeside.

Kisa upon seeing the creatures begged her father to stop the caravan so she could get a closer look. Vinceno agreed but also asked the adventures to accompanying her after everyone made camp.

"They are beautiful," Kisa looked at the creatures from the campsite.

"We don't get them this big in the south," Jase.

"Seamus so it's official, we're in the north," Seamus

"The western steppes, or the start of them to be exact," Xarona.

"So you can talk," quipped Callum looking at the redhead.

Xarona looked at the young lord briefly, " What does that mean.?" she said before cutting herself off, "Never mind," she quickly added.

Clare looked at the two and rolled her eyes, "You know, I'm not the only one noticing how you two are avoiding talking," she said in a matter of fact way.

"It's none of our business, but she's right," Seamus.

"It is none of your business," Sani spoke up, "But Yes It's annoying,"

Xarona looked at her familiar scandalized, " I have no idea what you're talking about," she said speaking far calmer than she felt.

"Me either," Callum added, "Now let's go see how close we can get to these things," Callum picked up his hammer and walked off in a manner that could be confused with storming off by some.

Watching the Adventurers and Lisa leave Bhang sat quietly next to Lisa on the driver's bench of a wagon. Lisa wanted a view of the mammoths but didn't want to get too close, unlike her sister exploration wasn't in her blood. In fact, the wilderness, in general, was seen by her as an enemy to be avoided at all cost and here she has trapped io it. She had begged her parents to stay home, in the large 10 bedroom home just northeast of Vallus, but her father would have none of it, he said it would be an insult to the future in-laws if one of them stayed and that everyone expected a matching set of twins once they heard about them. Lisa argued, but it was for not.

"Do you think they'll be safe," Lisa.

Bhang, who had not only proven to be a competent driver but very social shook his head, "Yes, Mammoths tend to be peaceful towards you as long as you're peaceful towards them," he said. "During my travels, I've heard people say they even mourn for their dead and lead travels to water.
"

"I bet they smell," Lisa spoke up to the driver.

"I'm sure we smell to them, look at those noses," replied the driver with a smile.

The girl laughed, "Kisa would probably say, The noses do something really interesting and blah, blah, blah," the girl did her best to imitate. Her sister as she spoke.

"You're sister has a passion for learning," Bhang

"I guess," Lisa spoke just above a whisper.

"I'm sure you have a passion for something," the driver spokes to the girl in the same way he spoke to his own young children

Lisa sat in thought for a second. "Does buying dresses count?" replied the girl in an abashed tone.

"If it makes you feel happy, That what I was taught. Life is about passion, finding that passion and passing it on. Be it something you love doing, something you believe in or even love". The driver replied remembering his father's words.

Lisa's eyes turned to face the driver, "Your father sounds wise?", said the teenager as she looked off into the distance.

"He is, but wisdom and enlightenment is his passion, hence time as a a Lotus Garden acolyte," said the man.

Lisa had no idea what the Lotus Garden was if it was a garden at a home of a specific Garden or what an acolyte was beyond it is a term reserved for a religious person. "I like it," the girl said running the man's words through her head again.

"I do too, my father taught me a lot," Bhang

"My father taught me about silk," chuckled the girl.

Lisa and Bhang conversation came to a halt as they watched Kisa and the five adventurers reach the lake. She could see Clare talking to Jase animatedly, Callum trudging off ahead his massive hammer in hand, Seamus and Xarona side by side near Kisa. and Sani flying above joyfully.

The Mammoths ignored the group for the most part only occasionally moving to circle their young. Kisa noticed that on some of the creatures were large claw marks and stab wounds healed over and partially covered with matted gray or brown fur. The animals were once again growing their winter coats having shed them in the spring. During the summer according to what the young girl knew they were mostly bald.

" I'm going to try to catch dinner," Jase moved towards the water unbundling a small net . Clare glared at him as he left her side, "I'm going to try not to get trampled to death," said the artificer feeling uneasy around the creatures. While the Mammoths looked harmless, they were massive and even more so due to her height. After watching Jase cast and retrieve an empty first net she walked back towards Seamus, Xarona, and Kisa.

"You should talk to him," Seamus looked at the witch who seemed to be ignoring him. The magician had known Callum all his life but never has he ever seen him so sullen.

"Why does everyone insist on butting into my business," Xarona spoke directly into Seamus' head startling him.

"What the hells are you doing ?" he thought.

"I don't want to disturb the large beasts around us, now leave me be," thought the witch back before shutting down the link.

Seamus glared at the redhead, he could feel whatever mystical connection she started was now gone, but in her communication, he could not only hear her voice but feel her pain.

Callum found a large uprooted tree and sat looking at the Mammoth and bisons, He tried to push his thoughts about Xarona away and why she was avoiding him. Instead, he thought about home, wondering what his family was doing, he didn't have time to send a message or crystal call back, but he knew through his nightly prayers Alomeg would let his grandmother know he was at least alive and well. She always knew when one of her grandchildren was in trouble. She would say she could feel them and their love across and distance thanks to her faith and had proven it to be true on more than one occasion.

When Callum's older brother was beaten and lying near death thanks to a fight with a Minotaur in a back Alley fighting den in Vallus she knew of it and sent Callum and his younger siblings to find him and bring him home. Callum, His younger brother, sister, and Seamus fought their way into the gambling den to find the third child of Lord Wimbowaradi laying in a corner with infected wounds and broken bones waiting for death. Only his will, training and titan blood keeping alive. It was the first time Callum laid on hands and the first time he raised his hammer against another living being in anger.

It seemed his brother owed the mobster running the den ten gold for losing the fight and since he could not pay, The young fighter was being held there and forced to fight despite his injuries to pay the debt off. When Callum his siblings and Seamus returned to the Oaken Cliff they had no idea that hot on their heels was the mobster, a dozen of his men and a minotaur kept in chains ready to be unleashed.

A day after returning with his brother, Callum awoke to the sound of the keeps bells ringing for war. Quickly placing on his armor, he made his way to the courtyard just in time to see the gates open and his father standing there, his great mace's sitting down on their hexagonal metalheads at his side. Next to the old warrior was his eldest , youngest son and two warriors wearing the wood and metal helmets of the Oaken Cliff military.

"That's them," said the younger boy wielding two custom dueling khopeshes.

"Let's try not to end this in violence," said the eldest son who despite his words of peace was wielding a staff that ended in a metal symbol of

alomeg each ray of the sun-shaped sharpened and as long as a dagger , a
gift from his late-arriving large hammer-wielding younger brother who
was adjusting his armor as he walked up.

"You boys be quiet," said Vilheim looking the leader of the group over,
a dark-skinned man in a bright purple and yellow shirt, blue pants, yellow
and purple jacket and foppish yellow hat. riding in on a horse.

"Quite a little house you have here," he said smiling with silver and
gold-capped teeth.

"Speak your business," said Lord Wimbowaradi, "It's morning, and I
haven't had breakfast," The broad shoulder graying man dressed in red
leader doublet, black pants, and boots smiled.

"Your whelps and their Wizard boy busted up one of my places and
stole something from me," said the man sliding off his horse to his feet
holding an ornate black cane with a small ivory skull on the head.

"Now, I know you by reputation to be reasonable, So get me my gold
or my property," the mobster spoke slowly and sinister.

Villheim looked at the man, "If you know my reputation, then you
know How this is going to end". he said, " My boy isn't property and taking him from you before you let him die was a courtesy on my part, because if he had died I would bleed Vallus like a stuck pig till I crushed
your skull.

The Mobster's eyes widened, "You're not showing me the proper respect," said the mobster before nodding to two of his men standing in the

small wagon that carrying a hunched over and chained minotaur in a cage . "cause I got something her even the Cyclone can't beat," said the man in yellow.

"I'll dice it up for the steak," Erv, the youngest son of the Lord took a step forward spinning his Khopeshes quickly, and with such precision, his father had to try hard not to smile with pride.

"Let the peace of Alomeg feel us," Igene the eldest son spoke softly but with authority. His words brought snickers to the mobster and his men.

"Boy this isn't a temple," said the Mobster, "but it can be a funeral real quick if I don't get what I want,"

Vilheim looked at his sons, and the guards, to his side. Nearby at Keeps great wooden front door he could see his mother, wife, and daughters gathering. Servants and workers some armed with farming tools, others with weapons from the armory were also gathering. He loved his son and was glad he was safe and healing now, but he also knew by the look of the men with the mobster that they were trained killers. In his prime, there would have been no negotiation, no quarter he would either be dead by now or standing over all their corpses, but today he had a lot to consider.

"Fifteen gold," he said to everyone surprised.

"Now we're talking," The man in yellow and gold took a step forward looked around, "Thirty Gold he said".

Vilheim looked at were the women of his family stood. He expected worried faces but instead saw ones of confidence. At the door, his youngest daughter stood holding a double-headed ax that even at her young age could feel a tree in less than a dozen strikes. His eldest daughter held a bow in one hand a quiver of arrows at his side, his mother old on a cane was being held back from hobbling forward by two servants. His wife, however, was not just standing she was calming walking towards the group.

"The lady must have the purse strings," said the mobster as the woman in long braids covered by a red scarf dressed in a simple red dress and red and gold shawl moved closer her hands hidden in wide bell sleeves.

Vilheim could see the anger in his wife's eyes, "Wife," he said holding his hand out as if motioning her to stop. "Did you bring what he asked for ?," The man. The woman nodded and walked up to the mobster who smiled as she moved forward.

"So M'lady, what do you have for me," he asked.

The woman looked up at the man and with a growl revealed the twin meat cleavers she held, the first one sliced through his neck up to the bone, the next one opened him up across the belly.

"How dare you come to our lands, to my home after my child," roared the woman to the stunned group of various lowlifes and muscle for hire. "Leave here and pray to the great and glorious Alomeg you never need to return," said the woman.

Callum never saw his mother the same way again, although, in hindsight, he could now see that for his mother there was no other real choice.

You protect those you love at all costs, he thought t as he stood and stretched. Near by the free-crusader could see his hunter friend in the water pulling a net full of small silver scaled fish and a few small fresh water crabs to shore .

Jase didn't notice his friend's eyes upon him but as he pulled the net to his side as a group of buffalo moved out of his way then started to walk off. As he pulled the nets closer, he could see the Buffalo was started to gather together in the distance , and the Mammoths move closer to the lake. Lowering his net he slowly he reached for his swords.

Callum watched Jase slowly and methodical reaction and started to look about. His eyes moved across the lake towards the wagon and back along the grass lines to a tree line in the distance.

"We're being watched," Jase walked past Kisa grabbing her arm.

Seamus raised his staff and tapped the ground with it, He started to feel the earth, the water, the animals around him, their hearts swelling with fear. Fighting past the animals fear, the magician began to spread his awareness through the grasslands nearby, till he was at his limit, sensing the energy of every living thing in almost a hundred yards in every direction.

"Something," said the blond, his voice straining.

Xarona placed a hand on the magician's shoulders and closed her eyes,

"Breath slowly, forget you, forget us and focus on nothing but what you feel," she said to him the softly.

Seamus slowed his breathing and moved past his own thoughts, fears and focused only on his spell and of what it was allowing him to feel. Suddenly his connection increased, he could feel the range increase slowly and not only could he feel the energy but he could see it and the shapes of everything around as a blur of color and lights dancing about. "There," he said pointing towards the higher grass near the tree line.

"It's not more eight armed monsters is it," Clare extended the Blade from her metal telescoping staff.

"No.," said Seamus who realized for the first time Kisa and Jase were moving towards the wagons, leaving him and the other behind.

"Come on," he said looking about as he herded his friends towards the hunter and the girl they were supposed to be protecting.

The group moved quickly past the bison and made their way to camp, Jase was already slinging his quiver over his shoulder and instructing the drivers to un-stake the Wagons and circle them.

Bernardo looked at the worry on Seamus' face then at his mother who was busy along with his father throwing supplies into their travel wagon.

Suddenly, Callum's bull reared up and started to move about as if they sense something as did the horses.

"We need to go," Sani twisted and expanded into her horse form just as the ground started to rumble. In the distance, the bison and mammoths started to move. Some towards the lakes, others away from the group. A small group of bisons however side stepped the main herd and turned towards the wagons.

"Everyone in the wagons," Bhang called out, We can gather the horses later" !

"Something is spooking them," Jase called out helping Kisa into her family's wagon. He then helped Isabella and Vinceno in before closing the door and running to another wagon where Clare and Seamus sat. Callum climbed onto the wagon driven by Bhang. From those watching, however, it was less climbing and more stepping. Looking around the free-crusader looked about to make sure everyone was accounted for just as the Bisons started to rumble through the campsite.

"Mistress... now" said the tiny voice of Sani who was flying over Xarona as she was trying to climb into a wagon. The redhead was straining up-ward when Callum's hand reached down and lifted her up as if she weighed nothing.

"Are you insane, woman," the Crusader called out.

'How dare you touch my person," said the witch.

"Why didn't you just levitate up here?," Callum looked at his friend who turned away from his gaze.

"Why don't you mind your own business!," the young woman growled in return.

"No!," Callum adjusted his seating on the canopy causing what was under it to shift, "Your either going to have to hex me, turn me into a slug or talk to me, those are the only options!" roared the Callum to be heard over the Bisons.

"I don't have to do anything," Xarona reached for her wand. She tried to focus, she tried to think of a spell, to find the confidence she needed to work her magic. The knowledge was there, she used to help Seamus, but every since Arden something was missing, something inside of her had gone away.

Across from Xarona, Bhang, Lisa, and Callum, Seamus sat next to Clare and Jase. The hunter was standing up looking past the herd to something moving. The figure finally rose just as a Bison somewhat slower than the rest ran by it. It was just under six feet tall, broad, with an almost no neck, long muscular arms. It had pinkish gray skin a heavy brow and a broad mouth full of large teeth. It was wearing a stitched hide vest, pants, and boots, Red tattoos covered its body and twigs and stones were tied into its long dark hair.

It tossed a large spear into the creature's haunches . The creature bellowed loud and raised both arms, from the high grass ran more of the same kind of creatures similarly dressed, males and females Some used spears, others Atlatls and slings. Jase watched one Bison fall after another in quick succession and called out to Clare and Seamus as he stood to get their attention.

"I've never seen people like that!" called out the hill-man to be heard of the stamped.

"Trogs!," Seamus spoke up.

Clare looked at the creatures, they were focused on the hunting Bison and didn't see to pay them any attention.

"I guess Callum's friend was right," she said standing just as a spear hit where she was sitting.

A half dozen trogs rushed the wagons roaring and brandish spears, wood and stone clubs and carved pieces of animal jaws as weapons.

"Trouble!," Called out Jase at Callum and Xarona who from his point of view was yelling at each other. The din of the stamped was decreasing allowing the two nobles to hear his alarm.

Xarona looked across to see Trogs heading towards the wagon tht turned out to be a distraction. Two other creatures were running directly at here . One leaped through the air to tackle her only to be tackled in midair by Bhang. As the two tumbled to the ground, Callum noticed the other one and leaped in front of it.

Jase fired an Arrow that stuck into one of the trogs thick skinned shoulders penetrating only up to half the arrowhead, "they're tough," said the hunter, drawing and preparing another arrow and firing again catching another one on the side of the head, The arrow pierced the skin but slid out after managing to only graze the creatures thick skull.

Clare reached for her belt and pulled off two fist-sized balls. Tossing one at a trog it hit and unraveled wraping the creature in eight tiny chains, that managed to trip up the attacker but do little harm beyond that.

"Seamus, you better start making the magic," Clare.

Seamus looked about, his firebolts though handy could leave them with a burning trog ramming into the wagon, A protective spell wouldn't last long, but could give everyone time to regroup, staff in hand he weaved golden energy from the air that the spun out encircling the wagons knocking near my Trogs away and leaving the groups members unharmed.

"That's not going to hold long," said a staining Seamus.

"We need to get out of here," Jase.

"Clare, except we don't have anything to pull our wagons. The Tinkersmith at a glance so not a single Goat, Bull or horse.

Vinceno peaked out of his Wagon's door, "What's going on," he asked looking about.

"Stay inside Boss, seems we have Trogs," said Jase.

The older man closed the door locking it from the inside, he had heard tales of Trogs ferocity especially towards travelers on the road. They were known for taking hostages and using them as slaves, food or worse. His eyes glanced fearfully at his wife and daughters.

"What have I done," he said to himself.

"What's wrong," Isabella,"

Vinceno sat in silence drawing his sword and waiting for what he thought was the end.

The Trogs circled the golden barrier. At first, they tried to rush through it, then hit it. After failing a few times, they let out a deep melodious yell and just stood watching it.

"Xarona, can't you turn them inside out or something," Clare looked at the witch as the group now on the ground stood in the middle of the wagons look.

"She's not feeling magical," Callum spoke up frustrated.

"I can speak for myself," Xarona.

"Just making sure," Callum

"Will you two lovebirds knock it off," Jase.

Before the two could protest Bhang joined the group, "We need to take care of the ones around us quick before the hunters finish their kills and join them," he said.

"I'm open to ideas," Clare, "Because My knoters didn't do much to them and everything else I have is one shot at best.

Jase looked at Xarona, "Fussy britches, we need you in the fight," he said concerned.

Xarona nodded, "I'll do my job," she said in a tone that should cause her self-doubt.

Bhang looked at Seamus then the group, " I might be able to help Mr.

Seamus hold on a bit more and help out in the fight," he said.

All eyes fell on the driver.

"Are you a Magician too," Asked Jase.

Bhang shook his head, "No, But I know about energy, internal and external". He said, "It something I picked up when I was younger," he added.

"If it works it works," said Clare,

Callum looked at the group," I want to try something". he said placing his hand over Seamus', " I need everyone to hold hands".

Clare took Jases hands and Bhang. , Bhang looked at Lisa who after a few seconds left the wagon and took the drivers hand then Xarona's.

Callum looked at Xarona, who to his surprise reached out and took his hand.

Callum closed his eyes and started to speak, " Eons ago, on a cold and desolate hill, they did provoke the right of the "warrior's wheel". Alomeg did bless them and their foes they brought to heel, For they spoke the pact and before darkness, did not kneel. We ask that our Aim is straight, Our will is strong, Our magic quick, and life is long. May Mizeriel guide us with as his wings unfold, Alomeg favors the just and his Archangel favors the bold".

"What was that?," Lisa opened her eyes. As everyone broke the circle.

"First, why are you not with your family, Xarona said, and second., That was the Warriors Wheel, It's an old Alomegian prayer for unity in battle and strength".

Lisa like most her of a family wasn't overly religious, but she could feel that something had happened, she could feel a connection, and she could tell everyone wanted her out of harm's way, "With a confident smile she walked towards her family's wagon, knocked and Vinceno let her in.

"So are we ready?," Jase.

Bhang walked up to Seamus and placed his right hand on the magician's spine, "

This should allow you to reabsorb more of your chi energy when you release the spell". He said".

"I'm going to release it?," Seamus.

"Better you have something for the fight, instead of running dry, blondie," Clare.

As the group readied Shamuses protective shield unraveled, surprising the magician

"I didn't do that," said just as a bolt of bitter cold flew into the group from outside the protection of the wagons.

CHAPTER 12:
NORTH BOUND AND BROKEN

Seamus struggled to his feet. All around him was a frosty mist and moving shadows. Felling as he had fallen into a freezing river , the magician felt a bone-chilling cold that caused his teeth to chatter.   As he struggled to stand a large hand grabbed him, at first, he thought it was Callum, but this wasn't a friendly help up as Seamus discovered the hand belonged to a trog who raised him to eye level and roared.

The blond southern magician screamed and tried to struggle free, and when he couldn't, he reached for his sword, drew it and swung, hitting worn hides and thick skin.   It was then he realized he didn't have his staff and kicking and squirming he found himself thrown from a wagon.

The trog said something in a language he didn't understand and licked his lips causing the magician more distress. As the cold mist started clearing Seamus body started to go from cold to the burning feeling of frostbite.

"Drop him!," Clare stabbed the creature as she roared digging her spear into the trog's arm and straining to push through. Coming to his feat the magician instinctively reached out with his free hand knowing his staff was nearby. To his surprise, the staff flew from the ground to his hand just as a wave of green mist flew into the group. The Magician raised his staff, calling winds to disrupt the cloud and push it away.

"They have a caster!," Seamus called out to all that could hear him.

"No Kidding," Callum stood trap waste deep in mud, as he got his bearings after the freezing mist. Taking a deep breath the young Nyumbani lord tried to scramble out of the muck only to watch in horror as it became solid packed earth. One hand in the ground and the other free, the Callum called upon his inner faith and Titan's blood to start crack the earth around him but not before a nearby trog 's foot landed on his chest. Callum knew he was sitting duck and struggled more cracking the earth and managing to free his hand and the hammer it held. Swinging he hit the Trogs knees sending it to the ground.

Jase knew when Seamus said there was another magician what he had to do. As quick as he could he dived under a wagon rolled and came out on the other side. Looking about he scanned tall grass nearby and started circling the perimeter, bow in hand he knew he would just get one shot. From behind the hill-man heard a shout as someone leaped out of the grass at him, someone he didn't smell or see before, someone taller and thinner than the trogs. The pale creature with bright orange hair worn in braids had pink eyes, long pointed ears and wore a shirt and clothing that look as if it was made from woven plants. Jase dodged the silvery blade it wielded and fired hitting it in the in the diaphragm and sending it to the ground bleeding silvery blood.

In the chaos Sani flew up high to get a better view, she was worried for her mistress but knew if the group was to survive she needed to help, and her flight was her greatest advantage, looking down she saw The Trogs entering the middle of the circled wagons, Jase shooting at sometall willowy human like creature and another nearby such creature hidden from human sight by magic, focusing energies to cast a spell. Circling the wing cat flew towards the hiding magician from above turning into her larger wild cat form and dropping from the sky clawing at her foe.

The enemy magician moved quickly to the side but still managed to be scratched. Looking at his foe and smiled. With a wave of the hand, the magician called forth golden pollen that upon being inhaled by the cat sent it peacefully to sleep and back to its true form. Looking up at the human boy he realized his invisibility spell was now compromised and that an arrow was about to fly his way.

In a blur, Jase watched the fae vanish and reappear a few feet to where he once stood. Without a hint of hesitation, Jase quickly fired again only to watch the magician vanish and appear mere feet away visibly tired. The enemy magician gestured causing the Hunter to fly back and to the ground just as the wagon closest to him turned over pinning the magician he missed twice under it.

Callum saw the pinned frail-looking man, who reminded him a bit of Seamus. He had pushed the wagon over knowing that Jase needed him to do it, the how and why he knew wasn't clear he just knew for a second, then he remembered his prayer. The Warrior's Wheel connected those in it for battle. He had never experienced it and wasn't sure it would work or how it would feel if it did. He knew however it wouldn't last long and moved from the wagon to a trog menacing Bhang who had just dodged a bone club swung at him behind and in a series of graceful motions was spin-kicking his first attacker while dodging a blow from another.

Clare ran past free-crusader an irate trog behind her prompting Callum to swing his Hammer just over the short young woman's head landing it in the Throgs chest and sending it to the ground gasping air and spitting up blood. Turning Callum found an Atlatl bolt plunged at close range into his arm.

The Throg that did its weapon was flung away by a flick of Xarona's wand. The witch was still focused more on her own melancholy than the battle and cast the spell more out of instinct than anything.

Callum pulled out the wood and stone bolt that had dug into his shoulders and cursed to himself for being caught unarmored. Walking towards Xarona, he could see despite the urgings of other she wasn't herself.

"I'm useless she said," to out loud.

"How about you protect the Salazars and we finish this," the free-crusader spoke with kindness and pushed the witch towards the covered wagon placing her back to it and himself in front of her. Callum then knocked on the door, waited for it to open, put the witch inside and closed it.

Xarona looked at everyone inside and started to cry; Isabella reached out to her in the carriages dim crystal provided light.

"Are you hurt in," she said.

"No," she said ashamed.

"Is it your magic, Are you drained, I hear that happens even to witches," Kisa spoke up.

The witch sat her head against the wall listening, knowing if anyone died it would be her fault. They depended on her, and she failed.

"M'lady, whatever it is , I'm here for you," said the older woman.

"She's right," Bernardo

Xarona looked about at the Salazars and their drivers. She then looked at a concerned Isabella as the older woman touched her hand.

"Thank you, she said," directly into her mind.

"This is new," Isabella thought back.

"I want to talk, but just you," she said," You've been kind to me, and I failed you and your family because I'm afraid of my own decisions ".

Isabella closed her eyes hoping it would help her ignore the battle outside and though to Xarona. "Like I said I'm here for you,"

Xarona unleashed her memories into Isabella, her betrothal, Callum, Dashale and the Arden Witch's threats and observations".

At first, Isabela was overwhelmed, but eventually, the thoughts and emotions became less alien, and more like her own, it was almost as if she had experienced everything herself.

"My dear," thought the older woman "That's a heavy burden, but carrying it alone isn't what you need to do,"

"They are my mistakes, my problem," Xarona.

"You're young; You are not perfect, no one is When I was your age I was also betrothed," Isabella focused on those thoughts and pictured her past and how she fought a duel against her fiancé's sister, left him and after many loves found Vinceno.

"Mistakes, obligation and the will of others should never define you, M'lady, You define you," thought the woman giving the witch a hug, just as the wagon lurched forward.

Jase returned riding one of the draft horses he found not far from a lake. Quickly he and Bhang hitched to the Salazar's wagon. Once Bhang lept to the driver's seat and grabbed the reigns the driver started to maneuver the wagon towards the road near the river.

"How did I live through that," said Claire climbing up on the wagon to sit next to the driver. She looked at up to Clallum and Seamus had sprinting in the wagon' direction. Not long one of leg she would have been left behind if she had not sprung forward using her telescoping spear and wondered if it could help her friends catch up also.

On Top of the Wagon, Jase helped the magician and Crusader on board and watched the trogs give pursuit for a good two hundred yards before giving up.

With his eyes on the road Bhang drove north on the High Road pushing the horse to exhaustion. The Chi-wise driver knew he could grant the creature more energy, but there was a chance doing so would kill the horse or cause it to fumble on its hooves and break a leg.

Looking back and seeing no chase the driver maneuvered the wagon to the side and than then slid back the door on a small opening behind him and looked inside. He could see all the passengers huddled and worried in the dim light.

"We're safe for now," he said before closing it and jumping to the ground and stretching.

Jase leaped down to his side and was soon joined by Clare.

"Trogs and fae were working together," She said.

"I thought they we enemies," Bhang.

Jase stood silently, he heard of the oldblood, everyone had, but he had never seen them before. Stories painted Trogs as savages and fae as the aloof tree-dwelling pacifist, but that wasn't what he saw, The Trogs hunted as a unit, and the fae were fierce fighters.

"Well it looks like they made peace, in that group anyway," said the Hunter.

Callum landed near the group, his wounded arm was visible, but the bleeding had slowed.

"You ok Callum?," Jase.

"I'm fine," he said looking about to see if he could any sign of the Trogs. When he saw none, he knocked on the door and listened to the latch move and watched it open. Isabella came out first followed by Xarona, Vinceno, Bernardo, The twins then the drivers.

"Is everyone accounted for," Asked the silk merchant

Seamus looked down from on top of the wagon, "Everyone but Sani, the Horses, and Enkidu the bull," , he said.

Xarona looked at Seamus and closed her eyes, she could feel Sani was alive but very cross with her.

"Sani is fine, she's heading here," said the witch feeling her familiar was approaching.

"We need to rest here, make sure it's safe and then head out to gather the wagons or what's left of them," Jase spoke up.

"Repairs shouldn't be an issue, If it's not too bad," Clare.

Vinceno nodded, "Fine, that's as good a plan as any," he said stoically.

On both side of the road was grassland as far as the eye could see, The rare tree stood out and could be easy if need be. Jase was sure he could find food and headed off on foot to hunt and scout around for possible hostiles as soon he made sure the wagon wasn't in immediate danger. Callum headed towards the nearest tree to collect firewood. His mind was so focused on Trogs, fae and his own heart, he didn't notice Xarona was following him. Seamus and Clare stayed at the wagon as guards.

Callum turned about halfway to the tree to see Xarona and stopped.

He didn't want to be mad at her, but he was, he knew she was hurting and the fact she was keeping it in and hurting herself made him furious.

"Come to ignore me in person," he said gruffly.

"I'm ready to talk," she said, "I need to talk," she answered while looking at her feet.

"The Lady Belasona I know doesn't look like that, she looks people in the eye," he said.

"This is hard Callum," she returned, trying not to cry even as his words stung.

Callum stopped and looked at her and walked towards. Gently he raised up her chin with his hand, "I'm here," he said.

"I'm betrothed," she said.

"Who isn't," he returned.

Her eyes grew wide with surprise.

"My Cousin in Arden offered me one of his daughters, and I'm the third son of a Lord with all my teeth, I'm sure my mother or grandmother or father has at very least talked about it to some other n oble family at least in passing," he said with a smile.

The redhead started to smile, "It's not funny, It's to Dashel Phelix,"

Callum shrugged, "Never heard of him, But If he's a Phelix he's a ginger I take it," he said unimpressed.

"You're not taking this seriously," Xarona.

The free-crusader turned and walked towards the tree, "How an I supposed to take it?" He said walking away slowing and hoping she followed, " I get it, He's from a big family, and probably rich enough to buy my families land twenty times over,".

"That's not the point," Xarona returned annoyed.

"What is it then?," Callum did best to sound disinterested as he answered, despite the growing anger in the woman's voice.

"Turn around in look at me Lord Wimbowaradi," demanded the witch,

"Or so help me I'll turn your liver into a porcupine!

Callum slowly turned smiling, "See that it, that's the fire, That's what I love," he said.

Xarona stopped upon hearing those words, her jaw dropped as what it meant processed in her normally quick, mind.

"You love me?," she said.

"Of course I love you, I mean I think I do, I've never been in love but, I think I am with you," he stammered taking a step forward.

"But," The witch held her hands out as if telling the young lord to stop, "You can't".

Callum rolled his eyes, " Xarona Belosonna, do you love me," He asked.

"I can't answer that," She said replied.

"Witches don't lie, They don't have to, I heard that somewhere," Callum.

"It could be infatuations," she said coldly.

"It could," the free-crusader replied, "But I think we should see what it is before we toss it away,"

Xarona stamped her foot, "You're making this hard," she said.

"I heard it's supposed to be," Callum took the step forward as he spoke, then another, He could see the confusion on the witches face mix with anger and then a hint of a blushing smile.. He would kiss her he thought regardless of the results and the possibility of a porcupine digging its way out of his gut.

Before Callum could take another step Xarona walked quickly to him and hugged him, Slowly he did the same, He leaned over to kiss her, but to his surprise, she did it first.

"So I'm forgiven," he asked after the first kiss".

'My situation was not your fault," the woman," Manhandling, taunting me and being a general cad, now that you're going to pay for," said the young woman playfully, kissing the young lord again. And holding tight to both his hands.

Jase had heard that cockatrice love the open grasslands, The small two feet tall feathered lizards had long serpentine tails ending in straightly pointed stingers where notorious even in the hills. They stung their prey with a venom that left them alive but as unmoving as stone while they ate them. In most cases, he had heard they hunted small animals, but if they were hungry, they would go larger. The conjure man in his village used the venom in a tea to promote sleep or in larger quantities to deaden an area so he could set a bone or stitch up a wound.

Also, more useful to his current situation, the hunter had heard they were good eating if you sliced off the tail and tasted a lot like chicken. Taking his bow he knocked an arrow and fired into a group of five of the creatures killing one with a clean neck shot. He expected them to start running for higher grass, but instead, they looked up from where they were nibbling on bugs Upon seeing him they moved towards him and started to circle.

Jase knew what was happening, they were trying to get him from every side. Stopping he waited and listened till one lunged forwards. Calmly the young adventurer fired , moved forward and turned and in mid-stride fired at the one attacking his rear. He felt something like a small needle piercing his boot and into his leg. Knocking and firing he pinned the one that hit him to ground.

He wasn't sure what one sting would doubt figured it wouldn't be much even as his toes started to go numb. Stopping and standing still he waited and fired at movement in a patch of taller grass hitting another one, leaving only one who with a screech leapt at the hunter with the stinger, tooth, and claw. Jase struck it to the ground with his bow, pinned the tail with a foot, drew a sword and chopped off the creatures head.

******

Seamus stood near the wagon, concentrating, his energy was returning and whatever Bhang did to him made it, so it renewed itself far quicker than usual. Looking around he found a nice patch of flat area and walked towards it, taking his staff he raised it high. He burnt the grass in a perfect circle and rendered the earth it stood on dry and smooth. He then focused on feeling through the earth for water and eventually find it. Tapping the ground with the staff he waited as water started to flow upwards forming a small pool. He then waved a hand over the wet area causing an indentation and a perfect little spring that he figured would last for the rest of the day.

"That's incredible," Bernardo

Seamus looked at the handsome young man and smiled, "This is easy, I lived on a farm, doing this kind of thing is one of the reasons I learned magic". said the magician.

Bernardo walked over to the blond young man, smiling. "So, is it me, or are you looking more... I'm not sure what to call it," The young man spoke matter of factly.

"fae, and that's a long story," said Seamus.

"We have time, Jase is hunting, Everyone else is plotting our next move, and the Bull and Belle are either working things out or growling at each other"

Seamus chuckled and started to talk about what happened in Arden castle, going into as much detail as he could remember and the truth he had discovered. Bernardo stood to listen intently and at the end of the story gave Seamus a quick hug. As he two young men looked into each other's eyes, neither one noticed a spying Isabella watched with a worried look on her face from near the wagon.

Jase hobbled back to the newly created camp with five tailless cockatrices over his shoulder. Clare upon seeing him ran out to help him.

Upon seeing the scaled and feathered creatures she took a step back, "What the hells are those?

"Cockatrice," he said with pride.

"And their food? ," She asked.

"Pretty good food I hear," he said walking into Seamus' circle and placing the creatures on the ground and then sitting.

"Don't they turn you to stone," Clare.

"They just make you go all stiff and numb if they hit you with their tale too many times," The hunter slipped off his boot to reveal a pale, stiff foot. with a spider web of reddish veins. "Like that".

Clare looked at Jase and bent over, Checking his foot; it was cold to the touch and stiff.

"You're an idiot," she said massaging the foot.

"So I've been told by all sorts of people," he said with a big smile on his face.

"Is that a cockatrice sting?," Bhang walking up.

"Yes it is," Clare.

"You do know that doing that can spread the venom," said the driver.

Clare dropped the foot, "No I didn't I just thought It'd help him get his feeling back".

Bhang chuckled and knelt and lifted the foot up, He then touched the reddish part of the leg where the stinger entered and pinched it, Jase yelped, and Bhang then touched his ankle and Achilles' tendon and knee all in quick succession.

Each touch was like a pinprick themselves. By the time he was done Jase could feel a cold sensation in his once numb toes.

"The Salazar's are not paying you enough," Clare.

Bhang, Clare, and Jase started to laugh just as Kisa entered the camp circle saying something was coming down the road. . Clare and Bhang helped Jase stand after the hunter slipped back on his boot. The three arrived at the road to see Sani in horse form leading A bull, two riding horses and draft horse down the road.

"They're not paying that cat enough either," Clare.

Jase, "I don't think the cat is getting paid," Jase.

Bhang, "I think we should at least buy it a large bowl of milk when we get to Kascee, Bhang".

Xarona was overjoyed seeing Sani, back in her winged cat form and rush to hug her, behind her, a mule pulled the shattered remains of a tree behind it.

"You found a mule"? , Vinceno.

Xarona kissed her familiar and then turned to her employer. "No, That's Lord Wimbowaradi". she said.

"You turned my best friend into a mule?," asked Seamus.

The Witch nodded, "Some lessons are not easy ones," she said pulling out her wand and flicking it to turn the Mule back into a man.

"I take it you two worked it out," Isabella.

"Yes," said Callum, And a resounding no, You don't turn your boyfriend into a mule," he protested.

"So you're her boyfriend now?," Jase.

"Well, we're figuring things out, together," Xarona looked at the Hunter and smiled but then playfully scowled at him, "Not that it's any of your business.

The Witch placed her wand back into her belt sheath and then took a deep breath, "On that note, everyone I'm sorry for letting my personal issues prevents me from being a productive member of the team," said the witch, "It will not happen again".

"You still turned me into a mule," An irate Callum spoke up removing the rope from around his torso.

"I heard you the first time," Xarona spoke haughtily, " And for now we're even".

Callum looked at the girl smiled, walked past her and kissed the top of her head before walking past her, "So Jase what did you find for dinner? ".

The hunter hobbled up to his friend,

" I guess you can say I caught us a genuine delicacy, my friend. ," he said.

*****

Xarona joined Callum who was sitting on a raised stone created from compacted rock by Seamus who had managed to create six such pieces of furniture before having to rest. Callum was using a knife he kept tucked in a sheath in the rear of his belt to skin the creatures before gutting them salting them and spicing them from a small pouch also on his belt.

"Do you always carry spices around," she asked.

"Of course," he answered.

The young girl woman cringed as he placed the skinned creatures the on their own skins,

"That's disgusting," she said

"It's how food happens". Callum impaled the long necked creature that now looked like skinless chicken on sticks and leaned them over the fire .

"Are you still mad at me? Xarona placed a hand on Callum's shoulders.

"That would be like being mad at the rain for being wet," he said,

"I don't like you because of your quiet and bashful".

'Well truthfully, I'm not sorry, but I don't want mad at me regardless," she said.

Kisa watched her two friends near the cook fire, she had read all about love, and from what she had read they were both definitely in it or at the very least close to it. She found watching people entertaining and identifying their moods and histories based on how they move, or a subtle facial expression something she enjoyed. She remembers when she was young, before the mansion when her Father ran their small silk shop in Vallus how he would be able to use the skill to figure out how to haggle with the potential buyer. How he would tell her and her siblings how to pick out people's "tells".

Lisa walked over to Kisa and pushed her aside to take up half of the stone stool. Kisa playfully elbowed her back, and the two smiled.

"I bet you're going to write a book about this". Lisa.

" At least two," said Kisa, " I've learned so much, seen so much, lived so much". The twin in glasses looked at her sister in a way she had never seen before. Kisa was always quiet, and bookish, Lisa outgoing, but now Kisa seemed to be in her element and it showed.

"Do you think I'm useless?," Lisa.

Kisa looked at her sister and leaned into her, "No, you are not useless. You ride better than me, you dance better, you look better.,".

"We're twins, we look pretty much the same," Lisa.

The girls started to laugh, neither one noticing Bhang walking up.

"Miss Lisa, Miss Kisa, I didn't mean to pry but did your sister say you could dance?

Kisa looked at the driver and nodded, "She knows all the waltzes and line dances and even a few of the old world dances". She said.

Lisa blushed, "Dancing comes easy to me, like knowing stuff comes to my sister".

Bhang smiled, "I know it may not sound like much, but if you like I can teach you to use those skills to protect yourself, and your family," he said.

Lisa looked at the man and laughed, "Mr. Bhang, I'm not a fighter, I saw you move, and I can't do that".

Bhang walked away from the girls and stood, slowly he started to move, arms encircling slowly, his legs taking precise steps and bends. After a few minutes, the driver stopped and looked at the impressed girls. Bowing he looked at Lisa, "what did that look like?," he asked.

"Dancing, very beautiful Dancing". She said.

"Actually, that's the first kata of Open Rose Style empty hands fighting" he corrected the girl politely.

Lisa nodded and stood and did her best to emulate what she saw as Bhang and Kisa watched. After she was done, The driver complimented her and walked through the motions with her again and again till she got it right.

After a dinner that was far better than anyone expected everyone sat around a fire, Plans was made for going back and seeing if the two wagons and Callum's cart was still there and to collect any remaining supplies. An hour into the discussion, to everyone's surprise, and the amusement of others everyone discovered that while the strange feathered lizards did indeed taste like chicken they enacted a gaseous revenge for their consumption.

Xarona sat mortified as even her normal illness resistant witch metabolism betrayed her. Callum and Seamus managed a near perfect retention of a childhood song using their temporary gas based abilities and Jase and Vinceno joked about using the gas as a weapon in a case of a Ttog attack while a shocked Isabella watched.

Eventually, the darkness and exhaustion claimed the group one by one as plans to keep watch failed and while wolves howled in the distance and the nearby patches of long grass shuttered there were no real disturbances that night save for a chilly dew that coated everything.

Jase awakened on top of the Wagon to the sound of Callum singing while he urinated on the other side of the road in a bush. The sun was up and fearing the worst he came to his feet looking around seeing only his party, the road and the green grasslands around him.   Leaving the top of the Wagon he looked under it to see Seamus, Bernardo, and Bhang asleep. The other drivers were huddled next to a dying fire. Walking towards where his friend was relieving himself the hunter checked the road seeing nothing in either direction as far as he could see.

"I haven't slept that much since I was a cub," Jase said as he took off his belt.

"Yesterday was something," Callum was tying up his britches and preparing to leave. Jase nodded and then focused on relieving himself as the Free Crusader walked back to the camp, he could hear others yawning and the creak of the travel wagon door where the Salazars (except Bernardo), Clare, and Xarona slept. He loved roughing it but knew they preferred only the illusion of it. With Kascee a good month away he knew that if they didn't find supplies or other wagons, they would have to risk turning back to Arden and possibly running into Trogs or even possibly worse try to make it to their destination with limited supplies. Either one wasn't something he or anyone else wanted, but it was something the group's guide and hunter he had to think about.

After everyone was awake and a quick breakfast of leftover cockatrice and coffee from a private stash the Salazars was keeping for a special occasion Jase. Callum, Bhang, and Vinceno headed south down the road in search of the lost livestock, wagons, and supplies. Finding the wagons was easy, they were more or less where they were left. The one turned over was still turned over its contents of bolts of silver, chests of clothing and boxes of supplies strewn about and obviously quickly gone through. Most of it was still there, just dirty and rummaged through.

The supply Wagon and Callum's cart were also there, the contents were thrown about and most of the dry goods bags were torn open and emptied. to Callum's surprise, however, his spices did remain intact with only a bag of powdered pepper being open(he expected the trog or fae that did it, tasted the peppers and ran off screaming)

Jase found Xarona's magical bag closed and near where the wagons we circled. Callum righted the turnover Wagon and the four men loaded it everything they could find from it and , hitched up Enkidu to it. The draft horse Bhang road was hitched to other wagon and Bernardo's horse to Callum's cart. The three men then started riding back while Jase hunted for the remaining livestock.

Jase spent two hours looking and found another draft horse alive but limping from a cockatrice sting. Near by was Clare's Goat and Vinceno's horse, both dead and partially eaten. Their flesh torn apart by what looked like large claws. Leading the stung horseback up the road Jase found another horse in a creek bed. After coaxing the animal back to the road, the hunter guided his two prizes back to camp

Regrouped the travelers decided to spend one more night at their campground. Clare, upset at the loss of her goat mourned it with the others telling the goats very colorful history including its love of drinking beer. As everyone listened to the impromptu wake, Xarona used her magic to clean bolts of silk, and some clothing.

"Do you think we can make it to Topic?," asked Vinceno after going over the supplies with Jase.

"Doubtful," said Jase, "we'll be hard press to push due north to Kascee-proper on what we have.

The older man nodded, "Stuck between the fallen and the deep blue sea," He said.

The nearby witch who was casting her cleaning spells looked up, stopped her magics and spoke. "I would be more than willing to added my supplies to the groups if that would help,"

Taking of her brown bag, she turned it 's normal large size and pulled out two small bags of flour, a bag of corn meal, two bags of rice and almost tree dozen cans of food.

"When we first started this endeavor I wasn't exactly sure about Jases hunting skill or Callum's prodigious cooking skills," she added shyly.

"So you brought back up food?," said Seamus

Xarona nodded.

"It's not a lot, but it might make a difference". Jase.

"Especially if we go to Kascee proper," Vinceno.

Callum glanced at the redhead, "My skills are not exactly prodigious," He said.

Xarona looked ready to comment when Clare spoke up, " I swear to avenge you, Henry Clay!," she called out after taking a sip of drink from a cup ending the discussion on supplies and restarting the wake.

CHAPTER 13:
WALIKING THE PATH

The road leading off the High road wasn't on the Salazar's map. The sign at the split in the road said 5 miles to the Freetown of Windspoint. freetowns were becoming more and more common as pioneers headed into the wild between the east and west coasts. Aligned with no kingdom or any nobility they lived by their own rules. Most free towns are eventually claimed by a kingdom and handed over to the nearest noble house to supervise. Those that avoid that faith either go on existing as self-sustaining villages of vanished, consumed by the wild itself or some other tragedy.

The road leading to Windspoint was mostly packed dirt with the occasional wooden log and strewn white stones marking what passed for upkeep. The amount of horse and wagon trails showed that very few people traveled in or out of the area Still after being on the road for twelve days the party was happy to see the sign and hoped that it wasn't another Lester.

Vinceno decided that the chance at buying supplies and a warm bed at night was too much to pass up. The caravan headed down the road with Jase in front. The hill-man looked about spying only the areas high grasslands at first. Eventually, however, the grass turned into farms growing wheat and corn . A mile down the road a small bridge crossed a flowing creek where a boy sat trying to catch tiny octopods. With a little wooden spear.

"Howdy," said the boy upon seeing the young man dressed in leather and hides. "Howdy yourself," said Jase, "What kind of critter are those things? ," the hunter asked. The boy picked up his wooden bucket and walked over to the stranger ignoring the wagons and other horses behind him. Holding it up for Jase got a better look, the bucket was full of it was full of crawfish, tiny crabs, tiny octopi and a few tiny fish.

"Their just "Crazy Legs," My mom's going to make soup out of them for us," he said.

Jase nodded, "So, What's Windpoint like," he asked the boy.

"It's nice enough, my grandfather started it, I figure he's in the family hall, in the center of town, you can't miss it. " The young man smiled and replied, "I'm sure he'll like to meet you, He loves meeting travelers hearing their stories and what not,"

Jase reached into a pouch and took out a newly dried cockatrice skull and tossed it to the boy who upon reviving the gift looked at it as if it was made out of gold.

"Thank you, Mister," said the boy who waved at every person and wagon in the caravan till they passed.

The group passed more farms, and Wind-powered mills, workers all dressed in gray in the field looked up at the strangers with concern as they moved towards their town. A half an hour from the bridge at the creek, the group spied a row of bee hives lining the road being tended by a man and woman in one dressed in simple but clean gray peasant attire and wearing hats with sheer cloth netting over their face.

"Howdy," said the man to the strangers., "What business do you have here?".

The woman looked at the man, "Don't mind my husband he's just concerned with what's going on and all. ," she said to Jase.

"Just passing through, hoping to buy some supplies, maybe rest in for a day or two," The hunter kept his eyes on the man and his hand on the hilt of one of his swords.

" We don't have an Inn," said the man gruffly

"But I'm sure Father Nick would be more than happy to sell you some supplies," added the woman quickly.

"Thank you," Jase

The caravan continued under the couples watchful eyes. They counted three wagons, the one that stood out was had a door dark glass shuttered windows and a door   There were three more people also riding, a ginger-haired woman, a skinny blond boy and a Nyumbani giant riding a bull pulling a cart. The strange group of travelers made their way to a fenced area with a sign saying "Winddpint," near the gates entry. Ynside was four small wooden buildings and one large long house with multiple doors and balconies. People, all dressed in the same style gray clothing moved about, some carrying farming tools, others bushels of wheat, and others doing various chores.

"A bell started to ring as a the-the group moved closer to the large long-house. Those outside the building quickly and orderly made they way inside.

Jase came off his horse to his feet and looked about the clean town center with packed dirt and stone streets and wooden walkways. It reminded him of many ways of his village in the hills save for the oddly dressed occupants and the large building in the middle.

"Now this is a strange little place," Seamus.

"I kind of like it," Jase.

" Because It's simple, just like you," Xarona quipped. Riding up on Sani.

"It's very clean," Sani.

"Shh, I think it's best if you stay quiet, some people's aren't used to magical things," Said Jase quickly.

"So you think there's going to be trouble," Callum rode up to Xarona and climbed of Enkidu and removed his hammer from its saddle bracket.

"I don't think so; I just think they're just reacting like most people would if we all came into their town," Jase.

Clare stood up on the driver's bench she shared with Bhang. "We don't bite!," she called out to everyone's surprise,".

" I guess that's one way to greet the locals," Xarona.

Clare looked at the witch, "I'm working on my diplomacy M'lady," quipped the tinkersmith.

As the two women spoke a door opened in the central longhouse and an old man in gray wearing a wide brim hat exited flanked by two muscular men in a similar simple outfit.

"Only thing bites around here are wolves, the wampus, and Brother Rylie's mule. " said the old man humorously with a kind smile. The man looked the group over, they were young, well-fed but save for the red-haired young woman had the dust of travel on them.

"Welcome to Windpoint," he added. "All those with peace in their heart" are welcomed,"

"Thank you:," said Callum, "We're definitely peaceful,"

Jase looked at the two young men next to the old, they were not armed not even farming instruments, nor did the place have walls to protect the group from the creatures of the wild or worse.

"No offenses," The hunter took a step forward as he spoke, "I've never seen the place like this or a house like that,"

The old man nodded, "It's an old-land style house, We all live in it, and we all own it," he said, "It may seem odd to you son but for us Walkers its tradition,"

Callum recognized the name "Walker," and then put everything together.

"You're Walkers of course," he said, "It all makes senses. His grandmother and bother had talked about meeting followers of a very conservative branch of their religion who lived communally, walked everywhere used livestock only for work. According to his family, they also had some unusual customs, which he now regretted not asking more about.

"And by that big fancy necklace, you follow the Bright-Father," the Old man spoke up.

Callum nodded and did a slight bow to the old man.

"So what brings you to our town," asked one of the burly men at the Old Man's side.

"We're looking to rest, and maybe buy some supplies," Jase.

The old man smiled, "Well we don't usually sell supplies, but we're more than willing to share some with you and maybe if your so inclined you can help us with a problem we're having,"

Seamus looked at Jase and then the others before speaking, "What kind of problem?".

We can talk about that later, Why don't we get you washed up and fed first my friends," The Old man clapped his hands once and in the distance, a bell ranged.   The people in the longhouse filed out orderly surrounding the group and their wagons.   Not sure what was happening Clare reached slowly for her telescoping spear.

"My children, these people are our friends, make sure they are washed, and their animals feed and watered. They'll be our guests for dinner and for the night" said the old man in gray

The very simultaneous person in gray said, "Yes Father Nick," Before returning to their business.

*****

A group of women, their heads covered in white bonnets stood around Xarona, Clair, Isabella, Lisa, and Kisa both admiring and scandalized by the audaciousness of their clothing.

"Come we'll help you get clean," said an older woman.

"Thank you but if you show us to some water and a private room," said Isabella before being cut off.

"Oh no, Father Nick said you must be ready for dinner," said a younger woman her hand on the Xarona's silk sleeve.

"The'yre going to try to eat us," Clare.

"I just think they have some quaint customs," Kisa.

"I heard there are towns in the wild full of cannibals," Clare continued.

"I'm sure they mean well," Isabella

"I think we have something more modest for you," said the older woman in gray, "personally I'm surprised your men let you dress like this.

Xarona eyes widened with surprise then narrowed with anger as she was about to say something Kisa spoke up, "Our ways are different," she said. The old woman nodded lead her group towards the building.

"If they eat me I'm haunting all of you," said Clare to the-the men in her group as she walked past.

The men were similarly lead off to another part of the longhouse by a middle age man and two younger ones. As they reached the door of the communal leading to the young boy who was fishing ran up to the group.

" You found them," said the boy,

"Actually, they seemed to have found us," said the middle-aged man in gray.

"Well tell Father Nick, I saw the first," said the young man.

"Now did you?," one of the younger Walkers spoke up and looked at the boy, " Never a day that an untruth doesn't flow from your lips little brother," The boy looked at group crestfallen. Upon seeing his face Seamus looked at the boy "Actually he did greet us first," he said.

The older man nodded, "I'll let Father Nicodemus know," he said in the almost emotionless way everybody, but the young boy seemed to talk in.

Inside the men were lead to a stark white room with simple wooden benches and a wooden floor. They were told their belongings would be safe and they could undress and enter the bath behind the only other door in the room.

"Modesty is just vanity's shy cousin," said the older male Walker after he gave the group their instructions, " He whose name is too holy to speak made all of us in his likeness,"

Callum was the first to undress, growing up with three brothers, he wasn't shy about undressing in front of others. Seamus followed then Jase and the others with Bernardo being last. The men were escorted into the next room where a stone-lined pool awaited along with benches, rough scrubbing stones, and willow branch brushes. No sweet smelling oils or soaps or warmth in the room. After the instructing them to clean themselves well the men in gray left and Jase picked up one of the rough white pockmarked stones,

"This is why I avoid churches and religious folk, no offense Callum," he said.

"From what I remember, and It's not much, Walkers tend to do things the old and simple way," Callum.

"This reminds me of an old bathhouse, minus amenities," said Vinceno before jumping into the pool and discovering it was not only not warm but cold,"

The merchant cried out bring laughter from the others in the room.

"I think cannibals would be better," Seamus.

"Any bath is better than none," Bhang said slowing entering the pool.

Jase touched the water and then looked at Seamus, "Would be nice if I knew someone who could warm this up with a wave of their hand," He said.

The magician looked at his friend and joined the driver and his employer in the cold water. He knew it was cold, but for some reason, it didn't register as uncomfortable.

"I'm not going to piss on another person's belief," Said Seamus before sliding under the water briefly and rising again. The willowy blond looked about and saw his reflection and for the first time realized how long his hair gotten.

"I need a haircut" he added to anyone who was listening.

"'I'm sure Isabella has scissors," Vinceno.

" I need one-two," Callum said after sitting in the pool and noticeably raising the water level. His once shaved bald head was now fuzzy with wooly dark black hair.

"Son, are you okay," the silk merchant looked at his offspring who was covering himself and standing nearby.

"Father... I never took a bath like this before," said the young man.

Vinceno laughed before answering his son, "We're all friends here he said.

The young tanned skinned man looked at the pool, his eyes falling on Seamus. Slowly he started to walk towards it. Once at the water, he closed his eyes and slid in next to his father and hoped that no one would notice him reddening.

The Walker dining room was a simple as the rest of the hall, on the second floor above the kitchen. The room like all the other was lit by candles, a single long table sat in the middle with over fifty chairs on each side and a single chair at the head. The tables and chairs like every other thing made of wood oak and well made despite the simple design and lack of any cushions on the chairs. The plates were also made of oak, and the cups simple hardened glazed clay as was the milk filled pitchers.

Father Nick was the first to sit, followed by the male guests than adult males than young males. Female guests, older women, then younger women and female children followed.

The guests were given either as gifts or so they didn't stand out too much gray clothing just as their hosts wore. The Males button-up collared shirts, Grey pants and black leather shoes and gray socks. The women wore long Grey one-piece dresses with collars that almost touched their chins. They also wore simple white bonnets that hid most of their now pinned up or braided hair.

"They itch," whispered Jase to his friends after sitting. He had never worn clothing so confining and uncomfortable in his whole life.

"I don't think comfort is something they place a high value on," Bernardo. Bhang nodded, he had visited the garden temples of his people and the even the who's days were focused on meditation and not coveting worldly things had more comfortable clothing and seating. They were also less concerned with the sex of their members treating booth equally.

Xarona sat in her seat, next to Isabella, It seems the women assumed she was the eldest daughter for no other reason than they could not conceive of a single woman like her and Clare traveling without family. Clare sat next to her fidgeting as women in gray entered the hall carrying platters of brown bread, a fishy smelling soup, meat boiled to the point of being grey and vegetables cooked to near mush.

Once the platters were set down. The women retreated against the wall and the Patriarch, Father Nick stood.

"The creator has blessed us with this food, this configuration, guests and our lives," he said, Let us all hold hands and pray for his mercy for our reward is not in this world but to the next. " All the sitting walkers and those against the walls linked hands, and after a brief moment of confusion, the congregation's guests did the same.

The prayer lasted for what seemed like an hour to the visitors; even Callum had a hard time focusing even though he recognized at least half of it. Once done the food was served, starting with Father Nick.

Cold and flavorless even the milk was mostly water. Eaten in near silence with only the sound of utensils and the occasional slight movement of chair or plate breaking the calm the bland food was consumed quickly and efficiently by the Walkers.

Once dinner was finished the serving ladies retrieved all the plates and platters, bowls and glasses and retreated from the room and one by one everyone followed save for Father Nick and his guests.

"Can we talk about what services you need now," asked Vinceno.

"Tomorrow said Nick, now is the time to sleep., " said man rising from his chair and walking out the door.

"Now we're fattened up," Said Clare, "We'll be tomorrow's lunch,"

" How could they do that to food," Callum sounded disgusted.

"I don't think they're going to eat us," Jase. "Although big man you would be the first to go... clean living, well muscled.,"

"You know he has a point, Callum would feed the whole group," Seamus said humorously

"No one's going to eat him," Xarona spoke up in a protective tone.

"True they might eat you first, being that your all plu.," Said Jase before a menacing gesture from Xarona sealed his mouth closed.

"Don't make me destroy you hill-man," she said in a tone both menacing and humorous.

Before the hunter could react, An old woman and a middle age male walker entered the room. The woman gathered up the women and left, as did the man with then men. Leading the groups in different directions and upstairs to identical rooms wirh bare floors, walls ceilings two slit-like shuttered windows, two candles, and mattressless wooden beds and with wool blankets. When asked about a latrine the group was told, they were to uses a communal chamber pot in a special alcove at one end of the room.

*****

Bernard opened his eyes, he suddenly felt a chill run up and down his spine. His eyes widened allowing him to see in the dim light, He hated using the ability inherited from his old bloodline. Growing up the merchant's son was taught that such a heritage was considered uncivilized by the nobles and royals whom his family did their best to emulate. Rising from the bed, he looked around the room to see everyone was asleep save for Jase who was missing. As he moved towards a window, the chill came again as did a feeling of far away terror. Opening the shutters, he saw the sparse grounds of the peculiar town under a quarter moon and bare feet just hanging ever so slightly off the rooftop over his head.

As he watched, something moved in the distance speedily leaping from a clump of trees to a field of corn. Even with his eyes taking in all the light the moon the figure appeared only as a large black shadow and made no sound. Watching it part the tall stalks of corn moving closer towards the village he suddenly realized he heard a purring noise and the chills came with the purrs.

Bernardo stepped back, closed the shutters and tripped over his own feet, causing him to fall to the ground. Moving to his feet, the young man watched to his surprise and horror as something came through the windows. Bernardo started to scream just as Jase hand covered his mouth.

"Let's not do that My friend," whispered the hill-man.

Bernardo took a deep breath realizing it was his friend and not the creature. "I thought.," he said.

"It was that big critter?," Jase, " I saw it too, felt it, heard it,"

"What do you think it is?," Bernardo.

Jase stood silent; he knew what it was, He had seen one before and watched it kill a dozen man back home. , "I think it's death," said the hunter.

The next morning Father Nick called for his guests to met him in the nearly dining hall. His people had already eaten and the sun had been up for an hour. The old men out of a sense of hospitality wanted to give the travelers time to sleep and prepare.

Sitting at the head of the long table the Walker patriarch ate a meal consisting of an oat and pine nut mush and water downed milk ,quietly and calmly. As the group entered he motioned them to a table where their original clothing sat folded, repaired and clean. Under the table sat their weapons, belts and scabbards and everything else they had worn polished and repaired if needed. On another table sat cloth bags of corn, ground wheat, oats and four large clay jars of honey as well as a bag of iron nails, wagon brackets, and other small metal work.

.

"I set my smiths to reshoe your horses and fix your wagons," he said after swallowing a spoon full of his dull mush.

"Thank you," said Vinceno looking at the old man and trying to read him and failing.

"Patriarch," Callum spoke up, "You said you wanted us to do something in return?"

The Patriarch nodded and stood, "We're a peaceful people, we don't kill, all our meat is from creatures that The great father takes from injury or age. He said, "It's our way, but It's not yours,"

"Here comes the eating," Clare whispered to herself before glancing around for signs of an ambush.

Slowly the old man stood and walked to the end of the table where Seamus' staff and Xaronas wand sat shined, "Nor do we truck in magic, hexxin, and conjurations," he added picking up the staff before placing it back down.

The old man patted the table and door his guests entered reopened, two men, brought in two oxen heads and another one brought in a still body of a child.

"Last night it took, two oxen and a boy," he said calmly.

The group looked at the body, Isabella gasped, Lisa started to cry, and one of the drivers threw up as the young boy who greeted them laid before them his chest opened and partially gone as was all his entrails, part of an arm and leg, his face frozen in horror.

"What did this?" , Xarona

"It was a Wampus," Jase.

The Patriarch nodded, "Aye, It was, and It's preying on us for almost one moon. The boy, his father, others and livestock. " he added.

"We saw it last night," Bernardo.

The old man looked at the young man surprised, "And lived?"

"Must have already been full," said Jase.

"Can you find it, son, can you end it," asked the old man in a tone that was as close to begging as he could muster.

"You want us to kill that thing?," Vinceno?

"I can't say the words," Father Nick faced Vinicio and lowered his head as he spoke.

Jase looked at his employer, "Wampus are death and shadow with six claws the size of Callum's chest, "I can find it, but I'm not sure if we can kill it," said the hunter.

"I won't make you do what you don't want to," said the father Nick, And you are of welcome to the supplies and our prayers for safe travel if you don't,"

Callum stared at Jase, " We need to try," he said.

"I might have something about them in my books," said Xarona.

"And I think I can help find it," Bernardo spoke up, "It seems tied to my family's old blood.

"Cat calls the cat," said Kisa.

Jase looked at his friends, he knew that at best they had a slim chance but the free-crusader was right, they had to try.

After plans were made, Seamus spent almost an hour trying to talk

Bernardo out of coming on the hunt. Vinceno was proud of his son's bravery, and he himself wanted to help, but Isabella said otherwise. The remaining Salazars, Bhang, and the drivers would prepare to leave while the adventures hunted for the Wampus. According to what Jase knew and what Xarona's books collaborated Wampus's killed at night and slept by day. Xarona also said the six-legged, two-tailed cat-like creature was "shadow and necro aligned, which meant it was vulnerable to light and life and healing magic. They also seemed to have the ability to travel through shadows for short distances, razor-sharp claws, dagger-sized teeth and thick skin. Attributes that made defeating it even with its vulnerabilities a daunting task.

The group gathered at where the creature slaughtered the Oxen, While it left no footprints, Jase could smell it and the blood it left on the ground. They followed it from there back to the cornfield, into the grasslands and after an hour lost the trail at the tree.

"Seamus used his magic to search the surrounding area for underground burrows but finding none.

"Maybe we should split up," Bernardo.

All eyes fell on the young man, some humorously, others angrily.

"You never split up," Clare, "I mean we did leave your family in the hand of possible cannibals, but when you're monster hunting you, really don't, and I know that and this is my second monster hunt... quest-thing".

"If adventuring history, guild log reports, and common senses have taught us anything, splitting up usually ends up in death," Xarona.

Callum smiled at the redhead, "Never have splitting up ever ended well in anything I ever read,"

"I think the book I read before being granted adventures papers actually said, "Don't split up, ever," Seamus.

Xarona nodded, "Adventures Guide to Survival, By Jorgenson and Murphy," page 134, chapter two. , paragraph 1. ," said the witch.

"Can I borrow that book?," Clare.

"Of course," Xarona.

Jase looked about for signs of the creature, "So is now a good time to say I never read that book?". said Jase .

"I'm still not sure you can read anything other than maps and, tracks and trails," quipped Xarona.

Jase was about to say something either witty or something that would end with him being cursed when the wind shifted, and the scent of blood filled his nostrils.

"This way," He said, bounding off through the knee-high grass. The others followed moving into a higher grass and stopping when Jase held up a hand. The hunter knew what he was about to see even before he laid eyes on it, it was. It was a large red deer; its head almost cut off by a single mighty swipe.

Jaser looked at the creature, then touched it. By its warmth, the drying of the blood and how it laid told the kill told the young man it had only died a few hours ago. The fact it was a kill that was just left lying there meant something far more disturbing.

"I hate this thing," Jase., "It's not like a normal critter, This bastard hunts because it likes it,"

"Bernardo, are you feeling anything?," Seamus.

Bernardo looked at the group, though he didn't tell them he was feeling something, nervousness, and fear that was almost overwhelming.

"I'm not sure," he said apprehensively.

Seamus walked to the young man and took his hand and could feel something wrong, "I'm here he," said softly.

The magician felt the young man's relief, he also felt something else, an energy Bernardo was connected too. Seamus concentrated, following the energy from where they stood in a cold dark place where sunlight never touches and hope didn't exist. He then followed it back to a place a few miles away, a river bed and to a cave, where something foul slept.

Seamus pulled his hands away from his friend. He was sweating and shaking.

"It's not far," he said pointing past the dead deer.

"What happened?," Callum looked at his friend. He could feel a wave of darkness and despair come through him.

"I'm not sure," Seamus.

The group headed north then east coming to a row of trees and a sharp cliff near a creek bed.

"He's going to smell us," Jase.

"No, he's not," Xarona took out her wand waved it at the group, pungent smell and green mist erupted from it covering the group.

"What the hell was that," Clare said fanning the green mist away with her hand.

"A spell I used to cast when I was a child, It makes things smell like skunks. It came in handy when dealing with annoying courtiers". said the ginger young woman as the green mist faded.

"It's not going to last is it?," Bernardo said almost gagging on odor.

"It'll fade in a few hours," the witch answered.

Moving through thick brush the group made their way to a cliff leading to a creek. Jase removed the rope from the buttoned clip on his belt and tied it to the tree. He then climbed down using the rope and waited for the others. Xarona casually walked off the cliff and floated to the bottom some twenty feet below. Clare attached a device to Jase rope gripped it and slid down slowly. Bernardo followed down the rope then Seamus, both taking their time as not to hit the cliff face. Callum descended last, sliding down more than climbing.

"Does this stuff wash off," Jase asked Xanora

"No," she answered, puzzled by the question until the hunter stepped into the creek itself. Callum followed as did Clare. Seamus, Bernardo, and Xarona kept to the continually shrinking bank until it was too thin or dangerous to maneuver on. Once everyone was in the water, they moved upstream until the bank increased again and cave could be seen against the cliff.

"I think that's it," Seamus.

Jase sniffed the air, smelling only the stench of the spell they were all under. "I can't smell anything but Fussybritches hex," he said.

Bernardo upon seeing the cave felt a chill, he knew it was in there.

"It's there," he said, his voice shaking.

"What's the plan?" , Clare. "I might have enough light crystals to blind it if we go inside,"

"I say we burn it out," Callum, "That way we fight it on our terms,"

Jase looked at his friend and smiled, "I like that,"

"But what if it has cubs or there are other animals," Seamus, spoke, resisting growing senses of dread he felt emanating from the cave.

"It's a Wampus, the cubs will be killers too," said Jase.

Clare removed her net bomb and readied her staff. Callum and Jase maneuvered to a side of the cave. Seamus stood in front facing the entrance his staff ready, quickly he conjured a protective spell around him and Bernardo, who stood at his side. Xarona cast a spell on herself and faded away becoming nearly invisible.

Seamus then pointed his staff at the Cave and started building heat around the end. Once the air itself started to shimmer from the heat, he released two fireballs into the cave. Illuminating it with orangish light and the sound of whooshing air. After a few moments smoke started to come out of the cave.

"You think It's cooked?," Whispered Clare who was now standing next to Jase, her shadow and his had merged in the sunlight and though neither of them noticed a large golden cat-like the eye was looking out of it at them.

"It's near, really near," said Bernardo as a chill ran up and down his spine, the purr only he could hear shock his bones.

"Alomeg, give us strength in this endeavor and let us do your will," said Callum. His faith flowed from him, filling himself and those around him with confidence.

The prayers blessing, however, was no match for the terror Bernardo suddenly felt from behind, turning he watched the Wampus leap out of his and Seamus' shadow with four of its six claws ready to strike. The large paw and talons struck the shield sending him and Seamus flying across the stony creek bank. Xarona prepared to cast her magical purple bolts but before she could release it, one of its thick snake-like tail wrapped around her foot and pulled sending her to the ground.

Jase fired an arrow that hit the creature in the shoulder, but like the Trogs the arrow didn't penetrate fully and slid out.

Callum rushed forward hammer raised Striking at the creature but missing.

"I fear not you or your darkness," roared the Crusaders as his swing missed.

Seeing the big man's shadow and a chance to vex his prey the wampus leaped into and vanished into the big man's shadow, instantly reappearing out of Jase's. Quickly the hunter dodged by crouching low. Seeing her chance Clare tossed her net-bomb at it. On contact, the wires wrapped around the creature pinning a leg.

"That actually worked," she said reaching for her belt and pulling out a brass disk. Tossing it at the creature, she watched it fly apart into tiny shards of metal.

"Keep on it," called out Callum, turning and attacking with his hammer.

Standing Seamus raised his staff and concentrated on the sunlight before he caused it to bend and wrap around his friends destroying their shadows.

Xarona still transparent fired a purple bolt of lighting at the creature that on contact tore through his leg, "Get it to stand still," she said as her aim was not for its leg but rather its horse sized torso, But even with one of its six legs bound the creature moved swiftly.

Upon hearing her words, Callumm instead swinging at the creature, focused his faith on speed and broadsided it with a tackle sending it sprawling on the ground and scrambling to rise.

Seeing an opening, Jase fired an arrow hitting the Wampus in its roaring mouth, before drawing two swords and charging the creature. Slicing at his head, he managed to cut it along its cheek and nose before a paw sent him flying against the cliff wall.

The wampus let out another roar as it turned to face Callum, Who was already swinging. The hammer caught the creature on the shoulder causing it to sidestep into Clare's telescoping spear as she stabbed it.

Managing to stand, Jase staggered forward stabbing at the Wampus and slicing off one its tail. "Howe's that," said the hunter coughing up blood.

'Callum, Jase needs you," called out Seamus as he focused on his spell,"

The young lord nodded and ran to the hunter, placing a hand on his friend's chest and feeling a broken sternum.

"I'm going to need time" Callum.

"We can finish this thing," Xarona released her invisibility spell and pointed her wand at the creature, causing its skin to erupt in blisters and lesions. Clare then reached into her pouch and removed a three-inch cylinder and connected it to the other end of her spear. Using that end to stab she then rammed it into the large cat creature. Upon impact, the cylinder made a loud popping noise and exploded in white flame burning a hand-sized hole into the wampus.

The creature hissed loudly turning from Xarona to Clare. Forcing past his fear Bernardo drew his sword and stabbed at the injured beast cutting a rear leg as Xarona struck again and in quick succession with her purple lighting before following up her damaging barrage with a curse that rendered the creature's bones brittle.

"Don't worry about me," Jase, "Bring that murdering thing down," Said Jase as his friend's hands glowed white on his chest turning broken bones to cracked bones.

Callum ignored Jase and focused on his healing.

Behind him Xarona drew on her last reserves of magic to cast a spell that shrunk the creatures head down to the size of a normal cat, confusing it enough for Clare to stab her spear into her burning wound again and Bernardo to slice it in the side with a sword.

Seamus seizing the moment released his "shadowless," spell and quickly fired a blast of concussed air at the wampus, shattering its brittle ribs and sending it over on its side. The cat-like monster on the ground convulsed, growled and kicked until Clare stabbed it in its shrunken head ending its life.

"How the hell did we do that," Said a relieved Seamus walking over to a stunned Bernardo.

"And we did it without our Hammer and Bow boys," Clare.

"Hey, we had it going, you just finished off," Said Jase as Callum helped him to stand The hill-man felt sore all over especially in his chest and ribs. "also, The pelt is mine,"

"You can have it," Xarona said waving her wand and releasing her pungent spell and drawing in as much of its energy as she could.

"You were magnificent," Bernardo looked at Seamus.

"So were you," The magician looked at his merchant's son, pulled him close and to everyone watching surprised, kissed him.

CHAPTER 14: THE CENTER

"Jase looked at the Wampus pelt and smiled. He had cleaned salted and nailed down the pelt in a secluded area, not far from Windpoint. The Walkers had offered the travelers their hospitality for an few extra days while they put the dead boy to rest and to show their gratitude. Jase ,sore from his injuries was glad for the chance, and though he was advised by Callum to rest, the hunter skinned his prize, removed some teeth, claws and helped his friends and the Walkers burn the creatures body.

After which both Seamus and Xarona collected a few bottles of the ash.

"So what are you going to do with it," asked Clare who was watching Jase from where she was sitting on a stump and tinkering with a new device.

"Hides pretty tough, but flexible, I'm thinking boots, maybe some kind of armor.

"That's going to be something," Clare. "I bet we can find someone in Kascee to do that".

"I reckon we can," Jase smiled at the young woman.

Clare looked at the handsome hill-man. He would never be anything more than an occasional comfort, romantically, she knew neither of them wanted anything else. After Jase finished looking at his work, the two sat quietly talking about their plans for Kascee-Proper , a city larger than Vallus and one of the great cities the Newlands.

At midday Jase and Clare joined the rest of their party for a final send-off by the Walkers, Father Nick prayed for them and a safe journey for half an hour before bequeathing more gifts upon them. The gifts included a set of sturdy walker sitting stools, six more large jars of honey, more corn, and wheat, a wooden cage with six chickens, dozens of eggs, blankets and a promise of hospitality to all of them among the walkers as long as they live. The walkers then escorted the group to the high road that borders their land and waved as their new friends headed north.

For the next two weeks, the caravan traveled north, Not long after the Walker land the High road took a turn for the better and became less lonely as travelers, cattle and sheep drives and more became not only frequent but nearly constant as did news of Trogs and fae attacking small villages and sighting of war parties being seen further east than they have been in years.

After crossing into Kascee controlled land, marked by a large wooden sign showing off the head of a Thunderbird in front of the stylized drum shield of the native kingdoms. The travelers found news of trog and fae attacks increasing as those they met on the road not only relayed what they had heard but spoke from personal experience including a group fleeing Topic for Kascee-Proper after an attack.

As grasslands became even flatter and rivers more prevalent the group started to see signs every few miles marking not only the closeness of the Kascee-Proper but directions to other towns and villages surrounding it as well as the Thunderbird heraldry of the ruling family.

It was common knowledge that the Kascee family were once members of a human tribe native to the Aerix who ruled over the lands of the mid-central planes. With the coming of the old races from the old lands they found their land being claimed by foreign powers and though shrinking in number, the "new land" tribes united to maintain control over the central road hub of the nation and over time adopted the technology and a few of the ways of the "new people," that came to their lands.

Kascee was also one of the few places east of the Sapphire mountains where majority native human villages could be found. In large numbers. Because of that, thee Salazars and their party wish they had time to stop at the over a dozen such villages they passed, but they had lost time and knew that once they reached the great river city, they could rest and prepare for the last leg of their journey.

As the capital of the plain lands grew closer, the great city of roads could bee is seen in the distance as could a series of walls each one higher than the next surrounding the city. Because of its unique position as a Native city unaligned with any old land families didn't turn before reaching the city but instead went directly through it where it branched off going in every direction.

To protect the multitudes of travelers passing through and its citizens the great city had large wood and stone gates at its walls, guarded by men and women in hard leather carapaces, feathered thunderbird bonnets and ornate spears and war clubs guarded the walls on foot while cavalry dressed similarly carrying bows and great lances patrolled nearby.

Between each wall was farmlands, full of corn, wheat, and cattle along with the occasional rice paddy. Hundreds of carts, wagons, and riders on various animals moved in and out of the gates as ships moved along the canals leading into the city and airships floated above.

"This is incredible," Seamus looked up as several airships ranging from galleys to large barrages floated above. Powered by Artificer made engines and magic they were seen as the future of travel.

"I saw a few over Vallus, but the sky here is full of them," Said Xarona riding on Sani.

"You'll never get me in one of those said Jase, "just not natural".

The hunter despite the farms on his side could feel the wilderness dwindling around him and civilization creeping in with each mile, farms soon gave way to buildings and homes of various designs. In the distance walls made of wood and stone sat carved, the giant face of former kings, queens, and elders starring eternally at the horizon

At the cities gates, the group was allowed to enter without inspection after a caravan of camels blocked the main entry for almost an hour as drivers had to coax the creatures inside using whips and loud yells. Once they had entered the Salazars and their employees followed down the still wide high road, past stone and adobe covered buildings and people of every shape and size.

Eventually, the road started crossing a series of canals with high arcing bridges that allowed sailing ships to the past.

"Any idea where we're staying Father?" Bernardo looked at Vinceno who was sitting next to him in the lead wagon.

"I've only been here once, didn't stay long, so anyplace that looks nice should do," said the merchant looking on amazed at the city that had grown even larger and more crowded since he had last seen it.

Looking about the Salazar patriarch spied a merchant he recognized from his travels and Vallus, selling beautiful tapestries and carpets out of a storefront. Vinceno quickly dropped in asked a few questions and left and instructed his drivers to head north then left at the next canal road.

The driver was not happy about being crowded by his boss and the bosses son grumbled something under his breath and did as he asked. Leading the group to a quaint looking inn overlooking a canal.

"Coin only," said the middle age woman with reddish brown skin of a Kascee native, in the simple but clean dress sitting on a bench outside the building, "And no Trogs, trog blood, squid worshipers or sailors!".

Vinceno stepped down from the wagon and walked over to the covered Travel wagon and opened the Door, Isabella exited followed by her daughters. He then strode up to the woman.

"We have none of those," He said, "and Ernesto said you have the best rooms on this side of the city,"

The woman looked the tall man over and smiled, " Silver a room per night," she said. "You can park in the rear; Livestock upkeep is copper a day, extra watching on the wagons is an extra copper a day,"

Vinceno nodded, "That includes room and board?"

The woman looked at the group, her eyes stopping at Callum, "That big fella looks like he eats a lot, so an extra copper a day for him.

Everyone giggle, except Callum.

"I don't eat that much," he said.

It's ok Lord Wimbowaradi," said Vinceno. Taking a pouch of his belt and counted out three gold coins. " We'll take five rooms for three days," he said, "Take whatever change is left over and have your cook prepare us a feast tomorrow night," he added.

The woman looked at the coins of Vallus, bit them and nodded, "We can do that She said," And welcome to the Lazy Rest,"

The man then turned to his groups, "Isabella and I will take one, The Girls and Bernardo another, and Lady Belasona and Clare one Our Brave gentleman and Drivers the last two," he said. The Driver's eyes widened.

"Thank Mr. Salazar," said one of the drivers after taking off his hat and bowing to his employer.

"All of you have done more than your fair share and I want you to know it's appreciated," he said his tone growing more solemn. "And to expedite the rest of our trip, I'll be booking Air service for My family, Our Adventures and just in case Mr. Bhang. The rest of you will be paid your full promised wages and a bonus of 2 gold each". he added.

The drivers looked at each other both relieved and excited but strangely sad. They had come a long way with the group and despite the growing danger was starting to look forward to the trip to the Sapphire Mountains.

"You are all still welcomed at the feast after which you'll be paid," Isabella spoke up. She knew despite her growing affinity for the drivers, especially Bhang they could not be trusted not to run off if they were paid immediately, Kascee was a place, according to what she had heard, where all manner of diversions could be found.

The drivers parked the wagons in an area behind the inn where a stable and small garden and the animal pens were located. Three young boys took the horses and the bull to stalls with wood awning and sloping tarred roofs. They then helped unpack the supplies into a cellar and joined everyone else inside the inn.

Children that looked like relatives of the three boys hurried about, some carried the Salazars and the Adventures bags, others brushed, moped and a few even darted in and out of the kitchen area.

"Everyone takes your shoes off inside," said the old woman pointed towards an area where the others footwear sat and a girl no older than eight was using a tiny metal pick to remove the mud. as she sat on a stool.

"Our Shoes?" Isabella looked at the woman who stared back at her as if waiting for her command to be heeded.

One by one shoes, and boots were removed and taken to the girl assigned to clean them. The girl smiled and pointed towards a small glass jar full of copper pieces.

"Well my boots are pretty big," said Callum who tossed a copper coin into the jar.

"I've seen smaller boats," quipped Clare.

*****

" Now this is nice," Seamus stretched out on a bed in his room. With a high roof and wooden floors it was just as large as the one he slept in in Arden, only instead of three beds, there were two sets of large bunk beds which according to the teenage boy that opened the door could have the top bunks removed and used as canopy beds.

"We should invite Bhang into our room," remarked Callum, "Jase is going to sleep on the Balcony anyway, said the young lord.

"And Maybe Bernardo," Seamus.

"No," Jase, said before correcting himself, " Yes to Bhang, But not our bosses son,"

Seamus looked at his friend, "Why not?' he said knowing the answer and fearing the conversation.

"You know why not," Callum, "Seamus, we're two days here and If I'm right two days from Colos by Airship, you have to end this buddy,"

The Magician glared at his friend's staff in hand, "I don't have to do anything," The furniture in the room started to vibrate as Seamus fumed.

"Yes you do, You gotta know Bernardo isn't going to disappoint his folks," Jase did his best not to sound as if he upset with Seamus and Bernardo.

Seamus looked at his friends stormed past them, magically opening the door and slamming it as he exited" He'll be okay, he knows we're right, he's just not ready to hear it," said the free-crusader.

341

Jase nodded. "And what about you and "Fussy Britches," he said with a wry smile.

"You do know she can turn you into a grub worm," Callum.

"You're not answering," Jase sat climbed on the high bunk and sat.

The young lord thought for a second then smiled, "Complicated, but worth it?," he said. "And speaking of complicated I better go to the post and let my parents know I'm alive" He added quickly exiting.

Xarona and Clare walked into the clean and wood-paneled room as two teenage girls were removing the top bunk of both beds and adding a canopy over them.

"Sorry Misses, we're just finishing up," said one of the girls.

"Take your time," replied the witch as she sat in a chair and stroked the odd-looking white cat that had lept into her lap.

"I need a nap," Sani.

"You're always napping," Xarona.

The girls looked at the redhead in the green dress, black corset, and wide brim pointed green hat.

"Did your cat just talk?," said one.

"Yes I do," Sani, "But as of late I've been told to be quiet,"

"I'm sorry for that, but the Walkers might not have understood," Xarona.

"And eaten us," Clare.

Xarona looked at her friend and rolled her eyes, "They were not cannibals".

"Did you taste that food? I'm pretty sure that wasn't beef, pork or anything else people would eat". Clare smiled and sat on the large trunk she insisted on bringing into her room.

Xarona laughed, she wasn't sure why, the joke wasn't that funny, but the was something about Clare's general forwardness and with and the fact she had confessed her burdens that made her feel as she could finally enjoy life just a little.

"You have a great laugh," Clare looked at her friend.

"I told her she should do it more often," Sani, but does she ever listen.

Xarona took the cat from around her shoulder and placed it on her lap.

"You are in a sour mood today," she said stroking the creature's soft white fur.

The cat purred and started to relax, "No, I just needed pets," it said.

The ginger lady rolled her eyes, Clair giggled and the girls after finishing their work slowly approach the Xarona.

"Are you a Witch Miss?," said the taller one, they both had dark hair reddish tan skin and high cheekbones typical of many of the Inn's owner and the other children.

"Yes I am," Xarona spoke with a hint of the haughtiness she reserved for strangers.

"and can you do magic?" asked the other girl.

Clare stood up and walked over to the girls who despite being at least five years younger were almost as tall as the stoutkin. .

"The Lady Xarona Belasona, magic is a thing of wonder," she said.

The witch glared at the artificer then at the girls, "Yes I can," she said.

The girls looked at each other, whispered to each other, the taller then pushed the other one forward.

"We've saved 14 copper," said the girl.

"That's a fair amount of money," said the witch.

"Our brother Danis, he calls us names and bosses us around, and puts tar in our hair". The girl continued.

"Then Danis is a right arse," said Clare.

The girls nodded and the taller one stepped forward. , " He is, But He's in charge, along with my grandmother while mother and father are on patrol for the month. "

"If you're looking for a blessing for your parents, I really can't help, but I do know of a Crusader who seems to be good at that kind of thing, Xarona said with a smile. The girls shook their heads and bowed,

"No we want you to put a curse on Danis," they said, "Turn him into a mouse, or a bird... or," said the tall one quickly.

"Not forever but just long enough to teach him a lesson," The other one said.

Clare started to laugh, "And this is why the great gear didn't see fit to make me a witch, because if I could, I would be turning idiots

into things all the time," she said.

Xarona looked at her friend then the girls, "Have you tried talking to him?"

"Yes, and he punched us and put tar balls in our hair," said the shorter one.

"He made me eat a raw egg," said the other one.

Clare, "For fourteen copper I'll punch him, repeatedly for you," said Claire.

The witch thought for a second, the girls seemed to be more afraid than malicious and she would, of course, have to get the approval of the local lead witch, a meeting she was not looking forward too.

"I will consider your request," said the witch gesturing cause the door to open, "Now begone," she said coldly, even though she was more amused than upset with the girls.

The girls ran off, almost knocking Seamus down in the hallway. The door closed and Clare looked at the young lady and giggled, "You know M'lady, you really have to know how to play up, the whole, scary witch thing when you want to. ," said the Artificer.

Xarona nodded, "There's actually a class for it in Coventry," she said.

. After unpacking and informing Bhang that he could stay with them, the lord and the hunter decided to seek out Their magician friend and run a few errands in the strange city. Jase hated all the sights, smells, and noise of city life and knew tracking Seamus would be hard. After looking at the inn's outside he did discover the general direction the magician headed off in.

The two adventurers along the stone side walk off of the bustling city. In the streets people, horse-drawn carts (and the rare magical horseless carriage) moved about avoiding pedestrians, people on horse and camel and large multi-car carts pulled by elephants.

Stores lined the streets and boats filled the large canals, somewhere flat bottom barrages, others pleasure galleys and fishers. Up until now, they thought Vallus was a big city, but to compared to Kascee, it might as well be a Lester.

The two Young men eventually found their way to a Post rookery where trained pigeons carried messages for a price to other Free kingdom Posts or riders could be hired to deliver packages along set routes. Callum and Jase entered the tall building where workers moved about in green uniforms bearing the gold crest of the Free kingdoms Post. A young woman greeted the adventurers and took Callum's information. She then vanished in the rear for what they thought would be for writing supplies but instead returned with a letter for the young lord from his family. He smiled knowing his Grandmother had an uncanny talent for finding her Grandchildren and in this case guessing where he was going to be. The letter was short stating all was well, and he was loved and missed. It also came with a bank draft for eight silver just in case he needed money. Only three weeks old he immediately had the postal worker write out a letter in return saying he and Seamus were doing well and he had had money and he missed and loved his family. He then handed the woman a ring form a pouch with the family seal. She pre- pared the letter, sealed it and after he paid two copper sent it to the Rock- ery saying It'll be in Vallus in a week and a half and in his families rockery a day after that.

Jase declined to have sent his family a letter knowing that post birds tend to get shot in Hills of his home and riders didn't fare much better.

After leaving the post, the two traveled down a street, brought some rolled fried bread full of clove-spiced honey and cream. Turning a corner, they were stopped in their tracks by what they at first thought was a funeral procession. As people gathered on the wood and stone walkways. As the young man stood they watched a figure glide down the street The woman was seven feet tall, had dark brown skin just a few shades short of black four arms and was dressed in a tight-fitting black and gold dress. Her four purple eyes glanced about and despite her unusual a appearance, her beauty was never in questions.

"She's old blood," said Callum.

"I figured that, but what kind," said Jase.

"We called them Getchi,   but in the Old lands, they were called Deva and Djinn.

They're mostly from the old lands my family is from and the spice lands to the old-east. , my mom has a bit of that in here," he said.

"How much, So If I ever met her I won't gawk too much," quipped the hunter.

"Not much, Why most of our old blood is from Dad's Titan side," he said.

Jase nodded, the woman continued down the road casually and eventually, the procession broke up. It was during that time Jase felt the tug on his belt. Quickly he reached down and grabbed the hand, which was connected to a little blond girl.

"Looking for something little lady?," he said.

The girl's eyes widened and she quickly pulled away and ran down the street.

Callum immediately checked his belt upon seeing what happen to Jase, everything was present and he figured his height may have been his saving grace.

"We better be more careful," said the Hillman.

Seamus wasn't sure he was going, he just wanted to be by himself. From the Inn, he headed along the Canal where the sight of ships and so many people in some many different styles of clothing almost lead to him being run over by a horseless carriage. The strange device looked like the Salazars travel wagon only the driver was set further back and covered on all sides and instead of a reign he guided the device with two bars.

He could tell by the ornate carvings and brass and silver framing on the carriages they were driven by the rich, most likely nobles or merchants. Once across the main street the young magician ducked into an alley and moved down it past a few vagrants and a family rats the size of small dogs. He knew he was entering a more rough part of town but didn't care. In fact, all he cared about was not wanting to think about Bernardo or what his friends said.

Seeing stairs leading down next to the canals, Seamus crossed another street to head down the stone steps to a walkway along the canal, their People rolled barrels, carried bags, and by there talked seemed to be sailors. Slowing down the young magician started to relax, he knew his friends meant well and may be right and maybe he felt so strongly because Bernardo was the first person like him who reciprocated his affections. He also had to consider during their travels Bernardo never said anything about calling off the marriage or advancing what they did beyond the occasional hand hold or awkward kiss.

Stopping under a bridge cross, Canal Seamus decided to sit on upward going stone incline that was part of the bridges under-structure.

"I'm an idiot," he said

"Hey, boys what do we have here?," a voice and the smell of rum brought the young wizard out of his melancholy stupor.

Three men staggered in his direction, "Is it a blond lass" said another of the men.

Seamus study, tightening his grip on the staff.

"Fancy a kiss lady," said one of the men moving closer and puckering his lips.

"You don't want to do that," Seamus.

"That lady sounds like a boy," laughed one of the drunks.

Seamus watched as one of the men rushed forward in a stagger hands out "I'll have a check," he said only to be sidestepped by the blond young man.

"Hey That's not right," said the other two moving forward hands up ready to grab, Looking at the large bottle one of the men carried Seamus focused heat from his staff into it, causing it to sizzle ignite and explode, sending one of the men into the canal.

"She's a wizard or a witch," said one of the men reaching into a short scabbard and pulling out a knife.

'You can't win this," Seamus said, again focusing fire, this time into knife causing to heat up and burn the man's hand. The other man who had been side step with a punch that managed to make contact across the wizard's face.

Staggering to the side Seamus raised his staff and swung in front of the man using magic to send him into the canal next to his friend. The last one who hand was burnt by the knife started to run but soon found himself thrown into the drink an invisible bolt of force from the wizard.

Seamus looked at the water, worried that the men might drown he reached into it with his power and caused it to rise and drop the men on the pavement.

"We're sorry ma'am... Sir," said one of the men.

Seamus laughed, "It's fine, I really needed that," he said reaching into his pocket and taking out a copper coin," next rounds on me", he added, tossing a coin at the downed men and walking back the way he came.

To her surprise among the dozen or so children in the inn, Xarona had no problem finding Danis. In fact, the boy found her while she was downstairs in the common room filling out the group's adventures guild logs. While she was sure Callum and Seamus would be happy to help she enjoyed working on the minutia of logging day to day travel, events, booty gained and setbacks, She made notes about Clare's excellent work as a new addition, wrote down spells used by her and Seamus and faith blessing used by Callum. She was told in Vallus that while most groups just gave the basics, the more successful ones gave very detailed reports knowing such reports could help future adventurers and travelers.

As she finished up writing Danis was poking a younger sibling with a broom and chastising them for being possible a changeling child and a horrible brass cleaner. Xarona folded up the loose paper, placed them in her group's journal and observed the tall young man who was just a few years younger than her smile as he bullied his chubby sibling.

"Young man," she said to the boy.

Danis ignored her even as his victim stopped.

"Young man," she said in her the disdainful tone of Lady of means and influence. this time catching the taller boys attention

"Yes Ma'am," he said.

"Why are you doing that?," she said pointing at the broom than the other boy.

"Doing what?," Danis.

"Vexing that poor child," she said.

Danis smiled and grabbed his sibling's arm tight, causing the child to wince, "we're just having fun," He said, Isn't that right "Dilb?".

The other boy in obvious pain nodded, "Just funning miss," he said.

Xarona looked at the younger boy, "You're dismissed," she said in a kind tone. As both boys started to leave she looked at Danis, "Not you," she added.

The Witch motioned the young man to approach and offered him a seat.

"You have a problem," she said.

"What?," said the lean boy.

"Two of your siblings, I won't say who, has hired me to teach you a lesson," she said, "Now in all fairness, I thought I would give you a chance before I teach you the error of your ways,"

"I see," said the boy, " Thank you miss, I'll try to do better,"

Danis smiled, stood and bowed to the young woman, "Is there anything else I can do for you, maybe some more tea?," he added politely.

"That would be great," feeling pride as she had succeeded in her mission without the use of magic.

Danis returned a few minutes later with a fresh pot of Tea, bowed and left. Xarona took a few tiny sips enjoying the batches unique taste. Once she done, the Lady headed upstairs to find Clare teaching Sani how to play a game involving three dice with different colors on each of the six sides.

"So did you do it?," Ask Clare

"No, I decided to talk to him instead and I think he learned the error of his ways". Clare looked up and smiled, then started to laugh,

"Really?" she said, "He learned his lesson?".

"Yes," Xarona sat on her bed

Clare started to laugh louder, causing Sani to look at her mistress.

"Mistress, your mouth," she said.

"What about my mouth?," asked Xarona.

"Look in the mirror," said the Chimera.

Xarona stood and walked to a hanging mirror in the corner. Upon seeing her face, she screamed. Her lips were dark blue and her teeth a lighter blue.

"Ink in the tea," said Clare, I used that one before

Xarona face turned from horror to rage, "Oh he thinks he can make a fool of me," growled young woman.

"It's just a prank M'lady," Clare.

Xarona looked at her friend, pulled her wand touched her face removing the stains.

"A prank he's going to regret," she said. Before storming outside the door wand in hand.

CHAPTER 15:
CROSSROADS AND CALLINGS

When Callum and Jase walked into the Armor shop, they were met, the smell of leather and metal oil. A plump man with a handlebar mustache wearing an apron over a white shirt, dark pants, and boots puttered about the room. At the counter, a thin, pale red-haired girl in glasses sat twiddling her thumbs.

Leather, plate, and chain mail hung from the ceiling, and on wooden mannequins, bracers of all types sat on a counter as did helmets and greaves. Jase walked up to the counter and sat the folded Wampus hide down.

"Are you the armorer," he asked the girl?

"No, Just the apprentice," she said quickly. , "He's the armorer,"

The girl pointed at the man who was looking over a leather carapace that covered neck, shoulders and upper torso.

"Excuse me," said Callum to the man.

"Aye, I see ye lads," he said without looking up until he had perfectly adjusted the armor on its stand.

"What can I do for you?," he asked walking to the adventures.

The hunter pointed at the skin, "I was hoping on getting something done with this he said. The man walked around the counter, unfolded the wampus pelt till it stretched halfway along the counter, he then held the hide between two fingers, and sniffed, " Wampus, That's a good kill lads," he said, "Piss poor quick tanning, though," he added.

'Jase glared at the old man, "I work with what I had," he said.

"No offense," said the armorer, "You boys are adventures, I can tell. The muscle by his size and the bowman by the calluses on your fingers," he added.

"Pretty much," Callum.

The man nodded, "But your no brute big fella, you carry yourself like a man with book learning and morals," the armorer added.

Jase smiled, "He got you pegged there," said the hunter.

"And you lad, A wild hill boy, lots of skill, not much discipline through," continued the older man.

The free crusader giggled.

"Lass, go in the back and get me that extra large Banded plate, bracers, and greaves I made for that welching eastern sword-hand," Said the gruff older man, "And take that skin back and toss it in the setting oil,"

The girl nodded, grabbed the skin and headed into the back through some curtains.

"We didn't agree oncost yet,". Jase

"Names O'Shea, I'm the best, and fastest armor in Kascee made second skins for kings, generals, and knights. A lad like you couldn't hope to do any better".

Jase looked around, the armor, in the room was beautiful, he wasn't sure if the man credentials were true, but there was no doubt he did good work.

"How much are we talking?" The young Hillman spoke up.

"I'm going to make you a leather doublet, cloak, bracers, trouser, and boots. One crystal mount on each, you're going to pay me seven gold if you keep the scraps, four if I keep the scraps," O'Shea spoke with authority and in a manner that said in his mind the deal was done.

"I need it in two days," Jase.

"That's an extra five silver either way," The armor, "And before you try, no negotiation,"

" Fine," said Jase, "But you're going to throw in a belt,"

The man laughed, "I was gonna do that anyway, now let's get you measured, then it's the big man's turn,"

"I have armor," Callum.

"but not my armor," said the Armorer.

Callum and Jase walked westward from the armorer, stopping at a shop that sold exotic talismans made from various materials. Jase showed him the Wampus teeth and claws he kept in the bag. The Talisman dealer made an offer of six silver for all of them; The two young man wished they had brought Xarona with them knowing her negotiating skills were better than both of them. Still, after some haggling, they managed to raise the price eight silver. From there they headed to The first Newland bank and money changer and cashed in Callum's draft.

Against Jases, protest the Free Crusader dragged his friend to the nearest temple of Alomeg where he gave three silver as tithes, Prayed (as Jase watched) and took the local priests blessing. Heading back they found themselves at a large fountain light in the setting sun by light crystals. The large fountains danced and magically twisted and shaped forming Kascee warriors, the Thunderbird, buffalo and more.

"Hello," From behind the two young men came a familiar voice.

Callum and Jase turned to see Seamus standing behind him, a large bruise on his cheek.

"Did you win?," Jase.

"Surprising I did," said the Magician.

The three stood in silence briefly looking at each other before Callum spoke up, "I'm sorry about what I said, That's not our business,"

"True It's not, but you both were right," Seamus.

"Didn't mean to start a ruckus," Jase added.

"Water under the bridge," said the blond with a mischievous smile.

Callum grabbed his two friends and hugged them tight before releasing them.

"I think you rebroke my ribs," Jase.

"Sorry," Callum.

"Just kidding Hoss," said the hill-man.

The Three men stood at the fountain, talking about their first impressions and adventures in Kascee before heading back towards the inn.

******

Lisa and Kisa walked next to their mother with Bhang behind them. When she had asked them to go shopping with her, they thought it would be for dresses, something equally frivolous. Instead, after asking for the direction, the group found themselves at a store specializing in ladies arms. The small boutique boasted swords and other weapons designed to be elegant and deadly.

Bhang watched Isabella walk up to the store's clerk and start a conversation. The store clerk then took from the walls behind the counter where the weapons were kept three sabers.

"These are three of our best; we sharpen after purchase, ones a Dimark and the other two Sabatu Steel, silver inlays, three crystal mounts. designed to be light for a woman's hand yet as strong as any man's," said the clerk. Isabella picked up each sword and did elegant flick and thrust move that surprised her driver and daughters.

"They're very nice," She said.

"We have some eastern style blades if that's more to your liking," the clerk.

"I'll take the blue steel Sabatu," she said, and my daughters will each take one of those stilettos on that shelf," the older woman pointed to a satin lined the shelf with raised wooden holders that held daggers and stilettos,"

"Of course Ma'am," the clerk removed the stilettos.

"Why are you buying us those?," Kisa.

"I don't think father will approve," Lisa.

"He can take it up with me," said Isabella, "After all the dangers we've had to deal with, we need to be ready.

The woman looked at Bhang who was standing by the door doing his best not to be seen.

"I think everyone should know how to protect themselves and those dear to them," he said in as neutral a manner as he could.

After money exchanged hand the sword and stilettos were sharpened on a grinder in the back, placed in leather and brass scabbards and handed over to the owners.   The group then exited the shop heading down the street to meet up with the rest of their family.

"Father, I don't think a mother is going to be happy," Bernard looked at Vincent who was eating roasted spiced peanuts and chickpea from a wax paper bag.

"Nonsenses, she's going to love it, not only is it a good ship, but the captain seemed like a nice fellow," said the merchant.

"He seemed, shifty," the young man took a hand full of the food from his father's bag, "And I think that tall fellow he called the "Custodian of client relations," had blood on his boot.

"You're just nervous," Vince returned, "But I would be too if I was about to be married.

As his father spoke, Bernardo suddenly became less hungry and dropped his hand full of food. He suddenly felt queasy as it finally dawned on him that in a few days he would be in Colos and meeting his future wife for the first time.

"Can we not talk about it father," Bernardo.

"Of course, but if you ever need to talk..," the older man said just as he spied his wife, daughter and his driver heading in their direction.

"Why does mother have a sword?". the young man looked at his father.

Vinceno eyes widened, "I have to know idea," he answered stopping and waiting for the rest of his family to cross the busy street.

Isabella walked up to her husband and son smiling.

"So did you find us an airship?," she asked.

"Yes, ten tickets to Greyrock keep, the center of Colos," said Vinco, while doing his best not to notice the sword.

"Mother, why do you have a sword?," Bernardo.

"Why do you have one?," Isabella

"A gentleman needs a sword, to protect himself," replied the young man.

"And so does a lady," the older woman returned.

Vinceno looked at his daughters, of which were carrying stilettos in sheaths hanging in a brass rings on the side of their corsets.

"Isabella, the girls, don't need weapons," Vinceno.

"The girls were kidnapped, attacked by trogs and almost eaten by an eight-legged beast," said the matriarch of the Salazars, "If not for the fact that you hired some uncommonly good adventurers, they would be dead or worse by now,"

"It's unbecoming," Vinceno.

"Podría darle un culo de rata, about what's unbecoming when it comes to my children's safety," Replied the woman slipping into the language of her childhood to make the point to her husband and hopefully not offend the ears of those nearby. The tone of her words was also a tone Vinceno hadn't heard from his wife in years.

"Mother, you could hurt yourself with that," said the woman's son reaching out for her blade as if to take it. Seeing the move, Isabella smiled and in a single fluid motion drew the sword and tapped her son's hand with the flat of it.

"I dueled seven times and killed six men and one woman before you were even born my dear," she said.

Bernardo took a step back, he had always seen his mother as the dour but typical lady of means, but looking into her eyes now, he saw something else, a fierce confidence.

"Bhang, what do you think of this nonsenses?," Vinceno spoke to the man in hopes he would at least out a sense loyalty be on his side.

The driver looked at his employers, "I find it's never good to get between a husband and his sword-wielding wife," said the driver.

Lisa and Kisa giggled as did Bernardo.

"Good answer," Isabella.

The woman sheath her sword and hugged her son.

"We need to talk," she whispered, "When we get back,"

Bernardo's stomach churned more and suddenly retiring to the comfortable little inn filled him with dread.

*****

Xarona stood behind the inn next to Clare who was moving a brass mounted clear gem about with her hand and watching it control a buzzing mechanical flyer the size of a large bird. The mechanical ornithopter was pestering Sani who was doing her best to nap.

" You didn't have to come," the witch looked at her friend who was piloting her winged device around a sleeping chimera.

"Yes I do," said Clare, "I want to see the idiot brave enough to pull the ink-tea trick on a witch,"

"I don't think he knows I'm a witch," Xarona.

"Red hair pointed hat, nose in the air all the time, everyone knows your a witch,"

The witch frowned, "That's not true," she said.

"Really," The stoutkin, looked around and spied one of the many children working at the inn preparing food for the livestock,

"Hey boy, what would you say my friend's occupation is?". asked the dark-haired young lady while pointing at the woman next to her.

The young man looked at the redhead for a minute, "I would guess a fancy lady or some sort of witch," said the boy.

"A fancy lady," An angry Xanora looked at the boy, and her smirking friend scandalized.

"Or a Witch," Clare.

"Bah," said the redhead as she crossed her arms and playfully pouted, "Fancy lady indeed, the child's lucky I don't hex ignorant peasant children,"

"Unless they put ink in your tea," The artificer added quickly.

"Ink and my tea, torture of siblings negate all restraints," said Xanora with a smile.

Danis watched the two women from the door, The one he had tricked was laughing, and the shorter one had something in her hand that seemed to be controlling some kind of buzzing metal bird.

"When you die can I have your shirt," said his younger brother.

"I didn't know she was a witch," The older boy looked at his sibling as he spoke, "and no,"

Taking a deep breath, the young man stepped through the door into the backyard and towards the two ladies.

"Please don't kill me!," he said vehemently.

Xarona and Clare looked at each other after hearing the words.

"It was on a dare," continued Danis.

Xarona rolled her eyes as the young man begged, "Who dared you?," she asked.

Danis thought for a second, he hadn't thought that far ahead and thought quickly through his lists of siblings to find the perfect patsy.

"My sisters Leaf and Norni," he said quickly.

"Are they the same sisters who're hair you tar," Clare spoke up.

Xarona stepped forward and drew her wand, "You do realize as someone one of noble birth I could have you flogged or placed in the stocks for what you've done," she said.

"It's Norni and Leafs's fault," insisted the boy.

"Mistress, get it over with, his sub-par begging is disturbing my nap," Sani.

Danis looked about, If he ran away, he thought, he could just wait for till the witch left. That would mean living on the streets, despite having all manner of extended family in the city. Like the witch, they didn't find his pranks funny either and would most likely drag him back to the inn.

Quickly Danis moved towards the side gate where the Salazar's wagon was brought through.

"Well, that's unexpected," said Clair watching the boy make it to the gate and fiddle in a panic with the lever used to open and close it.

Xarona looked at the boy with pity, a part of her wanted to let him run away, to let him get away with what he had done in move on.

But another part knew that if he got away, he would learn nothing and possibly think he could get away with troubling another witch or noble.

"Sani, please get the young man," said the witch.

The winged cat came to its feet and started to change into its wildcat form.

"My Mistress would have a word with you," Said the cat from behind the Danis. The boy turned to see the large white cat behind him and screamed. Sani, wanting to get back to her nap, grabbed the boy by the cuff of his pants, yanked pulled him away from the gate and to the ground. She then dragged him across the backyard through animal droppings, uneaten corn for the chicken and more till he laid before the witch.

"Stand up," Xarona.

"Running was a bad idea," Clare.

Danis managed to stand, "I'm really sorry," he said again.

"I'm sure you are, I'm sure you're very sorry you were caught," The noblewoman spoke and tapped her wand in the palm of her free hand. The boy nodded.

"But are you sorry for how you treat your siblings?" she asked. ,

"And keep in mind If you lie I'll know it,"

Xarona had, no such spell active of course, but knew fear would keep him as truthful as good as any casting.

"But, But," the boy stammered.

"You stand accused by a noblewoman of the crimes of threatening the innocent, Attempted escape from a rightful authority and sophomoric assault,"

"Is that last thing a real crime?," Clare

"It is now," said the witch, "How do you plead?"

Danis stood resisting the urge to soil himself. Finally, after the fear finally built to a point where he thought it couldn't go any further he accepted his faith, "Guilty," he said.

Xarona nodded, "Then I Xarona Belisona sentences you to 24 hours as a rodent," she said waving her wand then pointing at the boy.

Danis shriveled away till he was as she stated a small gray mouse. Upon seeing the creature, Sani ran over and swallowed him in one gulp.

"Sani!," called out Xarona in a tone that showed not only her surprise but fear.

Immediately the disappointed chimera started to cough and in in a few seconds managed to cough up the still live mouse.

"That almost turned out really horrible," Clare.

"Sorry M'lady," the cat reverted to her true form.

Xanora picked up the mouse carefully casting a refreshing spell on it as she did.

"Now, Let's make sure you're safe for the remainder of your sentence she said conjuring a small cage around him.

"What do you think Lord Wimbowaradi is going to say about this?', Clare.

Xarona looked at the Artificer, " I'm sure he'll say something about Alomeg and that fear shouldn't be used as a detriment to sin, or something like that,". said the witch

Clare nodded, "That's what I figured too," she said before walking back towards the inn's rear entrance, her flying contraption buzzing behind her.

"You turned him into a mouse?," Callum sat in Xarona's room after dinner. Clare had headed downstairs to play cards with Jase, Seamus, Bernardo, and Bhang allowing the couple to have some "alone time" as she put it.

" Yes," she said sitting in the young man's lap, her hand around his back, allowing her to lean over and kiss him softly on the lips.

"You know I'm not okay with that, right?," said the Free Crusader.

"I know, But He'll be that way for 24 hours regardless," she said,

"And don't worry, Sani is guarding him,"

"So your cat is guarding a mouse?," said Callum lowering his head into hands, "That's not helping," he added.

"He'll be fine," said the witch.

"Callum kissed the ginger woman on the lips holding her close he knew that she wasn't like him, she didn't follow his god or his moral compass, she was a good person of course, but things like revenge and casual bits of wickedness towards those that crossed her was something she saw as perfectly fine with her. He knew he couldn't change her, nor did he want to.

"Do you think I'm wicked," asked the witch kissing the young lord on the cheek.

Callum smiled, "No, just morally different," he said. , "I blame your Hecate for that,"

Xarona sat up straight and crossed her arms, "We never say any of her names," she said.

I'm sorry, truthfully I don't know much about it other than It's a goddess or goddesses and something about the moon". said Callum.

"This is a city of crossroads, you should come to her temple with me tomorrow, and I can educate you on my beliefs," said Xarona.

"I would like that a lot," Said Callum, "But what should we do till then,"

Xarona leaned over to kiss the young lord again, "I'm sure we'll figure something to occupy our time," she said while giving repeated kisses.

Bernardo sat in the inn's common area across from his mother at a small table; Isabella had made sure the rest of the family was sleep before meeting with her son.   She could tell by the way he fidgeted that he suspected something.

"Why didn't you tell me," Isabella?

"Tell you what," Bernardo looked about and then at the wooden table with a Go board carved in the top.

"That you're sly," she said.

"I'm not sly mother, responded the young man while looking at his hands.

Isabella smiled, "You are, but my darling boy, I don't care what you are," she said taking her son's hand and holding them.

The young man looked into his mother's dark eyes seeing tears in them that matched his own. He knew no matter how much he denied it; her opinion would not change.

"Does Father know?," Bernardo spoke barely above a whisper.

The older woman laughed, "Of course not, he's a good salesman and a good father and husband, but he's also very good at fooling himself," she said.

Bernardo smiled, suddenly feeling relief despite the fact a part of him wondered how much his mother knew and how her knowing would affect his families plans.

Isabella released her son's hand, and her smile vanished, replaced by a severe stare. "So what are we going to do?," she asked.

"We?," Bernardo.

"About the girl in Colos, are you going marry her, or do we need to turn back now," the woman asked, "Men of your persuasion marrying out of obligation isn't unheard of. but I rather you be happy then ruin your life in a loveless relationship,"

The young man nodded and sat in silence. The idea of deciding on the subject sickened him. He could feel his nausea returning and a nervousness in his hands that caused his fingers to twitch.

"I need...I need to do it," stammered the young man.

Isabella lowered her head briefly, feeling pride and fear for her son.

"No you don't," she said, "Your father will be angry, but he'll get over it," she said.

The young man fought his fear and sat up straight, "This isn't about me, It's about us, our honor and our family, If I do this it'll hurt our name, and It'll hurt Father, and I won't let that happen!".

Isabella sighed, "You are an adult, and I will do whatever I can to help you, but, from experience, this type of thing never ends well," said the mother standing, and looking at her eldest child with pity.

Bernardo nodded and continued to sit, long past his mother exit from the room and until the hint of a rising sun could be seen through the rooms windows.

*****

Callum walked through the quiet streets of early morning Kascee next to Xanora. According to the witch, the time of day was important when it came to the temples of the Lady (or ladies) of the crossroads. The free-crusader remembered his grandmother described as "Just a shade lighter than dark," he knew that among the four great faiths there was very little trust between them.

Alomeg was the most prominent among those living in the new and old lands even though each culture had their own way of looking at the "creator" and bastion of light. Some focused more on Alomeg as a force for good, others as a wrathful protector and a few saw the archangels as the center of the religion.

Dark was often seen as the opposite of Alomeg by many, but the Callum knew in a lot of cases that wasn't true. Dark from what the young lord knew was about the eventual death in everything and accepting that and revering the force that caused that. Most dark worshipers, he had met did there best to live relatively benign lives. However, if rumors were to be heard some of the more radical members of the religion practiced necromancy and performed human sacrifices in dark places in exchange for power.

Followers of Dark were a definite minority or at the very least very secretive. The Green-mother, however, wasn't. The Green-mother was a nature-based religion and from Callum's understanding (And what he had learned from Seamus mother who was a worshiper), was the second most popular among the people of the world in one way or another. The followers worshiped the planet as a living entity and a cycle of all things coming from the Earth and going back to it.

Like Alomeg it too had a large variety of sects and temples, only in the case of The Green-mother, those temples tended to be areas of pristine nature.

The Lady of the crossroads was like Dark either small or secretive and represented change or chaos; the young lord wasn't exactly sure. The thoughts of religion brought back a song he once heard in his youth that a traveling salesman who revered all gods (Unionist as they were called) would sing while setting up his stall in the market.

Alomeg in the light

The Dark in the night

The Mother is green

The Lady's magics night

The squid in the sea.

The dragon dreams you and me.

No one is right

No one is wrong.

We'll learn the truth, when we're called home.

"How do you know where it's at?," asked Callum, "Is that just something witches know?"

"All roads are the same road, all crossroads the same crossroads," said the ginger noblewoman as her and the young lord moved down a nearly deserted street towards the center of town. The witch could feel the power of the Lady, said to be the mother of all witches growing around her as she passed multiple crossroads.

"Here," she said pointing at a place where their roads met and circled a great structure of black and dark purple stone that from Callum's point of view seemed to fade into view as he got closer, behind the surrounding city around it.

"I feel strange," said the free-crusader as his connection to his ever-present faith ebbed.

"Because he's not her," said the witch, "She's both uncaring and selfish, hateful and kind".

As the couple grew closer, they could feel the very air around them change from the that of a city to something else that defied description.

"Where are we" Callum looked up at the sky, gone was the warm colors of dawn, replaced by a dancing bands of purple and a large bright moon.

"The crossroads, The place where all worlds meet," said Xarona leading her friend by his hand closer to the grand spired structure topped by a silver statue of a six-armed woman with three faces standing armed raised.

The young lord and lady could see people moving like ghosts moving in and out of the structure, most where women, but a few were men. Regardless all where dressed in a variety of clothing some styles he recognized others were garish or so odd he had no words to define them.

"So, is this real, an illusion?," asked the young man to his lady.

"Yes," the witch answered, tapping the air and watching it ripple like water.

"Who is brings his son to her place," said a woman's voice from above.

The young lord looked up to see a woman standing on a balcony above the great stone and stain glass front of the church. He swore a second ago there was no balcony or stain glass present, but there it was now.

The woman seemed more real than the other people moving about them was dressed in black leather armor with black feathers on the shoulder and along the forearms looked down. Her helm, made of black leather with a silver faceplate that covered down to the tip of the nose gave her the appearance of a great blackbird.

"I Xanora of Belisona," said the red-haired lady.

The woman on the balcony leaped down landing in front of the couple.

"And what is your name?," she looked at the man.

"I'm Callum of the Mwamba wa Mwaloni. ," said the free crusader regretting he left his hammer as he noticed the woman was armed with two large night metal chakrams tied to her side by a ring of black leather.

"I smell his sanctimony on you," said the woman in black., "I smell his order and apathy," Her voice seemed to the ego as she circled the two adventures only to vanish and reappear at the door once they had lost sight of her.

"You may enter, but his fate is in your hand, Xarona Belasona," added the woman,

The ornate silver and stainless door opened by folding in on itself and retreating into its framing.

"Don't touch anything," said Gilden woman to the Nyumbani man.

"Is everything here always so dramatic?," Callum said entering the door next to Xarona.

"This isn't dramatic; this is just how things are," She said as the doors reformed behind the couple who were now in a large open room that revealed most of the building inside was hollow and stretched from the floor up to the statue.

In the center of the room was a great fountain that danced around an obsidian and silver statue of three women, One in Armor, One wielding a wand and one dancing, The statue moved slowly as if alive, growing closer, merging into the six armed three face woman then separating into its three forms again. The acolyte of Alomeg looked around, save for them there was no one present.

"That's incredible," Callum.

"She is one and many, goddess and goddesses to call the ladies are to invoke their will and whim. That's why we use so many names for her/ them as not to invoke their same name too much and gain their notice," Said the witch.

"What about the Priestess," The Crusader walked towards the fountain, "That how you do it right, no Priests just priestesses?," he said.

Xarona nodded, "Indeed, and they have a tad more leeway," she said relaxing and feeling the intense magic energy. She knew all of their temples/temple were connected along ley lines of mystic power forming in a way one great temple transcending time and space as most people knew it.

"I think I'm ready to go," Callum looked about at the building, between the blinks of his eyes he saw subtle changes, stones shift, and stain glass images change then he remembered one of the name of the ladies the names of the ladies "Muses of Chaos," he said to himself .

"Why did you do that?," Xarona looked at her friend with frightened eyes.

"Do what?," Callum suddenly felt queasy.

"We have to go," the witch said grabbing the man's hand and running towards the door even as something formed behind them. The shadows of three ladies crawled past them just as they made it to the door and out of the building and into the streets of Kascee.

"What happened," The young lord breath heavily as if he was running for hours.

"You invoked that name, in their house, where they listen the most," Xarona said her voice calming, "We had to go before they arrived,"

"Why? I would love to revel in the light of Alomeg," Callum said walking to his surprise and in hand with Xarona out of the middle of the street and onto a sidewalk that to their surprise was right down the street from the inn.

"In the songs of Alomeg, has it ever ended well for any mortal who seen Alomeg?," asked the witch.

Callum thought of the prophets and their inspirational but often tragic lives. "No.," he said

"Exactly, now think of my less than forgiving and far more mercurial goddesses/goddess would be like," Xarona.

The couple, stood on the sidewalk calming their brush with the divine before heading back to the inn. In their relief, they did not notice a trio of blackbirds watching them briefly before merging into one and fading from sight.

*****

The rest of the day went by uneventfully, save for the hassle and bustle of food arriving at the Inn and the old woman and her grandchildren preparing a feast. Without Danis, things moved more smoothly for the children, and when he returned a few hours before the feast with tales of be-

ing a mouse and swallowed whole, no one seemed to believe him especially his grandmother who thrashed him on the rear with a wooden
spoon before sending him back to work.

The common room was clean and arranged for a great dinner. Bottles
of wine, mead, and sparkling juice sat on a beautiful tablecloth of bright
Kascee symbols. A plate of multiple kinds of cheese sat in the middle as
did fresh bread and a bowl of fresh fruit. When the Salazars, the Adventures, Bhang and Drivers, arrived two of the children who had been
working sat in a corner playing a rattle-like instrument and a flute.

Once everyone was seated, Callum gave a prayer of thanks to Alomeg
for his generosity and for allowing them to reach Kascee. When the
prayer ended, the two girls who had "hired " Xarona (and received their
payment back) came to pour drinks. A heavy set young boy then entered
with a tray of fresh grilled vegetables and peppers. Followed by another
child with a tray of grilled pig's ribs, chicken, and lamb sausage, behind
them another boy with a large beef roast. Sauces and relishes were laid
out by the old innkeeper as the salad of shredded cabbage, onions, carrots, and fennel mixed with a red vinegar and oil dressing.

Once the food was served, the conversation turned to the past and
those lost and the future. One of the Drivers would head east, Another
back to Arden. Vinceno told the tale of how he hired an airship and of
his pride in his son. As more drinks were consumed and more food was
eaten, Songs started to be the song, first by Jase, then Callum and Seamus.
Not to be outdone Isabella song a romantic ballad in Iberian that

brought tears to everyone present even Danis who did his best to keep the guests happy and not look Xarona in the eyes.

"That was wonderful my love," said Vinceno leaning over to kiss Isabella after he returned to her seat.

"Thank you," said the woman city.

"I had no idea mother.," Bernardo, "It's like I'm finally meeting you,".

Lisa nodded, "That's where Kisa gets it because it's wasn't from dad and his sailor's shanties,"

Clare looked up from she was doing her best to get Smoosh the baby octopod to drink from a cup of apple ale.

"Kisa, have you been hiding, even more, talents from us," said the tinkersmith looking up at the girl sitting across from her.

"My sister has a voice much larger than her," Lisa spoke.

"No," said Kisa in a scared, shy tone.

"Yes," Seamus looked at the girl, sing us a song. said the magician.

"No," the bespectacled twin sunk down in her chair while glaring at her twin.

"You don't have to sing," Xarona spoke up from where she sat rosy-cheeked and relaxed.

Kisa was about to agree with her friend when suddenly she realized, the shyness she was showing wasn't who she was anyone, she had spoken to nobles and generals and told them tales of here journey, she had seen and experienced so much and while her old self-was a comfort to her it wasn't her.

Standing slowly to her families surprise.

Fine," she said smiling at her sister be starting to sing a melancholy ballad she had learned long ago.

I'm wishing on a star

To follow where you are

I'm wishing on a dream

To follow what it means

I'm wishing on a star

To follow where you are

I'm wishing on a dream

To follow what it means

And I wish on all the rainbows that I see

I wish on all the people who really dream

I'm wishing on a star

To follow where you are

I'm wishing on a dream

To follow what it means

The girl in purpled watched as all eyes fell on her . Wanting to retreat into herself she started to sit; then a Driver clapped, then the old woman and so it went as the room exploded into applause feeding her with an energy she had only read about. It was what the great minstrels and performers would talk about a feeling of connection and power given by an audience for a performance well done.

"Thank you," said the girl.

As midnight approached the event started to die down, and everyone started to head to their rooms. It was a solemn occasion for all as everyone knew their journey would be ending soon, some that minute, others in a matter of days.

Morning came on the group's last day in Kascee was net by in many cases pound headaches and bright lights. The Colos bound group packed and moved one by one to the inn's common room for a breakfast of sweetened bread dipped in honey and fresh coffee. It was a quiet meal as everyone's mind seems to be in other places.

After the Breakfast, Bhang, Vinceno, and Bernardo drove the wagons to the Airship docks while Jase and Callum visited the armorer. Unlike the-the other days, there were no unforeseen events, the armor was ready and perfect, and unlike most, the hunter's armor didn't make a sound in fact unless he purposely stomped his feet or clap his hand as hard as he could it and movements he made was silent. Callum's was heavier than his chain and made of strips of a plate overlapping on the torso and a cloth covered metal disks on the legs and sleeves. The grieves were also metal as was the bracers. O'Shea placed the symbol of Alomeg on the chest and two brass bull heads medallions on the shoulder at no charge on asking from both young men that they show the world his work.

*****

Captian Kit Solen stood at the covered boarding platform leading to his ship the Resolute dressed in the long gray coat, black vest and pants and a dull tan shirt. His black hair was slick back and while he wasn't a vain man he knew passengers expected a certain amount of cleanliness when it came their-their captains.

The Resolute was wood and the brass airship that looked like an old man-of-war style sailing ship. Its top deck was covered curved glass and it mast, sides, and keel supported golden metallic sails that folded in when not in use. The bottom of the ship was storage and engine, above that more storage and stables for traveling livestock. Above that living quarters for the crew and above that Quarters and amities for passengers.

"They look like trouble," His first mate, watched the passengers head towards the boarding platform, The dark-skinned woman dressed in Blue shirt, and brown leather pants and vest was a former soldier and gladiator and even though she was missing an eye could tell by the look in a people eyes and they way they walk that they knew how to fight.

"Salazar said he has adventures," said Kit, " Nothing to be afraid Xel, they look like a bunch of pups first time from home".

" Maybe," said the woman., forcing a smile as the group she was watching got closer.

"Welcome to the Resolute folks," said the captain, "You Livestock and things should be board, this is my first mate, Xel she'll show you around and can answer any question you have.

"The Resolute flies smooth, but if it's your first time on an airship, you might want to stay close to the head or grab some of the mint-ginger candies from the common room.

"This is going to be so much fun, Kisa said, bounding up the boarding platform.

"I should have made an air sick potion," Xarona.

"I know some techniques that might help," Bhang said looking about as he boarded the ship. He could feel it was mostly floating in the air and be held at the station mostly by the wooden dock it pored in and rope,

"This isn't so bad," Seamus said feeling the ships magic move about him and circulate to what he had read was a combination of rare air and lift crystals. Seamus had read multiple books on Airships and would spend hours watching them fly to and from Vallas he sat on the roof of his family's farm.

"Ain't natural," said Jase already looking pale.

"You travel with a witch, wizard, and crusader, natural isn't a thing you tend to indulge in," said Clare. Who like Seamus was just as fascinated with the ship. To her, this was the height of manatechnology the perfect combination of mechanics and sorcery. Looking about the young tinkersmith made a note of every brass covered pipe, every crystal conduit, and every rune etching as she did her best to figure out the workings of the ship.

Once the passengers were on board, the first mate and captain entered and moved swiftly to the ships sleek raised wheelhouse near the rear of the vessel to wait for their launch signal for the Kascee airdock.

"So what are they like? asked The lanky blond man in a colorful patchwork shirt patchwork leggings that stood at the wood and brass control wheel.

"Like Trouble," Xel.

"You think everyone looks like trouble Sugar-Lumpkin," said the Ship's pilot before kissing the much taller woman on the cheek.

"Belay that, we need to look professional," The Captain spoke up knowing he would be ignored.

"Yes Sir," said the first mate after pulling away from her husband after a few more kisses.

The captain looked out of the thick glass windows and walked over to one of the brace funnel connected to rubber tubes that on hangers against one of the walls of the room.

"Engineer, are you ready," he asked into the cone.

A moment later the voice of a young female answered, "Aye-Aye Cap'n she's read to float and flow.

The Captain placed the cone back and picked up another one

"Sue, you got everything tight down in storage?," almost immediately a gruff male voice answered. " Kit, you see the size of that Bull? I bet It'll be good eating,"

"That Bull's a passenger and we don't eat passengers," The Captain returned before hanging up.

Xel smiled, "Sue's rarely right about anything, but I bet that pull tastes pretty good,"

The Captain rolled his eyes and spoke., "We don't eat other folks livestock, less we have to and right now we don't have to "

As the Kit finished the Airdock large horns sounded with two short bursts and one long one signally that the Resolute could launch.

"Get her up and out Winn," said the captain to the pilot, who turned to wheel and focused feeling the ship through his bare feet the blood man concentrated and pulled a lever to his right, twisted one of the many nobs above his head and grabbed the wheel as the ship started to for free of its dock.

"We're launching sir," he said feeling despite his enclosed place the air currents around him.

The captain nodded and walked to the wall of call funnels and picked up another one, "Passengers and crew, the Resolute has launched. We'll be heading High-Side for a quick cargo drop off and then to Colos and the Gray Keep air dock,".

The Resolute pulled away from the airlock, blew its launch horns twice to signal the port, circled and then headed west.

Switching funnels the captain spoke again to the engine room, "Minnie, I need three-quarter power and 20% lift "

"Aye," said the engine chief.

Not long afterward the resolute increased speed hummed turned west and started to move up into the clouds of Kascee.

386

CHAPTER 16: COLD WELCOME

Captain Kit and Winn watched as Clare moved the large wheel that controlled the Airship. He had known the girl had potential, but in such a short time not only had she learned the workings of the lift crystals engine that called the vessel to fly but had studied it's rigging and mechanical piloting mechanism.

"You sure I can't talk you into staying," he asked rubbing the mostly healed wound on his arm from the dark magical bolt.

. "Winn could use the help, and I'll pay full wages," he added.

The pilot nodded from where he sat next to his wife, Xel.

"I need to finish this," said the young woman. " I made a promise,"

The man nodded, "Aye that I can understand. But remember we run from Vallus to Kascee twice a month, if you're ever around there looking for work, it's yours".

Clare could not stop smiling. She had wanted to see the world, and now there she was piloting an airship heading towards the snow-covered peaks of the Sapphire mountains of Colos.

"I just might do that," she said as she felt the ship bob in the air currents and did her best to feel for the right time to head downward. It was during this time she realized why the Ship's regular pilot went barefooted at the wheel it gave him a stronger connection to the ship.

The machines', gears, and connections were alive to her, and she knew if she listened they would tell her what they wanted.

"Permission to signal the Colos air tower," she said.

"Granted Ms. Clare," the Captian returned.

The ships air horn blew loud as it passed a small tower on the side of mountain sporting the flag of Colos with it mostly green background a white stylized mountain peak, The ship followed similar towers for an hour blowing once at each tower as it flew over great pine forest, lakes, valleys and small villages till finally making it to a city on a great hill with roads and tunnels leading to its great stone walls and gate. The city of the Grey Keep was the capital of Colos, and while most kingdoms high cities were the kingdom named followed by Proper, In Colos it was different for some reason lost to time.

"It's almost as big as Vallus-proper," Seamus looked from the observation deck to city laid out before him . the great wall merged towards a mountain forming a great half circle. , geysers of steam shot up from large vents and green lights lined the streets. He could feel the power of the hot springs that kept the warm city year round and feel the trees below. More than Kascee, this city felt old and powerful.

His amazement soon turned to melancholy however as his mind went to Bernardo and what their arrival at the last leg of their trip meant. He knew his group would escort the Salazars to the castle, wait around for a few days and return to Vallus by the Resolute. Vinceno had made arrangements for the ship they were on to pick them up after it returned from a quick run to the Colos City of Rockport.

Callum sat his head in Xarona's lap, watching Sani chase Smoosh who despite the chimeras effort kept squeezing between its grasp.

He smiled at the witches fingers rubbed his bald head gently.

"I think Seamus familiar is frustrating yours," he said.

"Poppycock, if Sani wanted to eat that little thing she would have done so long ago," said the witch with a smile

Despite the past day's events, the Lady of Belason felt calm, even the idea of what was to come once she returned home didn't frighten her as much as she thought they would. While she would never admit it is with her friends and Callum her complicated life just seemed much easier.

"And I'll do that If it ever sat still," said the cat watching the tiny stubby legged octopod move about the floor. to Seamus before vanishing.

"Good boy.. or girl," said the Wizard.

"You still don't know it's sex?," Xarona.

"It doesn't have any... bits," said the bond.

"I'll check my books again; there has to be a way of telling," said the witch.

"Maybe it's like Gulp-Frogs, they can be boy or girl depending on what's needed" Jase spoke from the door where he stood," He still hated flying but had grown used to it and knew he would soon be on solid ground.

"I hate those things," said Callum.

'I thought Crusaders didn't hate, "Xarona

Seamus smiled, "A gulp Frog ate his dog when we were kids," he said before stretching , "Almost ate us too,"

And now you're courting a woman who can turn you into frog?," Jase snickered after speaking. "That's all manner of strange,"

Callum took Xarona's hand in his, "Oh I'm sure she'll never do that again," he said kissing it softly.

Xarona leaned over and kissed the young man on the forehead,

"I make no promises," replied Xarona, "I have a temper, and I'm good at magic,"

Callum looked at Seamus for support; the magician just shrugged as did Smossh who faded into view on his shoulder.

"She's right; she's very, very good at magic," agreed the jovial magician tone. Before anyone else could respond, the ships Horn blew twice signally they would be landing soon.

"Time to get to work," said Jase to his friends promoting everyone in the observation room to rise and exit.

The king of Colos stood on a balcony looking at the airship move towards a mooring tower. With long graying blond hair, green eyes and a well-groomed beard he often came up to the balcony to think and "escape,"

"It's them," said a dark-haired man in green and white robes wearing an ornate gold-trimmed hat and carrying a black staff with a broad octagonal headed sporting seven mounted.

"Thank you, High Magus," said the king

"Of course m'lord," returned the magician bowing slightly.

Turning the High Magus turned to leave, the king held out a hand signaling him to stop.

"You would tell me if you thought this was a bad idea, would you not the old friend," he asked.

The magician thought for a second, " The Salazars are wealthy and have connections, in the times that are to come both gold and allies will be needed, your Grace,"

The monarch nodded and turned to look at the airship.

"Anyway, what are daughters for if not to build such relationships," commented the king to himself and the man behind him.

The magician nodded before turning and walking into his own shadow and vanishing.

Vera Colos sat in one of the castles many small courtyards looking at a steaming pond. A lady in waiting had just told her husband would be arriving and the news was causing the blond young woman's stomach to churn from nervousness. She had never even been allowed to hug a boy, let alone kiss one. Still, while most of her wanted to hide, a small part of her wanted to meet the young man who had traveled so far to meet her.

Standing at the pool, the willowy blond who face showed a hint of her Avian heritage with her large golden eyes and elegantly hooked nose that did not distract from her beauty clapped once. Three Trogs females dressed in ill-fitting green and white tabards over gray dresses entered. Around each of their necks were metal collars.

"we need to prepare," she growled at her slaves who never once made direct eye contact with her. The trogs escorted the girl outside of the room walking behind her, head lowered down a tall arched hallway that came to the staircase that leads down to the castle.

"What need us do," said one of the trogs.

"Prepare my greeting dress, of course, your worthless Gritter," she said

"Yes," said all three grayish-skinned women.

Upon hearing the sycophantic voices, the princess smiled, turned and exited the small courtyard.

Bernardo stood dressed in his purple doublet over lavender shirt and pants. his sword in a black leather scabbard on his side as was the tradition for those seeking the hand of a betrothed.

His mother looked at her son nervously wondering what would become of him, especially if the truth about his slyness were to come out. She knew very little of Colos culture but had heard tales of angry Lords gilding sons-in-laws who proved to be disappointments.

"Are you sure you want to do this," she said to him softly.

"Ycs mother," Bernardo tried to sound calm as he replied.

"Of course he does," said Vinceno. , "He's my son".

Isabella glared at her husband, she wanted to tell him what she knew but could not bring herself to hurt the man she loved and knew, in the end, it was Bernardo's choice to speak or stay silent.

Jase looked at the carriages come up the road from where they stood just outside the airship tower in the heart of the bustling city. Like the others, he was dressed in his best clothing and had even endured a refreshing spell from Xarona and a shave from Clare. He would be meeting royalty today for the first time and for his part he would rather face the Wampus again.

The five open carriage each bearing the seal off of Colos was escorted by four mounted Colos riders in Chainmail, matching military tabards and armored horses.

"This is impressive, said Xarona," upon seeing the Colos carriages move towards them.

"Maybe not," Seamus could see at the rear of the carriages was two wagons and behind them four large Trogs in metal collars connected by chains to the rear wagon.

"What in the Hells?," Callum's eyes widened upon seeing the creatures, barefooted wearing dusty and dirty Tunics and pants.

He knew some lords and wealthy folk outside of Vallus and the southern lands had old-blood slaves, but he had never seen one before.

"Hold none in bondage least you be bound," the free-crusader said to himself.

"What's that?," Jase.

"It's from Book of Alomeg," said the Nyumbani lord.

Bernardo looked at his father, Are those slaves Father, you never said they had Slaves here!," said Bernardo angrily.

"I didn't know," he said, "They are outlawed in Vallus," Vinceno.

"That's horrible, even for Trogs," Lisa.

Kisa looked at her sister than her parents, she had read that Colos being so far west and surrounded on all sides by the wild was eccentric in its customs and that the family royal family had descended from humans who had mingled with the winged Avian -people native to the land and took pride in their stunted wings and the fact they had eradicated the Avians themselves. But nothing she had read said anything about slavery.

The carriages stopped at the group. From the lead, carriage stepped two soldiers followed by a middle-aged Gilden woman with white hair, golden eyes, and white fur hat. She waited why a footman opened the door for her, unfolded the steps to the ground and helped her out. Looking the group over first she then focused her gaze on the Salazars.

"Welcome to Colos; I'm Jazlyn, sster of king Palth, Princess of Colos and Majordomo of the High Castle.

She watched as everyone bowed and curtsey, even the hide-covered boy after some direction from the short dark haired girl next to him. Their bows, at least to her spoke volumes of everyone there, as did their dress.

The Salazars were newly wealthy and wore colors they had picked for their family. The father overdid his bow, showing himself to be a pleaser. The wife made eye contact and countered, showing her strength and the girls near perfect southern style courtesy showed they had learned it from a tutor. The Salazar boy bowed slightly, showing a defiance, she knew had to be dealt with eventually.

The others an odd mix of trained manners and forced grace. Her eyes fell on the blond boy with the pointed ears, he wasn't a full fae but was more than half-blood and wielded the staff of a magician. Her eyes locked with his and her mind reached out to his as she had been taught only to be blocked by personal wards against such things. Upon feeling the mentalist's probe, Seamus looked at the woman than to Callum and back to her.

"Welcome to Colos one and all," She said welcoming, " The carriages will take you to the high castle and the "Gritters," will load your supplies,"

"Gritter?," Kisa.

"I'm sorry dear, that's what we call the Trogs," she said.

Kisa watched as a footman unchained the Trogs from the rear of the Wagons and led them to the boxes, bolts of silk and luggage.

"I don't like this," Jase.

"I don't either but it's their custom," Xarona spoke holding Sani close to her.

Once the wagons were loaded, Jazlyn escorted Isabella and Vinceno to her carriage. In the carriage behind them sat Kisa, Lisa, In the next one Xarona and Clare and the last one Bhang and Seamus.

Jase on Horseback and Callum on Enkidu rode in the rear next to Bernardo who was also on Horseback as was the tradition.

The group moved through the wide streets past the city center with white stone buildings and stone vents that control the steam of underground geysers and springs to warm the city. Markets and merchant ran businesses gave way to well-kept neighborhoods and lined with light crystal lamps tree-lined roads as the road started upward towards the castle built into the side of the mountain.

Seamus sat in the carriage, he felt Jazlyn had tried to move past wards words he cast to protect his mind. Wards his teacher had taught him long ago saying that a wizard's mind was his greatest treasure. The fact she did a thing so blatantly violating worried him, not just for his thoughts but those of his friends, especially Bernardo. Focusing Seamus tightened the grip on his staff on his lap and closed his eyes He then reached out for a familiar mind. and found Xaronas's and out of courtesy asked for an audience.

"Yes," she thought.

"Princess Jazlyn, she tried a mind delve," though the magician.

"So that's what she was doing," Xarona returned, "I felt her try something on you and I felt you repeal it, good job by the way,"

"Thank you, I'm weaving some quick mind wards, and I need your permission to meld my protections into yours,"

Xarona smiled with pride, Seamus was thinking ahead and showing the power she suspected he had.

"Of course, It should be easy, Callum's Warrior's Wheel ritual still seems to be lingering, use that connection to set your spells up. " returned the witch relaxing her wards and allowing Seamus to weave his magic into hers. As he did, she released some of her energy into the bond the crusader ritual had granted her and her friends to help him.

Jase, Bernardo, Isabella, and Salazar was the easiest to add the ward too, they had no magical or faith training, and it was just a matter of connecting it to their auras and energy. Kisa's fast working and constantly moving brain made her particularly resistant to mind delving naturally and made her ward the strongest. Bhang's energy was next to impossible to find. He had so much control over it that Seamus had to lean over and whistler his intents to the man who was sitting across from him so the chi-wise driver could open himself up to the magicians' workings. Lisa's training with Bhang made her mind slightly more resistant than average as did Clare, but the later's place in the Warrior's wheel allowed the spell to work once she knew it was benevolent. And there was just he pure stubbornness of Jase that took more time than any other to negotiate with and ward.

Callum's connection to "wheel" as well being its center made him easy to connect to. Adding the spell to his energy was also easy as he trusted Seamus. However, while there Seamus could feel something powerful was also present, something old and while not harmful it was also very protective.

I'm curious to why the sudden paranoia?" asked the driver concerned. Seamus looked outside, the carriage was now entering the castle gate.

"I think the people of Colos are not as inviting as they seem," he said.

"Slavers rarely are," Bhang.

The magician nodded as to his surprise did Smoosh who was now fully in view on his shoulder. Seamus wondered if having such a pet in the open was a good idea, but then he realized it was no more exotic than Sani and would make him seem far more accomplished than he felt.

The carriages came to a stop inside the castles protective outside walls and before a series of high steps with landings bordered by statues the winged Avix people. At the top of the stairs stood the king, Queen, Princes, and Princesses of Colos and their retinue. From the side buildings at ground level exited guards wearing eagle shaped helmets of ivory and gold as well as metal and ivory breastplates. Each one had a large shield and spear.

"Here we go," said Jase sliding a hand to his sword,"

"I hope not said, Callum,"

The guards after surrounding the carriages then stood at attention before lining up along the steps much to the adventures relief.

Jazlyn walked to Bernardo and waited for him to get off his horse before taking his hand, "My niece awaits," she said leading him up the stairs.

Bernardo, without a word, just nodded, stole a quick glance at Seamus and then started up the steps. The carriage footman then started to fill in the procession as they had been trained to do over the past few days. The Slazar's next, starting with the mother and father, then the revenue based on social standing.

"He's handsome," said Vera to her mother.

"Of course he is," said the tall woman who looked like an older version of her three daughters, tall, golden eyes, blond hair and long neck. Like them, she was dressed in white, but unlike them, her dress was opened in her back to just below the shoulder allowing her small stubby birdlike wings to be seen.

"Who are the others?," asked the king to a man behind him the rear wearing glasses.

The lore keeper of the high castle of Colos looked the group over for anything that would tell him who was accompanying the king's future in-laws.

"Two minor nobles turned adventures, an Elf-blood whelp wizard, a backwoods bowman, the dark-haired man with the wooden beads is hard to read, but the other girl is obviously stout-kin. , My king" said the man.

The king nodded, The Salazar was not only showing their wealth and power with their attire but with their adventures. As Bernardo grew closer the king's eyes focused on him. He could see that his sword had some use and that his eyes had seen death. To monarch that meant the boy was a fighter and not the pampered merchant-prince he was believed to be.

"Welcome to Colos, Salazars," said the king raising both hands to greet them.

The Salazar's upon the greeting kneeled as did everyone else behind them. The king then gestured letting them know they could stand. Vera then stepped forward towards Bernardo and took his hand.

"It's good to finally meet you," she said with a smile.

"Thank you, m'lady," the young man in lavender returned doing his best to maintain eye contact and not vomit thanks to his increasingly nervous stomach.

Once Bernardo was standing next to Vera the king turned to leave, The queen followed as did everyone else. They walked towards the large stone doors, that to the surprise of the visitors slid open on their own. They then entered, moving down high walled halls of carved stone past tapestries showing past kings and queens as well as historical events including one depicting a war between the humans and the winged Avian people.

The group then headed up another long flight of stairs to the large hall where food was sat out on tables and a small group of musicians played. Two large fireplaces manned by collared fae in outlandish green and white attire warmed the room.

"Eat and drink till you're full my friends while our servants prepare your rooms," said the king in a booming voice. After the man spoke, his family and entourage clapped as did all the guests save for Seamus who's eyes were fixated on the collared fae.

"You okay?" Callum, carrying a large silver plate of meat, potatoes, cheeses, mushrooms, and bread walked to his friend after noticing the magician was standing by himself.

"No I'm not," he said softly.

"Yeah. I can see why," The free-crusader looked at one of the Fae servants toss a log into the fire than gesture at the flame willing it higher and shaping it to briefly take the form of a swan. "No one should be a slave," Seamus nodded, he could feel the despair coming from the fae. "Bernardo deserves better than this he said to his friend who nodded.

"M'lord, May I request your name as well as the name of the young Magus, for our records and to make you up proper writs of visitation," said the scribe holding a large book and a feather and copper quill that had its own ink reserves.

"I'm Lord Callum Wimbowaradi of Mwamba wa Mwaloni , third son and fourth child of Vilheim and Greta Wimbowaradi, crusader of Alomeg. " Said the young Lord in a tone that showed his annoyance with what was going on. The man took notes and smiled,

"Vilheim Wimbowaradi," the Cyclone, your sire's name is even known here," he said before turning to Seamus who's eyes were still on the fireplace tenders.

"And you?," asked the scribe. Seamus turned to meet the man's eyes with a steely gaze.

"I'm Magus Seamus Pathson of the Mwamba wa Mwaloni ," he said, his hair and robes blowing around him. The man quickly wrote the name and left.

"Calm," said the free crusader to his friend.

Seamus nodded slowly and calmed the air around him that to his surprise obeyed with the use of only the most minute energies on his part.

Xarona had been in castles all over the south and even in the east. Her family was asked to be guests at all manner of courts, from the swamp mansions of Lasana to great castle of the Emerald. and yet she had never seen anything like the Colos high castle. She was no builder, but she could tell most of it seemed hewn with great skill from the mountain itself.

"What beautiful hair," said one of the princesses who Xarona mentally noted looked almost exactly alike.

"Thank you Your grace," said the witch.

"It's like spun copper," added the slightly older young woman who liked her mother was wearing a dress that allowed her small wings to be seen.

"You flatter me too much M'lady," said Xarona.

"Please call me Tabia," said the Princess.

"I'm Xarona, of Belisona," the redhead did a slight curtsy.

"I knew you were southern by that accent," said the winged young woman. , "I do love your rustic way of talking," she added with a haughty laugh.

"Rustic," said Xarona raising an eyebrow?

"Yes with the yalls and ahs," said the Princess.

"My mistress is no rustic," said Sani who looked up from where she stood at Xarona side.

The Princess on hearing the creature speak took a step back. "Oh my dear the thing speaks," she said surprised.

Xarona watched the Princess lean over to touch Sana, who reluctantly allowed the woman to do so, "Is it housebroken," she asked.

"yes I am," said the chimera.

The Princess giggled. "It's so wonderful, where did you get it?" before looking at Xarona, 'Is it for sale?," she continued.

"It's my familiar?," said the redhead.

"You're a magician too? But I don't see a staff," Tabia.

"I'm a witch," Xarona spoke the words in a manner that would normally bring chills to most people.

The Princes smiled and started to laugh, "a Witch? We don't have those in Colos, the High Magis says they are nothing but trouble". said the girl in a matter of fact tone.

Clare stood nearby holding the plate full of multiple small cakes watching the conversation between bites of the delicious little desserts. She was finding Xarona meeting someone more prideful than her entertaining. Then she saw the witch hand move towards her wand.

"M'lady Xarona, you must try this!" she said walking up to her friend holding up a cake.

The princess turned to see the short dark haired girl in a leather bibbed dress walking towards her and the witch.

"Yes the lemon ones are the best," the Princess said, "I'm sure a girl your size would enjoy them even more so Lady Belisona,"

Clare's eyes widened, this was it, she thought, this is how she dies, Xarona disintegrates the Princess, The guard moves in, she helps her friend and dies in Colos.

Xarona smiled, "Of course Your Grace," said Xarona pushing back her anger and remembering her training and her position. The Princess smiled and took the cake from Clare and playfully placed it in Xarona's mouth.

"Well I'll leave you to it," said Tabia before heading off towards her family. Clare looked at her friend and was tempted to laugh but was stopped by the look on the redhead's face. it was anger held in check only by training.

"That waste of air?" growled Clare.

Xarona looked at her friend and pulled her away from the group.

"Watch your words, Clare, She's a princess, you're a peasant, she could have you killed with a word," said the witch.

"But the way she talked to you," said the tinkersmith looked at her friend who now wiping her lips with a lace handkerchief.

"You think that's the first time a royal called me fat?" said Xarona, " The highborn can be as uncivil as any lowborn".

Clare looked at her friend, "I swore you were going to blast her into next month" she said somewhat relieved and surprised at the witches temperament.

Xarona smiled, Blast her? Oh no, that would be too quick," said the young woman in a welcomed haughty tone.

Jase felt naked as he stood near the Salazar's, upon arriving at the room, he was asked to remove his weapons. The hunter after a few words from Callum and Isabella companied and to the surprise of everyone looking handed over his bow, arrows, two swords, nine daggers and a sharpened antler he hid in his boot. When no one was looking , however the hunter picked up a silver fork and palmed and slipped it up under his leather bracer. Feeling slightly more relaxed watched the royal family and the Slazars, not sure of exactly what his job was but staying nearby just in case.

What kind of hide is that?," a said a young man standing next to the Prince. The brown-haired young man with a thin mustache moved towards Jase and ran his hand over the blue-black leather armor on the hunter's shoulder.

"Wampus," he said.

"Wampus, impossible, whoever sold you this lied," said the man.

The young hill-man looked at the man and at his hand Like most of his people, he hated the idea of people thinking they were better just because of their family name or who their friends were.

"Don't buy it, we killed the critter ourselves," Jase returned, his voice just loud enough to cause nearby heads to turn including Kisa, Lisa, and Bhang. The Aristocrat, not accustomed to having a peasant raised their voice to him, face reddened as he figured out what to say next.

"It was amazing too, they saved an entire village," said Kisa.

"Liar, I've hunted all manner of beasts and neither I or my men have ever come close to killing a Wampus". said the mustached man to Kisa.

"Miss Kisa ain't a liar, and you best apologize for calling her one". Jase tried to take a step towards the man but was blocked by Bhang.

"I'm sure that's not what he meant," said the driver who was wearing the only court worthy clothing he owned, the gray and orange robes of a garden temple adept.

Jase started to calm down knowing his friend was only trying to protect him. Taking a step back, he was about to swallow his pride and apologize when the young noble spoke up, "Yes it was, that girl is just a big a liar as that hide wearing ragamuffin!," he bellowed out causing all eyes to fall on him. "and I demand satisfaction," he added.

The king upon hearing the words turned from his wife and his sister to see his son's oldest friend Gareth Applewhite, a young lord who's family despite being known braggarts were loyal and who's large winter apple orchards brought lots of taxes to the kingdom arguing with the scruffy young adventurer under the Salazar's employ.

"What the hell does that mean?," Jase asked out loud to no one in particular.

"I think he wants to duel". Kisa spoke up.

"Well then I.," Jase voice cut off, to his surprise and the surprise of everyone else.

Xarona moving her hands as if they were controlling a sock puppet cause Jases's head to lower and him to say, "I'm sorry, It's not my place to speak to one such as you the way I did". Jase could not believe the words coming out of his mouth nor could Bhang or Kisa.

"So you're a liar and coward," said Gareth,

Jases eyes bulged as he fought back against whatever was controlling him. Xarona could feel him fighting and reached for her wand to increase her focus. but was too late as to her surprise the Hill-man's hard-won stubbornness defeated her spell.

"The only low down coward I see here is you," said the hunter his mouth no back under his control.

"Then I take that as an acceptance, What's your weapon of choice ?" Gareth took a step toward Jase.

I get to choose?," Said the Hillman.

"Of course you do," The king spoke up. , "those are the rules".

Jase thought for a second, he could choose a bow and arrow, but knew every duel he's ever seen usually involved to much drink and swords.

"I choose swords," he finally said after some thought.

"Bully," said the king with a big smile, "Been a while since we had a proper duel, a perfect way to celebrate an engagement," he continued walking over to Gareth and Jase.

"Now gentleman, who shall be your seconds.. just in case you can't ful-fill your duties?," said the monarch.

"I will stand with Lord Gareth," said the prince. The king nodded at his son. He then looked at Jase. The hunter had no idea what a second was, in the hlls, if you ran from a fight you were coward and that was a label that branded you for life.

"I'll stand with Jase," Callum's voice boomed from behind his friend.

"Lord Wimbowaradi it is then," said the king.

The engagement part ended not long after the challenge. With no sign of malice The Salazars and adventures were escorted to the residences in the castle. For the Salazars they were given a small wing used by visiting dignitaries, the well kept and warm section of the castle not only had a kitchen but a full staff. The Adventures to their surprise was given a floor to themselves in the rear of the castle known as the "Third cousin's floor,". Xarona made a note of saying the term is used by many royals and nobles for a place you put unwanted family members. Callum and Xarona's room was large with built-in water closet and baths. and windows. and balconies that sat on opposite ends. Clare, Bhang, Jase and Seamus rooms were much smaller with communal water closet and small tub that had to be filled by one of the two servants assigned to the floor.

Once everyone was unpacked, the the Adventurers, plus Bhang headed to a common area near Xarona's room where a fire was already burning in a fireplace. For a time they sat in silence glaring at each other as if trying to find the words. Finally, Xarona, with Sani on her lap spoke. "You're an Idiot," she said to Jase.

"I was just defending Kisa," he said as he sat sharpening one of his swords. "he had no right calling her a liar".

Xarona rolled her eyes, "you don't get it," said the witch," He has all the rights here, He's a landed lord in Colos, Your just a freeman from the hills. He can kill you inside or outside a duel and no one in the castle save us would care.

"Aww, see I knew you cared" Fussybriches, said the hill-man in a manner that brought a giggle from Callum".

"And you," Xarona looked at the young lord sitting on a Sofa sitting on a bearskin rug on the floor his back against a sofa. "You should know better!," she scolded.

"The king seemed happy about all this," said Clare, "Too happy". Before the tinkersmith could say another word the witch drew her wand causing Callum and Jase to flinch as if they expected her to cast on them. With a flick, she made sure their voices didn't carry beyond the room.

"Now we can speak freely," she said,

"Good because, what gives these people the right to own other people," Seamus spoke up to everyone's surprise.

"Well I wouldn't call Trogs people," Clare.

Callum looked at the stoutkin and shook his head before speaking,

"They are people and Seamus is right, what's going on here is wrong".

Bhang looked at the group and then stood to speak, "You have all made me feel welcome and though I've oly known you for a short time I feel I need to say something for the good of all here. We should all think about our actions here before we do anything else," he said. The dark-haired man in gray and orange looked at Jase, " You are a good fighter, but I seen you use a sword, you fight to live not to win and dueling is all about winning".,

"I've bet that pampered peacock ain't never been in a real fight in his life said Jase.

"And I bet you've never been in an official duel," said Xarona.

The hunter shook his head, "no, but I ain't running from this," he said defiantly.

"We know," Clare spoke with a hint of sadness, "Just try not to die".

Jase smiled at the young woman and nodded, " That's the plan".

Everyone started to giggle at his words but stopped as soon as a servant entered the room. "Would you like some drinks," said the middle age man.

"No thank you," said Callum. The man nodded them looked at the group.

"His Grace loves sport of all kind, and hates to lose," he said barely under his breath look at Jase.

All eyes in the room widened as they watched the man leave. Once again everyone looked at each other as they wondered what the man's words meant.

"That was ominous," Seamus.

"Sure was," Jase

Callum looked up from where he sat at his friends, "It's never good when you risk speaking against the person who not only pays you but can have you hung for sneezing too loud," said the free-crusader

.

"True, I fear we've walked into a den of vipers and blindfolded," Xarona said in a concerned tone. "We need to find out what's going on before we leave the Salazars here".

"Yes we do," said Bhang who after speaking walked out the room and moved down the hall without a sound. In his travels, he had heard very little about Colos and the little he heard wasn't good which was why he and his family avoided it on his travels from the west.

Focusing his energy, he knew that most large castles had magical wards all about them, wards that detected the energy of those inside. Bhang's training allowed him to make his own energy vanish from such detections as did his physical training allows him to move swiftly and quietly. Making sure he was not seen the driver followed the servant that had spoke to them to a small room a floor down where he, collecting towels. Entering the room through an open doorway the chi-wise driver closed the door behind him.

"Tell me what you know," said Bhang startling the man.

The servant surprised and afraid took a step back, "I don't know what you're talking about," he said".

"I can tell this room isn't being observed," said the dark-haired man calmly, "I can also tell there is more going on here than we know and we need to know".

The attendant took another step back and sat down in an old wooden chair in the dimly lit room.

"The king, he's not a good man," said the servant.

"I'm starting to see that," Bhang

"Nor is his family, " the graying man continued, " They like seeing people hurt, they like hurting people. "

"Are we in danger?," Bhang.

The servant lowered his head, "As much as anyone is in this place not named Colos or related to them". he said. before standing.

"Applewhite likes cutting people, I bet he just picked your friend out because he saw he had a sword at one point". he continued.

"My friend can fight," Bhang.

The servant chuckled, "Applewhite's a never lost, and he faced real duelist, who either got sick or hurt before the fight".

"Magic?," the driver knew the answer to his question even as he said it and while the servant never responded verbally the look on the man's face and the ebb and flow of his energy said everything.

*****

Kisa and Lisa walked through the castles hall in matching lavender and purple dresses, their dark hair up in matching silk ribbons.

Lisa could feel her sisters distress and also see from her expression her brilliant mind was at work. Lisa, though she would never say it was impressed and occasionally in awe by how much her twin knew.

"This place is beautiful," said the more outgoing twin trying to start a conversation.

No, it's not, It's horrible". Kisa stopped and looked around.

Lisa took her sister's hand and looked into her tear-filled eyes. "It's not your fault," she said softly.

Kisa pulled away, "No it's not, But it was mine to fix, I could have spoken up, but I didn't!', she said balling her fist.

Both girls stood in the hall in silence while courtiers and servants walked past. Lisa knew her sister like everyone else was so caught up in the moment and so shocked, that silence was the only option. As the girl said she suddenly felt something not coming from her sister, a coldness in the air coming from a nearby corridor.

Bhang had told her in time her awareness would increase if she kept training and though her family did not notice she did, just that, waking at night to perform her "dances" and to meditate.

"Come on," she said to her sister, pulling her by an arm behind her.

"Lisa!," cried out the girl in glasses as she was guided back the way they came and down another hall at just short of a full run.

Lisa hoped whatever was happening would be something that would take her sister's mind off her problems. The two girls found their way to stairs going down.

"What's going on," Kisa.

"Shhhh," said Lisa finger to her lips, "I feel something".

Kisa rarely saw her sister excited by anything not involving romance books, shopping or other frivolous things. Yet today there was none of that usual hyper-activity, instead, there was a focus about her that was both new and disconcerting.

Both girls moved down the stairs as quick as there feet would allow, eventually coming to a walled balcony with slit-like opening overlooking what looked to be a large entryway connected to a door leading to the outside. The girls peaked through the slits at men gathering in the area below. Each one was dressed for the cold with Fur and leather long coats with hoods. Some carried long pikes, others swords and shields, and bow.

In the rear, a few carried large burlap bags.

"Where's your leader," said a man dressed in the green and white of a Colos soldier. Kisa knew by metal breastplate and leggings under his tabard and the high collar he was an officer. She also noticed a small raised area on the man's back, the kind of area that would cover small wings.

"Gravix is coming, he has a big one for you," said a grey-haired man with pale skin and multiple facial tattoos.

"Their Estahutten," whispered the girl in glasses to her sister.

"Esta what?," Lisa

"Northman, far, far north near giant lands," she returned keeping her voice down.

Just as the girl finished talking a shadowed darkened the group of men and sound of something large being dragged could be heard.

"Stop your lollygagging let's get paid and get back to camp, I got Flicks and Gritters to put in my stew," said a booming deep voice.

Kia and Lisa watched as a giant, standing close to twelve feet tall with pale blond hair, a matching beard, ice blue eyes and slate blue skin entered dressed in the fur-trimmed leather pants, shirt, and vest and wearing spiked iron-shod boots and gauntlets. in one hand he carried a great ax made of frost covered metal and in other, he dragged behind him a great long-necked white stag with four sets of horns.

"Alomeg no," said Kisa looking at the creature in knowing it was a roan one of the great beasts she had only read about. Known for being gentle and acting as guardians of the creature of the forest, according to some stories, killing them brought bad luck.

The Colos officer walked up to the Giant and looked at the creature,

" You finally caught the bastard that was killing our hunters in the Misty path," he said.

"Yeah, and a Gritter and Flick hunting party too," said the giant in a thick northern accent.

The man in the rear moved forward opening their bag and emptying out the heads of trogs and fae before the officer.

"They're a lot easier to hunt since they started working together". said the one of the Estahutten.

The soldier looked the heads and checked each one by hand. before standing.

"Twenty-three heads, Fifteen Gritters, nine Ficks, plus the Roan that's six hundred and thirty gold," he said wiping his hands on a handkerchief before gesturing to call a younger solider in the chainmail forward carrying two jingling bags of coin.

The band of hunters and the Giants watched as the officer counted out the coins from the bags and handed over to a thin older Estahuten dressed in a robe of leather strips and carrying a staff ending in deer antlers.

"Thank you M'lord," said the man placing the gold in a bag".

"Otis, divvy the gold up when we get back to camp," said the Giant, I'll have words with this chickened winged ponce".

The old man nodded and walked past the giant, all but three of his band of hunters followed.

"Be careful how you speak to me monster," said the officer fighting back the fear he felt.

Gravix looked down at the man and smiled

"You be best to remember what I am. The giant said grabbing the soldier next to the officer with his large hands biting off his head and throwing the still bleeding body against a wall.

"Because I can kill you and half this castle before you bring me down," he said after chewing the head and swallowing.

A woman's scream startled the men and giants from, bellow. Lisa looked at her sister who liked her was now crying. Both of them had screamed in unison merging the sound into one inside the hallway and alerting the men below.

"Get 'em," Gravix said to his men who sprinted up a nearby series of stairs leading to the balcony.

"Stop!" the officer yelled to the men only to be knocked to the ground by a Gravix, The Giant rushed past him and with a frost covered ax swung at the balcony, shattering a wall and chilling the area. .

Kisa and Lisa watched a nearby wall and floor collapse. Grabbing each other hand and turning towards the way they came the two girls ran.

"There ," said a man in furs and leather pointing at the girls before reaching out towards them as he cut them off. Upon seeing his intent, Lisa pushed herself forward and slid under his grasp pulling Kisa along. who despite stumbling kept step.

The two girls once past ran up the stairs the way they came even as a spear flew past them. Kisa glanced at her rear, three men were gaining ground and one was nocking an arrow on a short bow at full stride.

"Help," called out Lisa, her voice echoing in the halls just as she felt a stabbing pain in her leg.

Jase hated the fact his friends were right, his stubbornness and pride had not only put his life at risk but Callum's. As he sat looking at his friends he wished he had just backed down.

"I'm sorry," he said surprising himself with his own words.

"Nothing to be sorry for as far as I'm concerned," said Seamus.

"And it's not like at some point we didn't expect your bull-headedness to get us in trouble eventually," quipped a smiling Xarona.

"We're with you to the end," Callum stood.

"No matter how bitter or bloody," added Clare. "Even if you're gutted,"

Everyone looked at the girl and started laughing.

"That's one way of putting it," said Sani.

Smoosh climbed off Seamus and up to Jase,

Jase smiled and picked the creature up.

" Help, ," a far away voice that only the keen eared hill-man could hear .

Standing the Hunter moved quickly out the room, closing his eyes he sniffed the ear and listened as Smoosh leaped over to Seamus' hand

"Jase?," Clare spoke softly.

Something's wrong," he said from where he stood. a familiar scream in the distance that to his keen ears was little more than a whisper.

"Lisa!," he said running back into the room grabbing his swords.

The warrior's wheel was a rite that if done right, if done with the right people, or so Callum was told never broke. It granted a connection, an understanding that strengthens ties to those who fought together. Everyone in the room knew something was going on and that they needed to be ready.

Xarona released her spell drawing in any excess energy as Seamus touched the ground with his staff, using the stone itself as a conduit. The multiple wards in the castle would detect his magic but he didn't care. He felt Jase's panic and it added to his own.

Callum Sprinted down the hall to his room, opened the door and grabbed his hammer. He then sprinted back, catching up to his friends who where who were running down the hall towards stairs.

"Somethings blocking me," Seamus said frustrated.

"Don't fight it, use it," said Xarona.

Seamus still focusing on the stone, as he tapped his staff on the ground with each step he took found the energy of someone willing his magic to stop. Using his own energy Seamus pushed into the blocking ward and through it, connecting him briefly with the dozens of wards in the castle. Intruders signaled a ward in the lower military entrance corridors to another before yet another signaled to that ward, the intruders were temporary allies. It was a complicated setup and one that pushed his energy back after a few seconds.

"Down and to the left then right ," he said noticing a determined looking hunter was already heading in that direction, three steps at a time.

Lisa used all her meger training to ignore the pain in her calf.

"I'm not being kidnapped twice," she grunted.

Kisa nodded helping her sister the twins moved up the stairs calling out to anyone.

"Frails think they can get away from us," said the man with the bow reading another arrow.

"So you think Gravix wants them dead or alive," said a man moving in on the two girls his sword drawn.

"Who cares," said the third man, "He's gonna eat'em and better them than me".

Lisa could feel the blood pouring down her leg soaking into her dress and shoe

"Kisa, Get out of here I'll hold them off". said the injured twin.

"No Lisa," said the other girl just as she felt a hand grab her from behind.

Both girls started to fall. Kisa reached into a slit in her dress that her mother had folded and pinned and pulled out a stilelleto as the man drew her close.

"What do we have here," the man grabbed her hand at the wrist looked at the dagger and turned her arm behind her till she felt her elbow dislocate.

"This one was about to get all stabby:"he said with a smile.

Lisa saw the man grab his sister as she struggled to stand. Another man put his foot on her chest.

"Oh no missy, we'll have none of that," said the Eastahuten headhunter. drawing a small curved dagger from a special holder on the back of his belt and leaned over, place the blade to Lisa's throat, "Say one more word and I'll be putting your head on my wall back up north next to my last two wives".

CHAPTER 17: WAKING SECRETS

Lisa wanted to panic, and scream, but through her recent travels, she had not only been taught how to push back her fears but have seen others do the same.

Closing her eyes the young woman focused her energy knowing she would only get one chance. Opening her eyes, she grabbed the man leaning over her by the wrist, twisted it and pulled sending him to her and the floor. Without looking back, she rammed her feet into the head of the man behind her and sprung towards the man holding her sister.

The lithe girl in lavender ignored the slash a new arrow left in her side , hit the man in front of her square in the face releasing the "Kai," focusing yell that Bhang had taught her. The headhunter staggered back and released Kisa who fell to the ground crying.

"I'm going to skin you girl," said the man who Lisa had thrown coming to his feet. Kisa on seeing the man starting to rise realized she still had a weapon in her hand and with a rage she never allowed herself to feel moved up the stairs, her mind going through likely scenarios. The man had twice her weight, was armed, but due to the steps was standing off balanced. Stepping to the man's side and then pushing, the girl caused her foe to stagger ,opening him up for a well-placed stab between the stitches on his leather armor and into his kidney.

Lisa could-could feels her body growing weak from blood loss even as she swept the man's leg and spun to bring her foot down on the man's throat.

"Stand still you crazy Frail!," said a bowman who was reading another arrow as he watched his friend struggle with the foot in his throat.

Lisa turned just as the arrow left the bow and started to fly at her. Her thoughts first went to her sister than her parents then Bernardo. It then went to her wasting most of her life. Accepting her faith the girl suddenly felt a wind coming down from the top of the stairs that caused the arrow to changed course and hit a wall.

Kisa looked up from where she stood; her attacker slumped over her, her, She knew one stab wouldn't do on a man his size and had repeated her actions multiple times in a fearful frenzy that only stopped upon seen her parents hired adventurers heading towards her and her sister. Feeling the exhaustion of terror, Kisa relaxed and fell as did the man over her.

"You bastards don't know who you're dealing with," called the Estahutten knocking another arrow as a bolt of purple lightning hit him in the chest sending him into a wall. Small fires started to erupt on his body and as he opened his mouth to scream a gout of purple fire flew out burying his tongue to ash and charring his teeth.

Xarona lowered her wand; she knew witch fire was a painful way to die., it burned people and animals from the inside out if the casting was powerful enough. After casting her spell, the witch watched Jase move towards the man Lisa was holding down and Callum towards Kisa. The free-crusader lifted the man off the girl with one hand and slowly helped the dagger-wielding twin stand.

"Kisa?," he said looking into the girl's sad eyes.

The girl upon seeing her friends face leaned into him and allowed herself faint.

Lisa released her foot and for the first time saw what she had done, the man was purple in the face and dead. She had never even thought about taking a life before, but as she looked at the man, she felt no remorse. Turning she saw Callum with her sister and hobbled towards them falling only to be caught by Jase.

"Good job," said the Hunter who was now hearing footsteps coming from up the and down the stairs.

"I think there's more," he called out.

Seamus held his staff high sheathing it in flame illuminating the wide, steep stairwell. Xarona stated preparing a series of spells in her mind, Sani took on her wildcat form, and Clare extended her staff.

"Halt," called out the officer the twins had seen before, behind him was over a dozen Colos guards.

It looked like the cavalry arrived too late," Said Jase lowering his swords.

"Everyone releases your spells and place all weapons, wands, and staves on the ground," said a sergeant in a shiny breastplate.

From down the stairs came another group of guards.

"We're not the brigands here," said Xarona.

"Silence," said the young officer leading the guard from the top of the stairs. "You've disturbed the peace of Colos, and the king will decide who's the brigand,"

"The girls are hurt, let me help them," Callum asked.

"We have healers here Giantkin," said officials.

"What should we do Fussybritches," Jase spoke out loud raising his swords again. "these are your kind of folk,".

Xarona looked at the situation, they were outnumbered, and even with magic, there would most likely be casualties on their side.

"We surrender," said the witch.

The guard as commanded by their officers gathered up the adventures and twins weapons, staff, and wand. They then bound their hand in cold iron shackles, or in Callum's case thick chains. The Colos guard did their best to keep the incident quiet, yet despite their efforts news of the altercation had spread quickly. Vinceno, Isabella, Bhang, and Bernardo were already on their way to the king's audience chamber when the arresting officer, Lord Kenin, two court magicians, Jazlyn and the High Magis was arriving with the prisoners including their now mostly healed daughters.

"Kisa, Lisa!," called out Isabella. To her daughters who were wearing metal chains.

"What's going on here Your Grace,". Vinceno walked towards Jazlyn. Two guards stood to block him, but the princess moved past them.

"That's for my brother to decide," said the woman.

" Do I need to hire a barrister?," Vinceno.

"That's not how we do it here," said the white-haired woman, " The king has the final say and will judge the thenaccording to our laws and his will,"

The Queen's sisters then lead the guards, prisoners, and wizard into the audience chambers. The Salazar's and Bhang followed closely with Isabella's eyes filling with tears and anger as the group waited for the monarch of Colos to arrive, which for the girl's mother seemed like an eternity.

King Palth Colos, entered the room with a look of annoyance on his face. Walking to his throne the burly graying blond sat down and listened to his officers first, Kenin who was the officer talking to the Estahutten told the story exactly as it had happen, he, however, used the word spies when referring to Kisa and Lisa.

Kisa in great detail and with the tone of an expert storyteller told everything she saw and heard. Her words even managed to move a few of the guards next to her as they could almost feel the fear her and her sister felt. Jase and the others had a chance to speak towards the end, but by the look on the king's face, he by then bored and uninterested.

"Your Majesty the prisoners," the scribe spoke as he walked to stand before the king. The white-haired monarch nodded and gestured with a hand, signaling the guard to bring the adventurers forward.

"Shall I state their crimes, Your Grace," said. the scribe.

Ignoring the man, the king stood and looked the group over.

"No," he said. "Lady Belasona and Lord Wimbowaradi no matter their involvement cannot be tried for the death of those beneath their station.

," he said gruffly.

"The other three are licensed members of the adventurers guild who as I heard were protecting the Salazar's daughters who they are under contract to. therefore, they were just doing their job". he continued.

The scribe nodded, and the guards unshackled the five of the prisoners.

"Also, I'm still looking forward to that duel," The king's eyes fell on Jase, who nodded in return.

As the guards escorted the former prisoners to where the Salazars stood Callum noticed that Shane's wrist was raw and bleeding,

"What happened. he asked his friend.

"I think It's the iron," he said looking at the raw area and the discolored skin nearby. , "That's never happened before," the magician's voice showed the amount of pain he was feeling.

"I can try to heal them," said the Free Crusader.

"Not now," said the blond looking at Isabella who was still in tears as the king looked at his daughters.

"What of you two," he said, "You have no contracts or title to protect you, what was your part in this," asked the king.

Kisa took a step forward, "your Grace, I'm sorry about what happened, but my sister was just defending me and I her. " she said.

"So you said," Palth looked at the tan skinned girl, then to her sister before he continued speaking coldly, "Your story moved me, but someone needs to pay for the murder of those under my employ,"

"Then let it be me," Lisa spoke up to everyone's surprise.

The king nodded, "Very well, For your crime, which in the words of your sister was the murder of at least one of my men. I sentence you to death by hanging".

The room went silent until the Isabella wail filled the air.

"No," please I beg of you, cried out Vinceno.

"Please," Bernardo, "Not my sisters,"

Lisa looked at Kisa and lowered her head, She had no idea what her sentence would have been but was glad that at least her sister would be spared.

"This is horse Shit," Jase whispered to his friends as he started going over who he needed to kill first in his mind. From where he stood he could grab a sword and kill the guard next to him. And start his way towards the king. He would most likely die before getting there, but the hill-man had cheated death many times in his young life, and if it were to claim him now at least, there would be some worth to it.

Xarona looked at the hunter, "He's the king, and though I agree with you, here his word is the law,"

"We have to be smart here," Clara spoke up just as Vinceno moved towards the king hands raised,

"Please your majesty, take me, and spare my daughter," begged the silk merchant.

Callum saw it first, then everyone else, a smile, ever so slightly come across the king's face. The monarch leaned back on his throne, " As you wish, I don't care who dies as long as someone dies," he said.

Isabella looked at her husband only to see him glance at her and shake his head.

"Then it's settled," Jaslyn spoke up from when she stood next o her brother's wife. "As is tradition, Vinceno Salazar will be put to death tomorrow day after tomorrow sunrise,"

The king gesture after his sister spoke signaling to the guards to free the girls and place their father in shackles. The girls ran to their mother's side as she sat on the ground sobbing. Bernardo looked across the room at his father.

He wanted to say something to him, to the king but he knew the die was cast, and his father's fate was set, for now.

*****

"So what's the plan?," Clare looked at her friends as they sat on their floors common area once again under a sphere of silence cast by Xarona.

"We can't fight a kingdom," Xarona spoke solemnly, "And there is no way to get help from outside of Colos, we just don't have the time,"

"They hang people faster here than they do in the Hills, least there they give you a week to make your peace," said the hill-man who was now sharpening his arrows.

"That's the idea, "Callum looked up from where he was focusing white energy into Seamus' wrist, "My folks preferred hard labor over killing prisoners except when there was no choice, and even then we gave them time as Jase said... a week".

"So that's it, we let Vinceno die because the king here loves a good murder," Clare spoke stood her hands up in the air in frustration.

"Callum, if we get Vinceno to Arden, do you think your cousin would help?," Seamus spoke up looking at the large red scabs on his wrists. The pain had lessened but and he could feel the effects of the cold iron poisoning on his magic ebbing.

"Maybe, at the very least we will be in a better position," Lord Wimbowaradi looked at his friend wishing he could have done a better job. Cold Iron was used to ground the magic of magicians and witches and could in some cases leave large welts, but the effect they had of Seamus was more like a bad burn.

Bhang looked at the group, he knew they meant well. He also knew that if given a chance they would do something stupid and mostly end up dying.

"Vinceno's fate is set, our goal from this point on is to make sure no other Salazar's meet a similar or worse fate," said the dark haired driver.

"I don't think I can do that," Jase.

Bhang for the first time the group has ever heard raise his voice, "Yes you can, we all can. He accepted his fate, and we should respect that, but apparently, Lisa and Kisa saw something that no one wanted them to, and there may still be repercussions for that".

"He has a good point," Xarona looked at the group, "We need to get back to work and make sure the Salazar's get through this not only physically but emotionally," After a silence only broken by the cooing of Smoosh who now sat on its master's head, the group started preparing for what was to come.

*****

Jase stepped into the small arena that was built on a terrace near the bottom of the castle grounds. The arena had raised stone walls above which sat a single row of seats. The hunter had followed his friend's suggestions, after the meeting, he sequestered himself and ate and drunk only from their personal supplies. Also despite the lack of comfort he sad not slept outside but instead in bed under the watchful eye of Clare and surrounded by Magic wards set by Seamus.

Before dawn, he dressed in a leather doublet, his buckskin pants, and boots and headed towards the area escorted by Callum and four guardsmen.

Clare and Xarona had asked to come also but was told women were not allowed at duels. Thankfully for the guards, the free-crusader was present and talked the witch out of reducing each of misogynistic guards to the size of insects. Before leaving Clare kissed Jase on the check and Xarona, not one for public displays of too much affection took the tall lord's hand and had him lean over for her to whisper something in his ears that left him with a scandalized smile on his face. After the men had left Clare looked at the redhead.

"What did you say?," she asked unable to hold back her own smile.

"Don't make me kill you," said the witch in a manner both playful and cold. , "I hate killing people I like,"

Clare nodded and stayed silent.

Jase looked up at the seats, Bernardo and Vinceno were both presents. Next to them stood Bhang. Prince Arnic and Lord Gareth Applewhite entered from a door opposite Callum and Jase, at the same time above entered the king, The Scribe, High Magis, a few well-dressed generals and four guards.

"Ten gold on the scruffy hill-boy," said one of the generals.

"I'll take that," said the High Magis.

"Hmm, I bet you've already placed on spells that'll turn the lad into a sloth mid fight or some such," Said the general instantly regretting his wager.

"He better not, I want to be entertained with blood and steel, not with sorcery," said the king.

"I would never Your grace," said the man with the staff. The wizard had a few hours before tried to "hedge," his future bets by casting a spell that would sour Hunter's stomach, but could not find him magically. The "backwoods," a faekin wizard was far more skilled than he had thought when it came to magic and though he could break the wards the young man had cast, it would not go unnoticed.

The king looked at the combatants and opened a small drawer in the handle of his throne and took a cigar that his High-Magis then lit. Long ago, he was a duelist, and the loved of blood on snow and sand and the struggle of life and death.

After taking few puffs, the king stood, " Lord Applewhite and Freeman Jase," are you ready?" he asked.

Jase nodded at Gareth who was swinging his sword fancifully.

The hill-man could smell past the bravado and knew his opponent was afraid.

"Yes Your grace," said his son's friend bowing,"

The king then looked at the seconds. , "Are You Ready Lord Wimbo-waradi and Prince Arnic?"

The seconds nodded and bowed almost at the same time.

"Alomeg, bless this madness," said Callum.

"Is that all you got?," asked Jase sarcastically.

"That's all I dare," said the Free Crusader," I might need all my grace to keep you alive" after Callum spoke he found himself slightly amused by his own words as did Jase. Who had not drawn his sword yet?

Another door opened, and a short but thin man with pale hair and the hawkish nose of the lords of Colos entered. He was dressed in White and carried a white cane. Walking to the center of the arena he motioned the opponents forward.

"Single sword, if your weapon is lost or broken there will be no quarter given and he said to both of them.

"Die well peasant," said Gareth with a smug look on his face.

Jase looked at the lord and smiled.

The reeve took a step back and spoke.

"Let it be known that if any party would like to apologize and end this affair, they should speak up now,"

Both young men remained silent.

The reeve raised his staff. All murmurs and wagers in the audience stopped. Jase had never fought in a duel like this, but figured without instruction, lowering the staff meant it was time to fight. Locking eyes with his adversary he waited.

"Begin!," said the Reeve lowering the staff.

Gareth waited, he was taught to get the measure of a foe first. He watched the dark haired adventurer take a step back and draw his sword, then remain still.

Both men looked at each other waiting and watching.

"Well that's different," said the king. leaning in from where he sat.

"Are they afraid?," asked the High Magis.

"No, just sizing each other," said a general leaning forward in his seat.

Jase listened closely, he could hear the man across from him breathe, he could hear his heartbeat and the sound of his foot moving in the sand and snow. Suddenly Gareth lunged forward and stabbed with his sword and followed up with a swipe. Jase sidestepped the stab but rolled into the slice. The cut made on his arm was minor. Seeing his opponent bleed the young lord moved in slicing neck high but hitting only air.

Jase seeing an opening slid under the high slice and stabbed down piercing the Lords leather boot.

"Dirty Move," called out the High Magis.

" You can do it Jase!," called out Bernardo, forgetting where he was and feeling embarrassed by the jubilation he suddenly felt".

Gareth took a step back slowly unable to put pressure on his injured feet. Flashing a grimace at the southern hunter he expression was met with a smile.

"I'm going to kill you boy!" growled the lord, steadying himself and slicing. Jase seeing the man was hurt and unable to maneuver, parried the slice, then another and blocked a stab before finding an opening and stabbing catching Gareth in the side and running him through.

The crowd watched as Gareth fell to the ground holding his blood-stained side.

"Told you, " said the general. , "The scruffy boy waited, he took advantage and didn't get fancy. ,"

"How did you know he does that?," said another general opening a coin purse.

I used to be that boy, unlike you M'lord, I wasn't born into my position ," he said.

The king's eyes were still on the arena. Arnic looked at Jase and started to draw his sword. The hunter on seeing what the prince was doing took a step back and prepared himself for an attack.

The surprising sound of thunder filled the arena and shook the ground as Lord Wimbowaradi dropped his hammer's head on the ground while holding the handle. The Prince stopped.

Callum moved quickly to Gareth and kneeled, placing his hand on the young man's bloody side.

"What are you doing?," hissed the bleeding Lord.

"Trying to save you," The free-crusader spoke bluntly.

"No!," the king stood and spoke, "Let him bleed,"

Callum looked up at the monarch, "Your Grace, I think, I can save him," he said.

"He'll live or die by his own strength, not yours," The ruler of Colos raised a hand, doors at each end of the arena opened. Guards wearing leather armor and carrying spears entered.

"Come on Hoss," Jase placed a hand on his friend's shoulder.

The fist of Alomeg stood and took a step back.

"But.," he said softly.

"Let it go," Jase. the hunter moved his hand to his friends back and led him past the guards to an open door and out of the arena.

Xarona sat next to Kisa and Isabella. Fiddling with her gloves as Santi and smoosh played on the floor of the large bedroom. She had said her apologies to the family in passing, but despite that, she was racked with guilt. Maybe if she was more observant or more powerful, she could have figured out a way to save Vinceno.

Yet no matter how much she thought about it, there was no way out, nothing shy of a miracle and that was something the Lady of the Crossroads wasn't known for, at least not the kind of miracle she needed. She wasn't a priestess of her faith and feared more the result of prayer than her current situation. Still, the temptation was there.

"It'll work out," Kisa looked at her friend as she spoke, "Callum and Jase will walk through that door.,". Xarona shook her head,

"Those two idiots? I'm not worried about them and their men games. I'm worried about your father. " said the ginger lady.

Kisa lowered her head, upon hearing the witches words, the situation she had fought so hard to push away came flooding back and her eyes filled with tears.

"Please, let's not talk about it," said the girl.

Xarona nodded, her helplessness increased, even with her friends help if they would be fighting against an army. Even if she had a coven of witches she thought, they would most likely lose, she thought. Then like a wave it hit her, Witches she thought, when she came into town, there was no sigils, which marked the town as having a head witch.

"Muses!," exclaimed the Redhead.

All eyes in the room fell on her Xarona who stood, "Where are the witches?," she said out loud.

"Doing witch stuff?," Clare, "Which is causing trouble and being general nuisances, present company excepted, ,".

Xarona rolled her eyes, "I've been here two days and the head which hasn't made her presence known nor has any other witch.

Seamus looked at the woman, "On a similar note, On the ride here I didn't see a single temple spire or dome,"

"What do you think it means if it means anything," Lisa.

"I'm not sure, But I think it's about time I talk to my people," Seamus moved towards the door, then stopped, " That is if you think you'll be fine without me,"

"Go," Xarona said waving the young wizard away. , " We're short on information and if you think the fae here can help then by all means,"

Seamus nodded and left the room and headed down the hall almost running into Callum, Jase, Bhang, Bernardo, and to everyone's surprise Vinceno.

"What's the hurry blondie," Jase.

The wizard upon seeing his friends ran up to them hugging Callum then Jase. "You're alive,"

"It was barely a fight," said Bernardo doing his best to sound enthusiastic. "Our hunter made quick work of him,"

"Did you..," The blond young man looked at hill-man, "You Killed him?". he asked

Jase shook his head, "I cut him good, and I think Callum could have saved him, but his royal nibs made him stop, The bastard wanted to see a man die,"

Seamus' eyes widened with shock, "Do you think he's mad?" he asked.

"I think we shouldn't be calling the king mad in his castle's hall," Callum spoke softly.

"Good point," Vinceno spoke up.

Seamus looked at Bernardo "I'm sorry, I know he's going to be your father-in-law soon,"

Bernardo face turned from placid to furious, "Bull Shite, I'm not going to marry into house that plots to kill my father!," shouted the merchant's son.

"Again, not in the halls," Callum.

"I have an errand to run," Seamus spoke and started back the way he was headed.

"Do you need help?," suggested Bernardo.

"No, go be with your family, I shouldn't be long," The Wizard locked eyes with the handsome young man for as long as he dared and then turned away. Resisting looking back, he swiftly made his way o the stairs and downward. Not exactly sure where he was going he focused his energies and thoughts on his fae side and finding something to connect to the young magician moved to the entrance floor he passed a group of guards and turned down a hall to an opening on almost pure instinct. Past the opening was a small courtyard and garden. Flowers bloomed around a steaming pond.

Moving to the pond, Seamus looked into it to see tiny brown lizards with stone-like skin swimming in them.

"Blurp," On his shoulder a familiar sound

"I thought I left you in the room he said to Smoosh as the creature faded into view.

"Smoosh shook his head, Seamus knew it didn't want him to be alone. The connection between him and creature seemed to be growing daily, yet despite that Smoosh seemed to be able to vanish without any detection if it wanted.

The octopod moved to along the magician's shoulder then scrambled down Seamus's arm and leaped.

"Sorry little guy," You'll boil like a mudbug in there said the wizard catching his leaping familiar.

"You'll be surprised," spoke a voice from a nearby a small group of trees.

Seamus turned to a fae dressed in a white dress, "Octopods tend to be very adaptive," she added.

" Are you sure?', asked the blond young man

The girl who either looked more feminine then the usually androgynous or because of the wizards closer connection to his heritage was just more identifiable as a female walked up to then faekin and held out a hand, prompting the tiny eight-legged creature to jump to it. The girl then knelt and watched the creature test the water with its stubby tentacle pull back and closed its eyes as its skin folded and shimmered and became rock like Smoosh then let out a sound of glee and jumped in.

"Thank you," Seamus.

"It's a pleasure," you are a guest here, said the girl.

"I guess," "Seamus, "Although I'm pretty sure I'm not a welcomed guest,"

The girl looked about, after the wizard spoke and took his sleeve and lead him to the trees she was standing in, once then she gestured causing the trees barks to creak and the branches to close in closer.

"Watch your words, The king's wizard listens as does his sister," said the girl.

"Callum was right," Seamus spoke.

"Who?," the girl looked confused.

"My friend, bg guy with hammer that weighs as much as you," said the wizard.

"The Titankin," nodded and the girl nodded, "You keep powerful company,"

Seamus smiled, "we're not powerful," he said,

"I can feel what you are, what you can be," said the girl.

The wizard looked at the girl, despite her appearance, she sounded older, less like a girl and more like a wise woman.

" May I ask your name," he asked.

The girl thought for a second," the people here call me Snowflower, that will do,"

"I'm Seamus," said the young man holding out a hand. The girl looked at his hand then took both her hands and placed them on his cheeks, "This is how we do it," she said closing her eyes and opening her energy to him.

The wizard was almost overwhelmed with what he felt; she was old, older than his mother, older than Lady Soru Wimbowaradi who as far as known was just a few years shy of a hundred. Aside from age and power the magical also felt her state of mind, happiness mixed with fear.

Slowly Seamus touched her cheeks and relaxed. Snowflower could feel the young man's fear and his connection to his friends.

"You're part of a Fáinne contract," she said.

"A what?," Seamus questioned, lowering his hands, just as she did.

"You've made the pact, with your friends, you are bonded," Snow-flower.

Seamus nodded, "My friend called it the warrior's wheel" The magician upon saying the words suddenly felt the ancientness of the connection and its history.

"So brother," said Snowflower, "How did you earn your freedom?'

Seamus' eyes widened, "My freedom, I was born a free man," he said.

The girl smiled, "So you're not the bastard of a Colos Lord and a sister of the Great trees?," she asked.

"No, where I come from all are born free. We may kneel before a lord or king, but our lives are mostly ours,"

"You're lucky," said the girl., "Here we either serve the kings and his vassals, or we are slaughtered,"

The wizard could feel the sorrow in the girl, sorrow that fed his growing anger. "Why don't you fight,? he asked.

The girl chuckled, "The Avains, fought and they were killed and burned out hundreds of years ago, this castle was once their home. We fought, and our mother trees were burned, the Throg fought, and they were slaughtered in their cave warrens. I've seen thousands die and I've lost anything resembling hope,"

"Are there any more of you... use left," Seamus words surprised him, he had never considered himself fae, even when he found out his true parentage, but standing in front of Snowflower, hearing and feeling her tale of woe he suddenly feels connected.

"Yes, But Gravix and his northmen slaughter them and all the other creatures of magic the Colos cannot control,"

"What's a Gravix?," The wizard asked seeing his the fae girls face grow paler than it already was.

"He's a Giant, A full one not like your Titankin friend, And leads the hunters that kill our kind and the others for bounties set by the king. " Snowflower eyes filled with tears as she spoke.

"That's horrible, I mean we, have to do something," Seamus,

"As I said, they have slaughtered many of us, driven more into hiding, Even the witches hide their power in these lands,"

Before the young wizard could respond, he felt Smoosh climbing his robes and onto his shoulder. He could tell something had frightened the creature. Turning towards the pond and viewing through the leaves and limbs he could see Bernardo's fiance enter the courtyard flanked by two fae women.

"I must go," said Snowflower.

"I guess I'll stay here till she leaves," Seamus.

"No need, She's not the smartest human," said Snowflower leading Seamus out of the small grove.

"What this? ," said the Princess to the blond man and her servant.

after a quick curtsey, Snow Flower looked at her mistress, "I'm sorry, I was just showing the Young Wizard around," she said,

The Princess looked at the magician and nodded, " Did you show him the little basilisks?" she asked.

"Yes your grace," Snowflower lead Seamus to the opening leading into the courtyard.

"Thank you Snowflower and thank you, your Grace," said the magician. The princess upon hearing the words nodded and watched the willowy young man make his exit.

*****

Seamus made his way back to the Salazar's wing of the castle. Coming through the doors that marked the area's entrance, he a group of guards had gathered in the hall along with Prince Arnic

"I don't care what father says, I'm not letting that peasant get away with killing my friend," said the Prince.

The magician upon hearing the words moved into a nearby alcove before he was noticed. Focusing in any light near him, he willed them to dim, hoping it would make him harder to see.

"M'lord we're your guard, we do what you will," said one of the soldiers.

"Good, They have magic on their side, so be careful, try to spare my sister's man if you can," added the blond young man in white doublet, pants, and cape.

"I hate this place," said Seamus to himself," he knew attacking the prince was grounds for instant execution and despite what the Prince thought his dozen guards we're in for far more of a fight than they thought.

Taking a deep breath, the young wizard of the Mwamba wa Mwaloni released his dimming spell and stepped from the alcove releasing a gust of wind that alerted the guard.

"Your grace," he said with bravado, I know you may not wish to hear this, but I feel I must warn you, you can't win this,"

The prince turned to see the faekin magician behind him, hand on staff.

"Are you threatening me peasant?'

Seamus shook his head, "No your grace, I just know you are angry and upset and might not be thinking straight,"

The Arnics looked at his men then, "Your friend killed Lord Applewhite," He said in an angry tone.

"In a Duel, overseen by a reeve and your father," added Seamus.

"That has nothing to do with it," growled the young royal.

Seamus nodded, "Not at this moment, I know, but I would be remiss in my duties as a guest not to do my best to keep you from being harmed," said the magician.

"Harmed how?," Prince's voice calmed some.

"Well, you have twelve, of what I'm sure are capable men," said the magician. " Now keeping in mind that though I'm a simple country wizard but I'm pretty good at math, and from what I see you don't have the numbers needed to do what you have planned.

"My men are the best in Colos," said the Prince.

"Of that, I have no doubt," said Seamus, but this is a narrow hall, and if you rush in you'll be dealing with all manner of magic and the like," the magician walked towards the prince, hiding the fear he felt as he talked.

"Now Jase can take two, four if he has his bow," Bhang, our driver, is a Chi wise fighter, he's good for two or three. Now Lisa, who has already killed a man can occupy one. That's five, considering a best-case scenario ," The magical smiled.

"That leaves seven," said the Prince, "and me," The young royal drew a sword.

"Yes. Well, Clare our tinkersmith probably had the door rigged and whoever opens it wrong might lose a hand or two, so that's six. There will be some hesitation on your part after that and say Lord Wimbowaradi will be good for three if he's unprepared. Leaving you and two men left,". Seamus looked at the man with pity in his eyes.

"And then I guess we kill you first," The prince said coldly.

Seamus nodded, Of course, that goes without saying, but then there's the Lady Belasona , I hope you've said prayers because the only mercy you'll receive when facing her will be from the god of your choice.

The Princes' eyes widened, "We don't have gods here, All our actions, all our successes are ours alone," said the Prince.

Shrugging Seamus placed down his staff, "Really, then I guess your men being turned into mice and two-headed crabs," will be your folly alone, Your grace," continued the magician.

From down the hall, the door to the room the Prince and his men were about to enter by force opened reveling Xarona who had sensed Seamus was near and in distress thanks to her group's seemingly growing connection.

"Your Grace," she said curtseying, is there a problem?

The prince looked at the witch as she tapped her wand in her hand in a manner that both he and his men found intimidating

"Because if there is a problem, I would be happy to help," she added emphasizing her words with another tap.

"I was just talking with the young Magis," said the Prince, "It was a fascinating tale of Arithmetic,". said the thin blond man in white.

"I do love numbers," said the woman before smiling in a manner both playful; and intimidating

The prince looked at his men; there was no doubt they would die for him but would they endure a fate far worse?

Not wanting to find out, the young royal bowed politely at the woman down the hall, He then signaled to his men to follow him. Passing the magician, he looked the faekin in the face and nodded in a manner that showed his respect to the low-born wizard. It was after all either a well-worded ruse or a prodigious act of gall and luck. Either way, he knew that he could do nothing more than accept his friend's faith, for now.

CHAPTER 18:
XARONA'S GAMBIT

"If they can't control it, they either enslave it, kill it or ban it," Vinceno spoke from where he sat next to Isabella, "Then I guess I should feel honored," he did his best to sound mirthful.

"That's not funny," Isabella glared at her husband, tears in her eyes. The graying man held his wife's hand tight. "Just doing my best to accept my faith," he said before kissing his wife on the cheek.

"I'm still on the fence about accepting it," Jase.

'The walls here literally have ears and the fact we are magically blocking those magical ears I'm sure have not gone unnoticed," Xarona spoke up.

"Which means they know we can't escape," , Callum looked up from where he sat on the floor against a wall.

"Not without help," the witch looked at the young lord, " Which is why I need to find the witches,"

"Snowflower said they've driven away," Seamus.

"That may be true, but I wager, not too far," the redhead looked at her friends, "And I know places to look others don't, signs and symbols we use that even the High Magus may not know. ".

Callum came to his feet, "So when do we leave," he asked.

Did you ask Seamus to go with him?," asked the witch to the Free Crusader.

"No," said Callum.

"Then sit down, and stay here," Xarona glared at her friend, till with great reluctance he sat, with a sour look on his face.

"So how are you planning on getting out," Clare looked at her friend,"

Xarona smiled, "I'm the lady of a noble house, I'll exit out of the way we came in," she said walking towards the rooms front door and exiting, Sani at her side.

The witch headed down the halls and to the stairs. Moving downward she came to a hallway that leads to the main Castle Hall, Walking down the hall the witch, and her familiar made their way to the large exit doors guarded by four well-dressed guards.

"Open the doors please," asked the young woman.

" By orders of the king and his sister, we must ask where are you going," said a boy no older than sixteen carrying a long spear.

"That's my business," said the witch.

"I'm sorry, we have to know," said the boy looking at the other equally young guards for reassurance.

"If you must know, I'm going to the local adventurers guild to hand in my report," said the witch. The guard looked relieved.

"I always wanted to be an adventure," he said.

"Then It's best you don't get turned into a pillbug before you get the chance," said the ginger lady with a wicked smile.

"Do you need an escort, Ma'am," said one of the other boys.

Xarona rolled her eyes, "No," looking at Sani, she watched her cat turn into her large wildcat form. The boys looked on in awe, and before either the cat or witch could move, two of them had already started moving the crank to open the door.

The brisk cold air hit the witch as she exited the building. Quickly she gestured using a simple spell to alter her clothing into something more fitting for the environment. Her clothing material turned from fine cotton and silks to thicker wool; her cape grew a hooded and fur trim. Looking ahead down the great staircase the witch started to walk quickly. One at the bottom she looked at Sani, who smiled and turned into her horse form.

"Thank you," said the witch to her familiar as she reached into her pouch, pulled out a miniature saddle and returned it to full size and attached it to her chimera stead with a wave of her wand.

The woman on horseback rode to the castle wall, where the guards not only didn't ask questions but quickly opened the gate. With a tip of her hat and a nod the Lady of Belasona acknowledged their eagerness before heading down the road towards the city that just outside the wall of the castle.

"So are really heading to the guild?," asked Sani.

"Yes, If I don't they'll know, what they cannot control, they destroy and if there is a guild hall they control it," said the witch to her familiar as they rode into the cities street. Ignoring onlookers who had no idea what kind of strange "horse" Sani was, Xarona headed where all the streets met, it was a crossroads, and the crossroads were a place of power for her and her religion.

Once there the witch closed her eyes and relaxed. Feeling the energy about she waited for the lady and mused to connect with her. To her surprise, they did not Opening her inner eye she looked around for magic of any kind only to find very little beyond the normal background magic common to most places.

"No one can stop the primal powers and the old symbols," said the witch under her breath before closing her eyes again and concentrating. She knew what she was seeking had to be there, not because she felt it, but out of faith, Alomoeg creates, The Lady changes, The Mother nurtures, and the Darkness devours, four primal powers who's dance predates the universe.

"Excuse me, but are you lost," an old man with tanned skin and a bald head walked up to the strange multi-tailed white horse ridden by a woman in green. He could tell by what she wore she had money and by her attire she wasn't from Colos.

"Go away," said the horse.

The man took a step back and looked at the creature.

"Did you just talk?," he asked.

"Yes, now go away, My mistress needs to focus," said the creature.

"You're magic," said the man with a smile, "The north men will pay good money for you," the man turned, not noticing Xarona's eyes opening.

"Hunters?," asked the witch?

The man turned to face the young woman's piercing blue eyes.

"Aye," they look for magical beasts, and they pay well," said the man taking a step forward, "Of course if someone pays better, I might not go to them,"

The witch nodded, Do you know where the Adventurers guild is," she asked.

"Sure, take the west road towards merchants row, it's right before the market starts," said the man before adding " now as I was saying,"

"Yes that," Xarona pointed her wand at the man, a second later he was a bright green cockatiel, just like the ones her mother had imported for her garden. "

The witch smiled as the bird jumped about on the ground before flying away.

"I tried to warn him," said Sani.

Xarona looked at the bird, while she could have made the change permanent she had decided to set the spell to expire in a month or at any time the bird was in mortal danger.

Feeling better after venting with a bit of magic the witch headed down the west road. As she road she looked at the people of Colos, Everyone seemed busy, and the only eye contact made was looks of curiosity and contempt. In Vallus everyone seemed to smile, tip hats, bow and curtsey even to those, not of noble status.

The Southern noble lady first passed well-kept multi-level homes of wood and stone she crossed a small bridge and slowly the buildings gave way to shops with apartments on the top level. As the sun started to lower, the shopkeepers started moving things inside and closing door. The witch noticed there wasn't very much in the way of street lighting on this side of town. Even Lester had more lights per street she thought as she rode her familiar down the road.

After almost an hour of riding the young woman arrived at her destination, a small one-story building surrounded by a small fence. Out front was a sign showing the crossed Sword, bow and wand on a shield that represented the adventurers guild.

" Stand watch Sani," said the witch sliding to the ground from her side saddle position.

"Of course Mistress," said the horse.

Once on the ground the witch reached into her purse and took out a leather bound book with a metal clasp. The young woman then whispered a subtle spell into the book before entering the building.

Inside the Small guild main hall was empty, Two benches sat mostly covered in dust. In the rear near a small hall was a bench, behind it sat a middle-aged woman with green hair, large dark eyes, and pale skin, reading a book.

"Hello," said Xarona, startling the guild mistress.

"Leave your ledger and pick it up noon tomorrow," said the woman not looking up.

"If you don't mind, I would like to take care of this now," said the witch.

The green haired woman looked up at the redhead, "Fine," she said motioning young woman to approach.

Once at the bench, Xarona handed the book over and watched the woman open it.

"Well, I must say, your chronicler is done good work, most of the groups passing through, I can barely read the writing," she said with a smile,

"I make sure our notes and travel log precise and detailed" the Lady of Belasona smiled, It felt good to have the work she put into the log appreciated.

"A Wampus? cephlatherum? That's way above your rank. ," the Guild-mistress voice held disbelief,"

"The logs are enchanted so only the truth can be written on its pages, you'll find that spell unaltered," Xarona.

The woman looked at the book and ran her fingers through it, feeling the spell intact. "I'm sorry I doubted you, that's impressive,"

Xarona nodded and spoke, "If you don't me asking, is your guild hall always so empty?'

"The woman kept reading a few minutes before answering, " We tend only to get groups heading west or heading back from the west. A month can go by before someone darkens my door".

"What about local adventures? I personally heard a young guardsman saying he would like to take to a road". Asked Xarona watching the woman write into a large ledger with copper and brass ink pen.

"The king and his ilk frown on that kind of thing," replied the before looking up at the woman in front of her. "Take a seat, this is going to be while,"

Xarona nodded and took a seat, crossing her legs and taking out a book to read.

*****

By the time the woman closed the log book after stamping the first page with the mark of the Colos Guild Halls, the room's lights had dimmed marking the sun had set outside.

"Going to cost you three silver to get it sent back to the Vallus guild by my birds. ," The Guild Mistress.

Xarona rose, walked back to the bench and took out a gold coin,

"I expect it not to be seen only by the guild and if you can make sure a copy of it reached Arden,"

The woman raised an eyebrow and nodded and held up two fingers to her chest, Xarona without changing her expression added another gold coin.

The witch picked up the log book and placed it in her pouch.

"I'm sorry about the execution at the castle tomorrow; It's always hard to lose a client on the road," said the woman.

"Thank you," the witch looked at the woman and for the first time noticed she two small gill slits on her neck that marked her as Aquakin.

"Yeah they work, after a fashion," said the woman to the witch.

"Sorry I didn't mean to stare," Xarona returned embarressed.

The woman smiled, "Everyone does when they see them," she said.

Xarona nodded, "Thank you," said the ginger young woman promoting the Guildmistress to blurt out, "stopping to ask "Where the Colos and Silver rivers meet,"

"What?," Xarona

The Guildmistress looked puzzled, "I don't know why I said that," she said, shrugging and standing.

Witch smiled and exited quickly knowing her spell had worked, It was a minor one that made that asked one question directly to a mind and made the person answer before undoing itself.

"How did it go?"

Sani watched her Mistress exited the building. Xarona nodded at her familiar before taking to the saddle and riding south.

As the moon started to rise, the witch made her way to another wall, there two guards stood as farmers exited quickly. Seeing her chance, Xarona pulled her wand from its holder and gestured causing her and Sani to fade from sight. The two then maneuvered behind a wagon and exited to a small road leading down the mountain.

Once out of the guard's sight the witch released the spell startling the three children on the wagon she was behind who after their initial shock seemed more excited than frightened.

"How did you do that," said the blond-haired girl who's left arm was shaped like a large featherless and fingerless wing.

Magic," said the witch with a smile.

"Are you a wizard?," asked a young boy.

"No," Xarona, "She could tell her answer made the children both concerned and curious.

"Are you a .," started the girl again, before an older boy around ten cut her off.

She's kind, that's what you're supposed to say, she's a kind lady," he said quickly pushing his siblings behind him.

Xarona looked at the boy and nodded, "Who taught you that," she asked.

"My mother," he said.

"She's a wise lady," said the woman.

"Don't hex us, ma'am," said the child. "Lela was born cursed when her bird blood didn't come out right,"

Xarona looked at the girl knowing sometimes the mixing of species didn't work out well. especially if that species lineage was further from the human end of the heritage spectrum. She was taught at Coventry that all of the old-blood were once human who thanks to innate magic in an area had changed over the millennia. Those like the Fae, Stouts, Giants, and Vampyr while different were still close to humanity while Wyldkin and Avian, had become closer to animals than humanity.

The witch wondered how many members of the Colos noble and royal houses suffered from such afflictions and if they were allowed to live.

Xarona looked at the girl's arm, fixing it would be a simple transformation. But such magic could cause problems later on in her life. A transformed armed may react badly in areas of high magic, or it might not grow normally. What the girl needed was the good healer, the kind that could be found in a church of Alomeg, yet those like her church was missing.

"So do any of you know where the silver and Colos river meet," asked the woman to the children.

"We might," said the younger boy his hand out as if to accept money, before retreating back due to an accusing eye of his brother.

"Shut up you dunce, or I'll be telling ma and Pa how you're now a loaf of bread or a duck when we get home," said the older boy.

Xarona smiled and reached into her bag and pulled out a silver coin.

'I would rather reward you than hex you said the witch".

The older boy looked at his siblings, then the coin before reaching out and taking the coin and hoping with all its being it wasn't hexed.

"Take the second trial, after we turn off the road, follow it to a bridge, That's where they meet.

Xarona chatted with the children unnoticed by their oblivious parents, who view was blocked by a wooden board in the wagon's and several bales of hay and large bags of beans. After about a quarter mile the wagon turned down a road towards a farm.

The children waved at their new friend on the strange looking horse as she kept riding, down the road. A few hours later the Witch was turning down a lonely country road. Using her wand as a torch, she maneuvered along the wood-lined path. In the distance, a wolf howled, and nearby something growled.

"I'm starting to think the Alomeg worshipers are on to something, said Sani, bright Suns, meeting in daylight," she added. The Familiar could feel her mistress was nervous and hoped talking to her would ease both their growing fears.

"I really should have done this earlier in the day," said the noblewoman looking about the area lit by the green light of her wand.

As the familiar and rider move along the road, it started to grow narrow until one side of the road gradually dropped off showing a river flowing below. Sani walked carefully staying as far away from the increasing drop as possible as she rounded bend after bend. Eventually, the drop as replaced by a brush and the trees as the path cut through a forest.

"Ohhhk," from her right a sound and rustle in the trees. A figure was crossing the road with dark shaggy hair, short legs, a hunched back and swept back head it looked briefly at Xarona before moving into the opposite tree line.

Upon seeing the creatures, Sani stopped and prepared to rear up in self-defense. The abruptness of her halt almost caused her mistress to fall out of her saddle

"It's just a western skunk ape," said the witch recognizing the large simian. "They're harmless unless It's mating season or there's young nearby,"

"None of what you said makes me feel better mistress," said the familiar who once again started down the road eventually coming to a bridge that marked where two rivers met.

"Running water, a crossroads, the power here should be perfect for what I need to do,"

The witch slid off her horse to her feet and raised her glowing green wand.

"I hope we live to regret this," said the horse turning into a large two-tailed wildcat.

"So do I," said the witch.

Sani looked about smelling the wolves, skunk apes, owls, bears and more. "Any chance the boys decided to follow you? Because a Large Hammer or a bow would come in handy right about now," said the chimera only half joking.

"No, they trust me, and they know if they did I would do horrible things to them," said Xarona with a hint of mirth.

"Better horrible things for them than me," The familiar spoke just as just the hint of burning wood filled her nostrils.

"Witch fire," a voice from the woods called out as a blast of green flame flew at the young Lady. Xarona seeing the flame raised her wand and parried the blast with it, causing it to sizzle instantly while analyzing its strength. She knew instantly it was a witch, well trained but new to her power and not very focused, hence the incantation.

"Become a goat!," said the same voice as a snaking bolt of purple energy flew at Sani hitting her and briefly turning the wild cat into a white goat.

"That's not funny," said the familiar before turning back into a large wild cat and leaping towards the brush the spells were coming from.

"Sani be nice," said Xarona knowing whoever was casting the spell had no idea that alteration magic didn't work on natural shapechangers.

"I'm just going to nibble on them a bit," said the cat leaping onto her target who was smaller than she expected.

"Get off me beast," said a girl no older than twelve with golden eyes and wavy lavender hair.

"Not till I get my nibble". said the cat pinning the girl with a paw on her chest and another on a hand holding a silver wand.

Xarona walked over to the Sani, "No nibbles," she said looking at the girl in the yellow and orange dress.

"At the crossroads, we meet, with the moon we rise," said the older witch.

"we arc the storm before creation and the storm after it," added the girl.

"Off Sani," said Xarona to her familiar who instantly turned into her house cat form and walked to her mistresses side. reaching a gloved hand down Xarona helped the girl to her feet.

'I'm sorry Ma'am," said the girl, followed by a quick curtsey.

"No harm was done," said the witch.

"You weren't a goat," Sani

Xarona ignored her familiar's protest and looked about, she could now feel the power of the area under the half moon and the power coming from the girl.

"So are you out here alone dear?," asked the redhead.

The girl smiled and took the older witch by her sleeve and lead her off the road.

"What's your name child?," Xarona asked the girl as they moved through the brush, that despite its thick leaves and thorns didn't snag her long dress, but rather rolled off it like water against stone.

"You can call Cassadee," said the girl

"Nice to meet you Cassadee, I'm Xarona," said the red-haired witch.

" Lady Xarona of the noble house of Belasona," added Sani.

The girl stopped and looked at the woman. "Are you a Princess?" she asked.

"No, just a lady," the woman in green could now feel something ahead, well-woven magic and the smell of a cooking fire.

The girl nodded, 'I want to be Lady, and a warrior and a Manticore! " said the girl gesturing with a free hand at a tree directly in front of them causing it to split and form a door sized oval opening. Music suddenly filled the air.

"We're here," said the girl entering the opening.

Xarona looked at Sani who was entering the opening after the girl,

"Sani, I don't know if it's safe," she said.

"I smell fish," said the cat stopping briefly before entering,

"If I die I'm haunting you," said Xarona following the girl and cat.

Golden light from a central firepit of what the redhaired lady thought was a large cave until she saw the walls were made of trees that grew not only together but that formed most of the smooth wooden floor and domed ceiling.

"Mother, I found another one," said Cassadee running up to a blond woman standing at the fire, her wand levitating multiple large skillets, pots, and utensils. Near her, a dark-haired man played Banjo and danced a jig as children and others watched.

"Now what do we have here," A rotund woman with long brown hair and dark eyes stood up from where she sat on a bench, her accent reminded Xarona of the slight one Isabella had.

The trees creaked as she crossed her arms and the opening from which the witch and familiar entered, suddenly closed.

Xarona looked at the woman and carried, "I come seeking only knowledge" she said.

"We'll see about that said the dark-haired woman raising a hand and firing streams of silver energy at the young adventuress.

Xarona raised her wand and gestured sending the energy around her, only to have it snake back. With her free hand, she drew a silver sigil in the air, while aiming a spell at the woman who cast on her with her wand.

The dark haired woman watched her spells bounce off the sigil and fly into the trees cutting into them like an invisible ax blade.

Xarona's spell flew at the witch exploding in front of her and leaving a sulfurous yellow cloud in front of her.

"No one harms my mistress," said Sani leaping at the attacking woman and turning into her wildcat form. the magic user only to be pinned by something she couldn't see.

"Down girlie," said a female voice. Sani struggled under what felt like large paws. "She's only testing her,"

Sani growled as the face of a creature that looked like a black scaled bear with thorny spines and a whip-like tail appeared. With a gesture the witch caused the yellow cloud to vanish.

"That's dirty fighting', she said pointing at the ground and causing thorny vines to grow under her target and twist around her.

You say dirty, I say practically". Xarona floated upward and then towards the witch she was fighting.

"Old Tilda's bitten off more than she can chew this time," said a woman sitting on a log nursing a cup. of dark drink.

"Hush," said the witch in black gesturing at her heckler and turning her into a pile of rose petals.

Xarona upon seeing the spell tried not to react, that spell alone showed her opponent's power. But it also, at least her mind it also showed a weakness.

Xarona, spun as the vines gave chase. As she neared the wooden dome above her head, she cast a spell causing her to seemly divide into three copies of herself. Those copies then divided into three copies each.

"Novice move," said the older witch reaching out to feel the power of all the witches but finding none there just as the vines she summoned parted ways each chasing one of the redheads.

" Tilda stops it," said the woman at the campfire" in a stern tone.

"Not till I see what the girl's got!," Exclaimed the witch in black. Releasing the vines and causing them to retract.

I have this," A voice to her side followed by the appearance of Xarona. The Lady of Belasona gestured turning the ground into the under witch into the water, causing her to sink into it like a stone up to her head. With another gesture turned the water back into packed dirt constricting all her limbs.

"I warned you Tilda," said the woman at the fire gesturing at the rose petals and turning them back into a stunned woman.

"You may have the Hexing, but she knows how to fight". added the blond before pointing at Tilda causing her to vanish out of the ground and appear next to her. The woman then sheath her wand in her belt and walked over to the lady and green, "I'm Lizbeth ," she said while hugging the surprised well-dressed sorceress. "Leader of this coven and this camp". Once the woman pulled away.

Xarona curtsied and spoke , "I'm sorry I thought the other one was in charge" .

Lizbeth looked at Tilda "Tilda in charge of security and tended to cast first and ask questions later,"

Tilda looked at Xarona and smiled, "Sorry, been a while since I had a little fun like that," she said

"No harm no foul," said the young witch looking over to Sani who was being let up by the Newland-manticore that pinned her.

"Sorry Sister," said the larger creature to Sani.

"Hmph," Sani glared at her attacker before walking over to her mistress to sit at her side.

"Sani, play nice," said Xarona.

Lizbeth walked to the redhead, "Come and sit sister, " she said. Xarona smiled and found a place on a log near the stove and sat.

"I'm sorry about coming in unannounced but..," The young witch started saying only to be cut off by a plate being placed on her lap by Cassadee.

"Here you go Princess," sais the girl.

"I'm not a Princess," Xarona spoke up. only to be ignored by the girl as she placed a saucer at her feet, and then placed a cup of tea on the saucer".

"Cassadee, She's not a Princess, said the Lizbeth to her daughter, the girl was now sitting at Xarona's feet holding her own teacup and saucer.

"She's the closes enough," said the girl," smiling at the redhead.

Lizbeth looked at her daughter then her guest, "Sorry Xarona. my daughter has an unhealthy fascination with nobility despite the fact It was nobility that ran us into the forest," said the blond woman.

"Colos?" asked Xarona.

"Yes, and I pray to the muses you never run across them," said the head witch angrily.

"Too late, my adventuring group.. my friends are in the castle now with our charges, one of which is due to be executed tomorrow.

Lizbeth looked at Xarona with sad eyes, "I'm sorry," she said,

Xarona nodded, "I was hoping to find help," said the lady.

Lizbeth looked about at the families that depended on her and then at the young lady in green, "I'm sorry, We've lost too much, They killed three of our sisters, burned our temple, and have outlawed us, So now we wait to hope to outlive The current king and his bigotry,"

Xarona could see the sadness on her hosts' face and the fear in the faces of those nearby.

" But, we're the daughters of the Lady, It's our obligation to force revolution and change," Xarona spoke not just to Lizbeth but to everyone else who could hear their voice.

"They killed my man and my oldest to get to me," Tilda. , "I want to curse them as much as anyone, but I can't risk what I have left," she said a holding dark haired girl in a manner only a frightened mother could.

"The High Magius may be more puff than power, said Lizbeth," but he has two dozen wizards on his side and can call more from the across the land, add in the military, add in their Thunderbirds, and there is no way we can't beat them," Another witch spoke up from table where she laid out colorful cards used for divination.

Xarona had thought she was the only witch to ever feel fear. In her teaching she was told her kind were without such "low traits," yet looking at the members of her maternity in the hidden camp she couldn't help but feel sorry for them.

"Please, there has to be something," she begged to hope for anything that might spare Vinceno.

"We can't risk any magic that may lead back to us," Lizbeth.

"Then I guess I'll take my leave," Xarona stood, "Unless you feel me leaving would lead your enemies to you," The redhead's hand slid close to her wand sheath on her belt,

Lizbeth shook her head, "You are free to leave,"

"thank you for your hospitality," said Xarona before heading the way she came, Sani at her side. She could feel the magical exit nearby she felt it was now in tune with her, a gift from Lizbeth she thought. Reaching the "Entry Tree," she watched it open and stepped through. Thinking it would once again appear in the forest she was surprised to find it exciting near a place where two farm roads met near a grove of trees halfway up the mountain to her final destination.

Sani looked about to see if there was anyone nearby before taking on her horse form. Xarona once again placed on the saddle and ascended her steed. The witch looked at the sky and knew that if she did not hurry that she would be arriving at the castle not long before dawn and what that meant.

"I need you to run Sani," she said to the horse who upon hearing the words took off at a full gallop without so much as a word.

For most of the ride all, Xarona could think about was Isabella and her children, once strangers she had now grown close to them. She tried to force away Vinceno fate to the back of her mind as she started to consider options, could they take him and his family and make their escape, would Lizbeth take them in if they could find her. Could they make it to the Kasee border to the east or maybe to Myzonna to the south?

*****

" You asleep?" Xarona said while playfully kicking Callum after slowly closing the door to the Salazars main sitting room behind her. Looking about she saw Clare and Seamus sharing a sofa, snoring, Bhang sitting at the foot of another Sofa where Lisa and Kisa slept under a blanket and Jase eyes closed sitting next to the door leading to Vincent's and Isabella's room. Bernardo sat slumped over in a chair a glass of wine still in his hand.

"I heard you and Sani a while back, You were threatening to neuter a guard who didn't want to let you in, not sure what neuter means but I reckon it got the point across," said Jase

"It means... never mind," said Bhang smiling, eyes closed.

Callum looked up to see Xarona standing over him,

"Ahm not sleeps," he said before yawning.

"Sure you're not," she said sitting next to the man.

"Where the cat?," he asked.

"Outside in the hall, guarding the front door," she said leaning into the man's shoulder.

"Good Kitty," Callum

"She's going to bite you for saying that," Said the witch leaning against the crusader.

"I have armor on," Callum, "Also she's small,"

Xarona smiled and took the Free Crusaders hand,

"I found them," she said.

"Should we expect fire raining from the sky at dawn? ," The young lord looked at the woman leaning on him and saw only melancholy.

"No, Colos has them afraid too," she answered.

"I feel so helpless," Callum kissed the woman's hand after speaking.

"I'll protect you," said Xarona.

"Of that, I have no doubt," with those words, both the Crusader and Witch closed their eyes trying to find a few hours of rest before the dawn they all dreaded arrived.

CHAPTER 19: DARK DAWN

Isabella looked at her husband tears in her eyes as she made sure that his neckerchief was tied correctly and his hair was perfect. Vinceno kept his eyes on his wife doing all he could to burn the memory of her into his mind.

"You have all the banking information," he said to her as she adjusted the rose shape clasp on his dark purple cape.

"Yes I do," she said, "I'm not some dull housewife," she added forcing a smile.

"Lisa and Kisa, when they turn 18..," the man said choking on his own words and fighting back tears.

"If they are not married, they are to receive a third of the business combined, and Bernardo the other third when.," Isabella broke down leaning against her husband d sobbing. Bernardo looked at his parents, lowering his head exiting from his their chambers into the common area where his sisters and friends sat.

"This is madness he said," in protest to whoever would listen.

"We still have time to make a run for it," Jase looked up from where he sat dressed in armor and sharpening arrowheads,

"I wish there were a way," Clare spoke up, "But as Xarona said numbers, magic or not, it's not on our side and I trust her numbers,"

Looking at the floor to hide the tears on his face Bernardo walked quickly through the room towards the door that exited into the hallway.

Seamus started to stand shook his head and sat frustrated only to have all eyes fall on him.

"Go," said Callum to his friend.

The young wizard nodded at his friend rose and followed the young future royal. Bernardo stood in the hall his frustration building till half growling and crying he slammed a fist into the stone wall. His hand still throbbing and knuckles bruised he punched the wall again.

"Please, don't," Seamus' voice cut through his friend's pain.

"This is all my fault," Bernardo.

"It's no one's fault," said the blond, "at least not the fault of anyone not from Colos,"

Bernardo stood looking at his friend, "I could have stopped this, I could have stood up to my father," he said looking at the thin blond man who was now holding his bruised and possibly broken hand.

"Yes you could have, but your love for your family and your father stopped you, there's nothing wrong with that," the magician focused on the hand he held chilling the air around it as he spoke.

Bernardo looked at his held hand, "Getting into healing now?" he said softly.

"No, just something that'll help your hand till Callum can get to it," said the wizard.

Bernardo nodded and found himself smiling at his friend's words, and suddenly he realized his time with Seamus was ending and that his gentle companion would be leaving soon. The sudden feeling of loss and loneliness welled up in the young man to his surprise he found himself morning that as much as he mourned the idea of losing his father.

" And here we are at the end of whatever we were," said Bernardo.

"I could stay," Seamus. , "You'll need a friend here,"

Bernard placed his good hand on the wizard's shoulder, "No, I can't risk it, one wrong thought, one wrong moment and all is lost," he said.

Seamus nodded as he fought his urges and the wave of fear and attraction he could feel coming from the young man who hands he held.

"I hate this, all of this," he said. "This isn't how it's supposed to be,"
Seamus felt tears coming from his own eyes, then Bernardo's hands on his cheeks and then his lips on his. The two kissed, losing, ever so briefly the tragedy of their presence in their embrace and tender moment.

"What's this," A voice from down the hall. Seamus' eyes opened, looking over Bernardo's shoulder he saw the prince, his personal guard and two dozen other guards looking at them.

Bernardo hearing the voice turned to see his future brother in law.

"It's nothing," said the young man in Lavender,"

"It had better not be," snarled the Arnic as he walked up.

Bernardo looked at Seamus then at the Prince who was now within arm's reach.

"Please, Bernardo looked at the young man in white, "Can you talk to your father, save my father?" he asked,

The prince smiled, "I could, but I won't," answered the royal. "as my father said, laws were broken, and someone had to pay,"

With those words the royal walked past the young wizard and the merchant's son towards the door at the end of the hall, knocking he waited till Vinceno answered the door. Without a word Vinceno stepped into the hall and held out his hands as if they are to be shackled, The prince nodded, his gesture summoning a nearby guard to walk up with iron shackles that he clasped on the older man's wrist.

"Is that necessary as asked Isabella who was now standing behind her husband.

"Yes Ma'am," said the guard.

"Don't worry dear," said Vinceno looking into his wife's eyes before turning and walking down the hall.

The Prince, Vinceno, the guards, The Salazars, Bhang and the adventures moved down the hall and downstairs, turning towards the main hall and down it away from the entrance past high arched walls to another hall, before turning again down another narrow hall in silence

The corridor eventually ended at an open door that exited near a stable. The sky was just starting to turn from night to die, and in the distance, the group could see a gathering of lords and ladies, servants and more. Amongst them, to everyone's surprise, was a group of men in armor and furs standing near a giant twice as tall as most of them.

"Never seen this kind of hanging," said one of them.

"He kills my men, I should kill him," said the giant.

As Vinceno and his precision came closer the men in furs started to jeer, turning the solemn occasion into something even the king found offensive.

"Calm your man Gravix," said the king

"You hear his grace," said the Giant with contempt.

The Eastahuten grew silent.

Gravix watched the man in purple; he was told he had come to his daughters rescued and used a magical grenade and a hidden fury to defeat his men. It was a story that he didn't fully believe, but one he decided not to question, the money from Colos was more than he had ever made and would go a long way towards helping his people get what they wanted in the future.

The guards led Vinceno through the crowd towards an outcropping where a wooden arm on a swivel stool. Connected to the end of the arm was a noose. The king walked through the crowd flanked by his sister and the High Magis.

"That's a man of rare honor," he said.

"Not killing him, may gain you some favor Vallus," said Jazlyn dressed in her typical in a white dress under a white fur coat.

"How so?', asked the man in the white ceremonial breastplate over white long sleeve tabard and pants.

The woman looked in the audience spying Xarona and Callum.

"Belisona and to a lesser extent Wimbowaradi are vassals in good standing," she said.

The king thought for a second then shook his head. "Gravix demands blood and me rather it be his and not ours," he said to his sister.

"Palth...I told you that giant would be a mistake we'll regret ," the woman glared at the massive man in fur and into the dark and bloody halls of his mind briefly before pulling back and regretting what she had done,"

All eyes fell on the king who locked eyes at the doomed man and nodded. Thinking only of his family and friends Vinceno nodded back and bowed in hopes his death would allow those he cared for some modicum of goodwill . Not long after , two guards moved to the swivel arm turning it towards the king who without an ounce of expression tied the noose around the man's neck.

"No last words?," asked Jase to those around him.

He said all he had to say," Isabella who was doing her best to be as stoic as her husband. Xarona looked in the sky hoping against hope for a last minute reprieve as she grabbed Callum's hand.

"Alomeg, take you into his boundless heart," said Callum as the swivel was the move to lift Vinceno off the ground then to dangle over the cliff.

"It's all my fault," cried out Kisa as her father grimaced and gurgled, his face darkening and his life slipping away.

Lisa grabbed her sister and held her, both turning away from their father's horrifying end.

"I bet he shites himself," said one of Gravixs's man.

"Show some respect," growled a Colos Guard.

"I ain't afraid of you little birdie," said the Eastahuten drawing an ax.

"That's my father up there Northman!, said Bernardo his hand reaching for his sword.

The Eastahuten licked lips showing silver-capped teeth "If your feeling rabbity boy, then jump," he said.

The guard took a step back. Seamus in an attempt to calm Bernardo placed a hand on his friend's shoulder and could feel the anger and sorrow inside him.

The bereaved young man was about to apologize to the northern trapper when Jase stepped in front of him.

"I'm feeling all manner of hoppity," said the hill-man looking the man in the eye.

"Oh, this isn't going to end well," Clare casually bumped into Xarona and Callum bring their attention to Jase's face off. She then looked around for Bhang who was maneuvering himself between Isabella, her daughters fearing what he feared was about to happen.

Jase kept an eye on the Estahutten, he had seen men hanged before and did not need to see it happen again, especially to the friend. The Ax-wielding man kept an eye on the young hill-man, each saying nothing else as a man's death played out as spectacle.

After a Vinceno had stopped moving the king left, his family in tow, the Estahutten followed as did the other courtiers and servants. After half an hour only the Salazars and their friends and a few guards were left.

"Whenever you're ready," said a young guard to Isabella softly. Xarona recognized him as one of the ones she had threatened when she entered the castle earlier that morning.

Isabella just stood quietly.

"Now," said Lisa, who stood next to her mother and watched as the guards swung the wooden "arm" back over to solid ground. One of the men walked over and held up Vinceno's body while the other one cut him down. They then brought the body to Isabella and laid him gently in front of her before leaving.

Isabella looked at her husband's face, his eyes wide open, his mouth still looking as if it was gasping for air. Collapsing the woman fell on top the man and wept as those around watched, most joining in her lamentations.

Seamus unafraid held Bernardo's hand as he stood over his father.

"I'm going with you" Bernardo spoke matter of factually to Seamus, "I'm not staying here,"

Isabella looked up at her son and nodded, "We'll take him back to Vallus, bury him on our land," she said.

"Mrs. Salazar, I can cast some spells, one to make him look...more like himself and another to preserve him". Xarona spoke from where she stood next Clare and Callum.

"I never learned the death rites," said Callum, "But I'm sure once we're out of Colos we can find an Acolyte that can do it," The large man spoke as tears flowed from his eyes. The coldness of the execution and the fact it didn't have to happen had shaken the free-crusader far more than he expected. "why would Alomeg," allow such a thing? ," he thought noting for the first time he was questioning his creator.

"Look at them," Prince Arnic looked from the balcony overlooking what they called the Raven's roost, his father stood at his side smoking on his pipe.

"He's sly," Said the king to his son.

"Obviously," that milksop won't be giving you any grandchildren, father," said the blond young man.

"But that's, not the point, many a Sly man have seeded children for power and position," he said, "The point is that Vinceno Salazar, damn his soul sold me spoiled goods in his son,"

Arnic looked at his father, 'And what shall we do about the father?" he asked a slight smile starting to appear on his face.

The king thought for a second. "Tell Gravix and his men I have a special bounty for them," He spoke coldly, "Kill my future son-in-law" he added before taking another puff.

A soldier near him nodded turned on heel and left.

"I want that Hillman dead too," said the prince.

"Not on my coin, the guttersnipe isn't worth it," said the king.

"But if you want to pay, I'm sure Estahutten will give you a good deal,"

The prince glared at his father just long enough not to be noticed.

"Yes father," he returned in a submissive tone as he balled his fists.

*****

"Mother, I'm not staying" statedBenardo again as he looked at grief-stricken mother who sat in a chair, exhausted from her crying. He wanted to give her time to recover some before his announcement. The woman wanted to be left alone, she wanted to mourn, and a small part of her wanted to die, but she knew her priorities, get her dead husband and those she cared about back to Vallus.

"Your father would tell you, family obligation came first," said matriarch of the Salazar household, "But your mother says, to all the hells with these people,"

"The Colos' want takes that easily," Bhang spoke up from where he sat reading a book while he sat on the floor next to a fireplace.

Clare rolled her eyes, "At this point do we care?', asked the stocky young woman. , "Because personally, I don't care what they think,"

Xarona, who was sitting in a chair near the door suddenly felt magic at work. It was subtle, moving about not wanting to be detected.

"Seamus, your wards," she said to the blond comforting a distraught Bernardo by holding his hand.

"Seamus closed his eyes feeling the wards he had cast on the room to lock out spying magical eyes and ears and to raise the alarm if violent intent moved on them within the confines of the Salazar's wing. The Prince's guards near-attack had not only made such actions necessary but made the fact he didn't cast such spells earlier near folly. As he connected with them, he could feel multiple magics undoing them. First the alarms, then the ones to stop spies.

"They're being unwoven," he said.

"Mine too," Xarona spoke as she came to her feet.

"Six men, smell like hunters come upstairs behind a wall," Jase casually slung his quiver on his back and started to buckle on his dagger and swords.

"There's a hidden staircase?," Kisa.

"Sure is, I knew about it for a while," , Jase.

And you were going to tell us when," Callum looked at his friend who smiled before responding.

"Figured I would tell you when it became needed, It's needed now," said the hunter.

Everyone, we're leaving down those stairs now," said Isabella.

"Leaving as in not coming back leaving," Lisa looked at her mother who was now standing, the sadness on her face replaced by purpose.

"Yes, we'll have to leave some things, no time to pack," Isabella,

"What about Enkidu?," Callum.

Xarona looked at her boyfriend annoyed, "Silly man, I'll buy you a new Bull," she said.

Callum seemed ready to protest when Clair reached into her pocket and pulling out a crystal embedded in a copper and brass gearbox.

"Retrieve and find me," she said focusing on the box and placing her intentions into it,"

"Your spider and flyers," said a smiling Kisa.

"They'll grab what they can including the bull if they can lift it " said the Tinkered., "but that's going to be a might big if,"

"Chance is better than nothing," Seamus touched the wall feeling through the stone and finding the hidden door behind a wardrobe.

"Good place for a door," he said concentrating. He could now feel the feet on stone stairs not far away.

"They're almost here," he said,

" Alomeg who ways are mysterious and righteous, bless us, bring us success and keep all of us safe," Callum spoke out loud his divine energy charging the words and bringing confidence and focus to all in the room.

Jase walked over to the wardrobe felt around its edges; His father had told him about hidden doors before, they usually had triggers that were easily found if you put some effort into it.

"Moving a wall takes a lot of leverage," said Kisa, " look for something near the floor," she said.

Jase nodded, he trusted the girl's intellect and moved his hand along the wardrobes back near the floor than the wall. Finding a loose stone he pushed, the wardrobe slid to the side and a stone door slid down into the floor as the sound of steam was heard.

Without hesitation, the southern hunter stepped into the hall to see the glow of torches coming up a narrow corridor. With one smooth motion, he nocked and fired an arrow. The sound of the arrow hitting flesh and the gurgle of blood being swallowed was heard.

"Hop-Hop," he said preparing another arrow. As two more flew at him. With a spin, he stepped back into the room and prepared to fire.

"We're going to need cover," he said.

"We have cover. , "Callum grabbed the wardrobe and Lifted it off its mounts and into the once hidden hall.

Get behind me, I'll push it down the hallway, "he said,"

"No need for that," Seamus Staff in hand focused on the air behind the wardrobe, causing it to churn and push the piece of furniture forward.

"Now you can be ready to fight if needed," he said.

With a loud "woosh the wardrobe moved down the hall, surprising the six Estahutten hunters.

"It's magic," one said taking an Ax to it.

"Kill it," said another trying to ignore the arrow wound on the side of his neck that would have been fatal if it was just an inch to the left.

"The men pushed and hacked on the wardrobe splitting it with relative ease. However, the wind behind it still pushed forward staggering them back and blew out two of the torches.

The extinguished torches didn't dim the area as the men expected, in fact after the wardrobe shattered the hall filled with light from two light crystals, a wand, and a staff.

Without hesitation three of the would would-be assassins charged. while the other prepared another volley of arrows in the confined area.

"Which ones the mark!," said a scared faced man with a long brown hair.

"Kill'em all, let old' one eye sort'em out," said the Northman to his friend as he leaped to try to kick the bow-wielding youth to the ground.

Jase seeing the kick without hesitation moved to the side while nocking an arrow, Bhang who was behind him quickly move to block the kick with one of his own, hooking the attackers with his leg at the knee and spinning him to the opposite wall.

Releasing the wind Seamus raised his staff to fire a gout of flame down the hall, suddenly feeling them magic around him pulling away.

"They've set the castle wards against us he called out as what was going to be a fireball fizzled at the end of his staff.

Callum stepped past his friend, "They can't block the wraith of Alomeg," said the young lord channeling his divine resources into his body for speed and durability.

The Estahutten's ax made contact against his large attacker digging into his arm. The dark-skinned young man, however, acted as if he felt nothing. In fact, instead of flinching, he slammed his hammer into the man so hard it sent the northern mercenary into the stone wall, cracking stone and shattering bones.

Seeing a chance, the Estahutten bowmen prepared to fire on the big man, but before they could release their arrows, he barreled past their melee fighters and was on top of them.

Bring that shadow-skin bastard down!," Screamed one releasing his arrow. Callum knowing there was no room to dodge instead turned taking two if the arrows into his back and feeling no pain.

Coming out of the turn the free-crusader landed his hammer on one of the archers, sending him rolling down the hall with a broken clavicle.

With a determined look, Isabella drew her sword and entered the fray.

"You took my husband, "She called out., "But I'll be double damned before you take my children,"

Rushing, a staggered sword-wielding man the woman, slashed at his stomach with her sword and in quick succession stabbed in his throat. The trained northern warrior rolled with the first shot and blocked the other one with an ax. Moving forward the bearded man roared, knocking the woman back while raising his ax to strike with all his might.

Isabella knew blocking the heavy ax would most likely shatter her sword and kill her. Yet despite that probable outcome, she didn't feel any fear. She would be with her love soon.

Looking her would be killer in the eye the women prepared for the darkness of death, but instead of seeing the light of the next world, she instead saw two arrows pierce her attacker's skull.

The Salazar Matriarch looked up as Jase rushed past her dropping his bow and drawing his swords to assist his friend in the melee.

"Mother... you were amazing," said Kisa as she picked up the bow before running to her mother's side.

Isabella nodded at her daughter just as an arrow flew between them.

"Sani helps them," Xarona said as she focused on keeping the wards from undoing the magic in the items she wore, particularly the bag that among other things now carried the body of her former employer.

Sani nodded leaped off her shoulder and assumed her wildcat form.

The cat ran past Jase and was on top of a bowman clawing at him and knocking him to the ground.

"You foul-smelling creature," said the cat as the smell of weeks without bathing, tobacco, and cheap liquor assaulted her nose.

"You okay Hoss?," Jase moved past Callum slicing the archer across the chest.

"Alomeg sustains me," he said kicking the now injured man to the ground.

As an enemy archer tried to rise he was speared from through the gut by a telescoping spear that had extended it's full twenty feet to reach him.

"Short legs, long reach," said the tinkersmith retracting her weapon to five feet.

"We need to get out of here," Xarona called out in a voice that told them whatever she was doing was taxing.

Jase nodded and started down the hall, a finding the stairs that lead the man upward as well as the still living one Callum had sent down the hall.

"Lucky for you, my ma taught me mercy," said the young hunter as he stabbed the dying man in the throat as he moved past ending his suffering from multiple internal injuries.

Once past the man, he inhaled deeply through his nose seeking out the smell of the wild and finding it far away.

"Be careful it's a long way down he said, taking two steps at a time down the narrow passage into the dark.

*****

Hamston wasn't much a warrior, he spent much of the time feeding horses and helping keep the camp of Gravix and his men.

Today, however, he would wait in the small between two steep rising cliffs. Outside the castle near a cave that leads inside. According to the Colos soldiers that had talked to Gravix, the cave was created long ago as a way for the royal family to escape if needed and lead to hidden passages in the castle.

Gravix then sent six of his most stealthy men and Hamston to the cave, Hamston was to watch the horses and act as a guard. It as a job he often dreamed of, one that would allow him to be warriors without any real chance of being hurt, or so he thought up until without notice a sword was at his throat.

"Say a word, just one, and I'll open you up," Jase standing behind the man.

"Please don't," whimpered thin dirty blond man in leather and furs.

Jase knew leaving him alive was a risk, but unlike the other men, this one seemed cowed and was currently urinating on himself.

"Thank all the Gods we made it," Isabella exited the cave her daughters at her side and her son behind her.

"We're not done the mother yet, We should get as far away from her as possible," Bernardo spoke up looking around at the small area outside the cave with its high natural stone walls.

"I think I know a place we could hide, at least temporarily," Xarona.

"Lead the way, Isabella called out.

As the group prepared to mount the horses the sun dimmed overhead as if something large blocked it. All eyes darted up as a great bull descended.

"Enkidu!," Callum called out as his stead carried by Claire spinning mechanical pets floated to the ground. On its back was the clock work spider ising its grappling thread to hold a variety of things to the creatures back.

"Now that's something," said Lisa managing to crack a smile.

Claire looked at the strange table and smiled, "Well that worked," She said.

"How?," Seamus looked at the tinkered in bewildered and in awe.

"Jase said you had problems with river crossings... I thought I would come up with a set of routines for things that we might run across and also a flying Bull is pretty damn funny, even though lifting that thing probably burned through most of the crystals powering my whirly-gigs.

"Callum picked up Claire with his uninjured arm and hugged her tight.

"I owe Claire," he said tears in his eyes.

"Hey, everyone knows a crusader, and their noble steed is a thing... I don't get it, but it's a thing,"

"So you think the people in Colos will notice that," said Bhang in a sarcastic tone.

"I reckon, but then again, if they're working the castle magic against us they already know we're making our break," Jase.

Isabella looked at the group, her children and the young people she's grown fond of, " we need to go, now," she said in a calm but commanding tone. She then looks at Hamston.

"What are you still doing here?," she asked

"I thought I would wait till you leave. roll around in the dirt lay over by that rock till someone comes looking". said the man.

Isabella nodded, "That sounds like a good plan," said the woman.

Without a word and ignoring the Estahutten hunter rolling in the dirt, everyone started to mount up. On the six available doubling up as needed so that one could be used to carry supplies, Callum, starting to feed the pain of his wounds climbed on his bull, and Sani turned into a horse for her mistress.

The group exited the through the winding ravine to a creek. After getting her bearings, Xarona took the lead. Behind Jase looked and ahead for any sign of Colos soldiers or ambushes. They were now in enemy territory with trained soldiers most likely on the heels as well as Estahutten mercenaries and who knows what else.

Seamus could feel the magic flowing back into him; The ward blocking had not only drained his power but his spirit. But now that he was in the wilderness that started to change. He was suddenly feeling alive, and he wasn't sure if it was his returning magic or his fae heritage. Regardless it was a welcome feeling despite all that had transpired.

"Urgg," Callum grunted, the free-crusader he could feel the wound in his arm and the arrows still in his back move with each every movement. His divine power was almost done and while he knew it would return he wasn't sure if it would be fast enough. Fear was starting to creep in as was darkness at the edge of his vision. Ignoring the pain, the large man focused on riding on being there for Xarona and his friends.

"Say my name," said a deep voice in the back of his head.

Like his pain the young crusader pushed past the voice, he was sure was a hallucination.

As the sun started to set the group came to a small grove near a river where Xarona stopped and dismounted.

"Let me do the talking," she said.

"You do that anyway," said Jase.

Xarona ignored the hunter and reached out with her magic for the path.

"Stop!" a voice from a tree. The witch turned to see a fae with long blue hair with a readied bow aiming at her. "Take another step round ears, and you're done,"

"You first," Jase knocked and readied an arrow and pointed at the tall, thin archer he had not seen, smelt or heard until the moment he spoke.

Suddenly from in and around the trees came to a dozen more fae and behind them just as many trogs. The large gray skinned trogs, male and female carried large stone axes and clubs and wore buckskin pants and vests over ritually scarred flesh.

"Who be you!," said a large female trog to the group.

"We are travelers," Xarona, "And we're looking for a friend.

"No friends her daughter of the crossroads," said a fae.

"Yes there is". the voice of a young girl called from the trees.

"Cassadee!," The witch called out a purple haired girl ran into her almost knocking her to ground.

"Can we get these arrows out of me now," slurred Callum sliding off his bull to the ground. Xarona upon seeing her boyfriend laying in the dirt bleeding ran towards him.

Jase lowered his bow and ran to his friend's side helping him stand with the help of Xarona and to his surprise the trog, warrior woman.

"Giant Kin, needs healer," said the gray woman.

"He is our healer," Xarona.

"Follow me," said Cassadee. Moving back into the trees and down a path. The adventures and their allies along with Cassadee, and a few trogs and fae made their way through the trees to the large opening inside.

Lizbeth stood at a wooden table. Where frogs, fae and a few of her people sat listening intently. Upon seeing her daughter and Xarona she smiled, but the smile quickly vanished when she the motley crew that followed them.

"What's this?," She asked in a voice that held surprise and anger.

"Princess Xarona's giant friend is hurt,"

"A giant?," said a fae at the table wearing clothing made of woven cloth and vines and carved wood.

All eyes fell on the stranger's especially does of the witch with the colorful divination cards. Her eyes narrowed as she first drew and placed down the card signifying death and change, then the lighting card and the ice storm card.

"A giant will battle a giant," she said to herself drawing another cad, and seeing silver sword and silver wings. She had never seen the card before, but like most of her deck's cards, they appeared as needed.

"He calls," babbled the woman," knowing she was being ignored.

.

CHAPTER 20: RUN RABBIT

Seamus sat next to his Callum who was looking both embarrassed and sour. The crusader hated the fact he needed to be healed and even more so the fact the healing came from a witch he didn't know. He had nothing against witches on a hold, in fact, he was after all very close to one, but more than a religious difference it was a matter of principle.

"Still in a mood?," asked Seamus.

"I'm not in a mood," said Callum who was now sitting in his scale armor over red gambeson, the ensemble was topped by his long leather vest stamped with his family crest of the black bull on red and gold.

"How long have I know you?', asked the magician to his friend.

"Ten years, almost eleven," said the young lord.

"And you're in a mood," said the blond smiling.

Callum looked at the fire not far from them, "It's just embarrassing, having a strange healer... do their works on me," he said somberly.

Seamus smiled, " Now you know how I feel when Xarona does something utterly amazing," said the young magician, "what you're feeling is called humility,"

"I know what humility is," Callum

"You may know it, but you never took to it, I figured that what made you follow the path of the fist of Alomeg instead of the voice or the heart.

The dark-skinned lord smiled, "Don't go knowing me better than I know myself," he said patting his oldest friend on the back in a manner that almost knocked the thinner man off the log they sat on.

"So he's part Titan?," said Cassadee to Kisa. As the younger girl looked at Callum.

"Yes," the thin, bespectacled twin looked at the girl with the strange color hair.

"Strength of ten men?" asked the young witch.

"Well he he's very strong, Five men at least," Kisa looked at the daughter of the woman who had made her and her group feel welcome, offering healings, bath in a natural spring hidden behind the magical curtain of leaves, food, drink and something she valued more than that, information.

"And he loves the Princess?" Cassadee.

"I'm no expert on love, but I can say they do like each other a lot," after speaking the teenager took a sip from a wooden cup full of sweet berry wine, mixed with hot spiced tea.

"Well if Xarona likes him, I like him," Said Cassadee., "Even though he's the part giant,"

Kisa could tell the girl was sad by looking at her, Being able to read people, was a skill her father taught her and like all thoughts on him now it brought the only melancholy.

"Not all Giants are bad, in fact, Titans are among the most friendly and civilized..," said Kisa.

The one hunting us, the one with the Northman.. he killed my friends," Cassadee said softly.

"I'm sorry," was all the girl in glasses could say as the feelings that lead to her father's death started to overwhelm her.

Placing a hand on the girl's shoulder, Kisa moved her focus from her own conversation to another on the other side of the fire.

"If we fight together, we can defeat the Northman. Lizbeth looked at her fae and trog allies as well as Jase, Xarona, Isabella, Bhang, and Clare.

"You said they have almost two hundred men and a Giant.

," said Jase, "From what I see that's still not enough Miss Lizbeth.

"And that's not even taking into account the Colos," military, Isabella spoke up, "I'm sure they're after us even as we speak.

"We have an ally in the castle, we can talk about that when they arrive," said Lizbeth," But so far Colos has been letting the Estahutten do their dirty work.

"What exactly are your numbers," Xarona looked ay Lizbeth.

"My group has five witches counting my daughter and a dozen of so of our kin that can fight.

"We have a almost fifty that can fight in our tree said the fae standing next to the witch leader. "And some magic," he added quickly.

All eyes fell to the trog female who smiled, "we have many, she said not giving an exact number, Elk riders, Bear herders, clubbers, and spears," she said.

"I need to talk to my people," Isabella said.

Xarona, Bhang, and Jase all nodded at the woman who they saw not only as an employer but a friend.

Isabella stepped from the fire and walked towards the rest of her group who had gathered near Callum and Seamus.

Kisa looked up from a book she had borrowed from Xarona and whispered for Cassadee to leave as it seemed those approaching had the look of serious talks ahead.

The group moved to a quiet corner of the grove away from the fire and everyone else. The Salazar matriarch looked at the group and knew that if they were going to help, everyone including her children would have to be involved despite the danger.

"Pitting ourselves against a kingdom and a group of Northern merce-naries isn't exactly us going home,". said the woman to everyone looking at her in a dim light provided only by Seamus' staff.

"I'm not much for fighting a fight without being paid or it involving me and mine, "said Jase. before adding "But you'll are as much a family as I have back home, maybe even more, So I'll back whatever play you want,"

Bernardo nodded, "we need to avenge father," he said.

"This isn't about revenge; It's about justice. ," Bhang spoke up. , "Maybe instead of fighting, we should help move these people out of these moun-tains, maybe to Arden or Kascee.

Kisa and Lisa looked at the man they had just spoken than their mother, "I like that plan," they said in unison.

"It's something I haven't considered, Isabella.

"Better yet you have a Lord and Lady here who could vouch for the situation," Seamus.

Callum smiled, "I'm sure my cousin in Arden would at the very least consider it and if not we have room in the Mwamba wa Mwaloni for theses people and more,"

Or my family's lands," Xarona spoke up.

Isabella nodded and was about to turn and make the suggestion back to the group when a familiar voice reached her ears.

Without hesitation, the woman drew her sword and started to run towards the fire where the Lizbeth was holding an audience. Leaping gracefully over a log Isabella's eyes focused on a woman with the snow-white hair in a white fur coat. As the southern matriarchs sword moved to slice at the new arrivals neck.

Assassin," he cried out the Fae leader blocking Isabella's blade with his own and before the irate widow. In wind swing the found themselves knocked to the ground by a gust of the wind from Seamus' staff. Who like the others in the magician's group was now a few yards behind Isabella.

"I'm going to kill you!," Isabella looked at the Jazlyn as she prepared to strike again. Calmly the Princess of the Colos locked eyes on the woman and reached into her mind.

"Well fancy meeting you here," she said as Isabella suddenly fell unconscious.

Upon seeing her mother fall Lisa leaped through the air, dodging a trog's grasp and kicked the woman whose brother had ordered her Father's death in the stomach. As the woman started to vomit the girl then punched her in the throat then the nose. The Princess went to the ground.

"Everyone please stop!," Lizbeth called out hoping her words would do what her magic was prepared to do next.

"The trogs, fae, and witches halted as did the adventurers and most of their allies. Lisa, however, was not stopping and was now on top of the prone woman she had floored. The girl could not find the words to express the hate she felt for the woman she was about to pummel to death. Her father was dead, and she had done something to her mother, she could feel it. Was she dead too? Was she now an orphan.

"Lisa, don't !," Kisa called out to her sister as she attempted to pull her off the woman.

"She's our inside woman... our spy," Lizbeth added.

The thin dark haired girl, eyes still full of tears soften some as she looked down at the woman she had pinned under her. Her hooked nose was broken from a blow her throat bruised her hair now full of dust and blood.

Slowly, and without a word, the girl came to her feet and into her sister's embrace.

"That was unexpected," said the princess coming slowly to her feet with the help of the Female trog, "But not undeserved,"

"What did you-you do to my mother?," Bernardo looked at the woman who was dusting herself off.

"A little sleep spell," said the woman looking at the sword-wielding woman and willing her to awaken but calm, fearing a stab in the gut,"

"Looks like we're adding an assault on the Princess to the list of our crimes in Colos," Jase spoke humorously even though he still held his bow at the woman whose family had brought nothing but misery to him and those and traveled with.

"Colos has no legal warrants on any of you," said the princess, " You could walk to the borders and nary a soldier would raise a blade against you," she said.

"What ?" Callum sudden; felt relief, maybe Seamus' plan would work he thought.

"However," said the woman," he," pointing at Bernardo, "is being hunted by the Estahutten, It seems my brother thinks having s sly son-in-law is an insult, despite the fact his own son is hiding the same proclivities,"

"Your family is as small-minded as they are corrupt," said Isabella as she came to her feet with the helping of Clare and her own determination.

"True, we are corrupt as are most royal houses, although I don't share that particular prejudice," the Princess looked at Isabella with a look of both pride and pity.

"I won't let them harm you," Seamus looked at Bernardo taking the young man's free hand into his own.

"None of us will," Xarona looked at her friends then the princess, " If we were not here and you were not under the protection of my Sister Lizbeth... I would do horrible things to you, things that would twist my soul and I would do them without regret".

Callum raised an eyebrow, he knew the ginger young woman had a temper, but the coldness of her words gave him a chill.

The Princess smiled, "So is anyone else going to threaten me?," She asked. Looking first to Kisa and Lisa, then to her mother and everyone else in their group before turning Lizbeth, "If not I have news," she said calmly.

After a few moments to enforce the calm, Lizbeth gathered everyone around the fire and started to talk.

"So what's the news?', she asked the woman in white.

"My brother is starting to lose trust in Gravix the giant and his men," she said, " And fear them a bit, I think if they can be dealt with we might be a position to bring a peaceful solution to all of this,"

"How so?," Bhang spoke up.

"Simply put, The people don't like Estahutten hunters, and despite my brother's arrogance, he is a servant of the people. You get rid of a problem for them, and he may have no choice but to at the very least temporarily cease his removal of "Uncontrollable variables from our lands," The king's sister spoke calmly.

"and if he still wants to destroy us Uncontrollable variables?"., Lizbeth commented.

"Then the people would be less inclined to protest if my brother had an accident and a document making me the ruler and not my nephew was found," The princess added.

"What is wrong with you people?" Kisa called out, "You'll kill and lie, for power, without a second thought,"

The princess nodded, "Ironically that's how a family like mine gain and keep power. When my great-great-grandfather came to these lands, he was little more than Lord in name only, He married an Avian princess to gain their trust, then killed them to take their roost. When he could not control the religions, he drove them away, and when his son could not control the old blood he started driving them out till only a few small bands of trogs and one mother tree of flicks... fea was left. It's a history I'm both ashamed and proud of ". The woman in furs face showed no emotion as did her voice as she spoke, all eyes on her.

"While I appreciate your ruthless candor, your grace," Callum spoke up. , "I don't trust you, in fact, I opposite of trust you.

Xarona smiled and giggled a bit as did Jase and Cara.

"The fact the righteous crusader doesn't trust you pretty much tells me I should put an arrow in your brain by way of your eye and be done with you, Ma'am. " Jase shifted his bow to make the shot he just threatened.

The princess laughed, "Don't trust me, young hunter, trust my ambition. Turning away the woman walked away from the fire and towards the hidden glades' entrance path.

"Now, If were you I would get ready to put your arrow into some Estahutten. The woman exited the way almost everyone presented entered.

"I'm going to regret not killing her aren't I? ," Jase.

"Probably, but Alomeg will have his due," Callum.

"And if he doesn't the lady will," Xarona.

Lizbeth looked at the group, She also had reservation about the Princess, but if she ever wanted to return home, she would have to trust her or as she said at the very least her ambition.

"I think it's time we all got a little "rest she said to the group just as an arrow whizzed through the surrounding trees and hit the witch in the chest. In quick succession more bolts followed, the second one catching the witch leader in the neck and the third her right leg. Another then caught her in the arm and then her leg.

As the woman hit the ground, Callum called out," Seamus!",

The magician was already weaving a protective barrier as his friend's words made it to his ears.

"Everyone on me" the wizard called out expanding his barrier as much as he dared.

"Help him," called out a fae to one of his people. Moving towards the blond mage, a fae with green hair reached out with a hand hoping to add his energies to the spell, but before he could make contact, multiple arrows tore through his body.

"We need to get out of here, ," Someone called out just as the trees around them started to shake and the magic keeping the glade invisible from the outside started to vanish.

"They have magic," a Tilda holding up her hands as she tried to hold together the spell Lizbeth had cast some time ago even as a throwing ax caught her in the chest.

"I really hate Colos!," growled Xarona stepping near Seamus and pulling her wand and firing purple lighting blindly tin the direction the arrows came. The magician, thanks to the warrior's wheel knew instinctively know to let her spell pass through.

"This way!," Jase stood next to a barely visible deer path as he called out, " The untrained member of the witch's group, A few fae, and trogs rushed towards him as did Isabella and her family save for Bernardo who rushed to Seamus' side. Bhang and Claire brought up the rear.

"Are Nar!," Roared the female leader of the Trogs in her native tongue as she ran through the trees followed by half a dozen of her men brandishing wooden and stone weapons. Not to be outdone a group of fae followed their allies into the trees and an unknown battle.

I'll back them up," Callum said preparing a quick prayer of strength.

"No, we need to worried about getting out of here and the injured," said Xarona. "You can heal, that makes you important,"

The Witch looked about seeing the dead and injured, Callum looked at he nodded and moved towards Lizbeth while chanting "You are my rock, my hammer, and shield," over and over again as he ran to the down witches side and picked her. Please help her," Cassadee was kneeling by her mother in tears as the crusader arrived.

Callum saw the wounds and blood and felt no pulse yet still laid on his hands. The power granted to him flowed into the woman and back into him, there was no life to save.

"She's gone, there's nothing I can do," he said, resting the urge to add his tears to the girls.

"Bring her back," called out the girl. , "I heard your god could do that!".

Callum shook his head, "My Grandmother, a sanctified Healer on her best day could... I can't, That's not my path".

"Time to go, Hoss," Jase ran up to the crusader and young witch, grabbing the girl by her waist and turned towards the road he found. Callum, now carrying Lizbeth's body without hesitation followed, passing Seamus and Xarona who were providing protection and cover.

"Put me down!," cried Cassadee. c

"Not right now the little lady," said the hill-man as he ran along the trail with his friend behind him. In the distance, the young man could hear the sound of battle, the cracking of trees and the roar of a giant.

Jase and the others quickly caught up with the others that had retreated down the road earlier. Moving past them Jase took the lead and was surprised to see Enkidu had joined the party,

"You're a lot smarter than you look," he said to the riding bull who was moving alongside the trail through brush as if it was nothing

"He's following me," Sani spoke from where she perched on a tree in her wild cat form with a visible smoosh on her head.

"Can you fly ahead," asked Jase.

"I do so only because my mistress would want it," said the cat leaping from her perch and into her flying housecat form sending Smoosh flying through the air to land on Jase.

Jase followed the trail to where it exited near a river.

"You're dead... worse than dead!," said the girl he was holding.

"I've heard that before," said the young hunter looking down the river they way they came to see a dozen Estahutten moving towards them just out of bow range.

"Well, looks like the king of Colos doesn't skimp when hiring blood-thirsty Northmen," Jase dropped the girl

"Kill me later," he said drawing arrows and placing them point down into the soft soil.

Casadee watches the young man in black leather do a quick stretch, then nock an arrow.

"Oh you're not dying alone," Clare ran up to Jase, her telescoping staff in hand.

"Never figured I would, I knew one of you would be fool enough to hold the line with me,"

Clare smiled pulling a metallic egg-like device from her belt.

The Estahutten roared as they saw the thin boy and stocky girl along the tree line, Three prepared arrows in the bow as other raised weapons and increased speed, none of them noticing the river jumping its banks until it pushed them into the nearby tree line with such force the trees they struck shuddered.

"Last stands can wait," Seamus spoke from behind Claire and Jase.

Jase turned nodded, picked up his arrows and smiled,

"I wasn't planning on dying.

"Uh-huh," The mage smirked, causing Bernard who was at his side to giggle.

Seamus, still smiling leaned in to kiss the dark-haired young man who he had come to adore, but before their lips could touch something large hit him. From blond young man's perspective, time slowed down. As he tumbled into the air towards the river.

"Can't run from me little lambs!," Gravix strode from the tree line still holding the trunk of an oak he was using to clear a path for him and his men as he spoke. The giant raised the tree trunk again expecting a fight but instead finding the target of his hunt, the dark-haired boy in lavender lying halfway in the river his breathing raggedly, blood coming from his mouth.

"Looks like old king Colos is going to be happy tonight," said one of the Giant's man as he moved towards Bernardo.

"His fancy boots are mine," another man,"

"You can have'em, they look too prissy for me," said another Northman.

As the giant watched, His men stripped the limp and bleeding young man down to his pants. Once the men were done, The thin Estahutten with the staff walked up. To the body. Taking his hand, he touched the boys back.

The man with the staff looked Berardo over, he could feel the young man's life force slipping and knew he had to act quickly.

Taking a dagger, from a pouch he cut into the Young man's stomach, reached in and pulled out his liver and took a bite before

'I declare your strength as our strength," said the wizard. and handing the liver to Gravix who gulped down the rest.

Suddenly the north men started to cheer. After a few minute the men calmed and a red-haired hunter Northman spoke up. "Are we chasing down the rest?," he asked as if afraid his words would offend the giant.

'The giant smiled with crooked yellow teeth, " If they're headed south along the river they're going to once place, Aye Otis? ".

"The Tree," said the man in robes smiling.

Gravix looked at the wizard than his men as he spoke. "The

bird-woman said that's where they'll run and that's where we'll gut the rest of em'.

But first" he added, "let'em run a bit, get tired. Let them feed on hope, 'fore we take it and their last breaths away. ".

Once again the north men cheered, before turning back the way they came.

*****

Cassadee lowered her wand and the young witch, Jase and Clara reappeared along the river after the north man returned the way they came. Once they figured the Northmen were far enough away.

"What was that?," Clair stood, "that wasn't invisible, I've been invisible before,"

" The same spell my mom used to the camp only smaller," said the girl, exhausted from holding the spell for so long.

" We gotta find blondie," Jase without delay jumped into the river.

"He's dead !," Said Clare, "just like his boyfriend," as loud as she would dare. Fighting back tears.

Jase heard the words but ignored them, diving deep he swam looking above and below the water and seeing nothing. Coming back to the shore he started to gather his things.

"Not going to bury him till I find his body," said the hill man," in a tone that mixed sorrow with anger.

"But you saw what that giant did!," Clare could hear her voice crack as she called out. She wasn't mad at Jase, but at herself, and the giant and the north men.

"Be quiet, giants have good ears," said Casadee looking at the man and woman who seemed on the verge of either attacking each other or collapsing into grief.

Jase nodded, "Let's go then," he said following the river downstream as fast as he dared, knowing Claire and Cassadee weren't nearly as fast as he was.

Callum stopped in mid-stride. Pulling on the rope attached to his bull. Who now carried a witches body tied to its back. The free-crusader could feel something was wrong as they moved up a hill into the deeper forest and away from the river.

"What's wrong?," Xarona who walked behind him saw the big man go to one knee. "Seamus," he said," as if he was suddenly exhausted.

"Upon hearing the words, the witch felt something too, she had to go back to the river.

"Take the bull with you, We'll find you," said the young lord Crusader to a confused fae.

"Very well," said the thin warrior, who quickly made sure the witches body that was tied to the bull was secured tightly before he heads the bull away.

"Just follow this path," he said to the adventurers. I'll make sure my people are looking out for you," Callum nodded acknowledging the fae's word before heading down the hill towards the river.

Half way down the hill the sky darkened,

"M'lady," Xarona heard a voice from above and looked up. Above her, The remaining witches floated, their living and injured family members holding onto an uprooted levitated tree.

"I have to go," said the redhead," feeling a sense of urgency building in her.

"We're leaving," said the witch who was always reading the cards.

"You're running?," said Xarona.

"Call it what you like, Without Lizbeth, we can't win," said the short-haired witch before turning away and floating off on her broom, the tree and two other witches following.

"Cowards," growled the lady of house Belasona, in disgust.

Hiking up her dress the young woman finally caught up to the young lord who kneeling near the river. In front of him laid Seamus who was pale and soaked. Xarona speed up almost tripping as she came to Callum's side, looking about she saw the Wizards' staff floating in the water. Gesturing quickly she brought it quickly to her side.

"I know how to do this," Said the Crusader remembering what his grandmother had taught him, the breather's-gift she called it, could revive the near drowned. Leaning over he prepared to breathe into his friend's mouth only to find something there. Pulling back he saw Smoosh appear over Seamus' mouth. it's stubby tentacles spread across his friends face Callum looked at the creature and was about to pull it away when the wizard moved.

"Bernard," Seamus wheezed out as the small creature detached itself.

"He's not here," Callum spoke to his friend helping him into a sitting position and discovering the shattered left arm.

Bernard," Seamus said tears again in his eyes before slumping into the Crusader's arms.

"We should have stayed home," Callum.

"Maybe," Xarona stood close as the large young man stood with his friend.

"Is he dead?," Jase called out, obviously tired and distraught. , "I tried.,". He said before falling to his knees.

"No, Alomeg was kind today," Callum.

Claire looked at her friends, each one with a solemn look on their face. Her mind flashed back to the first time the meet, the freedom they represented to her. Her eyes then focused on Seamus.

"How is he alive?," exclaimed the tinkersmith, "A giant hit him with a bloody tree. Hell, how are we alive?',

Xarona was about to speak up when Claire continued.

"They have a giant! A real one, He ate Bernardo's liver..,". the young woman's voice became more frantic.

"Bernardo's dead? That's going to kill Isabella," said the witch with concern.

"They said the princess told them where to find us, That woman is playing all of us like a fiddle," said Jase.

"I'm going to kill her," Xarona growled.

Claire lowered her head before looking up at her friends,

"We can't beat this, They know where everyone is going, They are just giving everyone time to get there in one place," Claire spoke with urgency, " We need to get Isabella, Bhang, and the girls and get our arses to Kascee!".

All eyes fell on the stoutkin girl, deep in side they knew she was right, it was them and a few surviving Trogs and Fey versus trained hunters and a giant. As Xarona had said, the math wasn't on their side.

"We need to get Seamus someplace he can rest first," Said Callum.

"Then we run?," said Claire.

"Then we consider our options," Xarona looked up at the sky the way the witches had headed before looking at Cassadee. "Also we have to put Lizbeth to rest," she added.

With those words, Cassadee started to cry as the adrenaline left her body and the grief returned.

"Then we run," repeated Claire, this time not as a question but as something she felt was a matter of fact.

Jase upon seeing the path Callum and Xarona had exited started towards it in silence. He hated the idea of running but thinking about the giant and what he saw unnerved him far more than he liked. Giants were monsters, Oldblood for sure, but unlike Fey, trog and Avians and others they had more in common with great beasts than the others of their kind.

As the group followed the trail up into the hills that reminded the hunter of his home the brush around the path started to thicken.

"This is magic," said Xarona, feeling the energy of nature all about.

"We need Seamus," Claire spoke up.

Callum continued to walk, even as he was holding his friend he was healing him, fixing what he could with every ounce of divine energy he could muster. But despite him trying it was an uphill battle.

"There you are," a Fae with long blond hair sitting in a tree spoke up and was almost simultaneously skewered by an arrow and blasted by witch lighting for his trouble. Thankfully Jase and Xarona managed to stop themselves bore they accidentally killed their ally.

They fae jumped down in front of the group,

"This way," he said walking along the path causing the brush to part as he moved along a trail that in a matter of minutes turned from dirt and stone to a stone paved road.

"Amazing," Claire looked at the road, it wasn't just carved stones but a single piece of stone shaped into a road winding up and forming steps.

"Have any of you ever seen a mother tree?," asked The groups guide.

Once, but I don't think anyone lived there," said Jase.

"There are less than twenty left in so-called Free kingdoms. ," said, the guide. " Ours is the only one lefty in Colos. "

As he spoke the group noted great wooden arches running along a side road and crossing it and the tall oaks ahead being in what at first they thought was in the shadow of a forest covered hill. But as the group got closer they could see the hill was in fact. a great oak.

Moving even closer the adventures started seeing groups of fae with bows and spears sitting trees and groups of Trogs near cook fires on the ground.

"Bernardo," Seamus whispered.

"Did he just say something? ," Claire

"I think so," Callum.

The guide looked at Seamus, "This is a place of power for his people, It protects us and heal us,"

"Blurp," Smoosh moved from where it sat invisible on Callum's shoulder to Seamus's chest and relaxed as if it the creature was going asleep.

"Where are the witches and our people?," asked Cassadee.

Xarona reached out a hand to the girl's shoulder, " They left, they ran," said the witch glancing at Claire who suddenly regretted her words to her friends.

"A luxury we don't have," said the thin man in woven wood and vine armor, "Ths is our home, our center, as he spoke the group made it to a series of paths made of the mother tree itself leading up and through it. Glowing transparent fruit the size of watermelon lit the area and the path leading up. Slowly the group moved up the trail stopping at large terraces that held house sized tree knots hollowed out to make buildings and homes.

"Thank you,"Callum, spoke to guide.

"You're welcome, not often I get to use my Freeman's tongue," said the Fey.

"By the way, What's your name Pard," asked Jase.

"Norso," said the guide.

Eventually, the group moved past more small terraces to larger ones where crops and orchards grew to a slightly smaller one set against the tree where a great, beautiful carved building sat in a garden surrounded by great wooden carvings of former leaders, the great green mother herself, and abstract shapes.

"You made it!," Kisa ran up to her friends.

The girl was followed by Sani, the trog leader and the young looking fae scout Fey that had Callum had given Enkidu's reigns too.

"Where's your mother?," Jase and Callum spoke at the same time in a tone so serious it brought chills to the girl.

"With Harneli, the Fey leader," said Kisa who now notice Bernardo was missing.

"Where my brother? ," she asked, fearing the answer.

"Dead," Seamus whispered

The words from the wizard seemed to knock the girl off her feet.

"I'll take him to our healer, "Norso," walked over to Callum who was about to hand Seamus only, but instead was surprised to see the faekin stand unsteadily despite his obvious injuries and the look of despair on his face.

"Dead," said Seamus again to himself.

"I'm sorry," Claire walked over to Kisa who was on her knees. kneeling she held the girl sobbing with her.

"Father's gone, Bernardo is gone, what do we do now," sobbed the girl.

Claire sobbed for a second before speaking up, "I don't know," she said.

"I don't either," commented Jase who stood next to Cassadee doing his best to fight back the things that he was taught were a weakness. sympathy, connection, and tears. In the hills, men didn't cry unless they were drunk and even then they did their best to hid the true reasons for the tears.

The young hunter remembered crying only twice in his life, once when his mother died and again when his father struck him after the elder hill-man returned home in a drunken stupor. As he stood there looking at Clare, Kisa, Xarona, Callum and Cassadee the dam he had built long ago cracked then broke sending tears down his face.

"I best go and scout this place," said the hill-man under his breath before walking off.

"Jase," Callum spoke softly reaching out a hand towards his friend.

"I'll be okay big man," sad the young man in leather as he allowed himself to fully accept the fact he was hurting, that Vinceno Salazar was not just a friend or employer but a man he respected and a moreover a man that respected him like his own father never did, or least never openly did.

The young hunter walked swiftly around the beautiful buildings and found what he was looking for, arched buttress he could climb. Pushing away the exhausted the hunter started up the arched wooden building support, climbing at first then near the top, walking. Tired beyond words he sat and looked up.

"I never talked to you," he said, "We never thought much of you or the other gods atheist not till we were close to dying or at a funeral," said the young man, "But my friend says your there and through him, you've helped me get here".

Moving to his knees Jase continued his attempt at prayer, "I ain't one to lie or regret, and I don't like asking for things, But if you and yours can look out for Mr. Vinceno and Bernardo, I much appreciate it. ," he said. before closing his eyes and continuing to weep.

*****

Xarona looked at Casadee as she holding her hand.

"I'm sorry," said the older witch, "your mother seemed like a great lady".

Casadee nodded, "She was,". said the girl as if in a daze.

The ginger lady pulled the girl in close to hug her tight even as her thoughts moved not just to the anguish all around her but her situation and that of the child she must now at least in the meantime care for.

The rules were clear among her kind, Lizbeth was dead, The father had very little rights when it came to witches. In fact, in theory, Cassadee should do go to a grandmother or aunt, but as far as Xarona knew they were either dead or gone. That meant that as the witch present the girl was her responsibility until she could find a female witch relative or get her to the Coventry. or taken in by another witch.

Xarona walked girl to a nearby wooden bench that grew out of the tree they stood on.

"Is there anyone we should contact," she asked the girl as both of them sat, still in tears.

"I'm alone," said Cassadee. "Never knew my pa or other kin,"

Xarona nodded as the girl who was a few years younger than her sisters sobbed onto her blouse.

"You're not alone. By the Lady, The Muses and the thirteen sacred crones, I promise to protect and provide for you as if you were my own," vowed the ginger witch known that the promise she was making wasn't just words but a form of binding magical contract. If the young accepted the girl would be in the eyes of all witches and the Lady be Xarona's daughter. Cassadee looked into the woman that held her blue eyes and smiled, she still missed her mother but in "The Princess," she saw kindness and gentility and strength and though no words were said, the pact was sealed.

CHAPTER 21:
THE CALM

Isabella wailed in loss and frustration till her throat was dry. Around her, her daughters gathered to hold her in equal despair. Her son was dead, and she was not there to ease his passing or to save him, she was not there to do all the things that mothers do in such dark times, and so for that and more, she cried out.

A part of her blamed her husband who was also dead. The guilt of that thought and that blamed brought only more sorrow as she thought of what had brought her to a strange land surrounded by stranger friends.

Vinceno was always a dreamer. When they had met, she was the daughter of a wealthy family of free people from Myzonna, west of Vallus. Though they were mostly cattle ranchers, they also had a small heard of the large flightless birds they called Volos. Like her future husband, her family was Myberian, Part Mytec, Native and Iberians from the old world.

The Martinez clan more than most held tight to the Iberian part of their blood despite the fact they all had the tan skin and dark hair, traits that common among the Mytecs that lived on the other side of the Big River. Isabella remembered her terracotta roofed hacienda being full of paintings of family members from the old lands as well as high room, dark wood furniture and the near constant smell of cooking. The youngest daughter of eight children and the only girl, it was from her rowdy brothers and those that her family hired that she learned how to ride, use a sword and swear despite her parent's attempts to turn their daughter into a lady in hopes to marry her off to a noble or merchant family. Isabella, of course, wanted nothing to do with her family plans and as a show of her rebellion, she took her skills as a swordsman on the road as a duelist.

People would come from miles around to see a beautiful female duelist who was the match of any man in tournaments and dueling contests. A dullest who fought with grace not strength and who could run a sword through the cracks of men wearing plate armor with ease.

At one such tournament, the female duelist met a young sailor who had manage to come across a significant amount of silk and was trying to sell it at a nearby market. The sailor upon seeing Isabella fight made a deal with her. He would provide her with silk scarves to wear if she announced before the crowd where the silk came from. Amused Isabella agreed and so her and Vinceno's relationship begun.

At first, it was just business, but over time it turned to more, and by the time both of them turned twenty a few years later, Vinceno could afford to pay the young woman's dowry. Not long after that, the two left where the Big River ended in Myzonna for the east. Ending up in Vallus the new couple spent several years buying and selling silks and learning even more about the business including dying and producing the quality product.

Bernardo was born was born two days after Isabella's thirtieth birthday. It was a glorious party with friends and family and a special gift of a hand-carved wood and ivory folding fan from the queen of Vallus who had more than once purchased Salazar silk. The next day the long labor started and a day after that a dark-haired child came was born, and it was the merchant couples pride and joy.

A boy who she would never see the smile again, a husband who she would never argue with, makeup with or kiss.

"Father take my husband and son into your heart," prayed the woman. "And grant me forgiveness for the vengeance I will bring:," she added as her daughters who held her simultaneously said "amen,"

As Isabella lamented the people around them prepared for battle. The fae magicians who were also priests and priestess of the Green Mother talked to the mother tree, laying hands on it and holding their ornate staffs to reshaped the gigantic tree itself. Roots rose from the ground forming thick bark like walls at the base around the camping trogs and lower terraces. Archers roosts appeared in the trunk complete with winding stairs that allowed for fast access. In the terrace gardens food for a long siege grew even as the roots of the tree spread into nearby rivers in a lake to draw water into the massive hollow reservoirs inside the tree itself.

Knowing the enemy was coming would grant the last mother tree of Colos and its allies an advantage, but the fae knew other greater trees, the Great Ash and Pine of the high north and their sister Oak in the East near the Kascee border had fallen. Thousands had been slaughtered. Examination of the trees had shown the Estahutten had used a mixture made of deeply drilled black-water and other ingredients to coat the tree before setting them on fire. The mixture seemed to not only burn fast but prevented things from regrowing in the area.

Clare was asked to represent the adventurers who had right before the meetimg all but vanished into their own despair and problems. Standing next to Harnrli the fae's silver-haired leader now dressed in armor of hardened amber over woven wood and Zel an intimidating trog female who had inherited her tribe's leadership when the giant Gravix killed her father with one great blow with his ice crystal powered great ax. The giants men then slaughtered the rest of her family including her brothers and sisters.

The trog like Clare wished they were someplace else. In the case of Zel after the death of her father and brothers knowing her small tribe was outnumbered the new leader told her people to run and leave the caves, they had called home for generations. Seeking help, she first leads her people to where a small group of human missionaries lived. When she was young, they had taught her and few of her people to speak the free-speak in a small building that the Trogs found was now burned to the ground and used as a funeral pyre for the missionaries who by the look of the corpses were partially eaten by a giant before being tossed on the burned.

And so the trog chieftain and her people kept moving. Through cool summers and harsh winters avoiding the north-men and the Colos military. Warriors from other tribes wishing to fight and refugee from destroyed tribes bolstered her people's ranks enough to embolden her fight back.

It was while looking for the north men Zel discovered a small band of humans on the road. Zel and her people attacked only to frightened by the women in the group's magic. Zel herself was captured and thought she was going to be killed or worse.

The trog leader sat, thinking back on the first time she met Lizbeth and instead of being seen as an enemy she was treated as a potential ally. She offered the Trogs healing and magical assistance in exchange for food and supplies brought to her magically hidden grove. It was after returning from gathering supplies that Zel found the witch had been inspired not just to survive, but like Zel, fight back.

Now the woman whose kindness had saved many of her people was dead, laying on a slab in a fae tree and yet again her people had been forced to retreat. But soon the time to retreat would be over the all involved had decided to make the tree their final stand, and Zel herself had decided to die instead of running again.

"We need to be ready for the burning black water," said Harnrli to everyone present.

"It's called oil," corrected Clare knowing the liquid quite well thanks to its ability to lubricate devices.

Harnril nodded, Oil," he said before he continued talking. "We will do our best to occupy the north-men while our new allies deal with their leader.

Clare's eyes widened, the agreement the fae leader spoke of was one none of her group had fully agreed to, in fact, she was hoping to talk the group into making a run for Kascee and for her to live long enough to see her father again.

"You do realize, that's a Joltan, an honest to the Gear ice giant," said the tinkersmith. "I mean my group is full of some incredible people.. but... he's a giant".

Zel looked at the girl and smiled with her large teeth.

"Before my father was killed by him he made it bleed, and if it can bleed it can die," said the trog.

Clare looked into the tall woman's sad, dark eyes and found herself unable to do anything but nod.

Harnrli continued to talk using a large tree stump like table everyone was gathering around and his magic to shape it into terrain and miniature versions of troops that moved on there own. Taking advice from Zel's encounters with the northmen he outlined a plan of attack that took advantage of his people's natural magic, the great tree, and the trogs ferocious ground-based attacks.

"A lot of them," said the gray-skinned woman looking at the Estahutten's numbers.

"That's not an exact number, all we know is we're outnumbered," said the fae with a solemn look on his face.

Upon hearing his words Clare's mind started to race, that was a problem and fixing problems was what tinkersmith's did.

You're High Elfness," Clare spoke to the leader who looked at the young woman with indignation, "I can help there but I'll need a few things she said,"

"Go on my stoutkin friend," Harnrli

Clare walked on to the large stump-table and reached into her shoulder bag and took out her whirly gigs and started to explain what they did, how they flew and could be controlled by her control crystal device.

She then explained how the devices power supply was all but exhausted but if she could repower them and use them as spies that could report back on their enemies movements instantly.

After Clare made her case, Harnrli sent for his own artificers, and Zel sent for her lone shaman. The artificers provided Clare with four high-quality green crystals and worked with her to convert her flying devices from clear crystal power to verdant crystal. The new magic power caused the devices to look even more like insects. The shaman then took out small piles of powder and mixed them and poured it on the devices than on the tree stump table that the fae used to plan their war. The powders connected their energies and allowing the pets broadcast to the table.

Clare was taking apart her control crystal when Xarona walked up. The Tinkersmith looked at the witch and smiled.

"How's Grape?" she asked.

"Who?," asked the witch.

"The little witch girl," The tinkersmith laid out wiring and gears on a silk cloth

"Oh, the hair, she won't like that," said Xarona.

"I'm still calling her Grape," Clare

Xarona walked up to her friend looked at the various wires, coils, and dials on the table and tried taking a breath.

"She's fine and my ward," said the Witch, "I made the pact,".

The stoutkin shrugged and continued working

"I'm not sure I care, but it sounds important, " said Clare in a snide tone that caused Xarona to chuckle.

Changing the subject Xarona looked around the large wood room, and it vaulted ceiling and intelligently carved walls

"You hear about them read about them, But being here with them, it's just so different," said the ginger lady looking at the room as she tried to coax the change of conversation and ease the jumbled mess of things in her normally ordered mind. In fact, she had so many thoughts going on that her betrothal was now far down on the list as it was almost lost in the minutia of it all.

"I grew up hearing about how savage the trogs were but being with them, talking to them and seeing mothers nursing babies, elders telling stories, they are so much like us,". Said Chare.

"They are us, and we're them"m Xarona added, " The great scholars said we all spawned from the same bloodlines, It's just magic changed some of us along the way making the old bloodlines and the human ones. said the witch,"

"The Oldblood was born long ago.

One for the Fey up in the trees.

Two for the Avians wings in the breeze.

Three for the Stouts who dig and build.

Four of the Deva with webs they weave

Five for Giants, Titan, Ice, Fire, Hill, and Swamp.

Six for Wolfkin in hunting they romp.

Seven for the Vampyre, neither live nor dead

Eight for the Kitsune, self-changers and fox wives never wed.

Nine for the Naga they slither and shout

Ten for Trog, who do without. ," Claire song hey old nursery rhyme and the spite the fear she felt smiled.

"Papa Spider's book of songs and rhymes?," Xarona looked at Claire and spoke.

"Yeah, I haven't thought about that book since I was a kid," said the young woman.

"I still have mine, back home in my personal library," said the redhead.

The dark haired girl rolled her eyes, "Of course you have a library,"

Xarona looked at her friend with and spoke in a placating tone, "well I call it a library, It's just five thousand or so books. Not large at all, in fact, it's not even a quarter of the size of the family library or the public one in Bellstone.

"You do realize most people don't have libraries or own books," said Claire.

"Well, I'm sure everyone owns at least a dozen or so books," The red-head sounded scandalized.

Claire turned picked up the parts to her device and started reassembling them as she spoke one word, "Jase?," she said.

"Point taken," said the witch her spirits slightly lifted.

"So, how's Seamus? asked Claire her face turning serious.

"Our hosts moved him to their healing chambers, Callum is there watching him like a mother bear," Said Xarona, "According to Noros, he should but fine by now, but despite that   Lord Wimbowardi and Jase's occasional efforts he's been silent,"

Claire nodded, "I bet he's feeling guilty about Bernardo," she said.

The redhead threw her hands up frustrated, "This was supposed to be an easy escort. Our first mission, but despite our best efforts, we've lost two of our charges and maybe a friend. " as Claire watched both worried and amused the witch face grew red with anger, " I'm going to make that duplicitous cow suffer for this," added Xarona.

Claire nodded, "While I want nothing more than to see Princess Beak nose put down we have bigger worries like I don't know... north-men and a Giant".

Xarona looked at Claire, suddenly calmed again by her matter of fact words. "I thought you we were running? ," said the witch.

The tinkersmith lowered her head in shame, "You guys put me in charge the plans have changed. They want us to kill a Giant".

Xarona looked at her friend and without warning hugged her tight.

"Oh great, a witch hug, now I'm doomed," said the shorter woman.

The witch looked at her friend and pulled away curious about the reaction, "Excuse me?". She said.

Claire crossed her arms, "No offense, my name isn't Callum, and if you're all sweet, that means you don't think we're going to live through this," Claire.

Xarona was about to commit when Sani flew from the trees with two owls behind her.

"Mistress, You're needed near the fountain," Said the chimera.

"Which one?," ask Xarona looking up at her familiar.

"The one where Mistress Lizbeth's body is being mourned," said the winged cat ignoring the owls who were playfully circling her.

"Of course," said the witch to her cat, before turning to look at Claire, "I'm sorry, I have business to attend to with my ... ward ," she said.

"Don't worry and tell Grape hello. , "said Clare," I think I'll head over to the healing room or whatever they call it and see about getting our wizard out of his bed. "

***

Callum sat on the stump like wooden chair that formed out of the floor itself. Next, to him was a similarly formed wooden structure only slightly longer than the blond young man on it, laying on a thick bed of grass l and covered with blankets that looked like woven vines.

The stocky young lord had just awakened from a nap, hoping to see his friends moving, but instead, he found him as he was right before falling asleep. Curled up under his blanket his eyes occasionally opening and staring into nothingness.

"Buddy, you have to come back to us," said Callum picking up a wooden drinking cup and discovering smoosh squeezed into it asleep.

"Smoosh needs you," he said, "we all need you,"

The southern lord placed the cup back down on the floor and stood and looked around. The large round room held a few dozen empty beds, only the one next to him was occupied. Halfway up the walls were mounted pea sized pure crystals like the one his hammer was made of, they formed a ring of about fifty or so around the room and filled it with positive spiritual energy augmented by the trees nature energy. The result gave the magic a slightly green cast and kept it well lit along with the large light crystal in the ceiling.

"Alomeg helps me, help us," said the crusader as he walked over to where a small indention in the wall theld water. Taking the water Callum rubbed his face and looked into the water and to the young man's surprise heard the fluttering of wings, looking about he expected to see one of the large owls the Fey kept as pets and messengers or Sani, but instead, he saw nothing.

Heading back to his chair, The young lord opened up a bag on the side of the chair, inside sat a water skin, and a bag of old travelers mix he had concocted in Kascee. The small bits of jerky, popped corn, tried carrots, and apples were flavored some of the spices he had purchased and smoked salt. It wasn't his best work, but at least it had meat, something missing it seemed from all fae meals.

After eating a hand full of the food and washing it down the crusader walked to refill his waterskin, noting that despite the "leafy," tinge to the water it was both cold and of the highest quality, Once done filling the water he heard the wings again. Turning he spied for the briefest of moments something silver out of the corner of his eye.

"What are you he said softly to himself, expecting to hear nothing in return.

"Say my name," a voice like rolling thunder more in his soul then ears," staggered the large man.

"Who?," Callum thought to himself as suddenly a sense of peace and urgency quickly flowed through him before vanishing.

"What are you doing?," Clare saw the Crusader on his knees.

The Callum, on hearing the young woman's voice opening his eyes.

"Let me guess, Praying," said the tinkersmith walking past the

Nyumbani lord to the Wizard's bed.

Callum rose not sure what had happened remembering it not as something real but rather as a dream. "He moves in mysterious ways," said the free-crusader.

Claire looked at titankin lord and rolled her eyes,

"That's your problem, You make things complicated with all the religious stuff, "said the young woman walking over to Seamus' bead and unceremoniously throwing off the young wizard's blanket and with a raised foot pushing the convulsing adventurer to the floor.

"What in the name of the saints are you doing!," called out Callum who in but a few strides was at his friend's side.

"I'm getting him up," said the girl leaning over the blond young man and grabbing his arm to lift him.

Callum was about to protest when Seamus' eyes widened, and his face went from placid to angry.

"Get away from me !," He screamed his eyes glowing white.

Suddenly Callum and Clare found themselves tossed against a nearby wall and held there by an invisible force.

Slowly the wizard came to his feet and faced them. "Why won't you leave me be!," he called out.

Callum could see his friend was in pain and using a leg he pushed himself off the wall,"

"You know that's not going to happen," said the free-crusader using all his strength to brace himself against the force his friend was generating.

"Don't you see, Bernardo's dead because of me, there's nothing left for me," Seamus' eyes started to darken, turning from white to black as his anguish caused him to tap into power he that was both frightening and alive.

Callum slammed back against the wall. And closed his eyes, "Alomeg give me strength," using his divine energy to increase his strength allowing him to dig into the wood floor and push forward.

"Hey, you can stop now!," said Clare unable to move.

"No," Seamus called out in a voice that was not only deeper but sinister.

Callum could feel shadow slipping into his friend, the darkness of the void before creation that was an anathema to Alomeg's light.

"Don't let it in, Don't let your hurt open you to the dark," said the crusader puling free of the wall again.

Seamus now knew hat was happening, he wanted revenge, he wanted to hurt those that had hurt him, and like many a magical person had opened a door, some said could not be closed. The door to the magic fueled by malice, suffering, and death.

"It can help me, kill the Estahutten," said the wizard his simple white gown blowing in a ghost wind.

"It will break you and turn you from family and friends," Callum.

It will make me powerful," Seamus roared and for the first time noticed the pure crystals on the wall were dimming and cracking. He then saw his oldest friend, the man he loved like a brother once again thrown back .

"Think about your mother, your father, your sister and brother, think of the Mwamba wa Mwaloni, our home," said as he Callum, unable to move most of his body,

Seamus took a step back, knowing that the door was now open, that the darkness was there and he could call it at the cost of his soul being devoured spell by spell.

He could have revenge or most likely die trying to achieve it, but he would lose the capacity for love. The capacity to appreciate music, food and even a smile. That's the price the void took.

Focusing the wizard turned away from the door opened in his mind and blocked it' with thoughts of family, friends and his feelings for Bernardo, feeling that brought tears to his eyes.

Staggering forward Callum suddenly found himself free, turning he saw Clare slide off the wall into sitting position on the floor.

"What the hells was that?' she asked.

"Exactly what you said, the Hells," Callum moved towards his friend he could feel the darkness was gone for the most part. just the smallest sliver of its taint was left in his friend, the price for opening himself to the realm of shadow. Walking quickly the he he free-crusader without a word wrapped his arms around his friend knowing he had come to losing him.

"Don't ever do that again Seamus," he said.

"I won't, I won't," sobbed the Wizard.

"Good," Callum hugged his friend until thoughts of what he might have happened if Seamus wasn't strong enough to resist the temptation faded.

"Claire stood brushing herself off, "Well it wasn't what I expected, but it worked. She said walking up to the two young men.

"I almost tapped into shadow, do you have any idea what that means," said the wizard.

Claire shrugged, "Something blah, blah dark, blah blah magical and bad," said the tinkersmith in the sarcastic tone.

Callum pulled away from his friend, Well that's not an entirely wrong answer". said the large young man.

"Seamus nodded, turned towards his staff leaning against the wall and held out his hand willing to float to his hand.

"I need a bath and to talk to Ms. Isabella". said the blond.

"Are you sure you're ready?" asked, Callum.

"No, but I have to do it. ," said the wizard, "I loved Bernardo, she loved him, I can't let her hurt alone.

"Great, do that," said Claire, "and afterward we can figure out how to deal with a giant" The young men looked at the tinkersmith, knowing that despite her bluntness she was right. A battle was coming them, and they had to either be ready to receive it or ready to bring it to their foes first.

"Say my name," a voice only Callum heard followed by the fluttering of wings.

"You in there friend," Callum looked at his friend who was staring into space,

"Yeah," said the young lord. "I was just lost in thought," he said not exactly sure what was happening.

"Blurpdark" smoosh exited the cup he was asleep in and climbed up on Seamus to the top of his head and sat there.

There you are," said the wizard. "Have a good nap,"

"Glopspearman said the creature.

"Did it just say good?," Claire".

"Almost said, Seamus.

Callum, Seamus, and Clare walked towards the room's exit, "So It's going to talk. Like Xarona's annoying cat," asked the tinkersmith.

"One day," said the wizard.

"I wonder if Enkidu can talk?" said Callum.

Claire laughed, "If it does I'm sure its first words would be, m back hurts!".Callum smiled at the girl before playfully pushing her on the shoulder and lightly into a wall before exiting the room.

*****

The small group of fae stood behind a covering made of leaves and spun spider silk. In the small oak tree that like most of the nearby trees where little more than branches of their home mother tree.

"No sign of the northern barbarians they said a dark-haired fae in the green and autumn leaf gold colored armor of the Mother Tree's militia.

"All humans are barbarians," said a silver-haired soldier while sharpening arrowheads.

"True," responded another loyal member of the Mother Tree's militia spoke up just as an arrow pierced his side. As his friends watch the young fae fell off the branch, he was perched on the ground.

"By the Green Mother's magic," the bowman exclaimed as he stood, an arrow at the ready only to see something large moving towards him.

The boulder crashed into the tree splinter the branches and sending those hiding in it to the ground.

"Bring me their ears said Gravix clapping dust from his hands after throwing the large stone.

From out of the woods weapons drawn came a dozen Estahutten looking for survivors.

"Curse you," a fae leaped from the brush, ignoring the pain he felt he slashed at a human's wildly finding only a shield.

As he tried to get his bearing, a spear caught him in the leg than in the side sending him to the ground bleeding.

" Those ears are mine!," said the spearman lowering his weapon and walking to his dying victim.

"And this one's mine, growled another northern hunter as he shot a broken and crawling fae in the back of the head with an arrow.

Seeking other prizes, the Northmen spread out looking for any sign of survivors or bodies with ferocious intent. Beyond their search area, a fae with golden eyes watched them briefly, before limping off as quietly as he could manage.

Moving thru the forest, the fae warrior tried to ignore the pain. He had had to warn his people he had to live.

"I saw him go this way," said a deep voice in the distance,"

"I see blood," said another voice, "Stupid Pointy-ears, don't know when it's time to die,"

Upon hearing re his enemies words, the warrior increased his speed despite the pain he felt in his hip and thighs and buzzing in his ears.   As the buzzing increased the warrior stopped as a shadow moved above looking up he saw the largest wasps he had ever seen, each one as long as his arm.

Fearing he was delirious, he rubbed his eyes in the blink. As his eyes opened, he saw a large grey stone moving at him followed only by darkness.

*****

"They're coming 194 strong plus a Giant," said Clare looking at the intricate miniatures on the large stump table.

"Short girl do good," said Zel

Clare smiled, She had set her crystal control box to watch for the northmen, detect any magic from them and look out for Gravix and they had done their job well.

Harnrli noded at the Tinkersmith "I concur," he said before starting a series of command to Norso and the other fae commanders present.

"Bru-ack nor Zig Calo Mahr!," roared Zel in her native tongue before exiting with three of her largest warriors.

Clare watched unable to understand the words.

"May we meet in the Forever Fields!," said Norso in return to his Tog Ally.

"Is that what she said," asked Clare.

"More or Less," Norso assured, "Die with Honor may be a better translation?".

Clare nodded and moved away from the table towards the door to find her friends,

"The Gear turns, favoring none and favorsl. ," said the young tinkersmith quoting the holy book her father would read to her when she was young.

******

Jase leaped from branch to branch and occasionally shimming down giant leaves heading to the ground. In the distance, he saw Bhang doing the same with a grace he wishes he had. Bhang's chi-wise training was a mystery to him, according to the former driver it wasn't magic and was something anyone could learn given enough time and discipline.

As Jase made it to the ground, the hill-man landed as he was taught making as little noise as he could and staying low. Reading his bow, he looked about and spied the chi-wise boxer not far away. Both men started around the large tree finding their way to the trog camp and a pitched battle between the large gray-skinned people and the Estahutten.

The Estahutten, some in leather armor, other in the partial plate, scale or Chainmail fought savagely with large swords, axes, and hammers. The club and wooden spear wielding Trogs roaring with defiance used their great strength to their advantage, knocking foes down and attacking them with a brutality that made both of Jase and Bhang give their allies a wide berth lest they mistake them for the northern mercenaries. In the distance, both men could hear the sound of war chants who's words brought them unease, it was magic very similar to Callum's prays before and in battle, on this time it was being used against them.

Bhang had been trained to clear his mind and focus his surroundings and goals, in this case, it was to find Gravix and even the odds as best he could for him and his allies. Taking a breath, he silenced war chant in his mind and moved towards a stunned Jase.

"Ignore it he whispered to the young man who was looking about as if ever twig and leaf was a potential enemy.

"I'm trying," he returned doing his best to ignore the sound and the feeling of uneasiness and fearful-paranoia it brought. Seeing his allies nerve being undone the man from the west coast of Aerix reached out and pinched his friend's ear till it turned red.

"What was that for!," exclaimed the Jase suddenly focusing on the pain and not on the chant".

"Giving your mind other things to focus on," said Bhang.

The hill-man was about to argue when he realized he was no longer afraid, "Thanks, friend," he said nodding and looking about and spotting an Estahutten war priest at the rear of their lines chanting. Quickly he prepared an arrow and let it fly, sending it in a low arc into the crown of the man's head.

The war-priest fell, and the drummer next to him stopped dropped his instrument drew short curved swords.

"I can still hear more of them chanting," Said Bhang.

"We need to take them out, and any other magic types," said Jase.

"Exactly, If we're the only ones with magic, that could turn the tide," acknowledge Bhang before turning to see a group of northern mercenaries was now headed towards them.

Jase didn't take time to count, he knew him, and his friend was outnumbered and that the only way they would be survived is if he made every shot count. The first arrow he shot caught an ax-wielding man in the gut, the second one took out the eye of a man next to him. Bhang moved in after Jase's initial attacks caused the rushing group of attackers to slow their charge slightly.

Without any armor, he knew any blow against him could be fatal.

Dodging an Ax, the boxer threw a series of quick punches in his attacker's side. striking the kidney and pressure points and sending the bearded man to the ground in pain. He then Axe-kicked Another man knocking him unconscious despite the fact he was wearing a helmet.

"Kill the gold-skin bastard!," Said one of the Estahutten wielding a hammer and moving in on Bhang. The weaponless fighter turned to parry the shot, gracefully moving the hammer to his side allowing him to kick the man away.

"Got'em," said a burly northman grabbing the boxer from behind by the hair and pulling him to the ground. Two other Estahutten joined into pin their foe, slightly awed by the fact a man with no weapons or armor had done so well against them.

"Wonder what his scalp is worth," said one of the men kneeling on their struggling for to pen him to the ground.

As he raised a short sword to end the life of the struggling man he felt his hand go numb. In fact, he couldn't feel it at all. Looking up, he saw a metal pole had all but severed it at the wrist.

Clare retracted her staff across the field till it was only 6 feet long. She then whistled, sending her clockwork spider into combat. The creature climbed on top one of the men near t he chi-wise fighter, giving him a chance to push off the screaming man on top of him and roll to his feet just as an arrow fired by Jase whizzed past him to hit another mercenary.

"Who are we fighting? ," asked Clair loudly.

"They have some kind of magic chanters fortifying them," said Jase.

Claire nodded, pulled a grenade from her belt and tossed it as far as she could behind the approaching Estahutten. The grenade sizzled then exploded into green smoke that caused those smelling it eyes to go blurry throats to burn with pain.

"Pull back, you don't want my cry-babies anywhere near you," said the tinkersmith to her friends.

Jase and Bhang moved towards the girl just as a gust of wind flowed past them to hold the green smoke in place over the Estahutten.

"Don't worry, I'll keep it where it belongs," said Seamus walking up.

The young wizard had felt the wind was exactly what was needed for the connection he shared with his friend's thanks to the rite of the warrior's wheel. Staff in hand he focused on another spell hardening the air in front of his groups.

"My shield won't hold long," he said.

"Hopefully It'll draw out their magic and giant," said Xarona.

The witch looked about not only with her eyes but with her energy trying to feel anything mystical that wasn't from her, her friends or allies.

"What's going on?," Isabella walked up to her sword and, her daughters in tow.

"What are you doing here?" Bhang looked at the woman and the teenage girls".

"This is our fight too," said Lisa to her teacher.

"We had no choice, either I could waste magic I might need and put them to sleep, or they could come," Xarona looked at Salazars.

They killed my son and caused the death of my husband," Isabella spoke up.

"And where the Grape," asked Clare to her friend.

Xarona smiled, "I told her she was to stay and the tree and rain as much chaos on our enemies she could from there,"

Isabella looked at her friends and raised her sword, " For Bernardo, Vinceno, and vengeance," she called out.

"Vengeance is Alomeg's," Callum. looked at the woman with a saddened expression

"Not today,"., Isabella returned

"Giant!," A retreating trog called out to the group pointing to where small oak shuttered and the sound of battle and cracking wood could be heard.

"Here we go," Callum slung his hammer over his shoulder.

"Indeed," Seamus raised his staff sending the mostly dissolved green mist away, and from the crowd, it tormented and in the direction they would be heading.

The trogs started to push forward thanks to part of the Estahutten line was now on the ground crying and coughing up the contents of their stomach. As the group moved towards a confrontation, they both dreaded and sought they could hear battles behind and in front of them, Who was winning didn't matter to them. Instead, they focused on what brought them to Colos and what would get them home.

CHAPTER 22:
GRIT, SWEAT AND LOVE

Gravix stood in clearing holding a log with a pointed end in his hands. With a smile, he tossed it towards the Mother Tree like a human would toss a spear, arcing it high into the air. He knew he was still out of range and that a few of his men might be hurt or worse as his projectile came crashing down. The Estahutten under the giant's command knew the risk he thought and he knew logs raining from the sky would break the will of the most steadfast opponent.

The Giant looked at nearby sled, loaded with similar logs and stones that weighed more than a man. pulled by two large shaggy white creature that resembled a bear cross with a rhinoceros.   Even northerners used to the cold gave the animal a wide berth as its breath and skin caused the ground and air around it to frost and chill to temperatures even they found uncomfortable.

"We'll have those Flicks and Gritters scalped and burned before night-fall," said the giant to the man in thick fur robes at his side.

"So says the runes," answered Otis as he smiled with dark and crooked teeth,

"Hah, even Old-One eye is on our side," said the Joltan.

"The runes are his ways of letting us known his will," The robed man looked about, he could feel the magic in the air and the trees. Magics that would be attacking him and his leader if not for the wards he had person-ally tattooed in blood on the flesh of him and the giant.

He knew when they came south hunting the old blood trog magicians and priests were rare and would rather fight than cast and thus were of little threat. fae magicians and priests, however, were another thing. They were, in fact, the same thing as they believed nature and its magic was their sacred "Green Mother,"

For that reason, after arriving in Colos the Estahutten magician, killed a fae, drained its blood as it died, burned the corpse and said his spells over it. It was from that concoction of blood and sh that he made the ink for the warding tattoos he and others wore.

"Hhmmm, strange," said Gravix concerned as he hefted stone the size of a cows's skull in his hand and prepared to throw it.

"What?" Otis looks concerned after taking a drink from a wineskin full of fermented deer's blood.

"I don't hear'em," said the giant.

"Hear what," the Northman mage listened intently then spoke,

"The Skuld's," he said.

Otis was his most powerful magician, he also brought along half a dozen Skuld's, followers of their one-eye god who's music songs and words could tap into magic designed to inspire allies or break the will of enemies. Walking to his sled, Gravis playfully petted the shaggy beasts that came to his hip.

"I think it's time you had a bite," he said. "Kill anything, not of the north" he added before watching his pets charge into the treeline freezing the ground and frosting everything around them.

Best we end this quick," said the giant grabbing the chain connected to the sleigh and pulling it forward and barely noticing an arrow embedding itself into the thick leather on his chest. Glancing to the west of where his creatures crashed through the Joltan without hesitating grabbed a log and tossed it the way the arrow came barely missing a group of his men that stood guard nearby.

"What yeah looking at, find 'em and kill'em!" he roared to the stunned mercenaries breaking their stupor.

"It's Cryoboarh," Xarona spoke softly looking at the large creature moving through the trees.

"Oh this is not good," said Lisa standing between her mother and the witch, "Good hearing, excellent senses of smell," she said to herself just as the creature butted aside a group small trees as it turned to face them.

"Incoming!," Called out Jase running towards the group. As a pointed log crashed through the trees behind him, The hunter ducked and rolled to his feet and watched horrified as the log splinters and broken remains tore through his friends.

When the dust and snow cleared the Seamus stood, large pieces of wood and splinters stopping just feet before impact. The wizard seems as if he was about to say something when the Cryoboarh charged hissing frost and mist.

"Bring it down!," called out Callum moving towards the creature drawing its attention and reading his hammer. Not stopping the creature moved through trees as if they were kindling, knocking them to the side.

`"We need open ground to fight this thing!," Exclaimed Clare barely dodging a falling tree.

"No, we don't," Seamus spoke ramming his staff into the ground. Greenlight flew into the ground and into trees near the creature causing them to sway before branches reached out to grab the rampaging beast and small vines and brush twisted upward, wrapping around its legs.

Seeing his chance, Callum swung his hammer into the creature's side cracking at least one rib. Grunting the creature shifted to the side, its movement slowed by the entangling trees and branches.

Xarona finally having to time to think pointed her wand at the creature sending purple lighting into it igniting it's fur and searing its flesh under it before the frost the creature created extinguished the spell.

"Well that's unexpected," said the witch.

"Can't you turn it into a mouse?," asked Kisa.

Xarona nodded, "Probably, but transmuting something that size would use a lot of energy," said the redhead just as another log crashed nearby knocking her and those near her to the ground. Bhang could feel the pain on his side as he stood up from where he shielded Isabella.

"My girls," the woman said coming to her feet and then looking on in horror as she saw a piece of wood sticking out of the side of her former driver.

"Bhang!," she screamed.

"You and the girls need to hide," said the dark-haired boxer, in a strained voice.

Isabella looked about, Kisa and Lisa who were helping a dazed Xarona stand. Around them, the air was growing colder, and the sound of branches and twigs cracking could be heard.

" I know you," a gruff voice from where the logs were flying from.

As the girls watched a familiar Estahutten mercenary welding, a large sword flanked by two more with longbows stepped through the growing cold mist. Ignoring her friend, Isabella upon seeing the man who had almost started a fight at her husband's hanging moved forward drawing her sword and slashing at the bearded man.

"Looks like the widow has more guts than her hung-man," laughed one of the bowmen as he prepared to fire an arrow.

Instinctively the swordswoman remembered her training and moved, keeping the swordsman between her and the archers.

" It's breaking free!," Seamus called out as the frozen binds holding the creature snapped. branches and vines whipped about reaching out with a free hand Callum grabbed the creature's fur near the neck and pulled causing it to grunt and lead/drag him back towards the clearing it came from.

"Stand clear," Sani swooped from the sky, Smoosh on her head, In the distance the sound of smashing trees behind her. Xarona looked at her pet, and it swooped towards her.

"I told you to stay," she said.

"I'm a part cat, I'm allowed to disobey every once and a while," said the chimera just as Enkidu rammed into the shaggy white creature goring it with its horns and turning it on it's back.

"And also I brought help," added the winged cat.

Callum released the creature and stepped back. As he watched his usually peaceful War-Bull live up to its name. Enkidu reared up and brought its hooves down on its foe as it had been taught cracking its sternum. Not letting up the enraged bull gored the creature again gain eviscerating it before letting out a thunderous bellow.

"That was... amazing ," said Seamus

"I knew you had it in you boy," The free crusader said before looking around for other potential foes and ignoring his frost-covered gloves and numb fingers.

Less than twenty feet away from the downed monster a wounded Bhang, jumped into the melee next to Isabella employer. Throwing a punch at one attacker and a kick at the other at the same time in a manner so graceful even he was surprised by it.

Ignoring the pain, he prepared to attack the swordsman when once again the sound of an incoming log was heard.

Looking up he saw the shadow of the attack It would be close he thought as he leaps for safety only to find an arrow on his shoulder. The chi wise boxer could do nothing but stand there as all the pain he felt suddenly returned along with fear as above his head the log started to fall crushing trees and branches.

Suddenly the air heated, The log crackled and burst into flames than flaming shades. Bhang looked to see Seamus tossing another fireball towards him sending the archer that shot him away sheath in flames.

"Mother!", cried Lisa , leaping past her teacher and kicking the man attacking her mother in the stomach then in the knee.

"I got you," Kisa caught Bhang as he started to fall".

The man who had helped protect her family was bleeding and pale and only managed a nod before he failing to focus his chi on his wounds and losing consciousness.

As all eyes fell on Bhang the second cryobohr charged through the trees knocking Enkidu to the side. Instinctively Callum grabbed the creature's fur only to be swung into a tree, and the dragged away towards the clearing the creature came from.

"Sani help him," called at Xarona.

Without a word, the winged cat swooped upward over the charging northern monster creature and turned into her wildcat form. Falling to the creatures back she dug her claws in and held on for dear life.

The cryobohr exited back into clearing tossing Callum to the ground. Sani, however, held on tight clawing as it moved ignoring the cold till it made it to the creatures head where it swiped at its eyes before jumping free. Jase followed his friends into clearing spied Gravix who seemed pleasantly surprised by the return of his pet and the others.

" Ahh, brought me back something worth my while," said the giant lowering a log and pulling his frosty Ax out of the ground.

Jase nocked an arrow and fired only to have it blocked by the ax.

"Boy, you have to do better than that," Gravix rushed forward far quicker than the young hunter expected. covering the distance between them in a matter of seconds.

"Go for his ugly face," Claire called out to her pets. The clockwork spider and flying creature moved in quickly. Upon seeing them, Gravix turned and crushed the spider underfoot and cleaved the one flying machine in two with his ax.

"No toys going to stop me you little stump!"

Still moving the giant-headed towards Clare ignoring an arrow that stuck into the armor on his back that Jase fired.

Clair knew she wasn't fast enough to run and stood her ground reaching for her belt she pulled off a grenade and tossed it. The grenade exploded at the giant's feet releasing a green sticky gel.

"Now will someone kill the son of an ass!" she called out frustrated and fearful.

The giant brought his Ax down on the gel slicing at it as he struggled. "Your tricks won't save you" laughed the Joltan as the gel grew cold and brittle allowing him to pull free of the sticky mixture and swing his ax at the tinkersmith.

The girl instinctively moved out of the way but was too slow, and with a look, horror saw the large ax slice through her right arm just below the shoulder, Clare screamed as her arm flew through the air.

As the Joltan prepared a killing blow on the bleeding stoutkin, Callum, running at full speed rammed into the giant with his shoulders just at the waist. The attack lifted the ax-wielding giant off the ground briefly and before landing him on his back on the hard frost covered ground.

"About time you joined the fight Hammer-man," said Gravix with a smile as the Nyumbani lord on top of him hammer raised.

Before Callum could bring his weapon down the giant casually back-handed him away. Landing the southern lord landed on his back. Quickly the southern adventurer tried to move, but saw first hand the speed of giant the northern-giant stepped on his chest pinning him to the ground.

"Burn" cried Xarona and Seamus as their wand and staff shot normal and witch fire at the giant. igniting his furs and overpowering his wards and boiling his flesh.

"Real magic," declared the giant more amused than worried.

"Hardly," responded Otis who stepped from the trees. With a raise of his staff, the mercenary magician levitated stones from the giant's sigh before pointing his staff at the witch and wizard and sending the rocks flying their way.

Seeing a chance, Callum lifted off Gravix's foot and rolled out from under it and to his feet only to receive a punch that sent him to the ground.

"Boy, You have no idea how bad you're going to die," growled the giant as he lifted the Crusader and threw him at Xarona who had just managed to turn the incoming stone into a harmless mist.

Callum flew at his the women helplessly knocking her down before hitting the ground and rolling and skidding into a tree and cracking it upon impact.

"Now who do I kill first," Gravix looked about and licked his lips.

charging from the Tree line Enkidu moved towards the Giant only to be rammed by the surviving cryobohr.

Seamus' eyes moved across the battlefield taking note of the carnage. From the magicians' point of view, his fear and adrenalin made the world move in slow motion . Focusing he found the Estahutten magician and drew his sword. Holding his staff's curved top behind him, he released a burst of air that sent him to the clearing landing him within a few feet of his target.

"Never killed half-fae bastard before," said the North-man reading his staff and firing a jet of bitter cold at the magician who matched it with a burst of flame.

The two men stood blasting fire and ice at each other in steady streams, producing from where they met a heavy mist.

"And you never will," Seamus growled focusing his anger into his spell.

Callum sat against the cracked tree, Looking across the clearing he could see Xarona lying on the ground, His oldest friend was fighting an Estahutten wizard, and Jase was firing one of his last remaining arrows at the Giant.

"Big-man" Claire crawled over to the free-crusader, holding her bloody stump. "We need you back in the fight," she said.

Grunting the free-crusader looked at her and tried to stand despite the pain. He could feel ribs shift in his body, the pain in his arms and legs caused by cracked limbs. Ignoring that and the internal damage he knew he had, the third son of the Cyclone stood.

"Need a minute," he said fighting back the darkness at the edge of his vision.

"Don't we all," Clare manage to stand and face the giant,

"Come and get me!," she yelled.

"So eager to die girlie," said the mercenary leader with a smile.

"I'm going to kill you!," Jase said as his last arrow stuck into Gravaix's thick scale armor and skin.

"You first," The giant swung his great Ax at the hunter who managed to move back just out of its reach. As Jase drew his black metal dagger, he looked for an opening and then moved.

Running at full speed he ran under another Ax swing to the creature's side and stabbed, Gravix, ignoring the pain swung a fist at the Hillman, sending him rolling to the ground, "Gonna eat your heart for that boy," he said moving towards Jase.

Clare staggered forward with her spear only to be hit from the tree line by two arrows fired by a small group of Estahutten returning to the clearing to investigate the noise.

"Alomeg, please," said Callum trying to stand, "Let me die well this day," Staggering forward the young lord felt a chill in his body, at first he thought it was the cold of the Giant's pet, but out of the corner of his eye, he could see it was nowhere to be seen.

Taking another step the hammer-wielding adventurer eyes closed he body went numb and his saw only darkness. With a heart full of regret he knew it could be one thing, death.

"Lord Ziaiel, not now," he begged, after coughing up blood.

"I'm not Ziaiel," said a voice from the darkness.

"Who are you?," Callum tried to take a breath, but he could not breathe, in fact, he could not do anything. He had no body, no feeling and seemed just to be existing untethered in darkness.

"You know my name," said the deep, masculine voice that echoed like thunder.

Callum looked into the darkness, at its very edge, there was something there, silver and gold. The object moved turned towards him, folding about itself growing larger and taking the form of a man made of silver with gold hair, eyes of the purest light and six wings of white light, silver, and gold. "Say it and be called to my service!" , said the voice.

"Mizeriel," said Callum, "Let me be your hammer.

The Crusader's eyes opened, his wounds healed, as faith flowed into him, granting him strength and speed as he said, the name

"Gravix the Giant," You've murdered the innocent, Eaten your foes and, conspired to cause the death of thousands. ," Roared Callum with a voice that rolled across the field like a storm to the giant's ears.

"Drop your weapon, beg to Alomeg for mercy, or face his Judgment," he ordered.

Gravix turned from Jase to see the dark-skinned lord back on his feet, his hammer 's head glowing and golden energy fading from around him, In the distance, the giant heard passing of mighty wings,

"Too stupid to die, boy?," said the Giant as he started walking across the field faster and faster.

Callum could feel his faith flowing stronger than ever, but still, he knew like all energy given it wasn't infinite, He had to use it wisely. A good portion of it was already in him powering his body, what remained he could either save or use it to help his friends, for him there was no choice.

"Friends, We must fight back the pain, fight back the hurt and do what needs to be done, Alomeg's will is our wraith!" he exclaimed out focusing his energy through hammer into his allies nearby.

Seamus suddenly felt his weakening power increase. Spinning to the side of the shaman's icy blast he dropped his stream of fire and moved in with its blade. Slicing waist high he cut into his target.

"Bloody whelp!," the man called just as he felt something hit his eye.

The young magician watched as a stream of black liquid erupted from his shoulder hitting the northern magician in the face. Knowing it was his familiar he moved in quickly cutting again, this time at the man's throat then diaphragm.

Xarona ignored the pain she felt reached for her wand, Jase started to stir, and Clare's eyes fell upon the Archers that shot her. They didn't just feel confident; they felt the righteousness of their cause and the strength of their friendship. As his friends felt the call to righteous battle, Callum started to move again.

Hefting his hammer he charged the giant.

The Joltan could see the young warrior in armor wasn't going to stop, he could also see he was moving fast and gaining speed.

Once in range, Gravix swung his Ax at the Crusaders' head. Not slowing down moved under the attack and came to his feet to swing his hammer in one fluid motion, thunder rolled, and the hammer caught Gravix in the gut staggering him to the side and stopping his charge.

Repeating an attack that worked before Callum once again hit his foe with his shoulder to knock him to ground on his back

Knowing the attack Gravix managed to scramble to his feet quickly, "I'm gonna murder you hard shadow-skin," he said as he came to his feet, only to feel the weight of a hammer slam into his knee twisting it unnaturally to the side.

The large man managed to stand but could feel his broken leg and blood flowing free at his knee.

"My wrath is righteous, and you have but two choices... ," said Callum. " fall or be felled!". Choosing action to show his answer Gravix swung his ax down at the crusader who blocked it with his weapon and pushed it back against the giant.

Hobbling back the giant swung again, but this time Callum met the head ax with a head of his hammer. Both weapons vibrated their owner's arm but once again the sound of thunder was heard, and the ax's head started to vibrate before shattering into hundreds of pieces.

The giant staggered back and raised his' ax's shaft only to find it suddenly turned into a serpent. Xarona now standing turned her still glowing wand towards where a group of northman Archers had gathered to watch the fight and help if needed.

"I curse you, archers, I curse your bones to maggots, your tongues to salt, I curse you for all time," said the witch. Her magic was depleted, but she knew a witch was more than just her power, it was her reputation and the reputation of all her sisters.

"Please," one bowman begged staggering out of the tree line holding his bow and quiver high.

Jase seeing his chance staggered forward, throwing his black metal dagger at one of the archers puncturing the man's hand. Seamus seeing the Bowman's arrows summoned up his remaining energy and called a wind that sent the stunned bleeding bowman's quiver full of arrows flying, straining again he young wizard managed to move the bulk of the arrows near Jase.

Near by Isabella lead her daughters through the brush The woman glanced back to see her daughters carrying Bhang as best the could They had no idea where they were going but knew they had to get their charge as far away from the fight as possible.

"Can you help him," the woman to her daughters,"

"I read a few books on anatomy and non-magical healing," Kisa said in a tone that showed her lack of confidence in the situation.

Lisa smiled at her sister, " You never forget anything you've read," she said hoping her confident tone would help her twin.

Slowing down Isabella saw something moves up front in the brush near the clearing they were trying to avoid The woman held up a hand to stop her daughters.

"Stay here," she said, bringing her weapon up and slipping into the thick brush.

"Mother.," Kisa whispered reaching out, only to have her mother turn and smile before continuing through the dense foliage.

Three men sat in a makeshift blind made of leaves and vines.

"I can get the witch," said one.

"What about the boss?," Said the tallest one. another one

"The Shadow Skin is... Chtulhu's madness I think he's hurt him". The surprised man turned to his two allies.

"Take that shadow bastard down," said the taller one reading to shoot and not noticing a woman behind him wielding a blood-stained blade.

"Not while I live," said Isabella slicing wide, and cursing her sloppiness. She was rusty and though her and remembered how to fight, her flesh, however, was older and slower.

The bowman turned and instinctively fire, missing the woman in the torn lavender dress.

"Crazy old harlot!," the man called out, "I I thought you'd be dead by now!," The three other men turned And prepared to fire. ,

"You've tried and failed," roared the woman, before throwing herself into the group. She has had no fear of death, her son was dead, her husband dead and her daughters hiding nearby, or so she hoped. As an arrow struck her shoulder and grazed her cheek, the former duelist's blade found a target in the taller man's leg, causing him to call out and drop his bow.

Isabella then instinctively spun, pulling her blade free and to her surprise dodging the third arrow.

"When I'm done with you, I'm going to find those pretty daughters of yours, and if they're not dead I'm going to..." The youngest archer spoke up as he moved in dropping his bow and drawing a sword. only to have his words stop when Isabella sword plunged into his mouth.

"You'll never harm mine or anyone else's children again," she said as she pulling her sword free of the dying man to strike the remaining mercenary when the target of her attack, using his bow as a club hit her on the side of head and to the ground.

Dazed, Isabella only saw dancing lights in as she opened her eyes and heard, "I'm going to skewer you witch!" from what had to be the man who struck her.

Preparing to fire the man felt a sharp pain in the back of his head and his nose. The tan-skinned woman watched her attacker fall with an arrow sticking out of his face just as she cleared.

"Mother," Lisa reached into brush grabbing her mother and pulling her away and to her feet.

"What?," Isabella tried to speak and gain her bearing almost tripping over Bhang and Kisa.

"Jase," said Lisa.

Not far from the reunited Salazars Gravix grabbed a Crusader's head with his massive hands.

"I wonder what your brains taste like," said the giant

Callum felt the pressure on his head, and tried to pull away, the Giant staggered forward on one good leg, his grip was starting to slip.

With a roar, Callum pushed his hammer into the Giants' arms. Loosening a hand he then took a hand off the hammer to pull the other hand free and twist it back, breaking the Joltan mercenary's wrist and left arm,

"Brick by brick," said Callum kicking the Giant off him.

The massive man in the hide armor staggered back and fell to his knees.
"I break the wall," continued The Crusader continued as he slammed his
hammer into his foe's head shattering it like a ripe melon and exploded
onto the field.

Hamston looked at Gravix fall, and with a yelp, he started to run from
where he was hiding. Without looking back, he moved through the brush
towards a path that would lead back to his camp. Once there he stopped
to take a breath . as he prepared to move again the cowardly man felt the
sting of an arrow in leg. Looking about he then saw a trog welding a
mammoth bone club leaped from a tree on him. Out of the corner of
his eye, he saw fae bowman preparing to shoot as he hit the ground unable to move.

"Last one?," asked the trog.

"I think so, gather the others, we need to see to our allies," said the
green-haired archer.

Bhang eyes opened, he was on the ground, Kisa and Lisa looked down
at him

"I think he's waking up. ," said the twin in glasses.

"That's a good sign, right," said the other sister holding back hope.
Bhang had been more to her than a friend; he was a mentor who had
taken a useless girl from an upstart family and taught her how to fight.

"I hope so," Kisa looked at her work and didn't notice her mother moving behind her for a hug.

Xarona ran over to Callum who was leaning on his hammer exhausted

"Clare," she screamed gaining his attention.

Rising the crusader turned towards the witch and nodded.

Looking ahead the lord and lady saw Jase in tears over the convulsing body of the tinkersmith.

"You can't go like this girl," said the hunter as he held Clare's hand.

Seamus staggered towards the group with smoosh on his shoulder

"Please no one else Mother," he said feeling his friends anguish.

Upon arriving at the group, Callum looked down to see a pale Clare in a pool of blood, her right arm gone.

With a word, he placed his hand on her chest and focused his last reserves of faith into her.

"Not now, not today," he said in a wearied tone.

"We have to stop the bleeding," screamed Kisa running up to the group and seeing what was going on.

Seamus looked t the girl and suddenly knew what to do. "Stand back he said," pointing his staff at the bloody bleeding stump.

After everyone did as he asked the magician released a stream of blue fire at the stump to seal it.

Callum looked at his friend, "I hope between that and whatever healing I did it's enough" he said as he came slowly to his feet.

"I guess I'm up," said Bhang as he walked up leaning on Isabella and Lisa.

"But won't you to need your energy for yourself," a worried Lisa.

Bhang smiled, he knew she was right, but also knew he could never live with himself if he didn't do everything in his power to help his friend.

"I'll be fine," Bhang managed to stagger free of his helpers and move towards Clare falling to his knees at her side. Focusing he reached out to her energy and found it waning, death was near and he could feel it. Focusing his chi, the boxer started moving his hands to different energy nodes on the girl's body to unblock and steady them before he would add his energy to hers.

Taking a deep breath he raised his hands to touch her only to feel a hand on her shoulder. Looking to the side he saw Lisa, her eyes closed focusing her chi on him.

Nodding the man accepted the gift and focused it into the tinkersmith. The warmth of the chi at first sooth they then started to overwhelm him as more energy flowing through the Warriors wheel'. Taking another breath, he could feel everyone present giving to his task.

After a nearly a minute of his hands on the stoutkin, he felt her energy flow free and unencumbered and could hear her breathing become stronger and more steady.

Bhang stood in far better shape than when he went to his knees. Looking around he saw his friends, tears in their eyes

"I didn't think you'll save her," Jase looked at Bhang she spoke.

"Not me, we and It's going to take a healer far greater than me to regrow it," said the Chi-wise boxer.

"So it can be done?," Jase.

Callum nodded, "If we make it back to Kahsee or Arden, We can find someone, although the tithes for that at a temple will be steep,"

Seamus looked at his friends, " If we make it back? ," he said, "We just killed a giant, a monster, and Estahutten raiders, there's no if about it. "

Everyone looked at the blond who seemed far more confident than they expected.

"Colos still has military, and though the Princess said it had no problem with us, I don't trust her or the rest of family," Xarona spoke up.

Jase nodded and picked up Clair gently.

"We may still have some raiders to deal with on the way back to the tree," he said. "and we're not exactly in the best of shape.

As the Hunter started to turn towards the Mother Tree to the groups south, a row of small trees shuttered. The last Cryobor staggered forward and looked at the group who did there best to prepare for another battle.

As The creature move forward, it was hit on the side by Enkidu. The bull Horns dug into the creatures neck so far that when the Crusader's stead flexed its massive neck he almost tore the monsters head completely off.

"That guy's just earning all kinds of bags of oats today," mumbled Clare to everyone's surprise.

Jase looked into the stouts large brown eyes and kissed her forehead.

"Just too stubborn to die," he said.

"Look who's talking," said the tinkersmith. looking at her friends before fading back into a dreamless sleep.

Callum walked to Enkidu who seemed just as tired of him. The bull had a large bloody bite mark on its left hip and what looked to be a lame left limb.

" Good job boy," said the crusader,"

The Bull nuzzled his master playfully.

"HumphinMu," said the Bull in a manner that was just shy of a word.

Sani looked up from where she sat in Xarona's hand, " No need to brag," she said out loud looking at the bull.

Callum looked at the cat, "What did he say. I mean did he say something".

The cat relaxed her witch's arms, " Typical male... I am Mighty aren't proper first words for anyone". said the chimera.

Jase looked at his group and gently placed down Clare, "Might be best if I scout ahead to make sure there are no more surprises," said the hunter.

"No," said Isabella, " You'll do no such thing, I'll go with you," the woman stood cleaning her sword with a silk handkerchief. Jase was about to protest when Zel and Norso stepped into the clearing each one with sporting numerous wounds.

"No need," said the fae, "As the word of the giant, shaman and ice monsters deaths spread the north-men are starting to lose all resolve.

"Run like scared children," grunted Zel doing her best to roll her injured shoulder.

"We can still help," Lisa spoke up.

Norso looked at the group and shook his head, "Let us finish this," he said turning back the way he came after signaling everyone to follow him.

The group moved through the forest towards the mother tree passing bands of Trogs and fae hunting Eastahuten as well as frightened mercenaries who seemed to be more focused on getting away than fighting.

After half an hour of travel, the group arrived at the Mother Tree. To find the very lowest park burned and the bodies of the dead human, trog fae, Seamus s could feel that despite all the tragedy the tree itself was already repairing itself and bringing succor to those that had helped it. In fact, he could feel his all but spent energy returning.

Harnrli approached the group from above lowered by a vine controlled by his magic. Next to him holding on tight was Cassadee who upon touching the ground ran from the fae leaders side to Xarona almost knocking the witch and Sani down with her hug.

"I thought.," said the young witch tears in her eyes.

"No," said Xarona kissing the girl on the cheek.

Cassadee pulled away from her guardian and looked at the group and though everyone looked injured , all of her new family was present.

"You all look horrible," she said.

"Well, there was a fight and a giant and a less than nice Shaman and monsters. ," Said Seamus to the smiling girl.

"Two Monsters," added Bhang.

The girl rolled her eyes, "I know, I fought too," she said brandishing her wand.

Harnrli nodded, "That she did, vexing the northerners from above alongside me and our magicians," as he spoke the fae leader walked over to the girl and patted the witching on her shoulder.

Xarona was about to comment when she saw three goats wearing the helms of the northern mercenaries walk by.

"Never mind she said to herself,"

*****

Over the next few days, the adventurers found to their delight time to rest. The Mother Tree's healing had sped up everyone recovery but because there was so many injured no one was entirely healed and even with Callum's help almost everyone that fought still wore bandages and some of the wounds they earned in battle. Still sore and bruised Jase still found time to return to the clearing to gather the "spoils," of the battle there.

The young hunter took the hide of the Cryoborh, one of Gravix's hands, The giant's bags (The one holding fae and trog scalps were returned to their respective groups), The wizards bags and staff and weapons of worth from fallen foes. After recovering, he visited Clare who despite missing an arm was in fine spirits, mostly talking about how much she hated Colos and was looking to building herself a new arm. Despite having on one arm , the tinkersmith had managed to cobble together a signal beacon in hopes of contacting the airship they arrived on. Everyone figured they were long gone by the stoutkin swore that if they were within 200 miles, they would get the signal.

Xarona sat next to Clare as the Stoutkin fiddled with her new device tapping sailors code into it. Next, to her, Sani played with Smoosh and Cassadee regaled everyone with her heroics.

"And then I said... Become a goat!," and do you know what happened? " said the witch.

"He turned into a goat?," said Lisa who was eating from a bowl of grapes.

Yes" said the girl. "But unlike the other ones he only had one horn,"

Callum chuckled as he sat next to Xarona who despite enjoying her group's success was thinking of the future.

The red-headed Lady of Belasona knew she would have to return home, she owed her new charge a good life. She also knew that while it might cost her family, she would have to break off the engagement to Daschle. Her heart, against her trying, had been stolen by Callum and he was worth more to her than the trappings of her family's wealth or her good name.

Callum looked at Xarona and smiled and kissed her softly bringing a smile to all of those nearby. He had told her and the others what had happened. He had heard tales of the archangels choosing their followers through dreams or other means but in none of the songs of Alomeg, had he ever heard of anyone hearing the voice of one. Still, Mizeriel had made his choice and so had Callum, a choice that was for life and beyond.

It was also during their time of recuperation that Seamus finally found time to spend with Isabella. Jase and Norso had found Bernardo's body more or less intact save for a missing liver in the abandoned Estahutten camp along with a rite of work from the king of Colos for the mercenaries deeds. Xarona used her magic to repair the body to near pristine condition as she did Vinceno, earning a hug and thanks for a very appreciative Isabella.

The following morning Clare announced the Resolute was on the way to pick the group up and deliver them to Arden and then to Vallus.

Despite being ready to go home, the group was worried about their new fae and trog friends. Isabella decided it was best to put their cards on the table and write to the Grey keep telling the king what had happened in hopes of the leader pushing of Colos to show his hand Harnrli and I

Isabella expected the message to come from the king but instead it was from his sister stating that for the time being Colos will cease all hostilities between the Oldblood and magical folk and that it would be best for Isabella, her family, and their adventurers if would leave Colos and never return as soon as possible.

CHAPTER 23: HOME-PROPER

Isabella sat in the Airship observation lounge looking at the land below, gone was the high mountains s of Colos, replaced by the western hills of Kascee. Hearing the door open she watched Bhang entered the room, he was feeling not only better but relieved to be heading home to his wife and children in one piece. Bhang reluctantly allowed Xarona to add him to the group's adventures roster as freelancer turned member. The guild he was told would have the final say on his status, but more than likely he would receive his guild license after the proper interviews and investigations were done.

*****

The group also in the comfort of the room shared by Clare and Xarona opened up the bags and boxes collected by Jase from the Estahutten. The group had offered to split some of their booty with their new allies but were turned down as they had little use for human money.

Callum opened a small bag and poured out two dozen crystals. Most were less than jewelry quality, but a few, particularly the one from Gravix's ax and the Shaman's staff were of high quality.

" Ice, War, and Earth," said Clare looking the Crystal over.

"Big man gets the ice," said Jase looking at Callum.

"I think we should give them to Bhang, Kisa, and Lisa," said the Free Crusader. I mean we already have embedded weapons".

All eyes fell on Bhang who shrugged "What am I going to do? mount one in my forehead like the old war monks of the Wu" he asked?

Clare smiled, "I'm thinking a gauntlet or a bracer, I can cook one up before we get to Kascee," she said as she picked the lock on a chest found buried at the Estahutten camp with her remaining hand.

"Well, that would be nice to remember you all by," said the boxer, realizing that his words had a saddening effect on all his new friends as many of them will be going own their separate ways soon.

The tinkersmith tried to change the mode and spoke with an upbeat tone. "I can split that big ice one for the twins dagger things, mount the war for Bhang and maybe put the earth in Grape's wand. :

"Don't call me Grape Aunt Clare," said Cassadee with a pouty look on her face.

"You need to learn to take a little ribbing my dear," said the ginger witch to her ward, "After all, If I haven't Jase would be a two head slug a dozen times over by now,"

Jase looked ready to comment when he heard the lock on the chest pop. Inside was a wooden box marked with a magic seal.

"Ok, It's magic time," said Clare. scooching back from the chest.

Shamus looked at the ward and could feel its magic; it was a curse to be cast on anyone except its creator.

"Curse ward," said the magician standing up and holding his staff.

"We can do this," Xarona stood next to the blond faekin and raised her wand.   As the others watch, the two magic users focused on the ward moving their wands and staff in a manner that made the two of them look as if they were picking a largely invisible lock.

After a few minutes of wand and staff waving the ward started to peel off the box and float in the air as if it was old paint peeled from wood caught in a slow-moving cyclone. The ward then turned from painting to energy and started to unravel till nothing was left.

Shamus then tapped the wooden box with his wand to feel for any other spells.

"We're good," he said.

Clare moved back eagerly to open the box, but before she could, Callum reached over touched it himself

"No ill intent left," he said before letting his friend flip the latch.

"Oh, I bet this is going to be good," said Cassadee as the stoutkin opened the chest revealing a dozen small bags.

"Bags!," the young witch sounded downtrodden hoping for more magical trinkets.

Clare picked up the bag and recognized the jingle of coins. "I bet this was the Shaman's stash," she said spilling Colos gold and silver coins back into the chest,"

"Are we rich," asked Shamus looking at her friend empty bag after bag of gold.

"No, but I think we can live that way for a little bit," said Jase.

*****

Back in Observation deck Bhang stood before his employer

"What can I do for you Ms. Salazar," asked Bhang.

Isabella motioned for the man to sit and after he did she handed him a folded piece of paper,

"Read that please," she asked.

Bhang opened the paper, on it was a newly written contract stating Isa-bella Salazar would like to hire Bhang Zu-Mao as her estates' warden up until a time he wished to leave or was unable to fulfill his duties. The contract also offered a decent wage but included a Warden's house to be built to his specifications within reason.

Part of the Chi-wise driver wanted to take the job, another part wanted to return to his family's little home in Kascee while a smaller part enjoyed being an adventurer and thought that maybe that was his true calling. After some deliberation, he decided to take the job under the caveat his wife would have to agree to the move to Vallus.

*****

Gallen looked at the Estahutten's contract his cousin had handed to him, The message from Regent Jazlyn of Colos and a detailed and in his own words "rip-roaring," retailing of the events in Colos as written by Kisa.

"I do not like this," he said looking up at Callum, Xarona, and Casadee (who was dressed in a new dress and so overwhelmed by the fact she was standing in an actual castle that she had not said a word for over an hour.)

"It's true your grace,", said Callum,

"Cousin," corrected the king, "I'm your cousin,"

"Cousin," Callum.

The king looked at his wife and passed her the papers.

"The fae and trogs were running from Colos," said Gallen.

"Yes Your Grace," Xarona spoke up. "Although if and it's a rather big if, Colos holds to their word that should stop,"

The king nodded, "You have done us and those poor people a great service," said Galen.

"We hope you would reach out to Colos and make sure..," Callum looked for the right words only to have his cousin's wife speak up.

"That both Arden, Colos and the oldblood come to a mutual beneficiary agreement," she said with a nod at her husband.

"Yes," said the Crusader.

"Of course," said Galen, "And tonight we will celebrate your victory, and the lives of Vinceno and Bernardo Salazar .

king Galen of Arden then stood with a large smile on his face. To most, he was seen as a hedonistic monarch, who loved parties more than politics, but in truth, he understood the machinations of nations more than most. He knew that the politics of what was to come would not be easy yet a chance to increase his kingdom's relationship with Colos (and possibly Kascce) as well as returning the fae and trogs to there homes with little to no bloodshed on the part of his armies was well worth the cost.

He also saw the chance to partition the Free kingdom for damages from Colos and maybe gain some of the unclaimed frontiers between his small kingdom and Colos borderland in return for his grievances.

*****

"You fought a giant?," Bhang's wife stood in the largest room of their small cottage. The room was both living room and, kitchen and was currently being paced by a dark-haired woman with almond-shaped eyes in a red shirt and grey dress carrying a baby.

"I fought the Northman mercenaries while my friends fought the giant," said Bhang.

"So this driver job had very little driving?" asked the woman.

"There was a lot of driving up till we arrived in Kascee-Proper," said the boxer.

The woman moved towards the man and sat down on a red cushioned bench.

"Did you see a dragon father, I heard the mountains have dragons," said a dark-haired boy dressed in a white shirt with grey vest and black pants.

"No, but I flew in an airship, and saw so many things" Bhang reached out and pulled is the eldest son close. "Although none compare to seeing my family again,"

"And this job, in Vallus, will it be like the last one? Lots of fighting? ," ask the woman.

"No my love, I'll be in charge of the Salazar's lands and those that work it. I'll be little more than a manager," he said.

The woman, while still holding the child looked at the contract. She loved her husband and could tell he wanted the job, but Arden had been there home since before her six-year-old eldest child was born. Still, a new larger home and more money in a month than Bhang made locally driving wagons and she made as a seamstress in two years. They would be more than free-folk, they will able save, buy land, maybe a shop for her and afford a real education for their children.

"Fine," said the woman walking over to her husband. " Vallus it is,"

Bhang kissed the woman's free hand and smiled as she rubbed his back, " And no more adventures without telling me," she added.

"Yes My love," said the man before he stood and kissed the woman on the lips to the disgust of their eldest child.

*****

Clare watched her father Aldis, sit in his chair quietly smoking his pipe on their house small rooftop patio. To her surprise, the man had upon arriving in Vallas managed a drip back to Arden on Airship after winning a ticket in a card game.

"Look at you, A one-armed tinkerer," he said glaring at the girl.

"Not for long," Clare looked up from the table where sat with a quickly cobbled together arm made from old and used devices from her work-room.

"I hope the job paid enough," grumbled the man.

Clair smile, "Enough, to keep you from risking your neck smuggling hooch for a while," the girl touched the metal and rubber hand of her new arm with a crystal shocking it and causing it to close.

"Might even be enough to get you a proper liquor license and a little distillery," she said hoping her father would do more than glare at her with judgmental eyes.

The man smiled, "For that much, I'll cut off my hand too," said the broad shoulder great man, looking at his daughter and unfinished her hand.

"I think I have a life crystal, not high quality but not too many flaws that might help with your connection, ". said Clare's father.

"Maybe we can gestalt it with a pure crystal and a clear, get it some feeling in it," said the young woman. to her father who was already tinkering with arms shoulder connectors,".

"And a nice brass coating, mix it with that Phoenix feather mother gave me when I was six ," added Clare while reaching for another tinkering tool.

*****

The cities head witch looked at Xarona and Cassadee from where she sat in her chambers. She had not expected the ginger witch to return to Arden so-soon, let along bring another of their kind.

"What a cute little witchling," said Arati lifting up the girl's chin with her fingers., "Is she for sale?"

"No said Xarona as she did her best sound civil knowing the older and much more powerful witch seemed to get a perverse please from trying to get a rise others.

The witch gestured, conjuring herself a glass of wine before speaking again.

"Why are you and this child in my city," she asked.

"We are passing thru on the way to Vallus," said Xarona. "We will be gone tomorrow evening and expect to cast no spells beyond the usual day to day minor ones while we are here.

The reclining woman nodded and glared at the ginger witch, there was something about her that had changed, she was more powerful more assured.

"Fine," said the tan skinned witch. "Just don't break any of my toys," she added before taking a sip of the wine.

Xarona nodded at the woman then took Casadee's hand and prepared to leave only to find the door leading out close.

"How's Lord Wimbowaradi?" said a voice from behind,"

"He's fine," Said Xarona not only without fear but with a hint of menace.

Arati smiled, and the door opened, and the witch and her ward exited into an alley of the building.

"I don't like her," said Cassadee.

"Xarona smiled, "I'm sure she has her good points," said the ginger witch knowing that the she had not seen the last of Arden's lead witch.

*****

Jase stood playing with the collar of his new outfit. It was a fancy green doublet over a white poet's shirt with an ascot and tight dark pants and green boots. A gift from Callum and Shamus for the gathering being thrown in their honor by king Gallen and his wife.

"I don't like it, It's too tight and doesn't protect enough of me," said the dark-haired young man.

"You look almost presentable," Shamus said wearing the same clothing he wore on his last to Arden castle visit.

"I fell like a plum fool," Jase sat down on in a chair in the main room of the inn they had stayed in their last visit.

"You look good," said the inn keep.

Jase rolled his eyes and stood and looked in the mirror, his normally "free hair," was slicked back with a peppermint smelling concoction that gave it a shiny appearance.

"I look like a dandy," said the young hunter fiddling with the dagger attached to his hip in a green holder. "A peacock dandy,"

he added.

"If you embarrass Xarona we'll all be peacocks," said Callum.

"Or worse," Shamus.

Jase chuckled just as the door open, and Clare walked into the room in a beaded blue dress, silver bracelets and a brass covered right arm shined to perfection and etched with Mytec style designs.

"Howdy gentleman... and Jase". she said.

"Will you look at that, Callum walked over and touched the arm, "You finished it quick," he said the crusader

"Clare looked at her friends, "Not really, My dad and just got the basics and made it look pretty for tonight can't do anything but hold a cup or fork and not crush your hand when I shake it,"

"It still looks good," said Jase, "Heck all of you is looking mighty nice," Clare blushed.

"Why thank you Mr. hill-man". said the girl.

"Hillman huh? I guess that'll do for the last name. ," said the young hunter. "Never thought I would need one, then again never thought I'd be introduced to a king and such,".

"I like it said Shamus," strong yet.... You.

Said the magician.

"Keep it up Mr. magician, and I might accidentally stab you," joked the dark-haired young man,

"Pbbbt," Smoosh appeared on Seamus' shoulder reared up its legs to stick a tongue out at the hunter,"

Clare started to laugh and feared she would not stop. Luckily her father entered the room dressed in his a dark blue coat, white shirt and blue Kilt with a mytec pattern on it cooling her mirth.

"What's with all the guffaws?," Said the gruff older man. We're going to see royalty, not the circus,".

"Everyone, you remember my dad," said Clare.

The man looked the boys over. With stern eyes, "I'll be holding a grudge against the lot of you for taking my daughter off to Colos," he said gruffly. "But I also am beholden to you for bringing her home in almost one piece," the man managed a smile and then promptly started to shake hands.

"Did I hear Clare," said Isabella as she came down the stairs followed by Lisa, Kisa, Xarona, and Cassadee.

"Yes Ma'am," said the female tinkersmith.

"You look beautiful," said Isabella.

"My girl cleans up well," the elder stoutkin patted her daughter on the back playful before walking up to Isabella and kissing her hand.

"Ma'am, my heart weeps for you and your family. your husband and boy were good, brave men," he said solemnly.

"Thank you, Mr. Manohierro," Isabella

"Grape, your hair!," Clare looked at Cassadee, who was now sporting blue hair tied up in pink and green ribbons that matched her the colors of her dress.

"I got tired of being called Grape," said the girl in a sullen tone.

Clare smiled, "I'm sorry It rubbed you the wrong way... blueberry," said the tinkersmith.

"If I had my wand," said the girl looking frustrated.

"We know... goats... all of us. ," laughed Seamus.

*****

Bhang Ming hated being away from her baby; Luckily she trusted the neighbor who would be watching her nine-month-old or she would have stayed home instead of standing in a corner in a small banquet hall in Arden castle.

Across from her in another corner, six musicians played a melodious slow moving tune that involved a harpsichord, accordion, banjo, drums, guitar, and violin.   In the middle of the room, everyone danced including the king and his wife.

"You should dance," said Bhang to his wife.

"This is insane," she said to her husband as she walked up, "We're not the kind of people who get invited to things like this," said the woman looking about the room at the noble people, church officials, wealthy merchants and more dancing talking and eating.

"I don't like this kind of thing either, but It's a celebration not only of our deeds but of the lives of two friends," said the chi wise boxer taking his wife's hand. "And look at Li, he's having so much fun,".

Ming smiled and looked across the room at her six-year-old son who was playing with a prince just a year older than him and a small octopod creature. That was constantly changing colors.

"This will be a good memory for him," said the woman taking both her husbands hands.

"So will this," the man guided his wife to the dance floor, each one moving with a rhythm and grace no one present could match. So much so in a matter of minutes, everyone else dancing stopped and started watching the Bhangs.

*****

Enkidu sat in the stable trying to figure out which of the small troughs of oats to try next. The "Mighty" war bull looked about snorted and decided on the one in the middle.

****

"Done," Xarona returned from a hall leading into Adventurers Guild of Arden main room; the witch had delivered the journal. The guild scribe had agreed with the Lady that not only would copies of it be sent to Vallus and the Guild High Hall l in Emerald, Manheim on the east coast but it would also be sent to Colos.

Xarona met her friends with a smile "That was mostly painless," she said,

"So we're good with the guild?," Jase.

"Yes, and Bhang has been given special dispensation and added into our contract," said the witch.

"Again, that wasn't necessary said the tan, dark-haired man,"

"Fiddlesticks," said Clair," You're a.... What is our name again?".

"Thundereer," said a reluctant and embarrassed Xarona.

"That name is horrible," Clair.

"No, it's not," Seamus.

" I kind of like it," laughed Jase.

"You liking it just proves the point," returned Clair," "Personally I like Two awesome ladies, and those guys who kind of do stuff,"

The group's men were about to protest when a young girl in red robes and a god sun amulet walked up and said: " Excuse me".

"Yes Sister," Callum looked at the healer of Alomeg. The Thundereers stopped and looked at the girl, noting the newness of her robes and her general demeanor instantly marked her as the novice to the guild.

"I was wonder.. well actually me and group... friends... were wondering what is it like out there?"

All of the senior group's eyes moved past the girl at the group of people behind her, like here they were all shiny and new in appearance. A barrel-chested tattooed girl from the far islands carrying club festooned with sharks teeth. A bookish Nyumbani boy carrying a staff of a mage. A tanned skinned girl with long dark hair dressed in black and dark purples trying not to bee is seen and blond girl in blues and greens tuning a fiddle.

Jase spoke first looking at the young healer, "Dangerous,"

"Dirty," Xarona

"Life changing," Seamus

"Fulfilling," Callum added

Clair looked at her shiny new arm, " Things rarely go as expected,"

Bhang looked at the girl and his friends and backed to the young healer, "but worth it," he added bringing a smile to the girls face.

*****

Xarona had arrived in Vallus and after saying goodbyes to her friends, which included an hour kissing Callum and the two promising to see each other before their current fall turned into winter went about the business of trying to fix the parts of her life she broke by leaving.

First, she took Cassadee shopping for more clothes, a horse and other things a ten-year-old witch and ward of a lady might need. The two then went to the high side of town where each of the noble houses of Vallus had small homes.

Her Vallus home was much smaller than her actual one with just ten rooms including a large common room, two bathrooms with inside plumbing and a library sitting room on the first floor. The rest of the rooms were bedrooms that could if needed be converted into extra sitting rooms of offices.

It was there Xarona wrote her parents of her whereabouts, adventures, and Cassadee. She also discovered a three-month-old letter from them in her private bedchambers from her parents later that day asking her to come home and saying that they love her. After staying for a day at the Vallus home, the witches boarded a stage and headed south. arriving in Bellstone the largest city in Xarona's family lands three days later.

"M'lady," said the footmen dressed in green waiting for the stage.

"George," Xarona hugged the older man, surprising him. "I missed you,"

"I missed you too M'lady," said the man stunned by the fact the haughty girl she once knew seemed to have been replaced by one that hugs.

"This is..." Xarona looked at her ward who was holding Sani,"

"Miss Cassadee Belasona," said the man to the surprise of both witches.

"What?," Xarona looked at the man she had known all her life as he bowed before the girl and signaled two more men in attire similar to his to start preparing their carriage.

"Your father's doing, " he said.

Xarona had gone through what she thought was all the possible reactions of her family to Cassadee. Her sisters would most likely like the girl and treat her well if just for the fact they would no longer be the youngest. Her mother would be standoffish at best, more than any member of the family she was all about protocol and things being "proper," her eldest adopting an orphan witchling would scandalize her and everyone in her circle of gentry women in good standing just as much as her daughter being a witch did or the fact that same daughter ran away from home and became an adventurer.

As for her father, the Lord of Belasona would most likely retreat into his work of running the lands holding including touring the rookeries and wheel works and hunting with the low gentry that oversaw the smaller towns villages and lands around Bellstone and the other gentry. Henry

Belasona was on the best of days reserved and on the worst cold and distant when it comes to his daughters leaving their raising to his wife to the day to day running of their home.

Xarona watched the people of Bellstone stop to bow and curtsy as she rode through the streets. Realizing she had never taken time to explore the entire town nor has she visited most of the dozen or so villages in Belasona land, a situation she now wanted to remedy if her situation allowed.

"What's that smell?" asked Cassadee with her nose scrunched up in disgust.

Xarona pointed to the smokestacks of the rubber smelters at the wheel work's smokestacks in the distance.

"You get used to it," she said realizing that because she had been gone for long that the smell was affecting her just as much as it was her ward. ".

"We must do something about that too," she said.

"Like melt them?," returned Casadee.

Xarona smiled. No, but I'll write Clare, maybe she has some ideas," answered the ginger witch.

Belasona Manse sat in the middle of ten acres surrounded by orchards of peaches and apples. The three-story building was over a hundred years old and was built by Xarona's Great Grandfather when he was one of the few people of Gilden blood given land in the mostly Nyumbani southern lands in thanks for service against the Mytec Empire. With a dark green, white framing and pale green stone walls it was designed to look like the old lands Lord manor of the families homeland in Irie and sat unchanged save for the flags flying on poles on the roof, The family crests, her parents and for the first time Xarona's.

As the carriage rolled up the stone paved road past the front gates past workers picking fruit, each who upon seeing the carriage stopped to bow, tip a hat or curtsey, finally made it the house itself where all of the mansion servants stood outside along with the noble family and the various managers of the family lands and works as well as lower vessels.

The carriage stooped in front of the waiting group of people

"Be good," Said Xarona to Casadee who was gripping her wand for dear life. Still missing her mother, she was grateful to Xarona but was worried about her new family and how she would be treated.

The door opened, and a step was placed down to allow the witches to exit with ease. Xarona placed on her pointed wide brim hat, picked up her Chimera and exited first. The witch's eyes first went to her smiling auburn haired younger sisters than her mother and finally her father.

As she moved up past the servants and others present she saw her father smile

"My daughter," he said moving towards her and giving her a warm hug.

"Father?," Xarona looked at the man surprised.

"Look at you, fresh from adventure," said the man before moving to Cassadee, "And you, my newest daughter of sorts," said the man kissing the girls hand. Looking for the younger witch suddenly realized her dream had come true or at least in her mind, she was a Princess.

After the far more pleasant greeting than expected, the rest of the day was a blur as Xarona and Casadee were welcomed home by everyone and the younger of the two was given a tour of the house including her room which was full of with various stuffed animals and other gifts that sat crossed the hall from Xarona's Once the twin ladies of Belasona nursery it had sat used for some time.

Later that day after Xarona had rested Casadee was asleep in her room the eldest daughter of the Belasona family was called into her Fathers study. Entering the Ginger Lady found her sire sitting at his desk and smoking a cigar and sipping on brandy.

"Would you like some brandy, my dear," he asked as he poured himself one.

"No father," said the witch looking around the room at paintings and photos taken with the new Obscura devices and the heads of the mounted game on the wall.

"Sit then," he said.

Xarona sat and looked at her father.

"Adventurer, witch and lady," he said. "So young and so much life," he said.

"Thank you father," said the woman.

The man stood and walked to the window behind his desked to look out. "When you vanished, we hired the magician and skilled men to find you," he said. "Your prodigious magic, of course, blocked the magic, but at least when it did we knew you were alive and as for the men, I'm sure they found nice ponds to live out their days in,".

"I'm sorry Father," Xarona said, "But I had to, I couldn't marry Daschle Phelix,"

The man nodded, "Obligation can be frightening," he said, "And you are forgiven. Many a lord had left home to sew their wild oats, and I say what's good for the Gander is good for the goose".

The man turned to face his daughter.

" Then I'm truly welcomed home, and all this foofaraw isn't just for show?". asked the witch.

"Of course you are welcomed home, You are my daughter and my heir and truthfully you leaving did a lot to unify those of us left behind in a way I did not except,"

Xarona smiled even though her father's pleasant expression was starting to turn serious. "

"But as I said, it's good you got out and had a fling before you married," he said. "Or are the rumors from Arden of you and a Young copper lord not true?"

Xarona eyes widened.

"Father it's not a fling it's..," Xarona spike trying to find the right words but was cut off by her father.

"It's over, and in a few months young Lord Phelix shall arrive and formally ask for your hand, and you will accept," Said Lord Belasona in a tone that told his daughter there would be no compromise on his part.

*****

Jase was invited by both Callum and Isabella to stay at there homes while the Thundereers figured out if and when they would take another adventure. The hunter had decided to take Isabella up on her invitation knowing that the Mwamba wa Mwaloni was just over a days ride away and that Clare was the same by airship if he wished to visit from the Salazar's Vallus home.

The dark-haired young man was given a room in the large house but after a few days decided to move into a small shack near the woods behind the main house that Lisa and Kisa used to use as a playhouse growing up.

Still, despite being so close to the woods, the young man grew restless and felt hemmed in by the rules of the area, especially laws that prevented him from hunting anything more than birds and animals deemed as pests. Thankfully between the meager hunting, he occupied himself with, helping Bhang with his new job and sparring with Isabella and teaching Kisa how to use a sword and that, the hunter found some satisfaction.

After a month, however, Jase's wanderlust had grown so much that he took his horse and belonged and bided goodbye to his friends saying he would return before winter for a visit and headed towards the hills of his birth to the south-west.

Taking the back roads, the younger hill-man stayed in the woods following the path of raiders and poachers living off the land even as the warm southern fall started to turn rainy and cold.   It was after two weeks of such traveling away from another person that he made his way into the hills and into a village of Grange.

"Where are you going? ," asked a teenage boy on horseback blocking his path near the village's central well.

"Rand?. It's me ," said Jase looking at the boy he had known for years.

The blond haired boy looked at the young man on the scratchless brown horse. He was wearing fancy black armor a rabbit fur lined dark cloak, and store bought boots, The "city slicker" turned would hunter even his hair slicked back into a ponytail. Yet despite his store-bought look there was something familiar, a scar over a nose, focused green eyes and a bow carved from the local wood.

"Jase?," asked the boy unsure

"Damn right," said the hunter.

"Well look at you, all fancy and smelling like a rose," said the boy.

Jase smelt under his arms he had gotten into the habit of taking baths or at least washing off weekly thanks to Isabella.

"I don't smell like a rose," he said.

"Sure you don't," laughed the boy moving from Jase's path.

"My paw still around," asked the Hunter.

The boy smiled, " Yep, still in your house too," answered. "Although I think he figured you were dead or working off some bad behavior," said the boy.

Jase smiled and waved at the boy as he headed through town drawing looks from people who had known him all his life.

Moving outside of town he found a small road and turned to head down a tree-lined path to a small cabin that was dark save for a dim light in the front room.

Jase took his horse to the back to a small run-down shed that acted as a stable. Inside he saw a refuse covered floor, a coup with two chickens, a pig and a broken down grey mare.

Taking his saddle and saddlebags off the horse and making sure his stead was properly secured he headed towards the house through the back door with worn rope hinges.

"Pa," said the young man out loud knowing that if he surprised the man, he might end up with a slit throat.

"Who's that," a voice from the front of the house.

Jase walked from the small room that smelt of spoiled food into a front room reeking of alcohol and tobacco.

"It's my pa," said Jase looking about and spying a thin, balding man in the green shirt, buckskin pants, and boots wrapped in n old bison blanket sitting by fireplace holding only embers.

"Jase is dead," said the man.

I'm not dead," said the hunter.

"You come to haunt me then," said the man.

"I'm not dead Pa," the hunter walked up to the frightened and slightly inebriated man and touched his shoulders,

"It's me Pa," said the dark-haired young man.

The old raider looked at the well-dressed man standing in front of him for over a minute before realizing the stranger was his son.

"You ain't dead boy?," said the man standing.

"No, I've been on the road, seeing the world as a certified adventurer," said Jase.

The man eyes grew narrow and full of anger, " Leaving your family to starve!," growled the man as he attempted to strike his son with the bac of his hands to have his hand blocked with ease.

"No more of that, Pa," said Jase.

The man struggled for a few seconds before relenting and sitting down again and taking a drink from a brown jug".

"Look at you, to good to take a whuppin," slurred the man.

"Not too good, just too damned old," said Jase as he knelt in front of is the father before continuing speak "Now, I can go back the way I came, or I can help you get this place ready for the winter,"

The older man looked into his son's green eyes and nodded before falling into the younger man's chest expecting to be pushed back but instead receiving a warm embrace.

*****

Erv sat on the hill overlooking the old rundown Redstone keep where he and his family lived. In his hand was a simple wooden pipe full of sweet tobacco. Lighting it he puffed and watched the clouds move above from his perch in the old Pecan tree where the young lord came daily to hide his habit from his family. It had been a long week, and he and his father had helped out in the mine then in the field of one of their farmers. They then puttered around the keep, patching up the roof knowing the rains of fall were near and winter not far behind.

"All most Heaven, Mwamba wa Mwaloni,

Red Height mines, Cedar valley river.

Life is old there, older than the trees.

Younger than the mountains, blowing like a breeze"," sang a deep voice from a nearby road.

"High Road, take me home

To the place, I belong

Mwamba wa Mwaloni

Momma's waiting, take me home

High road," said another voice.

Erv upon hearing the voice put out his pipe and quickly slid down the tree, brushed off his red and-and black doublet and black pants and quickly moved towards the road with a smile.

Callum and Seamus had no idea how much they missed the tall trees and smell of pecans ready to pick of their home till they returned to it after a long journey. Callum sat mounted on Enkidu and the wizard on a grey stallion. The bull pulled a car weighed down in silks and chests and fine cast iron and copper cookery. As they sang, they noticed a shadow on their side. Stopping on instinct, they readied their hammer and staff respectively only to see the shadow climb up a tree leap off a branch and land gracefully in front of the adventurers.

Upon seeing his younger brother, Callum slid off his mount ran up to the shorter and thinner young man and bear hugged him.

"Erv!," he said with a smile.

"Big Brother," said Erv just as ecstatic,"

Callum held his brother for half a minute before putting him down".

Erv took a breath, "I forgot about how much those hurt," said the young dark-skinned man before walking to Seamus and shaking his hand.

"It's good to have you back," he said, both of you,"

Seamus nodded, It's good to be back". said the wizard,

"If we hurry we can get home in time for lunch," said Erv before taking a step back to look at his brother, "I can't wait to see the look on The old man's face,"

"How are the old man and everyone?," asked Callum.

Erv smiled, " He's still cantankerous but good. Mother is good, Grandmother good, the other lords and ladies of our house are good, and number two is expecting his first child in a week or so".

"Just in time," Callum said.

"Aye," Erv,

"And my family?," asked Seamus.

Erv walked over to Enkidu and rubbed the Bull's chin.

"Fine, we helped them bring in their wheat and pick their squash just a few days pass, They miss you though," said the young lord as Seamus wiped away tears.

The group continued to speak for a few minutes before Erv mounted his horse and escorted the two returning adventures down the road past small farms and through a well-kept village just shy of being an actual town. People moved about on foot and horses past houses of simple wood with curved roofs, each one painted red and black and gold in a style of the Nyumbani old land homes.

"Lord Callum and the wizard boy!," called out a woman who was selling apples in the small market.

"I heard they fought a Dragon," said an older man sitting on a stoop outside of a small cottage.

"Ring the bell," said a boy who moved to get a better look at the two lords and the young magician.

By the time the three young men had made it through the village to the wall of the keep the bell in the village center and the small temple of Alomeg where being rung loudly in a celebratory manner.

"That's too much," said Callum listening to bell ring as they came to the red stone wall of his families home.

"They are just happy you who are home," said Erv looking up to see a single guard on the wall.

"Keg, open her up," called out the youngest Lord to his friend, a tall, dark-skinned young man dressed in leather armor and the shirt of the local noble family.

"Holy Angels, there back he said the guard grabbing a rope and leaping off the walkway he stood on so that he would act as a counterweight opening the 10-foot tall double door.

Keg then tied off the rope and helped push the door the rest of the way.

"Heard you stole a Lord's daughter," said the guard to Callum.

"No," said the crusader in a scandalized tone.

"Less steal and more wooed," said Shamus causing his dark skin friend to blush.

"Now that's a story I want to hear," said Erv, and the fighting, was there fighting,"

"Too much of it," said the elder lord to his brother.

The group moved from the gate towards the old redstone keep with a black slate roof, and fading gold painted trim.

"Cal," a girls voice from near the large stable connected to the surrounding wall. The tall lord turned to see his broad-shouldered younger sister walking towards him, her head covered as was traditional among the unmarried women of their family.

" Vee," said the large young man sliding off his bull and running to pick up his younger sister who had since he saw her grown a few inches taller.

The muscular girl instead of being lifted by her taller brother actually manage to lift him briefly as a show of her growing strength.

"Look at you," said "still working with the lumberjacks," he asked. The girl smiled and slid her double-headed ax from the ring on her belt that heads it.

"With? I run the crew near the river and me, and Glory cut more wood than any three men. ," she said.

"I bet mom hates that," said her older brother smiling and know how much her mother wanted their eldest daughter to be a proper lady instead of a roughhousing, tree cutting free spirit,"

"Alomeg is praised," a familiar voice brought all conversation to a stop. All eyes turned to see a women one shade lighter than Callum with woolly snow-white hair, red robes leaning on a dark came with a loop at the end at one of the keeps smaller side doors.

"Maw-Maw," Said Callum moving towards his father's mother who wa far swifter he expected and met him halfway.

"Boy, you look as thin as a rail," she said.

"Hello Lady Soru," Shamus now off his horse waved at the old woman,

"Come here and give me a hug, boy. ," said the old woman.

Shamus smiled and walked over and hugged the woman who returned his affection before stopping her to   hugged her Grandson before pulling back to look at both young man with eyes that could see things others could not

"Been through a lot," she said, Good and bad," she said.

"Both men nodded knowing hiding anything from the former Acolyte of Alomeg was futile and that any lies would be met with a slap from her cane.

The old woman smiled, "But you're stronger, I see it," said the old woman before looking at Erv and Keg, "Keg, go tell Seamus family he's here, Erv, Tell your Ma we're having guests for lunch and that number four's home,"

The younger men both nodded and did as they told without hesitation even as Vee started to escorted the animals to the stables.

"Hold on," Callum waved for his sister to stop before moving to the cart to unpack a medium size chest and large bolts of red, gold, and black silk. He then removed his hammer from where it hung on his bull.

" You better had tithe that silk," said the old woman looking at the high-quality fabric.

"He did Ma'am," said the magician at the Temple in Vallus.

The old woman nodded at Seamus then her grandson before leading them into the keep with a step far more spry than one would expect from a woman her age.

The smell of home cooking filled the small side hall they traveled down that emptied a large dining hall with a long table of dark wood carved with the families symbol, a great bull. The table was brought from the old land and like a lot of the old furniture in the house was made of ebony wood from the old Nyumbani lands.

Callum placed the chest and silk on the table before following his grand-mother and friend down another hall past an open sewing room and a cluttered room where crystals from the mine were graded under bright clear crystal lights.

Sitting in the doorless open room was broad shoulder middle-aged man who's dark hair was starting to grey dressed in a black shirt and pants covered a leather workman's apron.

"Father," Said Callum to the man, moving his eyes from the Manor Lord of the land to the metal stand that held two large maces each with iron heads the size of a man's head. Maces that according to the stories he had not heard helped tame the wild lands of Vallus.

"Four," said the man looking up from his work and standing.

"You look, good dad," said the Young Lord before walking up to hug the man.

The Old man stooped looked and to the magician, " Thank you for getting him back Blondie Boy" he said walking to the magician and shaking his hand before giving him a firm grip on the shoulders, "Good to have you both home," he said.

Shamus smiled, he often told people the Lords of the Oaken cliff treated him like family but knew most people didn't believe. But he knew if those people could see what was transpiring there would be no doubt in what he said.

"Sir thank you for helping out my family," said the faekin.

"Bah, it was nothing," said the old man waving away the young man's words and walking to his mother.

"Does Greta know," he asked.

"Sent Erv and unless there was a pretty girl or a fight between the court-yard and the kitchen she knows by now," joked the old woman.

Vilheim chuckled to himself before leaving his work and walking to the dining area. And seeing the chest and silk on the table.

"Well that's a pretty prize," he said looking at the bolts of silk, "Booty or Payment? asked the Lord of the Mwamba wa Mwaloni.

"Part payment," said Callum walking over to the chest and opening re-vealing gold and silver coins more than half from Colos,

The Old man smiled, " Gonna buy your girl a big house with that,"

"Callum looked at his father who continued talking

"Oh we heard about Arden, Girl with hair like fire and hips," said the man with a grin.

Soru looked at her son and her Grandson, "Leave the boy alone, " she said in a chastising tone.

"My baby," the woman in the red headscarf and red dress ran towards the large man to hug him, "Look at you, skin and bones,"

"Mom, I'm pretty sure I haven't lost a pound," said the crusader.

"Boy, a mother knows, now let's get this table cleaned off and set up for lunch, I got fried chicken, Rice with Mushrooms and peanuts, Fresh cornbread, collard greens, and yams hot on the stove".

The woman then looked at Shamus, and said " Apple pie," knowing the boy loved her dessert.

"I love this place," said the blond magician.

A half-hour later Lunch was placed on the table present was The Wimbowaradi family, Servants, their children, A few visitors and Shamus's father who was called over from a nearby road repair gang. The man hugged his son and told him his mother and siblings would be there as soon as they could. Shamus looked at the man he thought was his father, and though he had questions, he held them to himself. Despite the fact burly redhead wasn't a blood relation he did raise him and that in the end might count for more than blood.

After lunch, Callum and Seamus were all but forced to relay the story of their travel by Erv, Vee, and others.   As they talked, Shamus's mother, younger brother, and sister entered in the keep escorted by Keg and was ushered to a chair and given pie and milk by Lady of the manse while the boys talked and showed off the spoils of their battle and travels.

And so it went, two adventures retelling tales of their exploits, which included the introduction of an apple pie loving octopod that surprised all watching with its appearance and ability to dodge a knife thrown by a surprised Greta.

Later that day a spontaneous party with music dance and food was thrown in the old red keep of the Mwamba wa Mwaloni. Everyone was invited, and almost everyone brought food and drink. The celebration lasted through the night and only ended when Callum sad goodbye to his friends and family walked down the hall to his room near his own personal workshop and smithy, waved goodnight to Enkidu across the yard in the stable, climbed into bed and went to sleep under the roof of the building he was born in .

APPENDICES

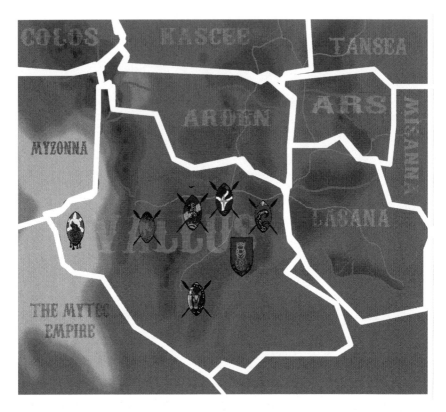

The Kingdom of Vallus is the largest Kingdom in the south and alone with Myzonna borders Mytec Empire, and thus by default acts as a buffer between the sizeable southern empire and the rest of the Free Kingdoms of Aerix.

Vallus -Proper (Capital City)
Population: 170,000
Current Leaders: Valnki Mlinziwajua III (King), Hasa Mlinziwajua (Queen), General Buso Batasi (General), Kysanoi Jawi (High Wizardess).

Built on the three rivers of the Nyotapeeke Vallus-proper is the largest city in the south with Atlani and Orle being close seconds. Surrounded by magnificent limestone walls risen from the ground by magic it is now a modern city complete with alchemical-methane powered water pump systems, Crystal water purification and crystal lit streets (in 85% of the capital). With the airship ports and dozens of taverns and Inns, Vallus is the picture of a modern Aerix city.

Vassals of Vallus

Ausnorbi

House: Ausnorbi
While Vallus-proper sits in the north, Ausnorbi sits in the center of the Kingdom. With hills, forest and the start of the Chita river, it is said to be the most magical place in the Kingdom. Home of not only it's the kingdoms wizard school, but numerous businesses that cater to magical folk in Austown (Home of the cities castle and keep) along with it's large cultural and artistic forward mundane community.

Ausnorbi also has a large community of Hill-folk living in isolated villages in their more isolated hills.

Belasona

House: Belasona
The Belasona family is the only Gilden noble family in Vallus and controls the once quiet orchard lands south and east of Vallus-proper, near its southern coast. While Belasona kept the Orchards and farms of the land, they over time added factories dedicated to wheel coach and wagon wheels as well as training hundreds of birds for long distance travel and mundane communication.

Diaz Pass

House: Diaz
The farthest west of the Vallus Noble lands has the big river at the south, the Chita to the East and the M, zonna and Caliph to the west.

Pass' past and people makes it one of the most Myberian, and Mytec influenced lands of Vallus. The Diaz family that rule the land are direct descendants of the same Diaz family that settled there long before the arrival of the Nyumbani. That same History also makes it the most rebellious of the noble houses as they see Vallus as "temporary allies".

Mwamba Wa Mwaloni

House: Wimbowaradi
Just twenty-five years old the Mwamba Wa Mwaloni sit south and west of Vallus-Proper. Up until Vilheim Wimbowaradi conquered it the lands were full of strange beasts and outlaws as well as multiple small communities with no real protection.

The Mwamba Wa Mwaloni and the Red Heights tree covered cliffs, hills, and valleys that no one wanted that is now quickly becoming a destination for those looking for

APPENDIX 1: Vallus

a life outside of larger cities and steady work. Growing rapidly, what it lacks in wealth, it makes up in community.

Ranger

House: Kuangaliambali
Ranger sits just west of Vallus-proper and sees itself as the gateway to the wild west lands of Vallas. Known for its cattle and the massive fort that now serves as the home of the noble family, Ranger Rock is one of the largest and most famous Noble lands in Vallus.

Tyro

House: Lugha
Those in Tyro will tell you they get no respect and are mistreated because of there house's noble houses of the kingdom of Lasana. East of Vallus Proper with its eastern border touching Lasana's western edge it is the rich in lumber and has the countries largest black water wells.

Those in Tyro tend to speak not common tongue but an old Nyumbani Tongue common to Lasana. They also tend to be far more superstitious than other citizens of Vallus thanks again to the influence of their eastern cousins and the dark magic and creatures commonly found around Black Water wells.

Other Houses and lands: as stated before, Vallus is large and full of minor noble houses and claimed lands including:

Angels Mound (House Hanusi): The religious center of Vallus.
Father's Island (House Ogano): A large Island, known as a port of merchants and pirates.
Juggernaut Plains (House Zulra): Flat prairies known for the giant (mostly peeaceful) Juggernaut creatures that live there.
River Bend (House Eshu): Land near the Mytec Border.
Wortni (House Wortni): a Small land between Vallus Proper and ranger.
Witch's Fall (House Kiswani): Noble land that has outlawed witches.

APPENDIX 2: Lexicon

The language of Aerix comes from a combination of cultures. Most people speak Freespeak, a common language that combines several of the major languages. Most people can also speak and or understand in two to three other languages.

Common Freespeak terms include:

Acolyte: a devoted follower of a religion who can use faith powers ort Chi Wise powers.

Dandy: A person (usually male but not always) that dresses fancy and is always clean and manicured.

Estahutten: Gilden people from far North Aerix,, barbarians and raiders.

Free Folk: People not beholden to a Lord. Because of their status, they pay Taxes directly to the lord)or no one at all) and come and go as they please. They have a higher legal status than peasants.

Gilden: Fair skinned people from the many countries of the north central old lands. More common Eastern Aerix.

Hex'n: To use magic.

Hoss: A large mal, usually one who's good natured.

Kin: A relative or in some case a type of Oldblood heritage such as Faekin.

Lady and Lord: Titles reserved for nobles who are vassals to royals. Often uses as "M'lord or M'lady."

Myberian: Decedents on some of the first old-land colonist to Aerix. They resemble Most have light tan skin and dark hair.

Mytec: People from south of the big river. Most have tan skin, dark hair and dark eyes.

Nyumbani: The dark skinned people from the many kingdoms of the "Motherland".

Oldblood: Members of the magical humanoid races.

Peasant: The lowest of the social order. They work for the lord of their land have no real rights beyond those allowed by the lord.

Proper: The Home city f a Kingdom, usually the name of that kingdom or terror followed by proper, i.e., Vallus Proper.

Qin: Dark haired dark eyed people with golden tanned skin common in Western Aerix and the Far East of the Old Lands.

Sly: Gay/Homosexual. Is sometimes used for any Queer person.

APPENDIX 3: Recipes

HEY CAL, MOTHER TOLD ME TO HIDE THESE RECIPES IN YOUR STUFF BE-
FORE YOU LEFT. I GOTTA ADMIT, I'M REALLY GOING TO MISS YOU BIG
BROTHER AND I CAN'T WAIT FOR YOU AND THAT BIG DUMB BULL OF YOUR TO
GET HOME.

TILL THEN, BE GOOD AS IF YOU BE ANYTHING BUT GOOD , HAVE FUN AND
SLAY A DRAGON FOR ME.

-YOUR BROTHER
ERV
FORTH LORD OF THE OAKEN CLIFFS.

Dear Four, I know you're doing what you think you have to, and I understand.
Just stay safe in your journeys. Speaking of safe, here are some simple recipes
to help keep you and the Pathson boy fed and to remind you of home.

May Alomeg bring you and your friend home to us.
Lady Gretta Wimbowaradi
High Lady of the Oaken Cliffs and your mom.

<u>Arroz con Leche</u>

Do you remember Mayra, The Myberrian girl who worked in our kitchen during the "Big Winter" before her and her family moved on to Austown after the
snows melt? Well, that rice pudding, love was taught to me by her.

Ingredients :
1 cup rice
6 cups whole milk
Pinch of salt
One cinnamon stick
½ cup sugar can also use brown sugar or maple syrup if that's all you have.
½ cup walnuts
One tablespoon butter
½ cup of sweet (condensed) milk
½ teaspoon vanilla oil.
1/2 teaspoon Nutmeg powder
1/2 teaspoon clove powder
One tablespoon rum - (Not for drinking you hear!)

APPENDIX 3: Recipes

<u>Directions</u>

Wash and rinse the rice very well, I mean really well and look out for dirt and bugs.

Put the milk (Cow is better, but goat or sheep will do) in a medium-sized pot (The one stole from the kitchen before leaving is fine) with the cinnamon stick, spices and pinch of salt. Bring to boil and add the rinsed rice.

Cook on a low until the rice is tender. Stir occasionally, increase the frequency of stirring as the cooking time increases.

Remove the cinnamon sticks from the rice (Your bull likes eating those)

Add the sugar and walnuts, cook for or until tender and creamy. Stir frequently.

Stir in the butter.

Add the condensed milk, vanilla and rum to the Arroz con leche and stir well. Remove from heat when everything is mixed well and melted.

You boys can eat the hot or cold, and it lasts a long time if you put it in a sealed jar in a lake or river.

<u>Grandmother's Fried Chicken</u>

Don't think I didn't notice how much Lard and butter you took.   Knowing you, that means fried chicken, and while yours is good, mine is better, and your father's mother is the best.

Here's her recipe and if you tell her I gave it to you, I'll switch your hide good when you get back.

3 cups wheat flour

One teaspoon salt

1/4 teaspoon fresh ground black pepper

2 cups milk or buttermilk

One egg

One tablespoon red pepper powder

One tablespoon of cummin powder

one teaspoon of dried garlic powder

1 or 2 3 to 3-1/2 pound chickens, each cut into 8 or 10 pieces with skin

1 and a half cup of lard

1/4 cup bacon fat

APPENDIX 3: Recipes

<u>Directions</u>

Remember that big pan you made that you could use to wallop people if something happens to your Whammer (Alomeg forbid) well put that over a fire and place in that bacon fat and lard and cook them down to they liquified and smoking a little and is ready fry. And in case you forgot, keep the pan high above the fire.

While that's going, take that milk (or water if you're out) and mix in half the spices till it looks like your ready to scramble them up for breakfast. Put in your chicken (or just about any chicken-size bird (And if you get ahold of some cockatrice, Alomeg has blessed you) in pieces and let it sit.

When the lard is ready, run that chicken through the flour mixed with the rest of your spices, back into the eggy mix and again in the flour then toss them in the skillet.

Cook them till the juices inside run clear and the coatings golden brown. Take them out and eat it up.   The most important thing here boy is you cook it till done, don't get in a hurry and a little char is better than you having to ask Alomeg to heal your stomach.

<u>Travelers Taters and onions</u>

Now this recipe comes from my father, you never knew him, but he was a cook on a boat ran from Lasana to the Oldlands.

Potatoes and onions are last a long time on the road, and when you cook them together, they taste better and are an excellent way to make a meal go a long way cheap. Serve them by themselves as part of a feast or toss in whatever meat and vegetable scraps you have added some water and its a stew.

1/2 teaspoon of salt
One teaspoon of black pepper
1/4 cup of butter
1/4 cup of bacon fat.
1/4 cup of water
Two pounds of potatoes.
One whole onion.

APPENDIX 3: Recipes

<u>Directions</u>

Time to use my pot again, Clean p your potatoes and slice them up not too thin, not too thick, so they're no thicker than a good plate. Boil them up in the salt and water and take them out before they go out. Try them out with a towel or the sun and toss them into your skillet after cooking down that butter and bacon fat till the butter is liquid and turning brown. Toss in the potatoes, cook till they start going brown on the edges and toss in the cut into rings and pour in the water, pepper, and cover till the onions are soft.

<u>Collard Greens</u>

As your heading north, you should be able to find all manner of greens on the road. While dandelion greens and turnips will work in a pitch, most good folk from here to Kascee have a patch of collard greens you can buy

A Mess of Greens (four bunches)
1/4 pound of bacon
Salt and Pepper how you like, less salt if you cook with Salt pork.
1. Milk Peppers (Jalapenos)
teaspoon paprika
A teaspoon of dried garlic.
Teaspoon of vinegar
A teaspoon of sugar.

<u>Directions</u>

This one ease as those taters. Clean your greens good then clean them again. A good soak for an hour won't hurt. Take your big pot and place over a medium fire. Toss in your bacon sliced up thin and let it fry and render than toss in your spices and pepper. Now start tossing greens till they cook down then cover and let them cook some more after adding the vinegar nd sugar. As long as you got water coming from the greens in the pot, you can let them cook. Two hours is just about right.

Once done your good

The best thing about his recipe is it works it also works cabbages of all types.

Malcolm Harris lives in Dallas Texas.

An award-winning comic book writer/artist and game designers. Inside his middle-aged interior lurks a grumpy old man that revels in telling kids how things were better in the old days and to get off his lawn.

A self-proclaimed Nazi-punching leftist, he believes in God, the innate goodness in humanity and that one day we'll get off this rock and explore the stars.

When not writing comics/ novels/screenplays or designing games, Malcolm can be found cooking for friends and family and be bringing the pain on the local Amtgard LARP battlefield as the Paladin, Sir Bloodmoon of Artenia, Count of the Emerald Hills, Lord of Ironcloud and Ambassador of the Duchy of Midnight Sun.

You can find Malcolm on Facebook because he's too cantankerous to switch to new-fangled social media.

Why just read about the adventure when you can Play it!

Made in the USA
Monee, IL
20 January 2024

51515742R00345